KATHERINE ASHE

*For Marilyn —
The very dearest of old
friends — love and
much merriment*

*Katherine Ashe
June 18, 2010*

Montfort

The Viceroy

D1364829

ISBN: 1450574238

ISBN-13: 9781450574235

Library of Congress Control Number: 2010902385

Printed by CreateSpace, An Amazon.com Company

visit: simon-de-montfort.com

katherineashe.com

Montfort

The Founder of Parliament
The Viceroy
1243 - 1253

VOLUME II

Acknowledgments

The actual, unquestioned events in the life of Simon de Montfort are so mutually contradictory, and there are such important gaps in the documentary evidence surviving from the thirteenth century that, to explore a plausible sequence of cause and effect, I've taken freedoms beyond those allowed a historian. *Montfort* is offered under the aegis of fiction.

Among those to whom I am indebted are Mark Peel of the New York Society Library; Dr. Henry Pachter, who urged me to pursue this adventure; Dr. Madeleine Cosman, founder of the Institute of Medieval and Renaissance Studies at The City University of New York, who encouraged and guided me; Dr. Karen Edis-Barzman and The Center for Medieval and Renaissance Studies at Binghamton University for their generosity in granting me access to their research facilities and lecture series; Prof. G. K. Martin of the University of Leicester for his assistance; the Viort family, castellans of La Reole who showed me their castle and provided invaluable information regarding the tower of Montauban de Casseuil; Marie-Noel Hervey for her researches in equestrian terminology; Emile Capouya, Jonathan Segal and James Clark for their advice; Clara Reeves who was my generous hostess in Paris and my traveling companion through Poitou and Gascony; Lucia Woods Lindley for her friendship, which has sustained me; and my husband, who has been very patient and helpful for so many years.

Contents

Book III

THE VICEROY

Prologue

BORDEAUX
1243

As he ran the echoing beat of his own feet upon the cobbled paving made chaotic din with the clatter of hooves behind him and the bursting throb of his heart. The house-fronts formed a narrow chasm, their whitewashed walls glowing in the moonlight, their dark shutters and doors bolted against the dangers of the night. The riders, three at least, were nearly upon him. Here. Here was the door with a dove with outspread wings carved in the stone of the lintel.

The runner pounded on the oak paneling. "Let me in! I'm Richard! Duke of Gascony!"

A knife blade thudded, driving its point deep into door. But the door-bolt rattled and the door swung open. A frightened servant dropped back as Richard forced his way into the safety of Guillame Colom's house.

The three horsemen turned and rode away before a torch could be thrust out the doorway to light the street and reveal who they were.

The next morning the vaulted beige stone hall of Bordeaux's hotel de ville was crowded as usual with Gascon lords swaggering in their fur trimmed cloaks, and wine merchants in their even more rich damask robes. The courtiers, petitioners and defendants milled about, talking in groups and casting impatient glances toward the dais. Servants came and went, bringing their masters refreshments for the morning had grown tedious as they waited.

Upon the dais steps a few English barons, still lingering on in King Henry's year-long stay in his last dukedom in France, sat frowning and muttering to each other. A new flag of red silk, embroidered in gold with a dragon, drooped with its dragon-tongue of long red streamers limply dangling – the battle flag of King Henry III of England, Lord of Ireland and Gascony – no longer Lord of Normandy, Anjou, Maine and Poitou.

For Henry had lost all of England's dukedoms on the continent save this one province, rich with the Bordeaux wine trade. Even his crown and his great flag with the strutting golden lions of Plantagenet had been lost to King Louis of France. But Henry had new ones now, and better. And if he could collect the taxes due from Gascony, he might even pay for them. It was his able brother Richard, Duke of Cornwall and of Gascony, who was charged with imposing submission upon the freedom-loving province and collecting the royal taxes.

Henry sat in a finely carved oak chair on the dais, his new gold circlet crown on his soft brown hair. The left side of his face sagged with palsy, giving him expressions that ranged from wry bemusement at best, to a look of agony suggesting the damned in Hell. And for him his twenty-four years upon the throne of England had been a hell.

Beside him sat his queen, Eleanor of Provence, her golden curls modestly covered by a veil of crimson silk with a white wimple framing her angelic, pretty face. Eleanor was thought the beauty of the era, with ice blue eyes and a bow mouth. A translucent pallor gave her sweetness an otherworldly charm. Rebel Gascons had poisoned her. For weeks she had lingered near death and was not fully recovered.

Near the queen's feet, among the English lords sitting on the dais steps, was the Earl of Leicester, Simon de Montfort, the king's councilor for war. Striking amid the courtiers in furs and heavy silks of brilliant hues, he wore the plain black woolen robes of a penitent. His skin was fair, his hair dark, his features finely made, with a handsomeness that for him was an embarrassment. His dark eyes peered nearsightedly about the room. The busy gossiping among the Gascon lords nearby, as far as he could clearly see, gave him alarm. He chewed his thumbnail, waiting for Richard to arrive.

While poor eyesight might seem a disqualification in a man of war, it was no bar in hand-to-hand combat, for at close range Simon's vision was perfect. At thirty, his skill with the two edged sword was such that no man wished to face him. And his knowledge of military strategy was unsurpassed. With Richard he had seized Palestine from the Saracens. On a narrow road not far from where the Court was sitting he had held off King Louis' army of thirty thousand with just a hundred English knights. He was the hero of King Henry's Court. But he was also the man least loved, least trusted and most suspected by the king. Only because Henry needed him, had he been brought back from exile.

King Henry turned and spoke in a whisper to his secretary, John Mansel. He seemed as perplexed and agitated as the rest of the assembly. Only one man appeared entirely at ease. The foremost and the richest of the Bordeaux merchants, Rostein DelSoler, smiled knowingly and nodded to his friends.

Every morning for a year Richard had been at his place, standing upon the dais steps with scrolls in hand, his clerks with more scrolls at the ready as he read accusations against the Gascon lords, or demanded accountings for the royal taxes. But not this morning. This morning he was nowhere to be found.

When it was nearly noon, a diminutive, finely dressed and curly-gray-haired merchant of Bordeaux, Guillaume Colom, arrived at the door at the far end of the hall. With his usually jolly face fixed in a firm scowl, he made his way through the crowd. Arriving at the dais, he bowed low. From the sleeve of his fur-lined robe he brought out a small piece of parchment closed with a large red wax seal that was almost too heavy for the little missive to support. He handed it toward King Henry, but the royal secretary Mansel stepped forward and took it.

The secretary broke open the seal and unfolded the parchment. As he read the hurried scrawl, his expression, as always, was carefully kept blank for the observant multitude. Then he bent and whispered into the king's ear. "There has been an attempt upon your brother's life," he murmured. "But Richard has escaped. He took ship with the tide this morning, bound for England. He ordered Colom to delay for fear he might be stopped."

The king looked to Mansel, then to Colom, stunned. He glanced toward DelSoler and saw the smiles and nods the merchant cast toward his fellow Gascons like a patron distributing largesse. A stab of recollection stung Henry – yesterday, in DelSoler's hearing, in a fit of pique at Richard's customary bold forthrightness, he had cried out that his brother needed to be taught a lesson of submission he would not soon forget. He had no doubt that DelSoler heard him. Had he seized the chance to rid himself and his friends of Richard's stern rule? His unctuous smiles would seem to claim the credit.

The king sat silently for some time. A worm of guilt was introduced into his conscience with a pain he knew would grow for he loved his brother dearly, and he feared greatly for his own soul. In that moment of frustration he had, but for Richard's escape, come close to the crime of fratricide.

But Richard had escaped. And the day's business was pressing. Henry saw he must take on the investigations himself, and that pleased him. He wished to be known as a kind and gentle king. Long experience had proved to him his subjects saw him not as kind and gentle, but capricious, possibly mad and certainly a vulnerable fool. But those depressing thoughts he struggled to keep far from his mind. Might this not be an opportunity to win his subjects' love? He felt a glimmering of satisfaction. He knew what they wanted and he would give it to them.

Henry steeled himself, composed his features to a calm smile, stood up and looked over the sly, covert grins of his Gascon vassals.

"Our brother, it seems, no longer cares for his dukedom of Gascony. He has returned to England. We have no choice but to relieve him of the burdens he has found so trying here. We offer, in his place, our own son Edward, who shall be henceforth Duke of Gascony."

A cheer went up from the Gascon lords and merchants in the Court. Edward was four years old. They need have no fear of a stern overlord for many years to come.

The English barons were shocked by Henry's betrayal of his brother.

Simon was utterly amazed. He felt profound unease, but could not fathom King Henry's intent. Glancing over his shoulder toward the queen, he saw a look of radiant joy was lighting her face. Her husband had done what she begged of him, granting what she knew her Gascon cousins wished, and bestowing the recognition that she wanted for her little son. If she thought of Richard it was merely with relief that he was gone.

Seeing Simon looking toward her, she reached down and touched his shoulder with her slender, pale hand. The smile she bent toward him might have seemed no more than a proud mother's happy victory – but to him her touch, her smile were as a shaft of heat, of linkage, of acknowledgement. Drawing his gaze to the frowning merchant, Colom, at the foot of the dais steps, he stifled his response to her with all the effort of his will.

Chapter One

CHRISTMAS AT WALLINGFORD
1243

IN SEPTEMBER OF 1243 KING Henry returned from his French duchy of Gascony, and the courtiers who returned with him were allowed at last to disperse to their homes. Simon, pardoned and restored to his full titles of Earl of Leicester and Steward of England, saw his home, Kenilworth, for the first time after four years of exile in Palestine and France.

Emerging from the green shade of the manor's woods, the view was a familiar play of colors before his weak eyes: the distant red of the massive sandstone block that was the fortress with its four square towers at the corners, the dab of gray that was the peaked roof of the chapel, the encircling red line of the bailey wall, the green swath of the outer yards with their dotting of barns and outbuildings, and the Mere as brilliantly blue as the sky, with the thin line of the causeway and the swing-bridge crossing its mirror-waters.

The Countess Eleanor, riding beside her husband, burst into tears. Five-year-old Henry, in a wagon with his younger brothers and their three infant-nurses, whispered proudly to little Simon and Guy, "That's our castle!" though even he was too young to remember it. Old Lady Mary, Eleanor's waiting woman, reached over from her mule and clutched Simon's squire Peter's hand – they had come through the bad years. Now would be the good.

From Kenilworth's tower, bells peeled out in welcome. The servants of the manor came running from the barn, the stables, the cooksheds and the wattle-fenced kitchen garden toward the causeway and the bridge to greet their lord and lady and conduct them home.

As Garbage the countess's kitchen boy, now grown to spindly adolescence, took Simon's horse's reins in the inner courtyard, Simon ruffled the boy's tousled head, but could not speak, he was so near to tears. He had borne up through years of shame, of hardship, of a future unknown, and now that power, honor and some wealth were won he found the relief almost unbearable, the joy almost too painfully welcome to embrace. He brushed his face with the back of his hand as he dismounted, lest anyone see he was crying.

Thomas deMesnil, Simon's loyal steward, helped the countess from her horse, his rosy, round face beaming. He had but lately returned with the Montforts' servants from Leicester, where they had spent the years of their master's exile under the protection of the Bishop of Lincoln, Robert Grosseteste, Simon's friend and councilor.

The countess laughed and wiped her eyes quite shamelessly. "There were bells... we didn't have bells before. And everything appears so tidy, so well kept!"

"The repairs to the tower and the bailey wall that were unfinished are completed now," deMesnil nodded. "And a good deal more has been done here."

"How thoughtful of my brother!" Eleanor glanced up toward the corner tower that had needed a new roof.

"Perhaps," the steward replied. "But, as you'll see, King Henry seems to have intended Kenilworth for himself."

The nurses bundled the three little boys out of the wagon, and Simon and Eleanor climbed the foyer steps into the tower's hall with deMesnil, as he continued, "Beside the bells, there are glass windows in the west chambers now, and a fireplace. And manacles set in the wall of the wine storage pit." He opened the door to the right of the hall's entrance. Light dimly shimmered off the oozing stones of the sunken chamber at the corner tower's base.

Squinting, Simon could see the darker shapes of iron chains, their massive staples wedged into the glistening, damp walls. "The simple comforts of a king?" he remarked wryly.

Kenilworth had been King Henry's wedding present to the Countess Eleanor, his sister, and Simon, his then best friend. But the castle had been a ruin when they received it and they had bankrupted themselves in making it habitable.

Simon looked about the hall. The great fork-tailed red lion rampant of Montfort, which Eleanor had ordered painted on the high wall opposite the door, was gone beneath whitewash. The soaring arches in the east and west walls now had draperies to limit drafts. For light, tall iron torchiers stood upon the dais by a fine, massive oak table and a pair of chairs carved with the strutting lions of the royal arms. Simon's feelings were a tumult of relief at homecoming and a strong sense of having been invaded.

"Henry never meant for us to come back, did he," the countess observed in a subdued tone. "Well, we shall repaint your lion, and enjoy the rest of my brother's unintended generosities."

In the weeks that followed, the earl and countess settled into their accustomed life at Kenilworth. Old debts for their improvements to the castle had not been fully paid and now appeared again. Simon sat at the table in the hall with deMesnil, studying his assets to try to repay what was owed. The stock from the earl's breeding stable of warhorses, preserved at Leicester, was brought down for inspection. The great white destriers, when trained, were costly – Simon's chief asset, for he had only some dozen fiefs that paid him rents. But the horses would need schooling before their full value could be gained. Simon felt indeed that he was home again, with the familiar strain of finances settling upon him as before.

In the garden by the castle's chapel Eleanor had Slingaway, the kitchen boy, plant the rose bushes that she had tenderly brought all the way from Gascony. She sat with Lady Mary upon the wattle garden-seat, cushioned with thick thyme, and watched her small sons playing in the nearby kitchen garden among the leafy tents of late French pole beans and peas. Mary called out sharply when they trod too near the woody rosemary or tender herbs and lettuces. A pungent, yeasty scent came from beyond the kitchen shed, where the brewster newly hired to make the servants' beer was busy at her work.

In the outer yard plums, pears and apples hung heavy on the orchard's trees. Arch-necked destriers neighed from the stable, as one by one they were released into the paddock by the stablemen to exercise. From the barn came the soft lowing of milk cows, while peacocks and chickens pecked grain out of the straw at the barn door.

On Kenilworth's great manor fields the winter wheat was being mowed, the villeins striding with a steady pace and swinging of the sickle. The spring field of oats, peas, beans and barley was near harvesting, and in the fallow field the villeins' long-horned oxen grazed. The cycle of manor life was as serene and steady as it had been for a thousand years.

"Are you content?" Simon asked the countess as they sat together in the hall one evening.

"With you... here, or in Palestine, or in Gascony... I am content," she smiled. Eleanor lived in wonder that she, the plain of face, the often erring one-time nun, was wedded to the man most beautiful of all the men that she had ever seen. She had followed him in exile, and would follow him to Hell if it were needful. In fact she nearly had.

Simon kissed her hand. But in England he could never be fully at ease, never sure how long King Henry's tolerant frame of mind would last. Never free of his sense of guilt. He still wore the black woolen robes and hair shirt of a penitent for cause.

In November the earl and countess were summoned to attend Court at Westminster. There was to be a double celebration – for King Henry and the Court's return from France, and for the wedding of the king's brother, Prince Richard. Richard was to marry the youngest sister of Queen Eleanor, Sanchia of Provence.

On finding himself stripped of his French duchy, Richard's first response was rage. But any sign from him of willingness to overthrow his brother, he knew would be met promptly with civil war. There were many of England's lords who would far rather have him king. Richard had no wish to be the King of England. He was already England's richest man. And now he began to think himself relieved of troublesome Gascony. He never for a moment thought his brother had prompted his would-be murderers. When Henry returned, Richard said nothing to him of the coup that bestowed Gascony on little Prince Edward. Instead he turned his mind to pleasant things. He was a widower. It was time to marry.

Three years ago the prince had met Sanchia, on his way through Aix en Provence to Palestine on his Crusade. He had remembered her, the shy and modest blonde, youngest of the four sisters of Provence, hailed as the greatest beauties of the age. The eldest sister, Margaret, was now Queen of France.

Though Richard seemed to have forgot that perilous night in Bordeaux, King Henry had not. To ease his conscience, he would mount a gorgeous celebration for the wedding. He was an artist at heart. Drawing and decorating were his fortes, the burdensome businesses of state was the misfortune of his birth.

"I want a hundred tablecloths of scarlet for the wedding feast. Have them edged with gold ribbon. Is a hundred enough?" he asked the queen's uncle, Peter of Savoy, whom he had made the Earl of Richmond – chiefly for Savoy's elegant taste. He was now Henry's favorite courtier.

"Two hundred might be better," Savoy, with a dainty flutter of his short yellow cloak, suggested. "You'll have them for your own use afterward." He would receive a percentage from the draper.

"Then we'll need a thousand candlesticks." Henry calculated cheerfully. "A carpet for the dais. And a canopy of crimson, with the lions of Plantagenet embroidered in gold thread. And let the service for the royal table be all of gold."

"My lord," the clerk John Mansel broke in, "the Treasury cannot..."

Henry cut him off. "I will have a fine wedding for my brother! Do you know no lenders?"

"Our credit is quite used up for your war in France."

Henry was unconcerned. His subjects had been forced to sell their horses, cows and household furnishings to meet the taxes for the war that had lost Poitou. Noble, prosperous families felt the touch of poverty, and the poor starved. But, when in a spending frame of mind, Henry floated on the happy thought that always more could be wrung from his people.

The wedding ceremony was to be in Westminster Abbey's chapel, beside the royal residence. With Abbot Richard Croxley, bent and fussing at his side, Henry viewed the little abbey church. He looked about the stark room with dismay, as if he noticed its cramped bleakness for the first time. He frowned at the glass-less windows, the plain whitewashed walls. Only the gilded, red and blue tiled shrine of Saint Edward, which he had commissioned four years earlier, showed any refinement.

Seeing the king's pained look, his palsy-drooping eye and sagging cheek adding such apparent agony to his expression that he seemed a soul in the pit of despair, Croxley hurried to say, "Good king, please notice the fine blue drapery we've put over the altar. And, of course, we'll use our best altar cloths!"

But Henry only snapped, "This place is a sty! We must have a better church here. Find a master builder who can make a suitable building."

"Before the wedding?" Croxley asked, terrified.

"Of course not before the wedding!" Henry retorted. "Something proper cannot be built in a week!" He strode away in a miserable mood, his plans for a magnificent occasion spoiled.

Sanchia arrived from France with her mother, Beatrice of Savoy. The bride, like her mother and sister Queen Eleanor, had masses of golden curls, a heart-shaped face and a brow high and rounded, with pale blue eyes. But she lacked the wit and challenge that gave Queen Eleanor such sparkle.

Richard's heart and mind were full of Sanchia. He was the very image of his red-haired, burly uncle Richard the Lion Hearted, but he was reduced to boyish simpering and gazing at his bride. In love, and touched by Henry's great preparations for his marriage ceremony, he forgave his brother everything.

The wedding was performed on November twenty-third. All England's high nobility crowded the little abbey church. From there, the splendidly robed party walked the short distance to Westminster Palace's hall.

A thousand candles lit the room to a brilliant golden glow; the hall's murals of the Battle of Antioch seemed alive with the moving shadows of the celebrants. Amid the scarlet-draped tables, pages in tabards of red and gold and caps with arching cock-feathers brought huge gold platters laden with the feast. Pastries filled with minced lampreys and eels, prawns and crabs, King Henry's favorite foods, were the first course. Then came custards of almond milk and squab; minced meat shaped as orbs and dusted with gold; lark pies with the birds' feet poking upward through the crusts; venison stuffed with frumenty, dried plums and medlars; and roast boar trimmed with gilded ivy leaves.

At the royal table Sanchia, then Richard were seated to King Henry's left. Queen Eleanor sat at Henry's right; next to her was Peter of Savoy; and after him, his sister Beatrice of Savoy, the Countess of Provence and mother of the queen and the bride. Simon was seated next in precedence, then the Countess Eleanor.

Beatrice, a connoisseur of manly beauty, studied her dinner partner with a practiced glance. Long of limb and muscular, Simon easily was first at Henry's Court for male comeliness. But Beatrice judged that his wife, though sumptuously dressed, was rather plain of face, her nose and mouth too large, no match for her own golden daughters. The mother of the queen and bride herself had been a great beauty, and her manner was vivacious, gay, eager to please. Flirtatious.

Despite his prejudice against the Provencals, his father's old enemies, Simon found he liked Beatrice. He chatted easily with her as the venison and wine were served.

"You too, good Earl, though French, coming from abroad like us, have found welcome in England," Beatrice observed, her voice audible to the far ends of the table. "This seems an open hearted land! Though when I saw those white cliffs towering from the sea, I thought the very earth itself rose up to throw us back." She darted a smile to her son-in-law the king, who nodded, much pleased with her compliment.

"It is true," Simon said thoughtfully. "I especially have felt the grace of England toward the foreign born." It was true, but a truth that in the past he had denied, insisting that his claim to the earldom of Leicester was his by right of inheritance through his grandmother, even though his father never claimed it. But it was not merely the festive night and three goblets of wine that prompted this mellow mood in him. With his success as foremost military counselor of the Crown, humility had come to him, tempered by his guilt for having wronged Henry. Though he spoke quietly, Henry, always attentive for praise, was leaning in his direction. Simon's eyes met the king's as he said earnestly, "I've been most kindly served."

Henry opened his mouth, but did not know what to say. There were in Simon's words and look a mildness so unexpected in his brother-in-law that he was confounded. He looked away from Simon, picking up the conversation on his other side with Sanchia and Richard.

Beatrice studied the Countess Eleanor's rich gown of ruby samite stitched with pearls, one of her treasures from her brief, happy time in Palestine when Richard's Crusade was triumphant and Simon was Mayor of Jerusalem, then Viceroy-elect. "Your wife is a very jewel!" Beatrice declared to Simon. "A holiday for eyes! My dear," she extended her talk beyond him, to Eleanor, "tell me of your wedding. Was your feast much like this?"

Eleanor colored at the question. "No, madam," she replied hardly above a whisper. In truth, there had been no feast, no robes finer than her plain russet nun's attire, no celebration whatsoever. Only vows spoken in a clandestine hush in the king's own private chapel.

"So modest! My dear, the sister of a king so great as this," Beatrice gave an airy wave at the splendid furnishings of the hall, "has no cause for modesty! I'm sure, had you no merits but your dowry alone, which is far from the case as I can see with my own eyes, that were enough for you to ever speak with a bold voice."

At these words Eleanor looked so upset that Beatrice reached past Simon to grasp her hand. "My dear, what is the matter? Are you ill?" Even Simon had to look away, embarrassed but amused. He covered his smile with his hand.

"I... I brought no dowry to my husband," Eleanor said painfully.

For a moment Beatrice was stunned. Her own daughters were dowerless thanks to the havoc and ruin the Albigensian Crusade, which Simon's father led, had wrought upon Provence. But this had not barred her daughters from marrying the kings of England and of France. Their beauty proved of greatest worth. Nonetheless she was acutely sensitive regarding dowries. She let go of Eleanor's hand and turned toward her son-in-law. "Can this be so, Henry? Your sister had no dowry?"

The king had not been following their conversation. The sudden question caught him by surprise. "Dear mother, you may be sure my sister had a dowry," he blurted. But seeing the look in Eleanor's eyes, he added truthfully, "She had a dowry for her first marriage. It has not yet been recovered from her deceased husband's heirs."

"Your sister went with nothing to her husband who sits by me here?" Beatrice asked, astounded.

The queen and Peter of Savoy were pressed between the king and Beatrice, Savoy making gestures to hush his sister, while Queen Eleanor laughed.

"We've tried to recover the funds." King Henry squirmed in his chair.

"If only I could regain my rents, we could pay off our debts," the Countess Eleanor said wistfully.

The queen regained her composure. "It is a shame that your sister has old debts to mar her homecoming, " she urged Henry. "But for Pembroke's stiff-necked greed, her dowry would be hers and there would be no debts! Can we do nothing?"

Beatrice nodded approvingly.

Henry succumbed. "I'll make good my sister's rents out of the royal purse. And I'll pardon her outstanding debts. Will that be satisfactory?" His drooping eye seemed so pathetic that the Countess Eleanor breathed a fervent thank you. The queen smiled triumphantly. Her mother cooed, "So fine a king and brother!"

Melting in the sunshine of such appreciation, Henry warmed to an excess of generosity. Leaning toward Simon, he added, "And I shall make a present to you of a thousand pounds to make good for your years abroad, and pardon any of your taxes that are in arrears."

"My king, your kindness is too much." Simon was amazed.

Henry met his gaze, "I owe you more for your aid to me, in battle at Sainte, and in the care you showed me in Blaye and Bordeaux, than can be paid in coin."

Simon was so struck with gratitude and remorse that he could hardly answer. "My lord," he stammered, "may I serve you always as your right arm, and as your friend." The closeness to the king, the affection he had once enjoyed from him, seemed all restored. Forgiveness, even forgetfulness of hurt, flowed in Henry on this night like honey from a hive. But Henry's moods were changeable.

The merrymaking at Westminster went on through December. Then, as Christmas neared, the royal revelers moved to Wallingford, Prince Richard's nearest castle. More than a hundred guests were housed in Wallingford's great, round tower. The floors were strewn with sweet rushes and pine, the doorways hung with holly and great branches of mistletoe. Huge braziers warmed the rooms.

On the night of their arrival, after a late supper of roasted beef, dried fruits and cheese, the guests went out into the castle yard. There, troubadours sang love songs by a bonfire that sent its sparks high up into the dark star-flecked sky. In the great hall and the chambers, servants swarmed to clear away the feast, take down the trestle tables and set up the curtained beds the lordly guests had brought with them, part of their customary traveling gear.

The guests, returning to the hall, found their beds crowded close together in the chambers. Their response was only the merrier. The Earl and Countess of Leicester discovered their bed was in a chamber shared with the king's elderly cousin the Earl of Salisbury William Longspee and his wife; the queen's uncle Peter of Savoy; the bluff Earl of Norfolk Roger Bigod and his wife; and the young Earl of Gloucester Richard de Clare and his recent bride.

"This is how it was in the times of Arthur," William Longspee observed, "when all the king's men slept together in the hall."

"And those were better times!" the wispy little Countess of Gloucester added with surprising force.

"You would say that," her husband teased. "In those days every man had to stay close to watch his wife. There could be a traveling about from bed to bed tonight!" he crowed. "Any man who goes out to the privy for a piss had better hurry back to see his place has not been taken!" Richard de Clare, the Earl of Gloucester, was just twenty-three. He wore his auburn hair in long, feminine curls, and his face was of that sweetness that had prompted Saint Augustine to say of the English, "These are not Engels, but angels." Coarse talk was young Clare's counter to his prettiness.

The Countess Eleanor lay back on her fur coverlet, feeling very languid from the travel and the evening's wine. She pressed Simon's hand as he sat cross-legged on their bed.

"In days of Arthur, King Mark was wise," Roger Bigod winked. "He sprinkled flour on the floor so he could trace the footsteps the next morning."

"Not wise enough," Clare countered. "Tristan could leap to the queen's bed."

"Yes, but he strained himself!" Clare's little wife added so vehemently that both her husband and Bigod burst out laughing. "I don't think that's funny at all. I think King Mark was very wise!" she insisted primly. But everyone was laughing now.

Savoy gallantly came to her rescue. "Indeed, how could Mark know how far a man can leap when he's so moved!"

"We'd better draw our curtains, one and all, before we have Gloucester demonstrating how far he can leap," the dour William Longspee said, but even he was chuckling.

Eleanor tugged Simon's sleeve till he leaned down toward her. She whispered in his ear, "Draw the curtains closed, I'd have you with me."

"Here?" he whispered back.

"Why not?" her eyes sparkled. "If new-wed couples have each other on their wedding night with guests still in the room, why not we who are in better practice?"

With a smile, Simon brought her hand up to his lips, then drew their bed curtains closed.

A murmuring went through the room.

"The first to quit the evening!" Gloucester proclaimed. "Sleepy so soon, Earl Montfort?"

Simon thrust his head out of the curtains. "No more than you, Earl Clare. But deeds speak louder than words," he grinned.

Bigod, Longspee and Savoy let out an approving howl.

"Well said," Gloucester parried. "The time for words is passed. T'is time for deeds." And he too pulled his curtains shut.

With the protagonist retired, the room quieted and curtains were drawn round all the beds. But soon there was a squeaky giggling from the Gloucester quarter.

"Ho, there! What deeds are these!" a voice cried from somewhere. Ripples of laughter came from all the curtained beds.

"Mind your own business, and I'll mind mine," Gloucester's voice called back.

"I am minding my own business. And we all hear how you are minding yours!"

So the night passed, with more laughter than sleep.

The next day was Christmas Eve. After morning Mass, at breakfast Prince Richard asked his haggard looking cousin William Longspee how he had slept.

"I've had no sleep at all," Longspee complained. "Gloucester brayed all night about his privy part as if nobody else had one."

A tactful shifting of the room-companions was arranged. The Longspees found themselves that night in more decorous company.

When breakfast was done, the guests, wrapped in their riding cloaks of miniver and vair, assembled for the morning's hunt. Out in the cold yard they inspected arrows, compared crossbows and tested the tensions of their strings. Sleekly groomed horses, their manes braided with bells, jingled as they pranced. Long pheasant feathers in the riders' caps bobbed gaily. Shouts and chime of bells filled the damp morning air, and then the blare of hunting horns.

But the hounds were quiet, already out with the game beaters in the woods.

Eleanor and Simon rode with the king and queen and the Earl and Countess of Warwick to their station at a clearing in the forest. There they sat their horses, speaking low, or keeping silent, listening for the dogs to bay. A few hardy winter birds sang in the bare branches overhead. Snow lay in white swathes upon the earth's brown leafmold. The sky was softly gray, and fog, drawn into long ribbons, wove among the trees.

Suddenly the hounds were heard. A horn trilled the notes of the chase. Bursting through the fog a stag bolted, springing over the ground at speed. The six riders at once spurred after him, dashing through the bars of mist. The horses ran headlong as their riders, straining forward, raised their crossbows at the deer. Six arrows hushed through the air. The stag faltered, then fell.

The hounds came like a shrieking torrent through the trees and closed upon the wounded, wild-eyed deer. Close behind, the Master of the Chase sounded the horn notes of the kill. He rode up, beating back the dogs with lashings of his whip. Dismounting, he quickly killed the struggling stag with his pike, then he pulled out the arrow that had struck most nearly fatally. It was the queen's.

"My queen surpasses my best soldiers in the chase!" King Henry announced proudly.

"It is no more than Mother expects of me," Queen Eleanor laughed. "Last night she set me to it with the tale of the girl who hunted boar in Caledonia."

"Not like the rough Atalanta do you down your game, my Queen," Simon ventured in a courtly compliment, "but like the goddess Diana herself."

Queen Eleanor's eyes lit. "Beware, good Earl," she tossed back playfully, "or you, like Acteon, may find yourself consumed."

A frown of jealousy crossed Henry's brow, but he said nothing.

The Master of the Hunt trussed the deer and gave the hounds their reward of the vitals. The winter sun burnt off the mist as the hunters waited for the hounds to raise more game. But the dogs did not bay again, and no more game was sighted.

When the bells of Wallingford announced the noonday dinnertime, the hunting parties went back to the castle for more music and the feast.

At table, as Savoy already had departed, Simon found that he was seated by the queen. Since his remark that morning, from time to time he noticed she was gazing at him. Now dreamily she nodded to the troubadour's yearning, lilting songs of loves bestowed and of loves lost. Her pretty bow mouth parted. Her hand, beneath the table's cloth, pressed Simon's thigh.

Her unexpected touch, her hand resting upon him secretly, and intimately, affected him with a force as if someone had flung him to the ground. The sensation lingered long after she drew her hand away. One touch and he was aching. Then the soft pressure of her hand again brought him to warmth that turned the ache to agony. He still wore penitential robes of black over a hair shirt, and it was not without cause. His rational mind was furious, yet fascinated by the force that, after years of penance and of exile, still had power over him. And he was annoyingly aware he had invited it.

She glanced at him, a knowing smile upon her lips. He turned away from her. But if he had supposed that this desire was conquered, he knew now for a certainty that he was wrong.

The Twelve Days of Christmas were spent in holy services, feasting and the chase. In the evenings, the queen's troubadours sang songs of yearning love, trouveres told tales of courts in times gone by, and on Twelfth Night the villagers of Wallingford performed a masque.

Simon kept distant from the queen. Feigning illness, he avoided the royal table where he would be seated by her side. Both Henry and the queen inquired about his health. But when a page reported to the queen that he had seen the earl eating ravenously at an inn, she understood. If he still felt a need to flee from her, her hope was confirmed.

On the morrow of Twelfth Night the guests were dismissed. Simon and the Countess Eleanor went home. The countess was aglow with the festivities. Simon rode in a pensive, withdrawn mood. He smiled to Eleanor, insisting he was quite recovered when she asked if he was still unwell. But his smile was melancholy.

A powdery snow began to fall as they neared Kenilworth. The lake and sky were a slate gray. The air between was filled with dancing flakes that caught upon the trees like fairy webs. The bastion's ruddy walls, muted by the storm and the gray light, showed pale rose as the dead brown grass turned white. Eleanor's horse shook its mane, its braided bells jingled. Just then, as if in answer, the castle's bells rang out.

Chapter Two

KINGSHIP AND TYRANNY
1244

DESPITE HIS TREASURY'S HOVERING NEAR bankruptcy, King Henry made good on his many promises given at Prince Richard's wedding time. Among the first to remind him of his words was the Abbot of Westminster, Richard Croxley. In January he appeared at Court with a master builder.

"Good King Henry," the Abbot bowed low, "such a holy work as you've agreed to undertake, to build a great church for Westminster Abbey, must please God and make your name forever sweet to Him!"

"My lord," the master builder, Henry of Rheims, bowed as low as the abbot, "I can build a church for you surpassing the most glorious cathedrals!" He brought out drawings: floor plans, elevations, designs for the details of a column, a portal, a pinnacle. He spread his drawings out before the king.

Though this was far beyond his intent for a chapel by his hall, Henry was enthralled. London had Saint Paul's Cathedral, monstrously tall and ungainly. There was no need for another such, to be built in the suburb of Westminster. Nor had Henry ever thought to build a thing so grand – until the artist in him saw this chance for his life's masterpiece.

Henry walked the abbey grounds. He spent hours with the master builder, working and reworking the plans. Croxley followed after them, agog at the expanding project as the design for his abbey's chapel grew more splendid with each passing day.

But even in the grip of this new interest, Henry's promise to his sister was not lost. Eleanor's debts were cancelled and she began receiving money from the royal purse – not fully equal to her dower rents, but enough for her and for Simon to live with less strain. And Henry managed to send the promised thousand pounds, which paid most of the earl's debts.

At Kenilworth, Simon's mentor the Bishop of Lincoln, Robert Grosseteste, came for a visit. Grosseteste was now gaunt and sixty-five. But like an aging elm, he seemed more sturdy, even more imposing than before, his gray eyes keener, his narrow jaw sharper. As Provost of Oxford and Provincial of the Order of Franciscans in England, he was one of the Church's most respected men of intellect. His liberal ideas often rattled Rome. For Simon, he took the place of the stern father he had hardly known, who died when he was five. His early education, as companion to the child King Louis in the Court of France, often met conflict with the bishop's new ideas, but he held Grosseteste in the deepest of respect on matters spiritual. The bishop was his confessor.

"I am writing a treatise on government," Grosseteste informed Simon, as they sat comfortably before the blazing hearth in the privacy of the western upper chamber, drinking the good Bordeaux wine Simon had brought back from France. "More and more, as grace gives me the insight, I see good government to be the surest means of tutoring the soul to its salvation."

"As a boy, I was taught that the business of a king is to rule so that each subject is led to live a good and honest life," Simon nodded genially.

"But who are the kings so able?" Grosseteste demanded. "God bestows our kings upon us, it is true. But they are far from perfect!"

"Indeed," Simon smiled, taking a sip of wine. He was too much at ease to be nettled by the bishop. "It would be hard to see King Henry as perfect."

Grosseteste drew himself up and looked at Simon earnestly. "You grant that kings aren't perfect. I suggest that kings are the means by which God leads us to understand His will." The bishop narrowed his eyes. "I've made a study of our old English ways, when the king was no more than a mediator, acting on the counsels of the Wittenmote – wise men who were chosen by the folk. The Wittenmote decided all matters of the public good. Not one man alone! There are other ways than rule by a king's sole will. And when God grants us a ruler who cannot be forborne, He leads us to recall His other ways!"

"Good Bishop," Simon was jostled from his comfort by his friend's words, "what you suggest is perilous."

"Is it not perilous to countenance misrule? Do we not have ancient Rome's example to warn us of the ills of kings' unbridled greed?"

"King Henry is far from a Tiberius."

"King Richard of the lion's heart, King John and now King Henry. Each has been more grasping than the last! Yes, we may see two or three generations pass before England has her Tiberius. But that will be too late. Your enslaved grandchildren will weep and curse our blind complacency!"

"Good father, you are speaking treason!"

Grosseteste ignored his cautioning. "Henry has summoned a meeting of the barons and high clergy. You know as well as I he'll ask for money. A new tax! The barons will kick against it, but then give in as they always do. That is, unless they have a demand of their own." The Bishop's features gathered to their sharpest focusing. "I shall offer a charter based on the old Wittenmote. When the king asks for money, we will demand a council! Permanent, and freely chosen by the people. Not just summoned when he wants a new tax! For thirty years we've had the Magna Carta. It brought war and death to King John, and has been toothless ever since! To be certain that the king does as the council wills, we must demand our own choice of chancellor and justiciar as well. They, and not the king, must keep the Royal Seal and administer the royal justice!"

"My good bishop," Simon said icily, "if I understand you right, this council would be sovereign, not the king."

Grosseteste's lips tightened in a thin, straight smile. "Nothing less will curb the growing tyranny."

"I see it not so!" Simon was appalled. Grosseteste's words alone were enough to have him hanged, drawn and quartered as a traitor.

But the old bishop seemed uncaring of the danger. He countered, "If you don't see the truth now, in due time you will! That is, unless the royal favors you enjoy have bought your heart and mind. Oh, but I forget! You are a foreigner. What do you care for England's good, so long as you're made rich!"

Simon's face turned white with anger. "Your words are unjust, father! I owe Henry much, but I do not owe him my soul! If I believed God's will was as you say, even my oath of fealty to my king would not stand in my way. But I do not believe it!"

Grosseteste's expression softened. He smiled, nodding approvingly, and even gave a little laugh. "I'm sorry. Please forgive me if I pricked you rather hard. You're still the man I knew five years ago. I trust Our Lord will show you, in His time and in His way, if our charter is to succeed."

Simon feared greatly for his friend, but knew not what to do to save him from pursuing his ruin.

In February of 1244 King Henry called a meeting of the barons and high clergy at Westminster. Simon went with deep concern and fear for Bishop Grosseteste. He found the meeting much like those he had attended years before. But now he had high standing in the Court. He was no longer just the king's hated foreign friend. He was the hero of the battles of Poitou and Gascony, and the king's respected counselor.

In the great hall, groups of lords and priests talked somberly. New arrivals wandered, greeting friends. Simon saw Grosseteste talking earnestly with other bishops, but kept a distance from him. He found his old friend from his student days in Paris, the Bishop of Worcester, Walter Cantaloup. Walter, tall and powerful, was leaning quite unbishop-like against a pillar near the front, observing the scowls of the lords with apparent amusement. Simon approached him from behind and cuffed his arm. "How is my guardian angel?"

Walter spun round like a fighting man, then saw his friend. "Simon!" His broad face spread to a wide grin. "It is so good to see you back in England! What's this I've heard about your being viceroy of the Holy Land? And stopping single-handedly the whole

French army in Poitou? Are you paying some trouvere to invent wild tales?"

Simon laughed outright. "Leave it to friends to always fear the worst and doubt the best!" At Walter's urging he recounted his life in Palestine and his reconciliation with King Henry, serving in his army in Poitou and Gascony. While they were still talking, the king entered. The noise in the hall dropped to a hush. Simon and Walter broke off and went to stand in their proper places.

The royal clerk Henry Wengham read the king's greeting and announcement. It was the expected plea for funds. This time the excuses given were the perpetual wars in Wales and the campaign in Poitou. No mention was made of Henry's grand new plan for Westminster Abbey's chapel. The king withdrew to his chamber. The meeting was turned over to the lords and prelates to discuss how taxes would be raised.

While the barons argued angrily, Grosseteste went among the clergy, drawing them off into a separate conference. Simon, distressed for them, tried to stop Cantaloup.

"Think what you are doing!"

"Father Grosseteste spoke with you?"

"He did. And what he said was outright treason."

"If treason it is, so be it," Walter met Simon's eyes, his pudgy face all earnestness. "We must act now, Simon. Would that you were with us!" And he hurried away to assist the old bishop.

After some hours, the clerics came back to the general meeting. To Simon's shocked amazement, they were nearly unanimous in support of Grosseteste's plan. His charter for an elected counsel, chancellor and justiciar was presented to the lords.

Grosseteste's dry, gray face was lively with expression, his voice ringing with force. "Good lords of England, I speak to you in urgency! The Church in England looks to you," his small eyes bored down upon the lords. "She hears the cries of her people, great and small! Government," he spread his hands wide, "is like a winnowing screen through which each soul must pass. When the screen is ill made, its openings too small, only some grains may pass through, while others that are good are cast back with the chaff and left to ruin! So it is, through the effects of ill-made governments, that many souls are lost to sin. When we of the Church see this happen, our hearts are torn. We must speak out. We beg you, heed our counseling!" He read to the lords his charter for a council, chancellor and justiciar, chosen by election by the people. No such thing had ever been proposed before.

To Simon's utter astonishment, the charter found wide approval. Absent from England, he had no idea of the rage that Henry had aroused through his ruinous taxations, or of the ruthless penalties that were being executed at his sheriffs' whims. Many of the lords agreed with Grosseteste outright. Others were so angered by the king that they seemed willing to accept any plan that could curb Henry's powers. The barons moved to choose an initial council at once, and have it present the charter as a thing already done.

Grosseteste, Walter Cantaloup, the Bishop of London Fulk Basset, the Earl of Norfolk Roger Bigod and Henry's nemesis, Gilbert Marshall the Earl of Pembroke were elected to the council. And lest the king see the council as made up solely of his enemies, Simon, Prince Richard and the new Archbishop of Canterbury – the queen's young uncle Boniface, in his early twenties, dim of wit and great of brawn – were chosen despite themselves. Two knights and two priests were chosen also, to represent the English people in general.

Grosseteste's intent was that the council decide all questions of the government, and publish its opinions for the approval of all subjects of the Crown. This was something truly new under the sun. Not in the democracies of ancient Greece, not in the small kingdoms where the Wittenmote had once held sway, had there ever been such sharing of sovereignty. Grosseteste had created a completely new concept of government.

When the lords and the clergy reassembled before King Henry, the council was their representative. The chosen lords, prelates, knights and clerics stood before King Henry. The rest of the convention waited solemnly, attentive and silent.

The appearance of good order and unity in the hall bore such a difference from the mass of contentious individuals that Henry usually faced, that he sensed danger at once. "What is this council!" he demanded, after the young archbishop had read the list of its members. Told of the new charter and the council's intent, he stood up, bellowing, "We will not recognize your council! Nor any other! Unless we choose to create one ourselves!" Stepping forward, furiously he spat out the words, "We would be no king at all to bend to such a thing as this!"

"If you object to our members, would you choose more of your own?" young Boniface offered innocently. The Archbishop of Canterbury was trying hard to fill his high rank as a mediator, but was far out of his depth.

Henry knew quite well that if he accepted a council that had originated in other hands than his, he would be giving up the very core of his power. Ignoring Boniface, in curt tones he told the assembly, "We will appoint a new justiciar and chancellor, if that will please you. But no council is needed! We will ourselves see to the wise rule of this land. This meeting is adjourned, to reconvene here six days hence. Use the days to reconsider the funds that we request!"

As they were leaving the hall, Henry summoned Prince Richard and Simon to his private chamber. "What is this new thing the barons have invented?"

"The clergy refer to the old custom of the English Wittenmote." Simon explained, trying as best he could to shield his friends.

"It is an abomination. I'll have none of it!" Henry retorted. Then his expression changed. "So this originates with the clergy? Well, we are armed to deal with that!"

News of the great abbey church Henry was planning had reached Rome, though few in London knew of it. The new Pope, Innocent IV, had responded with a letter rich in praise of England's devout king. The pontiff commanded the clergy to assist the king, by every means, to raise whatever funds he asked, and to support his personal rule as the Lord's Chosen Monarch. To act in accord with Henry's wishes was to be in accordance with God's will. Had Pope Innocent heard Grosseteste's arguments, his words could not have countered them more pointedly.

Henry called a meeting of the prelates that evening, and had the papal letter read aloud to them.

Grosseteste was not so easily halted. He knew nothing of the building of the stupendous abbey church that had prompted the Pope's letter. But the notion that King Henry's command had the authority of divine will was to him unacceptable in the extreme, even if the Pope himself proclaimed it.

Quaking with anger, he stepped forward when the reading of the letter was finished. He began slowly and thoughtfully. "We believe our Shepherd in Rome to be above error in holy doctrine. But, in issues of the governance of England, we know that he relies on men with interests of their own. Were he to hear the suffering prayers of the people with his own ears, he would be put in mind of Christ's own condemnation of the Pharisees. 'They bind heavy burdens grievous to bear, and lay them on other men's shoulders.' We obey our father the Pope as God's witness in things spiritual. But we must beware of the Pharisees in Rome. We must not lie undefended when their tongues drown out the voice of compassion from our Shepherd's ears!"

When Grosseteste finished speaking there was silence. The fathers of the Church looked at the floor, or away into the air, uncertain what to do. They were unprepared to contradict both the Pope and their king.

Walter Cantaloup broke the silence. "The Bishop of Lincoln speaks truly," he insisted, but his voice lacked conviction. Standing in outright opposition to the Pope was more than even he would dare.

King Henry looked from face to face. "Good Bishop Nicholas," he singled out the old, enfeebled bishop of Ely, "do you stand with Bishop Grosseteste?"

Terrified, Nicholas drew his lips down in a puffed grimace and shook is head.

"And you, Bishop Longspee?" Henry asked his cousin the Bishop of Litchfield.

"I think the Bishop of Lincoln holds strange views peculiar to himself," Longspee said acidly. "I mean to see that his words are heard in Rome!"

Grosseteste turned on Longspee, his eyes blazing, "I speak with Heaven as my witness! Do you suppose I fear to have the Vatican hear too?"

"There is merit in Bishop Grosseteste's warnings," Stephen Berkstead the Bishop of Chichester offered cautiously.

But Longspee sharply countered him. Soon the whole room was entangled in loud argument. Few of the clergy doubted Grosseteste was correct that misused royal power must be curbed, but few were ready to stand by him when singled out. Seeing he had succeeded in disarming Grosseteste's principal support, Henry ordered their meeting adjourned. The clergy were ordered to meet each night until they found means to fulfill the royal need for funds.

Henry was never more triumphant. The next day he created a council for himself. He did not entirely pack it with his own creatures. Simon and Peter of Savoy, and two knights in the royal service were appointed; but as a gesture to the rebels he added Walter Cantaloup, supposing Simon could control his old friend. He chose Simon to head the new council, and ordered him to meet with the clergy every night, to see to it they granted the new tax.

While Simon was allotted the work of bringing Grosseteste and his allies to heel, the king himself sent personal summonses to every lord in London, ordering them one by one to attend him in his chamber. During the six days of the adjournment, from early morning until late at night, Henry cajoled, threatened, argued and pled. Each day he grew more tense and frenetic. His fragile spirit crumbled with the strain. But he forced himself to go on.

Among the lords a bitter, set expression spread from face to face like a contagion contracted at their meetings with the king. Gathering at the inns of London and Westminster, they cursed and ridiculed Henry.

By the fifth day the king was looking ominously haggard. He talked in short, erratic bursts and busied himself in everything.

That evening, before the general reconvening of the lords and prelates at Westminster the next morning, Simon spoke to the fathers of the Church. Not he, nor anyone there save the Abbot of Westminster, knew of the plans for a stupendous chapel to replace the little abbey church. The project was still a secret held only by the king, the abbot, the master builder, the papal legate and the Vatican.

Simon argued from what he knew of the king's need of funds to quell the rebels in Gascony and Wales. If his own recent gains from the royal purse troubled him, they were as nothing to the costs of war, or even to the wealth that Henry heaped on the queen's kindred. He ended with, "You rail against King Henry for disorder in his lands and the loss of England's holdings in France. Yet you grudge the funds that he must have to bring peace! You counter-bargain for a council and for power for yourselves, while the wasters of England's dukedoms and the west country run rampant! Is this the wise benevolence of England's Church?"

The clerics listened. Grosseteste, in the forefront, frowned. But while the Bishop of Lincoln's look was dour, his feelings were mixed. The earnest youth he had first met in Leicester fourteen years ago was now a leader among men. There was conviction in his speaking that went beyond his words. This Simon had a power that could move men's minds and hearts, that could make them trust and believe in him. Grosseteste watched, and was pleased.

When the earl had finished speaking, the Church fathers, deeply moved, asked to hear the papal letter read once more. No one, not even Bishop Grosseteste, raised a word in contradiction. Simon had succeeded in bringing the king's cause to the brink of victory.

The clerk Henry Wengham entered and read the papal letter aloud.

But, before Wengham had finished, the king himself burst into the room. Henry was trembling. His whole body was quaking. He snatched the letter from the clerk's hands, crying, "Good fathers of the Church, it is beyond my understanding how you fail me. I've cherished your honor. But when I come to you in need of help, you turn your backs on me! Have I not honored each of you as if you were my father?" The king's drooping face was contorted and wet with tears. "I've loved you! Each of you! Why do you fail me?" Choking with convulsive sobs he sank, doubling over, to the floor.

Gripping his arm over his head, he lay curled with his knees to his chest, crying.

Simon, as astonished as the rest by the king's sudden appearance, stood helpless for a moment. But he had seen the king like this before – in Poitou when his lords there had betrayed him and given their fealty to King Louis. For weeks, Simon alone had tended Henry. It was this gentle service, above all, that earned him the king's forgiveness. Now he knelt and put his arms around Henry, raising him up until he sat hunched upon the floor.

Henry clutched at Simon, pressing himself to the earl's chest like a frightened child.

Looking to the astonished prelates, Simon said in a soft voice, "The king has not been well. I beg you, pray for him." To Henry he whispered, "My lord, everyone here is loyal to you. Only allow them their own voices. Let us go, and let them finish their approval of your funds."

He raised the king to his feet, supporting him, and walked with him out of the room. In an adjoining chamber Simon found a chair and Henry sat down, still trembling.

"I've done all that I could for them," the king rocked to and fro, his arms folded tightly across his chest. "I've shown them my love like a son. Why don't they love me?"

"They do, my lord," Simon assured him. "The fathers understand your needs. If they're not forced, they will grant what you ask. Have patience just a little while."

Slowly Henry became calmer, though he still clutched himself and rocked like a keening madman. "You advise me well," he nodded, smiling wanly. "I'm not myself right now. What should I do?"

The words struck Simon deeply. It was he whom the king was asking now. But whom might Henry ask another time? Whose self-interest might Henry's weakness serve, with papal force to place his every act beyond question? What would Savoy or Boniface do? Or other of the grasping or vindictive friends that the king kept by him. What results could be felt in distant shires? A helpless king made all his subjects victims. After a pause of some moments, Simon replied, "I would advise you to grant the charter, and accept the elected council, the chancellor and the justiciar."

Henry listened. Then he sighed and shrugged, "Why do I fight them?"

Simon accompanied the king to the royal bedchamber, where he left him with his clerk Mansel. Then he returned quickly to the meeting of the clergy. He found them dispersing. He caught Walter by the arm, "What has happened? Why are they leaving?"

Walter drew down the corners of his mouth in disgust. "They're afraid to take any position at all now! They won't stand in opposition to the Pope. Nor do they want to give free rein to a lunatic. So they're running home, fleeing from tomorrow's meeting like a flock of geese at a thunderclap."

Simon considered it was perhaps for the best that they left, having seen what they had seen. They would not be there to noise about news of the king's collapse.

The next morning the lords assembled without the clergy present. But the hall was an angry hive of buzzing gossip nonetheless. Each lord complained of his private abuse by Henry.

King Henry entered, leaning like an invalid upon Mansel. He fumbled with the chair as he sat down. Then, sullen and silent, he gripped his arms tightly around himself as Mansel read a new royal announcement. The lords were asked to draw up a charter for a council. The king would consider it, provided they agreed to grant him the funds that he asked.

The lords seemed deaf to his offer. They were not there to seek a charter any longer. They were there to vent their ire. Hardly had Mansel finished speaking when the Earl of Oxford, Robert de Vere, shouted, "The king's duty is to protect his subjects! Not to extort from them!"

"How much money have we given you already?" the Earl of Norfolk, Roger Bigod thundered.

Henry raised his drawn and ashen face to look at Bigod. "You think that I don't know? After Bedford there was a tax of two shillings on each plow. The year after that, the fifteenth part of all movable property." His voice was hollow, flat as a boy's reciting a hard lesson. His gaze was fixed on Bigod but his eyes were empty, as if he read the record of his spending somewhere in the recesses of his brain. "Then, when we went to Brittany, the clergy and the towns and Jews raised money. And again, when we came back, there was a scutage of three marks. And after that, a thirtieth part. Then, on the marriage of our sister Isabel..."

The recitation dragged on. The king recited every charge that he had made against his people since he came of age to rule. The sturdy Bigod looked away, abashed. He glanced to his neighbors uncomfortably. The king's fragile nature had been a secret shared among a few lords in Poitou, and he was one of them. But now it was displayed for all to see. William Longspee shuffled his feet and looked at the floor with tears seeping down his hollow cheeks. He cried for his lost noble generation. But no one felt moved to taunt Henry any longer.

The meeting was adjourned. In a few days it convened again. Simon read the charter offered by the lords. It called for an elected council of four lords or high clergymen who would be in attendance on the king at all times. It required the election of two justiciars to head the courts of law, and a chancellor to keep the Royal Seal which made the king's written commands official. The lords agreed to give Henry the money that he asked.

The king nodded his acceptance. But he spoke not a word.

The royal writ was sent out commanding the tax to be collected, and the meeting was immediately adjourned by Mansel. It all went very quickly and the hall was cleared.

"Do you really think the king will hold elections for the council, the chancellors and justiciar?" the young earl of Gloucester Richard de Clare asked Simon as they left.

"Of course," Simon answered.

"Small chance of that now!" Bigod scoffed. "We should have chosen the council members first, like we did before! I'll wager that he never summons us to vote. Henry's won this time."

"The king has given his word," Simon insisted.

"His word!" Bigod echoed derisively.

A page caught Simon by the sleeve and told him that the king wished to speak with him. Simon turned away from Bigod with only a glower for answer, and followed the page.

Henry sat in his private chamber. His secretary Mansel stood by his side with a wax writing-tablet in his hand.

"Well, we got the money," Henry bestowed a tired smile on Simon as he entered. "It was clever of you, getting the good fathers out of the way as you did. In thanks, I'm having your permanent title to Kenilworth written into the rolls."

Simon bowed, then asked, "My lord, when do you plan to hold elections for the council?"

"Council? I know of no council," King Henry smiled slyly.

Chapter Three

SORROW IN PALESTINE
1244

SIMON FELT BETRAYED. ANGRY WITH Henry, and himself. He went home to Kenilworth, determined to keep distant from the Court and Henry's petty connivings. He was troubled with an unshakeable sense of foreboding. But Henry's reign went on from one day to the next. The taxes were collected, and all proceeded normally whether the king was in sound mind or not.

Simon busied himself with his lands and the training of his destriers. The Countess Eleanor spent her days enlarging her household staff. Her servants from her early years at Odiham had returned with Thomas deMesnil from their safe haven in Leicester. But the countess added a fine cook, a baker, kitchen servants, maids, laundresses, gardeners, footmen, a lad who could ride swiftly as the wind to carry messages who was called Gobehasty, and a major domo, pleasantly known as Trubody. In high standing now in England, the Montforts needed a proper, lordly home and all the staff to run it.

Peter remained as Simon's squire, valet, barber and the household's surgeon. And Simon appointed as stewards two of his Leicester knights who had been with him in Palestine: Richard de Havering for Kenilworth, and Thomas Astley for the manse at Leicester. Thomas deMesnil was raised to steward-general over all the Montfort holdings. Lady Mary, deMesnil and Squire Peter looked upon the changes with deep satisfaction. At last the earl's household was becoming what it ought to be.

The rooftop rooms in the square towers that braced the four corners of the castle's walls were made into a school room, a nursery and servants' quarters.

Eleanor was pregnant with her fourth child. The future extended in a vista of quiet family life ahead, as placid as the limpid surface of the Mere.

Before leaving Westminster, Simon had invited Walter Cantaloup to visit. In a few weeks Walter came. The Bishop of Worcester strode into the hall well ahead of the footman who hurried to announce him. He seemed much agitated. Simon, working at his accounts at the table with desMesnil, rose to greet him warmly. But, seeing his friend so upset, he said instead, "Walter what is the matter? I hope your journey wasn't troublesome."

"If only the world were so right that the hazards of the road were our chief ills! You haven't heard the news?"

Simon dismissed desMesnil, who cleared the scrolls from the table as a footman brought a chair for the bishop. "I've heard no more recent news than that the king's infant daughter is betrothed to Scotland's infant king," he smiled. "That should give us peace on our northern border, at least until they're old enough to wed."

But the bishop did not smile. "Then you don't know. Simon, the Holy Land is lost!"

Simon looked at Walter as at someone who had said the moon was tumbling to earth. Then he laughed, embarrassed at missing the point of a gross jest. "I... don't understand. That isn't possible. When I left Palestine there were treaties... Alliances. The combined forces of the knightly Orders and the Outremerine lords of our Christian kingdom were stronger than ever before. And the Saracens were warring among themselves. All that cannot have reversed in just two years!"

"What I tell you is the truth, Simon. There's not a Christian left alive in Palestine!"

"Walter, leave off this tasteless jest! I had a letter only recently from the Master of the Templars in Jerusalem. It told of peace."

"I am not jesting! God save me from ever making mirth of such a subject."

"Then, whatever you have heard, it cannot be the truth."

"My information is the best! As I was on my way from Worcester, I stopped in London. King Henry had just received a letter from the remnant of the Knights Hospitallers of Acre. Of all the members of their Order in Palestine, only twelve men survive! Of the Templars, only nine! They, and a few of the lords of Outremere have found shelter in Cyprus. Your cousin Philip de Montfort is among them."

Simon studied his friend's face. "Walter, I cannot imagine what purpose such misleading news could serve, but it is not possible. There is the treaty with Ayub…"

"It wasn't the Saracens!" the bishop shouted. "Something no one could foresee! A people called the Khoresines from somewhere north of Persia! It's thought the Tatars drove them out of their own land. They have invaded Palestine – will you believe me, Simon!"

"I cannot." Simon leaned his elbows against the table and covered his face with his hands. "There is no doubt some purpose to these claims. The Emperor means to grind money out of Henry. Some such thing! What you say cannot be so!"

But the next day a letter reached Simon from Cyprus, from his cousin the Lord of Tyre, Philip de Montfort. It confirmed Walter's words. And it said more. *They came down like Pharaoh's locusts, destroying everything in their path. The Holy Orders, the Outremerines, everyone was taken by surprise. By the time the knightly Orders ceased their bickering regarding to what to do, it was too late. We were fighting for our lives on Acre's wharves and in the streets of Jerusalem. The Khoresines have spared no one. And no sacred thing. Even Our Lord's tomb is defiled by them. Would you had not left us! You alone were able to keep unity among the Hospitallers, the Teutonic Knights, the Templars and ourselves. With you still as our leader, we might have spared Palestine.*

In a voice growing more hollow and strained with each word, Simon read the letter aloud to Walter and the countess. Walter struck the table with his great fist. "Good God, why couldn't I have been there! I'd have sent some of those devils back to Hell!"

The countess, ashen, looked to her husband. Simon sat still, staring at the letter. Then he let it drop to the table. He had read it through loudly and clearly, but now his jaw moved yet he formed no words. He arose and stiffly walked out of the hall. The countess followed him. She saw him cross the courtyard to the chapel, go in and close the door. She returned to her guest.

"Is he all right?" Walter asked.

"He has gone to the chapel." She sat in Simon's chair and told the footman to bring wine. "In Palestine," she told Walter, "when the Emperor Frederic refused to grant Simon the viceroyship, though Richard himself, who won the land back from the Saracens, had pled for him... the lords of Outremere elected Simon to be their king."

Walter stared in amazement. "King? Of Palestine?"

"He refused the Crown. He felt that, with the Emperor opposing him, there would be civil war. We came back from the Holy Land to beg Frederic to grant his viceroyship. The Archbishop of Tyre had urged him not to leave. Only Simon was trusted by every one of the factions. Only he could lead them all. Oh, my God," she cried, "we should never have left!"

The footman brought a beaker of wine and two goblets. The countess took a long drink. The bishop rubbed his chin. "Simon... King of Palestine... and to turn his back on it!"

"We were so happy there..." the countess gazed at her reflection in the dark pool of her wine. "I have never been so happy. Jerusalem was abandoned when he was sent there by Prince Richard to be mayor. He brought the city back to life. Pilgrims were everywhere. And caravans... Agnes of Montbeliard took me in her camel palanquin and we bought gorgeous fabrics in the marketplace... I suppose she's dead... I suppose nearly everyone we knew there is dead." The countess tightly shut her eyes. "Our house was on the Mount of Olives, just above the Garden of Gethsemene, with the Holy City spread across the mountain opposite, filling our windows. Can you imagine how it is to waken every morning, to see the Holy City at dawn?"

"How could you leave?" the bishop's voice was hoarse. He took the countess's hand.

"We went to plead with the Emperor Frederic in Italy. We thought that, when he understood how Simon held the factions in a bond of trust, he would surely name him viceroy. We left almost all that we had in Palestine, thinking we would be back soon!"

"First Simon went to King Louis, asking him to be his advocate. But France and England were at war, and the Emperor is England's ally. Simon served Louis. Then Henry summoned him. He regained his earldom... but this loss... this is too frightful."

"Surely he meant to do what was right. How could he know? Ought we to go to him?" Walter asked.

"He is in the chapel. Let him pray. Will you pray with me, father?"

They prayed, then talked until supper was ready. And still Simon remained shut in the chapel.

Eleanor sent the squire Peter to call his master to the evening meal. But he could not open the chapel door, and there was no answer from within. Peter was alarmed.

Eleanor went and tried the door herself. It would not move. She pounded on the door and called out. Still no answer came. She thought, for a moment, that she could hear the sound of weeping. Going back to the hall, she quietly told Trubody, "The earl is at his prayers. We will dine now, without him."

The meal was somber. Seagrave and Lady Mary sat at the table on the dais with the countess and the bishop. The earl's chair stood empty. The household servants found their places at trestle tables set up in the hall. There was a buzz of curious whispers at the earl's absence.

Countess Eleanor met their questioning looks. "The Earl is engaged in prayer for the Holy Land," she said calmly. "We have had dreadful news this day. News the truth of which is beyond questioning. Palestine has been lost to a savage people called the Khoresines."

The Bishop of Worcester offered a prayer. Then, as the meal was served, the countess bade the bishop tell of the disaster. When supper was finished and the servants were retiring for the night, she took Peter aside. "Stay. I may have need of you."

Hours passed. Eleanor sat with Bishop Walter and the squire Peter, waiting through the night by candlelight. But Simon did not return. At last she turned to the squire. "Can you force open the door?"

"I can, with His Grace's help," Peter nodded toward the massive clergyman.

The three got up and left the hall. The countess took a lighted candlestick. They crossed the dark yard to the chapel. Walter tried the door. It was barricaded. Eleanor called to Simon again, but now there was no sound at all within. The bishop put his shoulder to the door, Peter put his back against it, and they both pushed. Inch by inch the door opened.

The faint glow of the altar lamp was all that lit the chapel, engulfing the room in shadows till the countess's candle added its soft light.

Simon knelt at the altar. He was naked to his waist; his back was bloody, flayed. Blood spattered the floor. The whip a priest had given him many years before lay near him, clotted with blood. His head was bowed, his bloodied hands covered his face.

"Simon," Eleanor called gently. He did not move. She gave the candle to Peter and went to her husband. Taking his hands, she drew him to his feet. He let her lead him. Silently, she brought him out of the chapel.

With the squire's help, Eleanor salved and dressed the deep gouges of the whip, and put Simon to bed. He would not speak. Nor did he sleep, but lay staring at the wall all night.

Days went by. Simon would neither eat nor speak, until at last he asked to see Walter. But when the bishop came to him, he asked him to retell all he knew of the fall of Palestine.

"I curse my tongue for having brought you this news! The recounting of it can only add to the Devil's work!" Walter protested.

Simon turned his face to the wall again and said no more. Later, when Eleanor came in, he said, "Send Peter to London. I would hear everything that's known of Palestine." Reluctantly, she did as he bade. But she also sent Gobehasty to Grosseteste, begging him to come at once.

The Bishop of Lincoln had his own pressing concerns. A house of Franciscans under his authority had complained against him to the Vatican. As Grosseteste believed a vow of poverty should be taken literally, he had smashed all of their better crockery. This was the latest of many such complaints against him. There had been too many. He was summoned to Rome. He knew that, before he arrived, Pope Innocent would hear of his arguments against the papal letter in support of Henry. He was preparing his defense on several fronts. Nonetheless, he left at once for Kenilworth.

After almost a week of wakeful days and nights, Simon was sleeping. When he woke, he found the old bishop praying at his bedside. He waited until Grosseteste finished and looked up.

"Father, I am as Judas," Simon said. "I have betrayed Our Lord's trust. Even his tomb is defiled."

"It is written, 'He is not here, but is risen. Why seek ye the living among the dead?'" Grosseteste answered. "Do you remember what Our Lord, when risen, said unto Simon, whom he called 'the rock'?"

"The Lord said, 'Lovest thou me,'" Simon responded.

"And what was the Lord's command to Simon?"

"Feed my sheep."

"He did not ask Simon to defend His tomb. But to look to the care of His living people."

"I've failed him!" Simon's eyes showed all the torment of his soul.

"The sheep you seek are here in England," the bishop's gray eyes looked deeply into Simon's. "Were it not so, the Lord would not have brought you back to us. Were it His wish, you too would have died defending Jerusalem."

"I was not worthy!"

"Our Lord alone is perfectly pure. He has no need of your perfection. Be not so proud of soul in judging yourself."

"Father, what do you see in me?" Simon asked bitterly. "Since I first came to England, you have held it in your mind that I would do great things. But you see how useless I am! I tried to gain your charter from the King. But I was only made a fool. If my sheep are here, I am a poor shepherd indeed!"

"Your father, the great Crusader, had an easy task. To fight, to win, to die in glory. You too could do that well, I know. But to you there is given a harder task. To endure. And by enduring, like the strong mountain of your name, to win at last."

Simon's dark eyes gazed at the old bishop for a long time. Then he said quietly, "Stay by me, father. Pray for me."

Grosseteste stayed at Kenilworth for several days. Hour after hour he, Walter and Simon prayed and talked. And slowly Simon was drawn out of the depths of his despair.

One night as Walter, Simon and Grosseteste sat by the firelight in the upper chamber, Simon asked Grosseteste, "Father, you have looked to me to be your advocate at Court. I mean to return to the Holy Land. But if, as you say, my place is here, uncover your full thoughts to me."

The venerable bishop was silent for some time, then he began, "Very well, I'll tell you what lies at the heart of my thinking. What is God's Kingdom but that place in which each soul has its allotted part, determined by its love of Our Lord and sharing of His burden? What is the Devil's kingdom, but enslavement in the coils of greed and lies?" He paused, meeting Simon's gaze, "To which of these two kingdoms does King Henry's realm bear semblance?" His lips turned downward in a smile. "Do not suppose that I take King Henry especially to task. Rare is the king whose works are done in open honesty, for look from where kingship itself springs. Not from Christ," he shook his head. "Kings ruled the earth before Our Lord came down to save mankind. There were kings among the pagans in Jacob's time. Only the Hebrews, who were God's Chosen, had no kings until they fell into the ways of unbelievers." He paused again, carefully considering the faces of his two friends. Then he said slowly, "Christ revealed to us that we are all Our Lord's beloved children. What man who truly knows himself a child of God would give power over himself to another?"

"Father, what of 'render unto Caesar that which is Caesar's'?" Simon asked, appalled at the implications of Grosseteste's words.

"The money Caesar coined is *all* Christ bade us render unto Caesar. Obedience he would have us render only unto God. The holy Francis, by living 'as the lilies of the field,' relying solely on Our Lord's grace, has shown that Christ did not ask the impossible in rendering *all* of Caesar's coinage back to him. Would that my Franciscans had the faith of their founder!"

"Truly, father, as even the brothers lack that perfect faith, how far is mankind as a whole from it," Walter, leaning forward in his chair, offered appeasingly. What Grosseteste spoke of seemed to him as distant from the limits of possibility as it did to Simon. "Does not God, looking upon the earth and seeing our faithless, evil ways, give us our kings to keep order and to guide us to the good?"

"When you stand before the Judgment Seat, will it be your king who is judged, or you?" Grosseteste asked.

"I, surely," Walter answered.

"You are answerable for your soul, and no one else is. Yet, as you say, mankind is feeble in bearing even that small burden. We are crippled in soul. Kings, with their laws and courts, serve as our crutches. We must gain strength so that each of us can stand firmly, and alone, beneath the final Divine scrutiny. That is the meaning of *salvation*. As crutches are cast down by the healthy man, so the rule of kings shall be cast away, as each man learns to bear the burden of his soul's responsibility."

"I wouldn't wish to see the day when kings are cast down," Simon gave a sardonic smile, humoring his old counselor, "for then we shall be ruled by every villein with a loud voice and a strong arm."

Grosseteste frowned at him. "Don't scoff at the commonality, lord Earl. It is the common man whose judgments in the hallmoote courts keep order in the countryside. And far more justly than in the king's courts, where judgments mean money in the judges' pockets!"

But he added quickly, seeing he was losing the trust of his audience, "Do not imagine that I advocate the overthrow of kings today. Were such a thing to happen in our time, our feeble souls would fall in such disorder it would seem a very hell on earth! No. We must proceed by steps. We are like children in a field overgrown with tares. First we must get us a plow and learn its use before we can begin to pull out the pernicious roots and plant the wholesome seeds. The Wittenmote I found like a discarded hoe. I fitted its blade as sheer for the plow. My council is the plow. Its election is the first handling of the tool. As the labor of plowing builds the plowman's strength, so may the responsibility of choice in governance build man's strength of soul."

Simon thought about the bishop's words then, in as kind a way as he could, he said, "I see merit in your council, father. But I was brought up by a wise and devout queen. I cannot believe other than that kings are God's chosen – to be aided when they are weak, and not to be overthrown."

Grosseteste turned from Simon, all his patience spent. Abruptly, almost at a shout, he cried, "Lord Earl, you're resting on a crutch that one day will, like Aaron's staff, turn serpent and sting you unto death!"

Simon recoiled, stunned at the bishop's outburst. But his emotions were too weak for him to rise to anger. "Father," his dark gaze rested on Grosseteste, "you have said before that I shall die in violence. Do not oppress me with your prophesies. I must live my life as best I can. And warnings never yet turned fate away."

The old bishop rested his gray head in his hands and muttered, "I'm a fool. I should know better than to speak out what wise men know better than to say." He looked up, "Forget what I have said, or credit it to an old man's ravings. God will work these things in His own way and time."

Soon after the evening of their talk, Grosseteste went on to Rome, and Walter Cantaloup returned to Worcester.

As Simon grew better, the one thought that filled his mind was the mounting of a new crusade to Palestine. The army would have to be immense to win back the Holy Land with no foothold in the East. He knew there was no chance of raising such a force in England alone. To raise a crusade from all of Europe would require a leader of the highest stature and respect. It would require King Louis.

Louis was still sick with the dysentery he had contracted during his campaign in Poitou. Simon heard that he was coming to England, to the abbey at Cirenchester, which was noted for its cures. He went to meet him there.

He found the King of France lying on a simple cot in a monk's small, whitewashed cell. Louis had refused finer accommodations.

Simon's heart fell when he saw him. Louis's broad, barrel-chested body was shrunken. Only the bone structure remained to hint that he had once been a tall and powerful man. His head seemed large beyond proportion, with staring eyes, a sharply pointed nose and thin lips barely covering his teeth.

"Oh, Louis!" was all Simon could say.

"The fathers will work their cure, if God wills it," the King of France smiled weakly. "I'm glad to see you, Simon. You've regained your lands and titles, I am told."

"Yes," Simon answered, too stricken by the sight of his childhood friend to rise to any easy conversation. "I had hoped to find you better..."

"So had I," Louis grinned.

"There's so much needing to be done..."

"You speak of the Holy Land?" Louis drew in his breath, and his gaze turned toward the ceiling. "I've taken the Cross. God willing I regain my strength, I shall mount a new crusade, and drive the infidels into the sea!" He turned back to Simon, his thin lips smiling with a weakness that made mockery of his bold words.

"God grant you health," Simon whispered, his heart breaking. "I had hoped to return and free the Holy Land..."

"And so you shall... in time," Louis cut him off. His friend's look of despair was unbearable. He shut his eyes. "My health is not the only bar. Our Mother Church is stricken too."

"What do you mean?"

Louis spoke with his fevered eyes closed, resting them. "I've received letters from His Holiness the Pope begging asylum in France. He fears the emperor. Pope Gregory knew how to parry Frederic's thrusts. Pope Innocent has thrown his strongest bolt and seen it miss." Louis opened his eyes and looked at Simon, "Frederic seems to have no fear for his soul. I'm told his response was to put his crown upon his head and ask his courtiers if he looked any different!"

"Having met him, that hardly surprises me," Simon replied.

"Innocent writes that he now fears for his life."

"But surely Frederic would not attack the Vatican!"

"Not directly. But the Romans have been rioting and pillaging. Innocent believes it is Frederic's work." Louis closed his burning eyes again. He was beyond the limit of his little strength. "God help us," he said softly, "that Christendom is wounded in so many ways at once."

The king was quiet, resting for a time, then he turned and looked at Simon. "You seem not well yourself... You hold yourself to blame? You think you ought not to have left the East?" Louis was as knowing of his friend as always.

Simon opened his mouth to speak, but tears welled in his eyes and his throat gripped.

"Simon," Louis said softly, "don't claim for yourself alone a blame that belongs to all of us. Or to none. I see your soul is as racked as my body. Let us both have time for mending before we go to Palestine."

Chapter four

THE CHILDREN
1244-1248

AT KENILWORTH, IN THE SPRING of 1244, the Countess Eleanor gave birth to another boy. He was named Amaury. Little Henry observed in his solemn way that, with Simon and Guy, he thought he had quite enough brothers already. Could he please have a sister next time?

After his visit with Louis Simon was convinced that there was nothing he could do regarding Palestine until the King of France was well. He turned his mind to the care of his estates. All should be in order when he left for the East. He was determined to remain absent from Henry's Court with its corruptive politics, and its temptations.

In early summer a royal letter arrived, followed by a guard of knights in Henry's red and gold livery. One knight held a small boy on his saddle. It was Edward. The prince, now five years old, had come to be schooled by the earl, as King Henry had promised. Simon and Eleanor, with their sons Henry and little Simon held by the hand, went out into the bailey yard to meet him.

As Edward was lowered from the tall horse to the ground, he looked about him with an attitude both cool and self-possessed. "The archbishop my tutor says that I'm to stay with you," he announced, making it quite clear that it was not his wish. "The archbishop says your son has known how to ride a pony for a year now. And that I'm to learn."

"That, and much else as well," Simon answered, restraining the temptation to add "beginning with good manners." He was not at all pleased with the boy's pettish bearing. "Here are your cousins,

Henry and Simon, who are to either side of your own age. You shall be schooled together."

Edward looked at Henry hostilely, taking measure of the infant wonder who already rode by himself.

"We have a pony for you. Would you like to see him?" Henry offered, ever the peacemaker.

Edward's expression lit at the invitation. But, struggling to remain in control as befit a future king, he replied coolly, "There shall be time enough for that."

As they went up the foyer steps into the hall, little Simon tugged on his mother's hand. When she looked down, he screwed up his face sourly. He did not like Edward at all.

Seeing him, unable to resist a return in kind, Edward covertly stuck out his tongue at little Simon.

Taking the prince's small hand, Simon walked over to his chair on the dais and sat, making the boy stand in front of him. "What has the archbishop taught you, Edward? Have you learned your alphabet?"

Edward nodded, confused and overpowered. The archbishop always showed him deference. He did not sit unless the prince sat also. But the archbishop was cold, aloof. Edward sensed that Simon was not cold and he was overcome with shyness. Forgetting about the other children and his need to be superior, he gripped the earl's hand tightly with his small fingers.

"Can you read?" Simon asked.

"Yes. I can read the Latin bestiary I've brought with me," Edward said proudly.

"That is very good for one so young. You'll be a learned king."

"I want to be a soldier!" The child looked into the earl's dark eyes, "You will teach me?"

Simon smiled and nodded to the bright blue eyes gazing into his. He kissed the child's blond head, feeling a flow of love for him as he had not felt for his own sons. "You will learn the handling of the sword and lance, and of whole armies. But you shall also learn from books," he added quietly. "For it is in them that the lessons of wise governance are found, without which all the armies in the world are useless to a king."

Little Simon, jealous of his father's warmth toward the stranger, came to the chair and leaned against his father's knee. Simon put his arm around him and kissed him too. "You must love each other as brothers," he said, with more truth than he dared even to think. But little Simon wrinkled up his nose.

After supper, Edward was shown to the small second-floor room prepared for him in one of the corner towers. Lady Mary had unpacked his belongings from the leather sacks the knights had brought.

"Is there really a pony here for me?" the prince asked the kind-seeming woman who reminded him of the nurse he had just left behind at York.

"There is," she nodded. "And in the morning you shall see him."

"Are there ghosts in this castle?" he asked, as she tucked him in.

"Not a one. If you hear strange noises, it's just the frogs out in the Mere, so don't you fret."

"I wouldn't fret if there was a ghost," Edward said staunchly.

Lady Mary laughed and said good night, blowing out the candle as she left the room.

When Edward awoke in the morning, his cousin Henry was sitting in a corner of the room patiently waiting. "I thought you might like to see our stable before breakfast," he offered tactfully, not to imply any special eagerness about the pony.

Edward dressed and, feeling very independent, went out with his new friend.

Lady Mary, finding the prince's room empty, flew in a panic to the countess. A search was launched. But soon the two were sighted as they trudged from the apple grove down to the stable yard with the prize of a green apple for the pony.

"Let Edward have some freedom, it will do him good," Simon told Mary.

At breakfast Edward was beaming, full of secret delight. He had seen his pony and, even more exciting, he had caught a frog. The creature suddenly gushed from his hands, aimed at little Simon's bowl of milk and bread-sops. Milky bread was splattered everywhere. The earl got up from the table, gripped Edward by the hand and took him to his room. The prince received his first spanking.

"I hate you! You are not to do that!" Edward cried.

"And you are not to bring frogs into the hall! If you don't behave like a man, and a prince, you'll not be treated like one! Little boys are spanked when they do wrong, and so shall you be!"

Edward sulked, humiliated. Yet he felt that the earl cared for him more than the archbishop had, though the archbishop never would have permitted anyone to strike him.

School began that day, in a classroom set up in one of the small tower chambers on the roof. Classes would be held every day but Sunday, from breakfast until dinnertime at noon. Bishop Grosseteste had sent a friar, Brother Gregory de Bosellis, to teach the children how to read and write in Latin and in French. Brother Gregory would also teach them history, arithmetic, geography and logic.

"Why do we have to learn about the wars that Caesar fought?" little Simon whined after the first day's lessons were done.

"We study the past so we can avoid those things that have been shown to be faulty or evil," his father answered. "And so we may gain from what has proven good."

Edward listened thoughtfully.

That afternoon the prince rode his pony for the first time. He stuck to his mount with fierce determination, his small, regal self all concentrated to do well.

As the days went by, Edward and Henry became firm friends. And, as was predictable, Edward and little Simon came to blows. It was a pitched battle, fought out with tiny fists in the privacy of an empty cattle byre. Edward appeared at the evening's supper with a bruised face. But little Simon had a black eye and a cut lip. They both looked guiltily at the earl and countess.

Simon bent his stern, dark gaze upon them. But he asked only, "Have you made your peace?"

Both boys nodded.

"Very well," the earl said, and he took no further notice of the matter.

But the Countess Eleanor was very much upset. She spoke to her husband about it afterward. "What if the prince were to receive some serious hurt while he was with us!"

"He wasn't seriously hurt," Simon replied. "For a prince who is to be a soldier, he had best learn to look upon the body's hurts as of small consequence. If he fears pain, he'll be in mortal danger from his fear. Let him learn not to think of the body's risks, and fear only for his soul."

The months, the years went by. Except for occasional visits to Court or a state excursion with his mother the queen, Edward lived as a brother to Henry, young Simon, Guy and Amaury for four years.

In the hall, by candlelight on long winter evenings, Brother Gregory would read aloud the works of Geoffrey of Monmouth, or of Wace or Layamon, with which Bishop Grosseteste kept him well supplied. Inspired by the tales of ancient Britain, the boys fought the battles of King Arthur at the River Douglas and Autun. With chips of wood for soldiers, spread about the floor, they learned how to deploy advances, flying wings, wedges and encirclements.

Simon watched their play. In ways that they could understand he taught them military strategy, pointing out their errors, setting problems of terrain and of attack, prompting them to calculate their moves. "Edward, your flank is exposed to Henry, there," the earl would say, suggesting a different deployment that would avoid the risk.

Edward was aggressive, plunging in impulsively. Henry, on the other hand, was over-cautious. But it was young Simon who gave his father the greatest difficulty. Left on the outskirts of the battle with Edward or Henry's reinforcements, he would lose interest, forgetting the conditions of the game. When he was finally called upon, he would charge with chips that represented archers, or bring his army up on foot across a lake. "You're dreaming again, Simon," his father would say sternly.

The boys also learned the use of the wooden practice sword and lance. A quintain was set up in the outer yard, beyond the bailey wall. Simon wrote to Peter de Montfort, his cousin in Gloucestershire, and asked if he would come to Kenilworth as Master-at-Arms. Simon could have taught the boys himself, but, as the one who had to discipline them, he did not think it wise. And too, he felt the need of practice for himself. He could think of no one he would rather have as sparring partner than his old opponent of the Cornish joust. Peter came gladly.

Mornings, while the children were at their lessons in the tower room, Simon and Peter, mounted and in full armor and caparison, would exercise and school their destriers in the outer yard. The clash of swords would send the children running to the high parapet. The servants too would stop their work and cluster at the bailey's gate to watch the two knights in mock battle.

"When I grow up I want to be like father," little Simon said. "I'll cleave Saracens' heads open! Crash! With one blow!"

Edward said nothing, but all his heart was in his eyes.

"Will there ever be a joust again?" Henry asked wistfully. Cousin Peter had told them about the Cornish joust where he and Simon had first met, but the laws against such mayhem had finally brought them to a halt.

"There will be jousting when I'm king, I promise you," Edward whispered with a passion in his voice.

The years passed peacefully. The three boys played and learned inseparably. As Guy grew old enough, he joined them, toddling after them when they went off adventuring. Henry looked after him, but little Simon told him he was just a pest.

The Countess Eleanor gave birth to a fifth child, a girl. She was named for her mother. Gazing at the pretty baby, Edward announced gallantly, "Eleanor, when we grow up, I'll marry you and you shall be my queen."

"You can't marry her. She's your cousin," young Simon pointed out pragmatically.

"I know. But I would if I could," said Edward, who was not so particular regarding rules.

Once they could ride well enough, the boys were allowed to cross the Mere to ride their ponies on the road as it passed through the woods and down into Kenilworth's village. One afternoon they came from the woods out onto the road just as an old pilgrim woman was passing on foot.

"A penny for a poor pilgrim?" the crone begged, holding out her alms bowl.

The Royal Exchequer kept Edward supplied with pocket money, though the prince had no need for it, and nowhere to spend it but on charity. He rode over to the woman and dropped a silver penny into her bowl.

"Thank ye! Blessings on ye, lad!" the woman bowed and nodded. "And blessings on yer brothers too!"

"They're not my brothers," Edward corrected her. "We're cousins only."

"Mercy! An' ye two look as like as any twins I ever see! Jus' one fair an' t'other dark," the amiable hag gurgled, pointing at Henry.

"He's not my brother!" Edward answered, becoming upset.

But the crone went on with her babbling. "As like as two peas in a pod!"

"Stop saying that!" Edward struck her with his riding whip.

His pony, getting out of his control, lurched forward, knocking the old woman down. She began to scream, her toothless mouth gaping in terror and her boney arm held up to ward off the whip's blows. Her bowl with its few pennies broke, scattering her meager wealth across the road.

"Edward, leave her alone!" Henry shouted. "She meant no harm. Can't you see she's not right in her wits?"

"She's lying!" Edward cried. But he kicked his pony and rode back into the woods with his friends.

Later that day the sheriff came to Kenilworth. The old woman had lodged complaint. No civil action could be taken against the prince, of course, but Simon assured the sheriff that the boy would be punished. That night he took Edward aside and confronted him.

"The sheriff has had a complaint against you, Edward. He says that you struck and knocked down a pilgrim woman on the road."

"I did," Edward admitted sheepishly. He did not lie to the earl.

"Don't you know that pilgrims are under Our Lord's special care? But worse, that you should raise your hand to strike any woman shows a lack of self-governance unfitting to a man, much less a prince."

"I... I couldn't help myself," the boy broke into tears. "She said I looked like Henry."

"That's not unusual for cousins," Simon said quietly.

"She said that – but that I'm fair and he's dark – we look like twins." Tears poured down the boy's face, wetting his flushed cheeks. He burrowed his head against Simon's shoulder. Through his sobs the words came out, "Why couldn't it be true? Why couldn't you be my father? Not Henry! I love you, not him!"

Simon hugged the boy, suddenly close to tears himself. He stroked the boy's blond head and said in a hushed voice, "Remember Edward, if you were my son, you could not be king."

Chapter five

MATTERS OF STATE
1244-1248

IN THE COURSE OF EACH year the Montfort household went on eyre of the Leicester manors, visiting first Chawton, Odiham and Sutton in the south, then Leicester, Ashby de la Zouche, Chorly, Compton and Desford, returning to Kenilworth for Christmas and the winter months. At each village, when the visit coincided with the meeting of the hallmoote court, the earl himself presided, listening to the complaints and the villeins' presentations of their local, customary laws. Often he had Edward and Henry sit by him on the judge's bench, and he would discuss the sessions with them afterward.

"The business of a king, or any lord," he told the boys, "is justice. And justice, in England, is made up of the common customs of the people and Our Lord's right."

"But what if they aren't the same?" Edward asked.

"Then the king or lord who judges must be very certain of what is right before he acts against the people's custom. But," the earl added, "if he truly believes the custom to be harmful, then he must act as he sees fit, no matter how much he is criticized."

"King Henry's criticized for asking taxes beyond the common custom. Is he right?" the young prince asked pointedly.

The question gave Simon pause. "King Henry shall have to bear the Lord's judgment for that," he answered carefully.

"I don't think he's right," Edward replied.

"Then, when you are king you will do otherwise." Simon perceived the prince's mind was taking shape from the mold of Grosseteste's radical teachings, by way of Brother Gregory. He did not interfere.

At Christmas of the year 1246 King Henry held a feast for all his direct vassals. The Earl and Countess of Leicester, and of course Edward attended.

The prince now was seven, fine-featured and long-limbed, with a mass of golden curls like his mother. King Henry smiled on him. Edward shifted from foot to foot, embarrassed under the unfamiliar gaze of his father's drooping eye. In his heart the sight of Henry pulled at a tangle of feelings. His growing mind was critical of the king, yet he was fascinated by the royal power. Toward Henry personally he felt repugnance, the sagging eye and cheek paralyzed by palsy, the sardonically curled lips; the body that seemed feeble and effeminate compared to the earl's. Henry was thirty-nine but looked much older than his years. To the boy he appeared decrepit. Edward felt guilty that he had no love for him. Ashamed, he took refuge in shyness.

Queen Eleanor seemed anxious about Edward's stay at Kenilworth. She sought to have the prince with her as often as she could, though Henry countered her with arguments that a future warrior king ought not to be overly tied to his mother. At the Christmas Court she was as aloof from Simon as the customs of the Court allowed, for which he was grateful.

What Henry's intent regarding Edward was, or what her unusual cautiousness portended, were both past his fathoming. But he found the stay at Westminster less trying than he had feared. He did note, with a stab of pique, that the elegant, auburn-haired young Earl of Gloucester, Richard de Clare, was often in the queen's company, jesting with a verve that she seemed to enjoy.

During the holiday Simon was summoned to meet privately with Henry. The king was in his chamber, standing by a table littered with parchment finance rolls.

"I've discovered how much the Church in Rome every years extracts from England's parishes and convents!" Henry was tense with excitement, his voice breaking in his rush of words. "The clergy's been complaining ceaselessly – and with good reason! Can you imagine, Simon! These cursed legates of the Pope are gathering three times as much as our royal revenues!" He was livid. "Pope Innocent issues blank orders with the papal seal, and his legates fill them out on whatever pretext they can contrive. And for every penny they can find! What, I ask, is all this money going for? To rescue Palestine? No! It's going to arm the Pope against the emperor – our ally!" Henry struck the table with a blow that made the tight rolled parchments jump. "I've given generously to Rome! I've never interfered with the legates! And now they rob my clergy, and thrust a knife into my back! I'm summoning the barons. I mean to put an end to this!"

It was not news to Simon that Rome levied huge taxes on England. Brother Gregory railed against the legates almost daily. King John, Henry's father, in a desperate reach for aid against his barons, had granted England to the papacy in hope that God would take his side. Since then, the Vatican had acted with a free hand in taxing England's clergy.

"What outcome have you had from the letter of complaint you sent to Pope Innocent months ago?" Simon inquired.

"Nothing! One could as well leave honey pots in front of bears and ask them not to eat. Words are no use. It's time the honey pots were locked away!"

"What do you mean to do?"

"Close the Cinque Ports to the legates! I won't let them into the country!"

"You'd sever England from the Mother Church?" Simon was shocked.

"The Mother Church has shown herself a stepmother to England!"

"My king, don't act too hastily. These are large matters, involved with the good of your subjects' souls – and with the planned crusade."

"What do I care for a crusade-to-be!"

Simon finally lost patience. Meeting the king's pitch of voice, he urged, "Henry, do not offer open breach with Rome, or we shall see all Christendom divided! If you break with the Church, the Emperor Frederic will join you, and Louis will be forced to give aid to the Pope. There'll be no crusade to the Holy Land, but Christian will fight Christian in the largest conflict ever seen!"

Henry shrank at Simon's words. They struck a chord, carrying the argument further than he had yet thought it through. He said nothing for several moments. When he spoke it was in a tone subdued. "I have information that Pope Innocent has offered my Crown to Louis."

Simon frowned. "Of what quality is this?"

"One of Richard's spies in France. A lord who attended Louis at his recent meeting with the Pope. He heard it with his own ears, he claims. I too find it incredible. But you're right. It is a time for caution."

Summoned by the king, the barons met. But only another modest letter begging relief from the legates' taxations was drafted.

The next legate to reach London arrived in a fit of fury. He had been intercepted in the Channel and all of his baggage had been thrown overboard. Henry listened very sympathetically. "Good father," he answered mildly, "the pirates are so out-of-hand this year. Alas, they are beyond my reach." He sighed apologetically.

Plans for the crusade proceeded haltingly. Louis visited Pope Innocent to work a peace between the Emperor Frederic and the Church. The meeting was a failure.

Simon gained Henry's permission to go to France to confer with Louis on the prospects for the crusade. "There is matter I would have you negotiate for me in France," King Henry told him. "The Truce of Blaye will end soon. Treat with Louis for renewal of its terms."

In late September of 1246 Simon was in Paris as England's ambassador. He was admitted at once to the King of France's private chamber.

Louis seemed well at last and in high spirits. Coming in from the garden that opened off his private apartments, he greeted Simon cheerily. Like the earl, he was wearing black. "How is our friend Mars, with whom we are in color now?" he asked brightly.

"I'm well," Simon bowed, grinning at Louis's teasing him about his military fame. He was overjoyed at the sight of his friend's health and bantering mood. "I'm glad to see there's crimson in your cheeks, my lord, if not your clothes. How came this change of color?"

"My clothing or my cheeks? No matter, the answer is the same. As I lay sick, my body died, my soul was gathered to the Light. But my mother's prayers that I be spared for the crusade were heard, and Our Lord sent me back. Don't you think that, as I'm risen from the dead, it's fitting I wear mourning?"

"This hardly seems a jesting matter," Simon frowned.

"I don't jest," Louis smiled gently. "To know the happiness of Heaven, and to be alive again in this troublesome world is cause enough for mourning. But only those who've died could know of what I speak, so I speak jestingly."

"I have serious business with the king. If he is not in fitting frame of mind, perhaps I should return at another time?" Simon asked curtly.

"Simon, there are times when even kings must be allowed to shed their gravity."

"I come on urgent business of the Holy Land, which has been postponed for two years, to our eternal shame – and I find you making jests about your death!"

"Don't hold my merry mood against me, Simon. I'd be merrier still if we could leave for Palestine today. You can blame His Holiness the Pope for our further delay."

"I thought the emperor was the cause."

"The emperor, though he's a proud prince, bent his neck most humbly to the Pope's demands. Innocent flatly refused his petition, which I myself had brought to him from Frederic. Christian Palestine, or what is left of it, is part of the emperor's domain. As is nearly every seaport along the route from France to the East. We must make landfall in the emperor's lands if we are to reach Palestine. But Innocent has sworn to place the crusade under interdict if we accept assistance from the emperor! You look amazed, Simon? Hear more! Innocent offered Frederic's Crown to me. And King Henry's too. With full financing from the Church, if I will move my armies against them. It gives me pause, wondering to whom this Innocent may offer my Crown if I don't do his will – which I will not."

Simon stayed in Paris through the winter and the spring. As England's ambassador and the confidant of two kings, he was an honored man at Court, and Louis's guest at dinner every day.

Louis's queen, Margaret of Provence, was neither so arresting a beauty nor so witty as her sister, England's queen. She was kind and rather shy. Conversation passed primarily between Louis, his mother Queen Blanche, and a select group of courtiers and scholars from the University of Paris. Louis made a point of inviting to his Court the most popular or controversial lecturers.

"I have an Englishman coming today," Louis informed Simon. "A wild-eyed young reader of Aristotle who practices alchemy. He has applied to me for protection from the university. It seems they've forbidden his experiments due to the foul odors that waft from his room."

"Can't he move his workshop down wind of the complainers without aid from the king?" Simon asked, amused.

"He wants financing to expand his work. The university opposes him, and I'm not about to go against them for one Englishman who makes bad smells. But I want to hear him out. Perhaps, once we've heard him, you can offer some suggestion."

The alchemist, whose name was Roger Bacon, turned out to be both wild-eyed and highly entertaining. He held the company at the royal table fascinated.

"God created this great work," he spread his hands above the tablecloth as to embrace the world, "so we might stretch our minds throughout it. We are meant to look upon the gross creations of the earth, the sea and sky and, through penetrating study of them, come to comprehend the numbers, the proportions and conjunctions that lie at the core of All. Numbers, proportions, interlockings – here lie the keys of God's Creation. Keys He places before our eyes, and in our minds, to find! It is no sin to grasp and use them. Rather, it is sin to remain blind and ignorant. To shut our eyes to God's magnificence. The earth is good, and all therein is God's Own work. To deny its sciences is a heresy!"

That evening, meeting with Simon, Louis was thoughtful. "I suppose Bacon may be right," he mused. "What greater mark of heresy did the Albigensians commit but to hold that the earth is evil and all dealings with matter are the Devil's work? Still," he temporized, "I don't want to force Bacon upon the university. Might not some place be found for him in England?"

Simon thought for several moments. "Perhaps Bishop Grosseteste will receive him. The University of Oxford is now in the care of his follower Adam Marsh, as Provost. I believe they would find Bacon's views intriguing. I'll give your alchemist my commendation to the bishop if you wish."

A few weeks later, Roger Bacon left for England to establish his new laboratory upon Oxford's bridge, with Bishop Grosseteste's and the Earl of Leicester's patronage.

Life for Simon in Paris was high pleasure, congenial to his spirit and challenging to his mind. But the work at hand was the mounting of a great crusade. He urged Louis to postpone no longer, but to find means of transport that could carry enough food, water and fodder to pass by the Emperor Frederic's lands with no need of landfall for supply.

Genoese shipbuilders were commissioned to design and construct vessels that could make the voyage in five weeks, from France to Cyprus, without touching land. The fleet must carry forty-thousand men, their horses and provisions. The Genoese drew plans for immense ships, each to hold five hundred horses or eight hundred men-at-arms and all that they could need. Louis ordered a hundred of such ships to be built.

From his father-in-law Count Raymond of Provence Louis bought a stretch of coastal marsh for the crusade's port of departure. The place was called Aigue Morte. Masons were sent to build a castle, warehouses and wharves. Word soon came back: Aigue Morte was as forbidding as its name. A sandy, wind-swept marsh, dark with mosquitoes that rose up like smoke and covered a man in an instant. Fever was killing the workers. But Louis was not deterred. The marsh must be drained, the harbor dredged – and dredged to double depth for the great ships that the Genoese were building.

With work begun, the date was set for the crusade's departure. The English forces, raised by Simon, were to join King Louis at

Aigue Morte. They would take ship together for the Holy Land in September of 1249.

Together Louis and Simon planned their campaign. No one in England or France knew Palestine better than Simon did. Or so well understood its terrain from a military point of view. The battle strategy and ordering of armaments were Simon's work.

Aigue Morte was rising on the Mediterranean coast. In Genoa the ribs of a hundred ships as large as Noah's ark were curving skyward in the shipyards. Everywhere through Europe wagons painted with the fleurs des lis of France were trundling, collecting money and provisions for the great crusade.

For Simon, it was as if the wrong he had committed in leaving Palestine at last was to be righted. The Khoresine invasion could not be eradicated from the past, but he would spend his life in *the* mending the catastrophe as best as he was able. The crusade meant far more to him than it did to others: they went for adventure, for forgiveness of their sins, or of their taxes, or for a genuine desire to see Palestine again in Christian hands. For him it was the reversal of the cardinal error of his life.

It was May. The Earl of Leicester had been in France eight months when, one day as he met with Louis, a courier from England brought him a letter. The messenger wore Henry's strutting lion livery, and the royal seal weighted the folded piece of parchment. Simon broke the seal's tab and read the brief note. He was recalled to England. Henry was appointing him the Governor of Gascony.

"This is nonsense!" Simon protested. "Let him find someone else to beat his Gascon dogs into submission. I have better work!"

Louis turned away from Simon, motioning for the courier to wait outside. Simon watched him with a questioning look. But Louis walked away from him, to the far end of the room and looked out of the doorway to the garden. There was what seemed to Simon, and to Louis's lords and clerks in the room, an interminable silence. When Louis turned from the door to face them his expression was strained. His eyes met Simon's. "I had expected you would be with me."

"And so I shall!" Simon said emphatically. "I've taken the Cross. Henry cannot stop me."

"Without Henry's permission, how can you lead the English knights? Your first duty is to your king. And he has the means to enforce it."

"My duty above all is to Our Lord!"

Louis made no further opposition, but he closed the meeting and dismissed Simon.

Days went by. Simon was not admitted to the king's presence at meetings, nor was he invited to dine at the royal table. The Steward barred him at the door. He sent messages. But when at last King Louis sent for him, it was for a private interview with Queen Blanche. Simon was ushered into a sunny room in the queen's private chambers. Louis was there, standing beside his mother's chair. But it was Blanche who spoke.

"Provision for France in the king's absence in the Holy Land has not been sufficient," she began in a quiet tone. "All my sons and all our ablest lords will be gone. I shall serve as regent, but I'm growing old, and Louis's heir is very young." She looked at Simon earnestly. "It would give my heart ease, knowing that you were nearby in Gascony."

"Good queen," Simon replied as gently as he could, "I must go to Palestine for my soul's sake. I bear a heavy guilt for having left the land ill-guarded."

"Simon," Louis broke in, "I will not take you with me against King Henry's wishes."

Simon's fragile patience broke. "Are you, the King of France, so much afraid of Henry?"

Louis's look went icy, but he pursed his lips and said no more.

Queen Blanche still spoke calmly, "Simon, I brought you up as though you were my son, but you try our love for you. Louis cannot take you in defiance of Henry, and then leave his own domains unguarded. We have no wish to have this crusade open more troubles with our neighbor kingdoms – or give occasion for temptations. You are King Henry's vassal, pledged to him, as you once reminded me many years ago. You must do as he wishes."

Simon returned to England. He was furious at Louis and at Blanche. But it was clear that his only hope lay in making Henry change his mind. He arrived at the Court in Westminster wearing his black robe with the red Cross of the Crusade.

Henry greeted him warmly, carefully avoiding any mention of the massive plans for Palestine which were the chief topics of conversation everywhere. "Governor de Gray is back from Bordeaux," he told Simon. "He's brought petitioners with him. You must hear their stories! Pilgrims on their way to Santiago, robbed and held for ransom!"

"Why hasn't de Gray brought the criminals to justice?" Simon asked, unmoved by Henry's blunt appeal.

"He says he can't." The king shrugged helplessly. "He hasn't collected a penny in taxes either. De Gray, d'Urberville, neither of the governors I've sent could bring order."

"I would advise..."

"I want you to go, Simon!" Henry looked firmly at him. "Speak with de Gray and d'Urberville, and bring me a full list of all you'll need. I want you to crush those vipers for me as your father crushed the Albigensians!"

Simon did as he was ordered. He met with the two former governors. They discussed each town and every faction in the province.

"The rebels have support from Thibaut, from King Alphonse of Castile, and from the King of Aragon as well," warned the lean, soldierly d'Urberville, under whom Simon had served in Wales and at the emperor's siege of Milan.

"We were told, when we were still in Bordeaux, that Thibaut, since he had come into his kingdom of Navarre, was plotting with the Gascon lords against Henry," Simon mused. Navarre was Gascony's southern neighbor. Thibaut, the Count of Champagne, since his youth had been an aggravation, raising rebellion against Queen Blanche, then writing torrid love poems to her. Simon could not recall a time when he had thought of Thibaut with any feelings but loathing.

"The Gascon barons are all traitors, have no doubt of it!" the sturdy, red-haired de Gray put in emphatically. "They'll raise problems along every border of the province if they can. The only way to deal with them is to throw them in prison. Or better, have them hanged!"

"Why didn't you do as you advise me, Lord Richard?" Simon asked pointedly.

"I didn't have the power! Don't let Henry send you as governor only. See to it the king gives you full powers as his viceroy!"

Simon had no intention of going in any capacity, but he had to contrive some means to discourage Henry. "What do you advise, Sire," Simon asked the more cool-headed of the two. Since serving under d'Urberville, he had a deep respect for him.

"Truly, lord Earl, one could as well attempt to hold a court of law amid the hurly-burly of a battlefield, as to expect justice be done by normal means in Gascony," the old soldier answered dryly. "What use are trials and fines, when you are fighting rebels sworn to making chaos of your rule?"

"Would you advise the seizure of noble men, putting them into prison without trial?"

"I would."

"Lord d'Urberville," Simon bent a piercing look upon his former commander, "if it were England we were speaking of, not Gascony, could you countenance imprisoning your fellow lords without fair trial?"

D'Urberville blanched, but answered steadily, "I thank God it is not England. And Englishmen have never yet behaved so treacherously."

When the meeting ended, d'Urberville caught Simon by the arm, drawing him aside as he was leaving. "Good Earl, I've been experimenting with a weapon that may interest you. Do you recall," he pitched his voice to an undertone, "when we were in Milan, the Emperor Frederic had a certain device that roared like thunder on the battlefield?"

"I do remember," Simon met his look. "It threw round stones or steel quarrels, not so well-aimed as a catapult but far more powerfully. And with a noise to raise the dead," he laughed shortly.

Hardly above a whisper, d'Urberville went on, "I studied that device closely. I've had cast from bronze just such an object. And I have a keg of that same black powder that was used in it. But I've not yet found the secret of its operation. As I'm preparing for the Holy Land, I've no more time to try its use. If you're interested, I will entrust it and the keg to you."

"I'd be most interested," Simon nodded, disturbed at the furtive tone, but curious. "There's an alchemist whom I sponsor at Oxford. If you would send the device and the powder to Roger Bacon, in my name, I'll have him study it."

The next day Simon met again with King Henry. He brought with him the draft of a contract so onerous that he felt certain Henry would not sign it. Or at the worst, would make his appointment to serve in Gascony quite brief.

Henry sat at an oak table in his chamber, reviewing the accounts of the Wardrobe, his personal finances, with several clerks. He took the contract from Simon's hand and read it. "You ask a viceroyship?" he asked, incredulous.

"Your governors, limited to act within the laws, have not had much success," Simon said tartly. "If I were to go to Gascony, I would require that the province be given over to my hands for no less than seven years. All taxes that could be collected would be retained in Gascony for the subduing of the rebels. I would have the liberty to do however I saw fit, not subject to recall or interference. And I would require the power to appoint what surrogate I chose to serve in my place so that, within a year, I may leave for Palestine with the crusade." Simon thought there was no chance at all that Henry would agree. But he added, "Short of this, I could do no better than your governors have done. I doubt that I could do as well."

"You say, 'if you were to go...'" Henry raised his one mobile eyebrow.

"Perhaps you won't wish me to go. You've not yet finished reading."

"So you've put further matter in here to dissuade me?" Henry smiled wearily. He bent his head again to read. Then, "You ask a force of fifty knights, armed and funded by the Crown..."

"Fifty mercenaries of my own choosing," Simon pointed out the exact words.

"And you want *all* of Gascony's taxes?"

"If the taxes can be collected, it will take that much and more to suppress the rebels, to hold the land securely, and to negotiate with the duchy's bordering princes." Simon straightened, looking narrowly through his dark eyelashes at Henry. "And I cannot be held responsible for any wars that might arise between England and the kings of Castile, Aragon and Navarre."

"You really do think you'll put me off," Henry chuckled, cocking his head to one side, more amused than offended. He returned to reading Simon's list. "You want full reimbursement for whatever of your own monies are spent – that of course. And you ask a fee of two thousand marks for your services? Two thousand, Simon? I thought my liegeman's services were mine to call upon."

"Your liegeman is pledged to the Cross," Simon said coldly.

"Simon," Henry handed the contract to his clerk Mansel for copying, "mend matters for me in Gascony and I shall grant you whatever you ask." Then, as the clerk moved to leave, Henry reached to take the contract back again. "In fact I shall make our agreement sweeter." Taking up a quill, he wrote: *The Earl of Leicester is released from all taxes owed to the Crown for the remainder of this year. And...* he raised the quill and thought a moment, eyeing Simon with a sly twinkle. "We don't want you to deplore your service to us in Bordeaux entirely." He wrote again and looked up. "We license you to keep a ship of your own, and to import wines duty-free for your own use. In seven years you should be able to stock your cellars at Kenilworth for generations to come." He handed the contract back to Mansel for copying. Turning to Simon, "Do we not try to please you?"

Simon watched Mansel leave, then he turned on Henry. "This is absurd! I must go to Palestine!"

Henry smiled. "I'm aware that is your wish. But first you must go to Gascony."

"What of the crusade! I'm leading England's forces!"

"I will appoint my cousin Longspee to take your place."

"In the name of all that's holy!" Simon exploded, "I must go! It is my fault the Christian kingdom fell!"

"Your fault?" Henry frowned and grew cool. He rose from his chair. "Simon, I have treated you as my own brother, married to my dearest sister. I've restored your earldom." He drew breath, "I've come to overlook, forgive, nay, even to doubt... certain matters. But now I need your help! Louis will reconquer Palestine, with Our Lord's strength. Not yours. But, abandon me now in my need, and may you ever be damned as an ingrate! I've given you my love and care... and set aside the words of those who speak against you. I've treated you far better than you deserve! Now you must help me!"

The king moved toward the door, bringing the confrontation to an end. "In four months from today, on the first day of October, you will be in Bordeaux to begin your services as our viceroy for Gascony."

Chapter Six

GASCONY
1248

SIMON WAS VICEROY OF GASCONY. But the crusade would not embark for a year. He believed that with firm, swift action, he could restore order, then leave the province to de Gray with all the powers the former governor had wanted. Aigue Morte was only a few days ride from Bordeaux. He wrote to Louis that he expected to meet him there shortly before the crusade departed, and he went home to Kenilworth to make his preparations.

The Countess Eleanor also had taken the Cross, to serve as nurse with the Knights Hospitallers. She was furious when she heard that they would not be leaving with the English knights. "How dares Henry to interfere with our vows! He worked his wheedling ways upon you and you gave in!"

"I had no choice. He is my king," Simon replied curtly.

She pursed her lips and tossed her head in a gesture of unquenched frustration.

The quiet years at Kenilworth were at an end. The eldest boys, Henry and Simon, were sent to Bishop Grosseteste to complete their education. Edward was returned to his mother at Court. Little Guy, Amaury and baby Eleanor would remain at Kenilworth with the countess, Friar Gregory and Lady Mary.

By mid-September Simon was in London to collect the funds the king had promised him. The Treasury issued him writs of receipt for two thousand marks, but that was all.

"The payment for the mercenary troops is due also," Simon told the Minister of the Treasury Peter de Riveaux.

"Nicholaus de Meulles has been charged with raising your knights."

"They are to be of my choosing!" Simon protested.

"I'm sure you'll find them satisfactory," de Riveaux smiled pleasantly. "De Meulles will have them for you at Bordeaux on October first. I am not empowered to grant any further funds to you."

The king had gone hunting at his manor of Woodstock, there was no time for Simon to go after him to lodge complaint. He sent Henry a strongly worded letter of protest. Then, taking what funds he could, he left England for France to make his preparations for acquiring a mercenary force. The Belgian Duke of Brabant maintained a Paris office where he made market in professional fighting men. Simon arranged that sufficient tax monies raised in Gascony would be transferred to him through the banking houses of Bordeaux. On credit of those taxes, he hired a force of a hundred archers.

Paris was quiet, nearly empty of all but shopkeepers and laborers. Louis had begun the crusade's year-long progress to Aigue Morte. Nearly all the nobles of France were with him. And many, many more from every Christian land would join him on his march. Simon felt more keenly than ever that he had been torn from his proper place. It almost seemed that he alone would not be there, he who above all bore such guilt for the fall of the Christian kingdom of Outremere. Filled with bitter anger at Henry, and at Louis for forcing his return to England, he rode south to Bordeaux.

The turreted, cream-colored spires of the city proclaimed the wealth of the great mercantile center of the wine exporting trade. After London, Bordeaux was the richest city in King Henry's domains. And as a city of the French south, it was the most luxurious. The Gascon lords and the powerful families of the wine trade, basking in their warm clime and flow of money from their exports, saw no reason why they should be under the dominion of England or of France. They wanted independence.

Gascony, the twin province with Poitou, of the duchy of Aquitaine, had passed with the marriage of Eleanor of Aquitaine to Henry II of England. Still provinces of France, the region, since the battles of Richard the Lion Hearted, had ceased to pay homage to the French kings. But Louis lately had regained Poitou in the brief war in which Simon, though on the losing English side, had served with such distinction that King Henry preferred to forget his crime.

Simon arrived in the splendid southern city in time to see his soldiers, led by Nicholaus de Meulles, debarking. "These are the fine warriors I was promised?" Simon stared incredulously at the brutish, ragged men who gathered, slouching, on the quay. "By what standard did you choose these men, Nicholaus? By their tenancies of fleas?"

De Meulles looked mortified. "My lord, these are the ones who were given me. They are all true knights. But most of them were prisoners of the Crown. King Henry gave them clemency in exchange for service here."

"I should have known that Henry's promises were nothing but stale wind! He raises his best knights for me by opening his jails!"

"My lord, no better men would come. By your own work for the crusade, nearly all of England's knighthood is pledged to the Cross."

De Meulles meant to be placating, but his words were like salt in Simon's wounded heart. The earl studied the dirty, surly men who looked down at the ground or glanced at him through narrow, hostile eyes. "See that they are bathed – and keep themselves clean from now on," Simon ordered de Meulles. "Have all their armaments – swords, helms, shields and chain mail – made with steel of good quality. Buy fifty sound horses, swift and spirited, the best that can be gotten reasonably. Dress the men and caparison their mounts in full and proper style for battle, and in the king's colors of red and gold. Oh, yes, and have a flag of Henry's triple lions made. Let them at least look like a royal force!" He handed de Meulles the receipt for two thousand marks. "Take what's needed from my funds, and use credit if need be, then send Henry the bill for what he owes me!"

Day and night the clang of hammers sounded in the armorers' street. Late into the nights the lights from oil lamps winked through the shutters on the tailors' street as padded pourpoint shirts, surcoats, stockings, horse mantelings and a flag were sewn. In little more than a week the troops were ready, mounted in the castle's bailey yard for the viceroy's review.

Beside the furling flag of the lions en passant guardant of the Plantagenets, fifty hardened criminals – men whose families had disowned them, leaving them to die in the king's prisons – stood in new surcoats and mantelings of diagonal stripes of red and gold, the gorgeous livery of King Henry's royal guards. Their fine mounts pricked their ears, alert and tense. Their new armor flashed like silver in the brilliant sunlight. The men, well bathed, clean shaved and some even perfumed, grinned broadly at their viceroy.

Simon, in black chain mail with the red cross of crusade sewn on the breast, sat upon a fine white destrier. The horse's long mantel was white, blazoned from arching neck to hock with the red, fork-tailed lion rampant of Montfort. Easing his mount to a collected walk, the viceroy studied his soldiers, considering each face closely as he slowly passed. When he reached the line's end he wheeled his horse and galloped the few strides back to face the center of the line. There he addressed his company.

"Any man," Simon announced in a voice cold and ringing with clarity, "who commits a crime, or fights among you, or who fails – for any reason – to obey me or my captain, will be returned to England with his hands cut off. And every man who serves me well will have a new life, and be well rewarded."

The next morning the viceroy and his soldiers rode out of Bordeaux. They traveled south to the city of Dax. While his forces were being dressed and armed, Simon had sent summonses to the lords of the western Pyrenees to come to court at Dax. And the town had been ordered to have its taxes, now long overdue, collected and ready for payment.

Dax was an ancient Roman bath resort, still renowned for its curative waters, and brimming with prosperity. Simon and his knights crossed the Roman bridge at the walled city's entrance and rode at a brisk trot down the main fork of Dax's market street. On their left the columned, roofless white marble spa spewed steaming mineral spring water from ancient lion-headed bronze spouts into a trough beside the street. Behind the wall of spouts, in the great rectangular pool of the bath, waders moved in the same slow dance of pained feet and rheumatic limbs that Dax had seen for more than a thousand years. Dressed in white cowls, rich invalids, and pilgrims on their way to or from Santiago, the shrine of Saint James, further to the south, held cups to the gushing lion-heads and drank the healing waters.

Toward the center of the town the streets were no less crowded. Jewelers' shops, busy with customers, displayed fine gold and gem-encrusted settings for the scallop shells that the pilgrims brought from Santiago. At inns, filled to capacity, the gouty rich pursued their lavish diets, and pilgrims celebrated their return from the shrine of knighthood's patron saint with heady drafts of Bordeaux wines, or stronger Armagnac. Money poured into Dax always, but even more just now as lords cleansed their souls through pilgrimage before joining Louis's crusade. There was no lack of funds in Dax to meet the king's taxes, only a lack of willingness to pay.

News of the viceroy's coming had already reached the town. Shopkeepers watched uneasily through the half-moon arches of their shop windows. They waited grimly for this Simon de Montfort, the son and namesake of that crusader who, in the service of an enraged Pope, had slaughtered twenty thousand of their kin and neighbors during the crusade against the Albigensian heretics. What they saw trotting down their street were burly, scarred knights in the king's colors, and the stern-faced viceroy in arms emblazoned with the all too well remembered lion rampant of Montfort.

On the first day of court, held in the town's castle, Dax's overdue taxes were delivered at once.

The Pyrenees lord Bertrand d'Aigremont appeared in response to his summons. The baron, called a second Herod by his enemies, turned out to be an elderly and dapper gentleman with very courtly manners. "You have, good Viceroy, no doubt heard many tales of me," he opened in a genial way. "Gascony is a land of gossips, some of whom make profit out of calumny."

"I've heard that you hold pilgrims for ransom," Simon replied bluntly.

Bertrand gave a short laugh. "Good Viceroy, in this city you see pilgrims spending money as if they weren't on humble pilgrimage but had come to a fair. They've all passed through my lands. Their purses were not cut."

"You will accept a royal garrison, placed in your castle for protection of the roads." Simon spoke as if the thing were ordinary.

"A garrison? Most certainly not!" Aigremont sputtered. "By what right do you offer to impose such a thing on me?"

"By your oath of fealty to England's Crown, Lord Bertrand. That oath acknowledges that all a vassal holds is held by the king's grace, for the king's use and for the land's good."

"That may be the custom in England," Aigremont protested, "but I assure you that oaths of fealty never meant such in Gascony!" He took the document de Meulles handed to him. After a brief glance he tried to give it back. "I see no royal seal here, only the seal of Montfort. On what grounds do you take this supposed royal power to yourself, lord Earl?"

"My letter of appointment as viceroy grants me the full powers of the Crown. Sign, Bertrand."

Aigremont's bearing turned rigid. He tore the parchment into pieces and threw the pieces on the floor. "I would not sign this if King Henry himself bade me!"

"Then you will lodge here in this tower until you change your mind."

"You would imprison me?" the baron asked in utter disbelief.

"Will you sign and go home free, or stay?" Simon said crisply.

Bertrand pressed his lips into a thin straight line. "I will not sign. Imprison me if you dare."

The viceroy said no more, but motioned to two of his knights who were standing by his chair. They led the Count of Aigremont to a locked room above the castle's hall.

One after another the barons of southwestern Gascony appeared at Dax: the lords of Bidache, Peyrehorade, Saint Vincent, Saint Martin and Labastide. All joined Aigremont in the locked donjon. Simon sent de Meulles and thirty knights to search their castles. He ordered that the taxes overdue be confiscated from each baron's treasury, and used to fund a mercenary garrison to be placed in each castle. The safety of the western reaches of the pilgrim route was to be made secure. Simon was establishing nothing less than a swift military occupation of Gascony in the name of the Crown.

With their lords in the viceroy's prison, the castles surrendered to de Meulles. Out of their cellars and towers came a few pilgrims and merchants taken from the roads for failure to pay high tolls. But most of the prisoners were Gascons: neighbors, cousins of the barons, the flotsam of family feuds, boundary disputes and Gascony's divided politics. Through Dax a stream of freed men came on their ways home. They were loud in their praises of the new viceroy, this "new" Simon de Montfort.

With the taxes collected and the western castles of the pilgrim route garrisoned for the king, Simon was ready to leave Dax. In the open square before the castle, the viceroy mounted with his knights to ride on to Saint Sever, where court was due to open in two days. The square was filled with people: merchants, pilgrims, minor landowners. They shouted "Vivre Montfort!" and "Down with Aigremont!"

Simon was astonished. "I never thought that I would hear the name Montfort cheered in the southern tongue," he smiled to de Meulles as they rode through the crowd.

When the viceroy arrived at Saint Sever there was a shipment waiting for him, forwarded from Bordeaux. Several small kegs and two crates were stacked against the whitewashed wall of the hotel de ville. They were from Oxford. Roger Bacon had succeeded in analyzing and compounding d'Urberville's mysterious black powder.

Simon had the kegs and crates moved to a stable. That night, with de Meulles and two stablemen, he had the strange bronze device and its oak stand unpacked from their crates. A letter from Bacon was included, describing the method of the object's use.

"It looks like a jar, or a bell, with a little hole in the side," de Meulles remarked, running his hand over the burnished bronze.

"I look forward to a chance to try it," Simon smiled.

The next day court opened with the same procedures as at Dax. The nearby towns had been summoned to bring their taxes, and the local barons to appear on specified days. The first of the barons to come was Arnaud de Gramont. Simon offered him the warrant for the garrison.

"I have no need of a garrison in my castle," Arnaud edged away. "I do well enough with my own people."

"Yes, you and your people have been doing very well to bring anarchy to Gascony. Sign, or stay here as my prisoner, Sire Gramont."

"I came to you in good faith, lord Montfort. Will you abuse that faith to entrap a loyal subject of the king?"

"If you were loyal, you would welcome the king's garrison."

The vicomte drew himself up. "We Gascons do not bend to force. The son of Simon de Montfort should have learned that lesson." After years of ruinous and bloody war, Simon's father had been killed by a stone hurled from a mangonel, and his son Amaury was forced to relinquish his conquests to the King of France who restored the Gascons' lands to them.

Without offering an answer, Simon beckoned to his knights. The vicomte turned and went with them with great dignity to his imprisonment.

Also due at court that day was the Vicomte of Soule. A messenger arrived to say that Soule could not come. He was sending his attorney in his stead. The court waited through the appointed time. Neither Soule nor his attorney appeared. As the session's allotted hours ended, Simon turned to Nicholas de Meulles. "When court is finished here, we will see how our 'bell' from Oxford rings at Soule."

The next day the court received taxes and liege pledges from the towns. All went smoothly as the towns' aldermen plodded to the dais, took their oaths and delivered up their sacks of coins.

Until it came the turn of the small town of Saut. "Lord Governor, the commune of Saut wishes to recall to you its ancient privileges." the chief alderman opened, full of the swagger for which Gascony was known. "We pay our taxes into the hands of the king himself, when he is at Bordeaux. At all other times the governor must come to us, and pledge to us in our city. Only after the observation of that honor are our taxes due."

The alderman's manner did not amuse Simon. It was a blazing hot day, the room was full of flies, and he had already spent several dull hours at this task. "I am not here as your governors of the past," he answered pettishly. "I am the king's own viceroy. I have no wish to be in Gascony at all, much less to visit Saut! Have your aldermen here with your taxes the day after tomorrow, or it shall be the worse for you!"

In two days the aldermen of Saut returned as bidden, but without the money. They staunchly refused to pay, except in Saut."

"My lord," the court clerk put in, "be not amazed by them. They refused to pay even to the king himself."

"Have you proof of this?"

"Most certainly, my lord. It is recorded on the roll of 1242, when the king was in Bordeaux."

The parchment scroll of 1242, the transcript of the court's records, was unpacked from the clerk's traveling chest. It showed Saut had refused to pay.

"I am holding you as defaulters," Simon curtly told the aldermen. "Let your fellow townsmen be warned. I will not tolerate this insolence!" He turned to the clerk, "I want an audit of the payment of all of Saut's taxes for the past twenty-five years." Then, to the aldermen, "You will be set at liberty only when *all* of your town's taxes have been paid."

"You're holding us to ransom!" one of the aldermen cried out as they were taken from the room by Simon's soldiers. "You're no better than a highwayman!"

Nettled, Simon turned to de Meulles and said, still in the aldermen's hearing, we will first march on Saut."

The broad shape of Gaston de Bearne filled the doorway as the aldermen were taken from the court. The Count of Bearne stood aside, then watched them go before he had himself announced. As he ambled toward the dais, the court clerk whispered to Simon, "Don't trust a word that this man says, my lord. Never was there such a snake in Eden!"

A look of amusement crossed Simon's face at this description of Queen Eleanor's cousin. He knew Gaston well from his time in Poitou, when the Bearnaise and his mother wheedled an immense annuity out of Henry.

The lord of Bearne smiled at the clerk, "What is this, Guillaume? Sharpening your tongue upon our viceroy's ear?"

"Gaston, I listen only to what you have to say," Simon said coolly. "I offer you a warrant for the garrisoning of your castle by King Henry's men. Will you sign it?"

"Most certainly, good Viceroy," Gaston replied lightly. "Anything you wish, you'll find me ready at your bidding." When the document was signed with Bearne's seal, the count asked, "Am I free to go?"

"You are," Simon answered. "But I would have you come to court again when it meets in Bordeaux. Come to me there on Saint Clement's day."

"Until November, then," Gaston bent his rotund shape in a suggestion of a bow.

A contingent of the royal knights was sent to Bearne's castle. They found nothing amiss. Bearne, of all the lords, was the most frequently accused of harassing the eastern reaches of the pilgrim route. But there had been sufficient time for him to hide the evidence. The advantage of surprise was spent. Time had run out on Simon's opening gambit. The viceroy moved on to his next strategy.

Chapter Seven

THE VICEROY'S STRATEGY
1248

"IF I MAY HAVE FULL keeping of the land as count for the next seven years, renewable for seven more, I will defend Bigorre."

"We accept your terms," Alice de Chabannais nodded to her uncle, Simon. "But my mother must give her consent."

"You'll have all Bigorre, in exchange for a fee of seven-thousand shillings Morlaas per year," Jourdain de Chabannais said, finishing the contract. The three were seated at Simon's supper table in the hotel de ville of Saint Sever.

"To the new Count of Bigorre," Alice raised her goblet in a toast. During Simon's father's holding of lands in Gascony, to protect his southern border he had his second son, Guy, wed the Countess Pironelle of the little independent country of Bigorre, in the Pyrenees. Guy soon died in the Albigensian war, but Alice was Guy and Pironelle's daughter.

"To peace in the south," Simon returned the toast. "As soon as I may, I shall visit your mother myself and confirm our agreement."

The next day Alice and Jourdain left for Bigorre with the contract.

When the court session at Saint Sever ended, Simon, with his knights, marched south. At Orthez they divided, the army going on with de Meulles to Saut and Soule, a small guard continuing with Simon to Bigorre.

The Countess Pironelle was at her citadel at Lourdes, and Simon met her there. The aged lady greeted Simon with sparkling eyes. Her gray-brown braids were coiled about her ears coquettishly. Though her skin was pale and creased, a touch of rose coloring had been added to her lips and cheeks. After five marriages of state, Pironelle was incurably accustomed to linking politics with romance.

"My daughter Alice has told me the terms you offer, and I accept them," she said decisively. "Bigorre shall be yours, for seven thousand Morlaas shillings a year for fourteen years."

Watching the tall, black-robed earl from England as he watched her clerk affix her seal to the charter, the old countess smiled wistfully. "You're so much younger – and better looking, than my third husband, your brother Guy. Though he was a handsome man..." She was regretting her age, her nun's habit, and that it was money, not herself, that was the bargaining token this time. "Alice tells me that you mean to close the Santiago road, re-routing the pilgrims northward out of Lourdes."

"Yes. I mean to cut Gaston de Bearne off from his prey."

"The pilgrims won't be pleased with the detour."

"It is for their protection."

The countess raised her boney shoulders in a shrug. "Do what you will. I'm sure you know what's best."

Simon paid the seven thousand Morlaas shillings with a note against his Leicester rents, collected at the Hospitallers' banking house at Leicester and transferred to Bordeaux, and he left Bigorre the same day. The king would have to reimburse him.

On the road, de Meulle's courier met Simon with word that Saut had capitulated at first sight of the army. The Vicomte of Soule had taken refuge in his castle at Mauleon. De Meulles was marching there.

Simon rode on to join his forces. At Pau, his first day's stop from Lourdes, he was met by the Count of Armagnac, Arnaud Otton. Though he had not seen Otton since the Pyrenees lord was in his early twenties, and Simon barely five years old, he had remembered him as one of his father's most trusted captains. He had summoned him.

The man who met Simon at Pau was balding, massive of build, and rather shy. "I served your father proudly, and would gladly offer my liege to his son," Otton said in a modest, husky voice.

Simon was deeply pleased. In the common room of the little mountainside inn, the Lord of Armagnac knelt on the wooden floor, his head bent, his hands placed together before him as in prayer. Simon, standing facing him, grasped Arnaud's hands in his, as Arnaud pledged new fealty to Simon de Montfort.

Simon raised the count up and embraced him. "I know you served my father well and loyally, and that all who know you speak your name in praise. I would have you serve as my Steward in Lourdes. For the next fourteen years, I am now Count of Bigorre."

With full instructions as to taxes and defenses, and the re-routing of the pilgrim route, Arnaud left for Lourdes.

Simon, with his southwest border secured, rode on.

At Mauleon he found his soldiers camped outside the village. Above, the stronghold towered, its brown stone walls rising from a steep, rubble-strewn slope. The hundred mercenary archers he had hired from the Duke of Brabant had arrived. Propped here and there among the rocks they had set up their screens: woven wicker panels behind which one or two men crouched with a barrel of arrows.

Simon squinted at the brown crease that was a road crossing the slope in front of de Meulle's archers.

"On the other side," de Meulles nodded toward the northeast, "there's a sheer cliff of rock. We have the vicomte close held, but it's going to be a long siege."

"I mean to leave for the Holy Land. I have no time for long sieges," Simon retorted impatiently. "When dark comes, we'll set up d'Urberville's contrivance. May it do what I saw done at Milan!"

The viceroy toured the siege site with his captain. To the west, a shoulder of the mountain dropped gently for a few hundred yards below the castle wall before falling sharply away. Simon pointed to the spot, "We will place the thing out there."

That night a patchy mist crept over the mountain and clung about Mauleon's walls. Clouds swam across the moon, their ruffled edges showing silvery, then brown as they dragged their shadows over the moon's face. High up, between the streaming sky and the black, motionless crown of the battlement, there glowed a yellow haze where the watch-fire of the night guards on the castle roof lit up the mist.

Led by de Meulles, the archers silently picked their way across the broken ground, carrying their wicker screens and, slung from poles upon their shoulders, the bronze device, its stand, the barrels of black powder, and several barrels of quarrels: heavy steel arrows. Before dawn the device was set into its stand, the screens were propped in place and the archers were ranged for the assault. The mist was gone and the moon had set. In the clear night no light reflected from the castle's roof. The mountain and the fortress were a single mass of black against a sky scattered with stars.

Carrying a cloth bag and a small pierced-metal lantern, shaded on the side toward the enemy, Simon picked his way cautiously across the rock-strewn slope and joined his men.

He had spent the night studying Bacon's instructions. Taking a length of twisted, fat soaked cloth wicking from the bag, he carefully threaded the tip of the wick through the little hole in the side of the bronze vessel. The captain of the archers knocked open the lid of one of the powder barrels for him.

"Watch carefully, I'll have you do this," the viceroy told the captain. By the light of his lantern, he made careful measure as he scooped out the black powder, then he poured it down the vessel's flaring mouth. He ordered the archers to bring several of the steel arrows, as many as would fit easily down the vessel's mouth. They set the quarrels in, on top of the black powder.

"Gently!" Simon whispered.

When the vessel was fully loaded, the viceroy cautioned his men, "Don't be startled by the noise. At dawn we'll make such thunder that proud Soule will be brought down."

As the sky grew deep blue with the approach of morning, the fortress and its mountain loomed, a mass of blackness in the east. Gradually the air lightened and paled. The archers, still in shadow on the castle's western slope, took aim for the first volley.

At the viceroy's command a hundred arrows arched into the morning sky. And Simon touched the loose end of the fatted wick to the lantern's flame. Then he stood far back from the device.

The yellow fire fluttered up the wick and disappeared into the hole in the vessel's side. The first arrows in answer from the castle's battlements were plummeting into the rows of screens when there was a great light and a blast that rocked the earth. The morning shook like shattered water in a pool. From scarp to slope the Pyrenees echoed and reechoed the boom.

Simon and his archers were doubled over, coughing in thick smoke that had a sulfurous stench. Recovering, the viceroy squinted at the castle. The wall showed a deep wound. A swath of dressed stone was broken away, leaving the rubble core exposed. No arrows came from the parapet.

Simon moved as close to the wall as he dared, straining his nearsighted eyes to study the damage. Satisfied, he gave the order to the captain of the archers to refill the empty vessel with another wick, more measured powder and more quarrels.

At the viceroy's command, the archers let a second rain of arrows fly, and flame was put to the wick. The second blast of quarrels opened a long crack in the castle wall, jigging downward from the parapet. A pall of white smoke blanketed the slope. The viceroy and his archers coughed and rasped, choking. But the damage to the fortress was such as never seen before. The archers grinned one to another, and glanced toward the viceroy with a mix of pride and wonderment.

Simon ordered a third volley. The hot vessel was loaded again by the archers' captain. Again a hundred arrows sped upward from the crossbows. But this time there was a louder blast and a blinding light. A fountain of steel quarrels and white fire blazed from the vessel's mouth, turning the smoky air white as the sun and raining red-hot quarrels upon the archers.

As the thunder strode away across the mountain ranges, the groans of wounded, dying men and a piteous high shrieking became audible. Amid the choking smoke that covered the slope like heavy fog, dying archers lay scattered among their toppled screens, flames flickering on their cloth hauberks where the hot arrows had struck them. It was the archers' captain who was shrieking. His surcoat was burnt away, his leather pourpoint tunic was black and gaping where his chest ought to have been, his face, his hands and arms were black as charcoal.

De Meulles, a few yards dstant, ran to him, coughing in the smoke and stench of sulfur and burnt flesh. The captain raised the remnant of his arm a moment, then let it fall back. His shrieking ceased. Archers were running to the wounded men. Some came and gaped in horror at what remained of their captain. They glanced at the bronze vessel fearfully.

Running from his place further up the slope, Simon reached them. "You men, care for the wounded. The rest, go back to your screens!" he ordered. "Nock your arrows for another volley!"

Cowed, they did as they were told.

"Have the captain wrapped in his horse's mantle," Simon told de Meulles. "I don't want any more of his men to see him."

De Meulles stared at the burnt corpse, then at the smudged bronze vessel. "My lord, do you want someone to take his place?" he asked hesitantly.

"No. I won't use that damned thing again. It's the Devil's own tool! Have it put into its crate. And, Nicholaus, I'd have you vow that you will keep what you know of it a secret." The archers nearby knew and could be expected to spread word of the infernal device, but the specifics of the weapon Simon wanted to be certain went no further.

"By the arm of Saint James, I'll tell no one," de Meulles, in a hushed voice, swore.

"Have the wounded brought away to camp. As for the dead, let no one be exposed to enemy arrows for their sake. We'll remove them after dark." Simon turned to give the order for the next volley of arrows. But as he did, an archer shouted, "Look, lord Viceroy!"

The cloud of smoke had thinned away over the castle's walls. High on Mauleon's battlement a white flag was unfurling in the breeze of the bright morning's sky. The Vicomte of Soule had surrendered.

At noon the viceroy sat at dinner in the castle's hall. The vicomte, a young man with dark eyes, fair skin and a blue tint of beard on his shaved chin, sat dejectedly at the viceroy's left. De Meulles sat at his right, counting as Soule's clerk put Morlaas shillings into leather bags.

"Six thousand and twenty," de Meulles reported when the last coin was bagged.

"I tell you truly," the vicomte pled, "in a year my rents in total are not ten thousand shillings!"

"You should have considered that before you chose to make war on your king," Simon said coolly.

"But the six thousand here is far more than I owe!" Soule insisted.

"Your taxes and your fine together are ten thousand," Simon said flatly, touching his napkin to his mouth as he finished his meal. "You will remain the king's prisoner until the fine is paid in full. I will not have the king's summons ignored, or his forces resisted."

The confiscated shillings went to support garrisons at Mauleon and at Soule. Simon sent the young vicomte, under a guard of his knights, to join the other prisoners at Dax. The bronze device, its powder and its oak stand, packed in their crates and barrels, were sent along with the vicomte, also to be locked away.

With the main body of his knights, Simon moved on to Ainhoa, on the border of Navarre. There he was to meet King Thibaut.

Simon had despised Thibaut since childhood, when the Count of Champagne had raised an army of French lords in rebellion against the newly widowed Queen Regent Blanche and her son Louis, who was then but a small boy. Ever adept at diplomacy, Blanche had met with Thibaut and, rather than play the part of offended royalty, had cast a gentle glance at him with such effect that he abandoned his program of military assault in favor of an amorous campaign.

He claimed to be love-smitten, and wrote some of the most lauded love poems of the age to Blanche. His passionate poetry dwelt upon the exquisite pain of his love, and upon each of her perfections with obsessive versifying. His heart was a tortured prisoner, the queen its cruel warder.

Blanche, a homely woman even in her youth, had been mildly flattered. But she and her counselors knew well that, were she to allow him to win her, beyond his proclaimed love was his true goal: the Crown. Her power as regent could be nullified, and even the life of her son might be threatened. The child-king Louis, and his companion Simon, ever after looked upon the elegant, handsome count with profound disgust.

Now there were rumors, and even witnesses, who swore that Thibaut was the chief instigator of the revolt against King Henry. Having inherited the kingdom of Navarre only a couple of years earlier, he appeared to have developed an ambition to add Gascony to his domains.

News of the extraordinary fall of Mauleon spread quickly across the mountains. There were dark rumors that the viceroy had conjured thunderbolts to burst Soule's walls. The barons of the Pyrenees smiled at the peasants' superstitious ravings. But Mauleon undoubtedly had fallen very quickly, and they were afraid.

"I see you've come as King Henry's right arm. Or is it Jove's?" Thibaut smiled, still sleekly handsome, and witty in a way that Simon found especially annoying. He dismounted amidst his knights and walked to where Simon, sitting on the low stone wall bordering the cobbled terrace at the foot of Ainhoa's watchtower, was waiting for him with his clerks and mounted guards.

"I've come to see that there is peace in Gascony," Simon, rising, answered him.

"Do you think force can hold men who don't want to give their fealty to Henry?"

"Perhaps not. But it can make their treachery costly. You, and your ... partisans are seizing travelers on the roads and holding them for ransom. They must be released, and this practice must cease."

"Who told you I did such a thing?"

"Ah," Simon smiled, recalling one of Thibaut's heated verses to Blanche,

> *"'The prisoner cries*
> *But is unheard,*
> *His warder's heart*
> *Is hardened by its power.'"*

Thibaut laughed. "So even you, Montfort, are civilized enough to know my poetry? But do you know also, later in that same song:

'He sees not in himself,
The faults he sees in others.

It is you who holds prisoners unjustly, I believe, and will not hear their cries."

"I act under King Henry's expressed commission."

After a moment Thibaut sighed, then gave a philosophic shrug. "Why are we here, when we both ought to be going to Palestine?" Changing his smile to one of easy, practiced aplomb, he offered, "Let us not raise hand against each other, Christian brothers. I'll be content to arbitrate my claims in Gascony."

"*Your* claims?" Simon fixed Thibaut with a look that pierced his pose of ease. "Very well, I will agree to that. But only if all matters that the arbiters cannot agree upon are submitted to King Henry for his final decision."

Thibaut's face puckered. "Is that what you understand by arbitration?"

Simon's look was cold. "As you say, we ought to be going to Palestine. I hold you as one of the chief causes that I'm not with Louis yet."

An agreement was drafted, set with the viceroy's and the King of Navarre's seals, and sent on to King Henry for approval.

As Thibaut and Simon mounted their horses to take leave, Thibaut remarked bitterly, "You are a bully, Simon, as you've ever been! It will be your downfall in Gascony. Mark my words!"

Simon straightened. "I, at least, shall not leave chaos in my wake – as you did in Palestine, and mean to do here!" He turned his horse and galloped to the gate with his knights following.

It was the beginning of November. Simon had been in Gascony just one month and had already broken the rebellion. The chief and strongest of the castles were garrisoned for King Henry. Travel was re-routed out of reach of the remaining brigand lords. The rebels' principal supporter was cowed. And most of Gascony's taxes had been collected. His methods had been harsh, but lesser methods had no effect.

As he rode to his next court session, at Bazas, Simon composed a full report for Henry. To the Countess Eleanor he sent a happy letter telling her that he expected to be back in England by Christmastide. And that, with peace achieved and the land placed in the hands of honest stewards, they should be able to join the crusade at Aigue Morte in the spring.

Throughout the five days travel from Ainhoa to Bazas, peasants trailed along the roads, following the viceroy and his knights. "Long live Montfort!" the bold among them shouted, or, shaking their fists, "Death to the Vicomte of Soule!"

Women brought sausages, breads, cheeses and wine for the soldiers. A troubadour joined the viceroy's company. In his parti-colored satins he swaggered and twirled in front of the flag bearer's horse. Shaking his tambourine, he sang in a high, fluty voice:

"He chains the lords and sets the pilgrims free.
He raises up the meek and humbles the mighty.
The Mountain Strong felled Mauleon,
Simon, Savior of Gascony."

The cheerful peasant mob sang with him. To their choruses, he spun verse after verse. Simon was their hero. Defender of the common folk, scourge of the lawless lords. In a triumphal progress, the people conducted the viceroy to Bazas and swung open the city gates for him.

At the third provincial court there was again the round of pledges and collecting of taxes. But now a case at law was brought before the viceroy for judgement. At issue was the rightful seizon of the town of Bezaume. There were four claimants: Amanieu d'Albret, Guillaume de Rion, Bernard de Bouville and Rudel de Bergerac. Each lord had attorneys with him who produced elaborate genealogies, charts and marriage contracts to support his client's claims.

Simon listened through their lengthy arguments. When they were done and stood awaiting his decision, he sat thoughtfully for a long time. His personal experience of the intricacies of inheritance made the issues vivid, but here the claims were each counterbalanced by valid circumstances among the other claimants. The choice was a hard one. And his recent dealings with Gascony's lords gave new color to his thoughts on the matter of rightful seizon. At last, looking from face to face among the four lordly claimants, he said, "I have seen, here in Gascony, numerous rightful heirs who disregard all that is right, who are traitors to their king and cruel lords to their people. Is the question perhaps not which of you has the more rightful claim, but who will be the better lord for the people of Bezaume?"

The attorneys and the lords stared at him, perplexed. Then one of the attorneys laughed dryly, "The viceroy makes a jest? He would presume to judge who has the purest soul? Perhaps the viceroy is advised directly by Our Lord above?"

"I am not jesting," Simon cut him short. "I'm weary of men who flout the laws because they are well-born. I know nothing of any of you, beyond what was presented here. That's true. I cannot judge who is the most worthy among you. But I would like to hear the choice of those who do know you, and who will be the greatest sufferers if their lord is evilly inclined. I will call upon the people of Bezaume."

It was unheard of. It was against all custom and the law. It was unnatural for common men to judge their lords, and even choose among them. Title to land in Gascony was ancient, stemming from the conquest of the land by Charlemagne. Title was as innate as an inheritance of one's mother's brown eyes or one's father's baldness. The issue brought before the viceroy's court at Bazas was only *which* of the four lords possessed the most points of inheritance. Simon tossed that very issue out.

The lords were confused, enraged. Their attorneys ranted. Simon turned them a deaf ear, and summoned all the male heads of households in Bezaume to come to court at Bazas and name their choice.

In a few days the people came and chose Rudel de Bergerac. In the minutia of the law, Bergerac's case was the weakest. But the viceroy upheld the people's choice. Bergerac received the title to Bezaume. The three lords who lost, Amanieu d'Albret, Guillaume de Rion and Bernard de Bouville were made laughingstocks. Victims of the will of common men, they seemed three eagles done to death by mice.

The three, who had been bitter enemies before, met at d'Albret's villa and bound themselves by oath to have revenge. By every and any means, they vowed they would bring down this viceroy. Conspiracy against Simon in Gascony formed its first bud.

Court convened last in Bordeaux. The capital was less troubled than the rest of Gascony. The rival merchant families of Colom and DelSoler had gone to England where King Henry himself was hearing their disputes. The viceroy's court received more taxes and heard one more case.

Like Bezaume, the suit was for the lordship of a town. But, unlike Bezaume, this town was crucial to the defense of Gascony. It commanded Bordeaux's access to the sea.

Old Rudel of Blaye, who had sheltered King Henry in his flight from the French army in Poitou, finally had died. His nephews, Geoffrey and Elie Rudel, were his heirs. But the lords Amaubin de Barres and Raymond de Fronzac, at war between themselves, also both claimed Blaye. Each commanded an army enough to take the fortress from the two Rudels by force. But Raymond de Fronzac had pledged his liege to King Louis. Amaubin had served King Henry faithfully. Simon knew him as an able soldier, and loyal beyond reproach. For Gascony's security he overrode the Rudels' claim, giving Blaye to Amaubin de Barres.

Outraged, Fronzac and the Rudels joined cause, and secretly they too met with d'Albret.

The court term ended in December. Before returning to England, Simon appointed Nicholaus de Meulles Steward of Gascony. The viceroy would return in the spring to make final arrangements, before joining the crusade as it gathered at Aigue Morte.

Richard de Gray arrived from England to compile a report on Simon's work. He was astounded. Gascony seemed tamed. For the first time in anyone's recollection, all taxes had been gathered and the highways had been made safe. The viceroy held in prison most of the known rebel lords.

On December the nineteenth, after a splendid feast given in his honor by the Colom family, Simon set sail and went home.

Chapter Eight

THE PANIC OF 1249
1249

CHRISTMAS AT LONDON WAS GLORIOUS. The Countess and the Earl of Leicester were the guests of honor at lavish celebrations. News from Gascony set Simon as the hero of the day.

In the newly built and sumptuous Savoy Palace, on Twelfth Night, Peter of Savoy, the Duke of Richmond, gave a memorable feast to honor the victorious earl. The vaulted ceiling of the grand hall was covered with gold leaf. Clusters of gilded columns were wound with ropes of holly and ivy. Murals depicting classical revels enlivened the walls. Here Bacchus lounged with his wild bacchantes, their hair streaming, their bosoms bare, their lips red with wine. There Cataline embraced the forbidden Vestal Fabia. And there Aeneas dallied with Queen Dido. The light from hundreds of tall candles in gold candelabras reflected from the burnished ceiling, illumining the ancient lovers and the guests alike in a gold haze. Lushness of every sort was Savoy's theme.

The guests, in fur-trimmed, rich brocades and silks as vivid as a summer garden, stood in groups chatting, waiting for the entrance of the royal guests and the guest of honor. Pages in the livery of Savoy moved through the throng, bearing gold trays laden with goblets of wine, or with small savories and sweet-meats: pheasant pate and minced hare pastries, tarts filled with candied violets and fruits.

A herald blew a fanfare on a brass horn hung with Savoy's banner. The Earl and Countess of Leicester were announced.

Eleanor was magnificent in her emerald colored samite gown embroidered with seed pearls, embellished for the winter with a short surcoat of dark miniver. Even Simon was neither dressed in his accustomed black nor his crusader's cross. He wore a vair-lined robe of his own colors: white with a dotting of the lion of Montfort embroidered in red.

Peter of Savoy hurried to receive his honored guests. "Welcome, Caesar of that God-forsaken bit of Gaul. And Caesar's wife," he added archly, kissing Eleanor's hand. "Gascony agrees well with you, my lord Earl. You look the very crowning point of high spirits."

Simon, in a merry mood, parried with a play on huntsman's terms for antler points. "If I am at the crowning point, Lord Peter, you surely are at point-gallant."

"Ah, be there no horns upon my head!" Savoy winked sagaciously. "But here comes the point-royal himself."

Simon turned to see King Henry entering with Queen Eleanor. Involuntarily he colored. He wondered how much Savoy knew of Henry's cuckoldry.

Savoy beamed. With his hands held out in welcome he walked to the king and queen.

Simon peered around the room. Nearby, William de Valence, the king's half-brother of Lusignan, now a tall, slender heart-faced youth of seventeen, stood amid a crowd of admiring ladies who were fingering his robe. It was of the new Florentine fabric, velvet. The Countess Eleanor had gone off to speak with someone. Simon found the old Earl of Salisbury, William Longspee, by his side. Longspee followed his gaze toward Valence. "Leeches!" he growled. "They're bleeding Henry white! These Lusignans, these Savoyards. Look at this place! What corner of it do you think the rents of Savoy paid for?" Longspee shook his gray head. "They're wringing Henry dry."

Simon glanced back at the king. He was wearing the same robe he had worn on Christmas Night. "I can't imagine he would go so far with his largesse as to be suffering," Simon replied.

"Largesse! You mean doting idiocy!" Longspee sputtered. "He's given away so many of his rents, he can't afford his own household expenses. Except for Christmas, there has been no feasting at Westminster for months! Not even adequate to feed the ordinary guests at Court. Henry goes from one bishop's manse to the next, inviting himself to dinner."

"And he hasn't summoned the barons to raise a new tax?" Simon asked archly. Never in the past had Henry missed a chance at that expedient whenever his funds were short.

"Of course he has. But the money raised was for the Pope. Henry stopped the papal legates' collections, and Pope Innocent retaliated by accusing him of collusion with the Emperor Frederic – threatening him with excommunication, and interdict for all of his domains. Churches closed, no weddings, funerals or baptism! Henry hasn't Frederic's disregard of Heaven's wrath. He managed to negotiate the papal demand down to a firm figure. But it was clear that if England didn't pay, Henry would be named an enemy of the Church and condemned, as Frederic has been." Longspee put his arm familiarly around Simon's shoulder. "I can tell you, there were plenty of us for not paying. Henry got eleven thousand for the Pope, but nothing for himself. And why should he? If it weren't for his giving away titles to his foreign friends, his Poitouvins, his Savoyards, and now, worst of all, these brats from Lusignan, he'd have all he could use and more!"

Simon noted that he was no longer being counted among the king's cursed foreign friends. Longspee himself had been the most outspoken of his detractors. The old earl had not mellowed. But Simon smiled at how – whether he was Henry's former foreign friend or not – he was no longer included among the undeserving. "I hadn't heard of the Church's levy. I've had a tax relief these last few months," he prodded, curious to see how far Longspee would go in his forgiveness.

"Well timed, Montfort!" Longspee squeezed his shoulder. "That eleven thousand was the breaking point for many of us."

As they waited for the trestle tables of the feast to be set out, Simon and Longspee went on talking. They were joined by others, and the topic shifted from King Henry to King Louis' crusade. Longspee was now head of the English contingent. They were due to leave in June for rendezvous with Louis at Aigue Morte, and embarkation for the East in September.

"I shall be sailing with you," Simon said confidently. "Gascony is pacified. I've appointed able stewards, both for Gascony and for the border country of Bigorre. There's no need for me to remain there." The English lords were very pleased to know the earl, who knew the military needs of Palestine so well from his time there, would be going with them.

A few days after the feast at the Savoy Palace, Simon met with King Henry to discuss spring plans for Gascony. The meeting was in the king's bedchamber with only the royal secretary, John Mansel, for witness.

Henry sat in his bed amid heaped pillows and fur coverlets. He had a cold. A brazier on the floor gave off a pungent smoke. He chewed narcotic henbane seeds and loudly blew his nose into a towel as he listened to his viceroy.

"The knights you sent will end their term in June. For their replacements, I insist on men of my own choosing, as my contract specifies," Simon said firmly, suppressing comment on the troop of criminals Henry had sent. Arguing would serve no purpose. He was learning to master his temper.

"Hire whatever men you wish. I'll pay you when I can," Henry replied, daubing his nose with the towel.

"My king, you've not yet reimbursed the monies that I spent to equip the men you sent me in October. I've had to use my own two thousand marks, and more, for them alone! The taxes and the fines that I've imposed have gone entirely to fund the garrisons, and for the cost of archers to augment your fifty knights. I cannot finance hiring the knights' replacements."

Henry's drooping eye took on a depth of sadness as he gazed up at the earl. From the little box by his bedside he took another henbane seed and put it in his mouth. "Simon, I'll repay you. What else can I do?"

"I expect you to keep your word!" Simon retorted, beginning to lose the close hold that he had on his civility. He turned away and walked some paces, thinking what to do, as King Henry and his secretary watched him. He wanted above all to be in Aigue Morte, to leave with Louis' crusade. But he knew if he were on bad terms with Henry, Louis would not be pleased. At last he let out a short laugh and turned back to them. "I suppose I have no choice!" he said angrily. "I'll have to use what credit I can raise. You're forcing me back into deep debt!"

Henry sighed with relief and daubed his nose again. "I'll reimburse you. And reward you, Simon. Just as soon as I can."

Simon left for Leicester to raise funds for Gascony.

In January of 1249 there were rumors throughout England and Europe that the English silver penny was going to be debased. People were hoarding all the silver they could find. Then, as if in confirmation of their fears, a proclamation from the Royal Treasury went out recalling all of the old silver pennies. A new coin would be struck.

Panic hit. No one doubted that the new coins would be debased. Country markets instantly fell back on bartering: a hen for so much wheat, a loaf for so much beer. The Earl of Leicester found the getting of a loan at any price of interest was impossible. No one knew how much a hoard of silver might be worth. There were wild stories that the new pennies would not be of pure silver but of silver alloy, or even plain copper.

By mid-spring the first of the new coins appeared. They were silver. But they were short in weight. No one wanted to accept them. A chicken that had cost a penny in the autumn rose to four and then five pence. Goods became precious and money cheap. Starving wage-workers stole sprouting vegetables from cottage gardens, and lined the roadsides begging for a piece of bread. There were riots in the cities. Merchants were paupered overnight as they could neither sell their goods nor buy food with their money.

In May King Henry called a meeting of the barony to deal with the crisis. The Clerks of the Wardrobe, who were in charge of the Royal Mint, were brought before the lords. With great care the new pennies were weighed. Their weight was found short.

"We struck the coins at the exact weight we were ordered!" the senior clerk protested. De Riveaux bellowed above his cries, "I want a full accounting of these men's finances!"

The clerks were held confined while a full inquiry was made. The search revealed that the funds of the Wardrobe had been badly overdrawn by King Henry. For the last six months the clerks' salaries had been cut to almost nil. De Riveaux found the case was clear: the clerks had made up the difference by pilfering from the Mint.

The men were brought before the assembled lords again and a vote was taken. Opinion was unanimous. The under-weight pennies should be recalled at once and new coins struck at full weight to restore confidence. The two clerks should be publicly denounced, and hanged.

As they were dragged to the scaffold set up before the gate of the Tower of London, the clerks cried out that they had taken nothing for themselves, but struck the coinage short in weight at King Henry's own order. De Riveaux had them gagged.

The hanging of the clerks and the minting of new coins restored fiscal order to England. But by that time Simon had gone to France to raise the money that he needed for Gascony. Queen Blanche's favor opened credit to him, closed to others suffering from England's panic.

From the Duke of Brabant Simon bought the services of fifty knights of his own choice. They were to meet him in Bordeaux in June.

By mid-May Simon was at Kenilworth. Eleanor was pregnant with their fifth child, due in November. Blissfully anticipating that the child would be born in the East, she spoke as though, with such a start, he surely would become a bishop, already foreseeing his brilliant future in the Church.

"And if it is a girl, she'll be an abbess?" Simon grinned.

"It is a boy," the Countess announced with finality.

Young Henry and Simon were still at their studies under Grosseteste at Lincoln. The small children: Guy, Amaury and little Eleanor, remained in the care of Brother Gregory de Bosellis and Lady Mary at Kenilworth. If the parents were torn regarding leaving their children, they healed the wound with plans to bring the children to them in the East, once peace was restored to Outremere. All was made ready for the earl and countess's return to the Holy Land.

In early June Simon and Eleanor embarked at Dover with the English crusade. They traveled with the crusaders through France as far as Clermont, then they turned southwest for what they intended to be a brief visit in Gascony. After the court's spring session in Bordeaux they would rejoin the crusade at Aigue Morte.

At Bordeaux, on the twenty-fifth of June, the viceroy opened his court.

Chapter Nine

THE COLOM AND THE DELSOLER
1249

"To our return to the Holy Land!" Simon toasted happily as he and Eleanor ate a late supper in their private chamber above the hall in Bordeaux's fortress. The countess wore the loose white woolen robe of the nurses of the Knights Hospitallers with the red cross upon the breast. And Simon wore again his black robe with the crusade's cross.

"What I must find, and quickly, is a good steward for Gascony," he said thoughtfully. "De Meulles has done well, and proven there's no more need for me to be here, but I cannot leave him here for the full seven year term."

"What of Guillaume Colom?" the countess asked. The jaunty little merchant's quick wit and apparent solid loyalty to England had impressed her. She had met few others to suggest.

"Actually I have considered him. There's also Amaubin de Barres. He's a good, honest soldier, but I think he lacks the patience to withstand the deviousness of the towns. I don't doubt Colom's able in that way. And he has his partisans all over Gascony. That in itself commends him. Whoever leads must be able to raise his own forces. If Henry doesn't send the money that he owes, the mercenaries will leave in December."

Eleanor pursed her lips. She wanted to say he was a fool for lending Henry money and putting himself in debt, just when they needed every penny for Palestine. But she had said it several times before and they had argued. The intimate supper, with its talk of returning to the East, was all too sweet to spoil with argument. "How soon will we be leaving here?" she asked instead.

"Not later than the first of August," Simon smiled. "We'll reach Louis at Aigue Morte in good time to leave with the crusade at the beginning of September."

"Let's drink to that!" Eleanor raised her cup. They drank, and drank again in Bordeaux's heady wines, and went to bed in a loving and contented mood.

Simon was sleeping soundly when, late that night, there was loud pounding on the castle's outer gate. Church bells were ringing, and through the open window of the viceroy's chamber a noise of distant shouting carried on the summer air. Simon awoke and pulled back the bed curtain to listen. He reached to the rack at the head of the bed where his clothes were hanging. By the light of the candle night-light on the wall he could see that his squire Peter was not on the bench where he slept by the chamber door. Eleanor was still asleep.

The pounding ceased and now there was loud talking in the hall below. Simon quickly got up, put on his shirt, his under-drawers and stockings, then, pulling a light robe over his head, he left the room to find out what was happening. As he opened the chamber door, Peter came running up the stairs.

"My lord," the squire cried excitedly, "Master Colom's here! He says there's fighting in the city!"

There was a scuffle in the hall below as the wiry little Colom tried to push his way past Simon's knight on guard and come up the stairs after Peter. Simon motioned for the guard to let him pass and Colom came up panting, out of breath. "Lord Viceroy, the DelSoler have killed the curfew wardens! There's riot in the Saint Eloi market square!"

The mercenary knights, who were lodged in the hall, already were awake and arming. Simon called down to them, "Be mounted and ready for me at the gate!" He went back to the chamber, pulling off the robe and putting on his heavy, padded pourpoint shirt and leggings.

Colom followed him into the chamber, talking rapidly.

"What's happening?" Eleanor asked, wakened by the noise. Seeing Colom in the room, she drew the blanket over her bare shoulders. Frightened, she asked, "What's going on?"

"Riot," Simon answered briefly as Peter helped him pull his chain mail hauberk over his head. He slipped the long chain sleeves onto his arms and Peter laced them to the hauberk. He pulled chain leggings over his stockings and buckled them to the leather straps on the underside of his hauberk. Then he buckled on his sword belt as Peter buckled his spurred slippers onto his feet. Taking his sword, testing its edge, Simon thrust it into the belt's scabbard and hastily left the room with Colom.

At the castle's gate the fifty mercenary knights were already assembled. William Blund, the young flag bearer from the first company, had stayed on though his term was done. Intelligent, able and grateful for the chance of a new life after months in prison, he had become a favorite of Simon's. Mounted, he held the viceroy's horse at ready beside him. The great white destrier shook its head. Its long white mantle rippled in the torchlight and the blazon of the red lion rampant seemed to paw the air.

Simon mounted, unhooked his helmet from his saddlebow and put it on, slipped his shield onto his arm and ordered that the gate be opened.

Outside, the bridge to the Saint Eloi quarter was dark and vacant. But the noise of rioting was clear. Simon started at a trot in the direction of the sound with Colom riding beside him. Blund rode at the fore with the viceroy's flag of royal red and gold. The clatter of the fifty mercenaries' horses on the cobbles racketed above all other sounds. They crossed the bridge, then paused at Colom's house as a group of men on foot, dressed in light armor, came running up. They were Colom's sons.

"Rostein's raised the town militia!" Raymond Colom shouted. "They're raiding the armorers' shops on the Rue Saint James!"

Simon ordered his knights to divide. Blund, with the flag, was to lead half of the men by way of the Rue Devirade, around to the Saint Eloi Gate at the far end of the Rue Saint James, cutting off the rioters' retreat. Simon, with the remaining knights, would advance straight toward the square.

Now the two forces moved forward at speed.

In the open market square orange light and dark shadows tumbled and roiled up the whitewashed house walls. People hung out of upstairs windows shouting, pelting the struggling crowd below with flowerpots and garbage and the contents of urinals. Blazing torches waved and jerked over the dark mass of straining, fighting men. Steel caps gleamed. Here and there a steel blade rose high enough to catch the light. The din of shouts, the clash of metal, the scuffling drowned even the sound of the viceroy's oncoming horses.

The viceroy's mercenaries struck the mob at full gallop. Their swords clashed down on the surprised men on foot, cutting through the riot's edge as a knife cuts through a crust. The shouting turned to screams. Panicking, the rioters pressed inward, then broke, running for the Rue Begueyre, the Rue des Ayers and the Rue Saint James.

In the dark, cavernous street of the armorers' shops, the knights led by William Blund with the royal flag, met the fleeing rioters head-on. At impact the flag went down. Blund's horse was stabbed. The young flag bearer was dragged from his saddle, bludgeoned and trampled. The knights behind him struck at the shadowy shapes that dodged between them and the building walls and shuttered shop windows. Ahead, there was a sudden glare of light on the Saint Eloi Square, making silhouettes of the approaching, darting rioters. In the marketplace dropped flares had set a rubbish heap aflame. Against the background of bright yellow light more dark figures came running. They vanished into an alley that branched off the Rue Saint James.

Two mercenary knights drew their horses around the downed and wounded flag bearer. The rest spurred past his thrashing, dying horse to chase the fleeing shadows through the alley and toward the Begueyre Gate.

Simon, in the market square, saw Rostein DelSoler. Urging his horse through the struggling mob, he forced his way toward Rostein. But the crowd surrounding the old man suddenly broke, running toward the Rue Ayers. Rostein disappeared among them as they fled. Simon sent ten of his knights after them.

The riot was dispersed. The viceroy ordered his knights to search street by street and house by house for Rostein and the city militiamen who had risen at his bidding.

In the abandoned square, fire billowed through the market's heaps of trash and the debris of the riot. One after another the barred doors of the houses opened and men and women hurried out with buckets to put out the blazes. Dark figures of monks appeared, moving among the dead and wounded sprawled on the cobbled pavement. The monks bore the dead away for claiming by their families for burial. The injured they took to the Convent of the Holy Cross for care.

It was nearly dawn when, at last, Eleanor saw Simon coming into their chamber. He had taken off his hauberk and chain sleeves. His padded shirt was soaked with sweat, the right sleeve stained with blood.

"Are you hurt?"

"No."

"Is it over?"

"Yes." He sat beside her on the bed. "These Gascons have no care for our sleep," he grinned. He seemed cheerful, exhilarated. He reached to kiss her but she pushed him away.

"You're dirty!"

"I'll wash. Later," he said, not to be put off.

This was the first time Eleanor had seen him right after a battle. She had heard the grisly screaming coming from the marketplace, and had not recovered from her fear.

Simon pulled off his shirt, his chain mail leggings and his underclothes, then he lay down beside her. He put his arms around her and pressed his mouth to hers.

She turned her head away. "It is exciting to you?" she asked, appalled.

"Yes," he answered simply, bending to kiss her neck.

She pulled away from him, sitting up and drawing the covers around her. "It sounded like men dying."

Looking at her frightened face in the dim light that filtered through the bed curtains, he sat up, turned her chin toward him and kissed her on the lips. "Out there," he tried to explain, "I feel... a freedom. There is nothing but the present moment. If there is death, then I shall have died as I should."

She met his gaze, not understanding.

"There is a sense... almost of joy."

She stared at him. "God help you!"

"God help us all, then," he said, kissing her and drawing her to him again.

It was still early in the morning when Simon went down to the hall. The straw pallets the knights slept on were strewn about the floor. Many of the men were just waking. The captain was sitting on the floor, breakfasting on a thick slice of bread, but he got up at once, seeing the viceroy.

The viceroy's flag hung in its place over the dais. It was torn and smeared with dirt and blood. Seeing it, Simon demanded of the captain, "Where is William Blund!"

"They took him to the Convent of the Holy Cross, my lord. He's badly hurt."

Simon's jaw tightened. "How many others?" He began counting his men.

"He's the only one hurt seriously. The rest who aren't here are still searching the city."

"Good. You say the Holy Cross?"

"Yes, my lord."

Simon sent his squire Peter to ask after his flag bearer. Then he prepared for the morning's opening of court. The knights cleared their makeshift bedding and housekeeping away.

Guillaume Colom arrived. And the prisoners taken in the riot and its aftermath were herded in, shackled together. Rostein DelSoler, who was head of the city's militia; the Mayor of Bordeaux; the entire militia and the city's Board of Aldermen were there: Bordeaux's foremost citizens stood in chains.

The viceroy, sitting on a tall chair on the dais, looked at them sternly. "For what reason do you men, above all, rise up to make war in the city's streets at night?"

"It is not us, but *you*, who makes war on the militia of Bordeaux! We were doing our duty!" old Rostein, in the forefront of the shackled group, protested vehemently. "This is the work of that grinning ape you favor!" He raised his iron-cuffed hand and pointed at Guillaume Colom, who was standing by the viceroy's chair.

"My lord, don't believe a word from the old deceiver," Colom responded coolly. "You saw for yourself who was fighting in the market square."

"I, and my sons, as is our custom," Rostein shouted over him, "assisted the militia in putting down a riot! A riot, lord Viceroy, that was started by the Colom family stealing armaments in the Rue Saint James! It is Colom who deceives you!"

A chorus of agreement went up from the chained prisoners.

Simon looked from DelSoler to Colom.

"That's a lie!" Colom burst out like a cornered terrier. "A wicked lie, Rostein! I heard the noise, and went there with my sons and found you stealing!"

Simon studied both men thoughtfully, then said in a low, firm voice, "I will conduct my own inquiry." He turned to the captain of the mercenaries, "Arrest Guillaume Colom and all those of his family who bear arms."

"You will release us?" Rostein gestured to his chained companions.

"You, too, will remain my prisoners until the inquiry determines who is telling me the truth."

The squire Peter had come in. He stood waiting at the back of the hall. As the prisoners, loudly protesting, were led off to the fortress's securest chambers, Simon motioned for Peter to come forward. He came up, reaching his master as the last of the chained men went out escorted by the mercenary knights.

Simon turned to Peter and said grimly, "Pray that Our Lord guides me, Peter. They could all be liars. How is young William?"

"My lord, he's dead. The monks are preparing him for burial."

Simon's expression went darker. He had grown very fond of his flag bearer. But he said nothing.

After some moments, looking up at the torn banner. Peter inquired, "Shall you order a new flag to be made, my lord?"

"Yes." Simon emerged from his thoughts and added somberly, "Have this one taken to the Convent of the Holy Cross. Let it be buried with the man who died defending it."

At noon, as Simon and the countess sat at dinner in their chamber, one of the knights searching the houses of the DelSoler brought in a letter. The question of who was treacherous was answered. But the answer was more ominous than the worst Simon had feared. The letter bore the seal of Amanieu d'Albret, and in it were the names of Raymond de Fronzac and Geoffrey and Elie Rudel – the losing claimants of Blaye; the son of the imprisoned Vicomte de Gramont; and Guillaume de Rion and Bernard de Bouville – the losing claimants of Bezaume. The letter referred to armaments the DelSoler agreed to supply, for a general uprising of the lords of Gascony to overthrow England's rule. It was quite clear who had been stealing from the armorers' shops.

Simon sent at once for Guillaume Colom. The merchant came into the chamber looking very shaken by the morning's turn of events. The viceroy had a stool brought up to his table and gestured for Guillaume to sit and have some wine.

"I believe, from evidence just found, that you've dealt with me honestly," Simon said guardedly. "But I ask, as a pledge of your loyalty, that in exchange for each man of your family whom I now hold, you will render to me a Colom boy to serve as a page and honorable hostage." He was placing the entire Colom family in acute vulnerability to the viceroy's displeasure; yet he was treating Colom not as a bourgeois, but as a fellow-nobleman. At Paris, as a child, Simon himself had been such a page-hostage, ensuring that the his brother Amaury observed all the terms in ceding the Montfort conquests of Toulouse, Carcassone and Foix to the French Crown.

"My lord," the merchant blustered, "our sons will serve you proudly. I'll see they're brought here today!" He knew what advantages an early life in a lord's retinue could bring. He stood and bowed clumsily again and again, like a flustered, bobbing hen.

"We will be happy to receive your family's children," the countess smiled, suppressing an impulse to laugh at Colom's comical performance. "I will myself see that they have a proper tutor here." She was charmed by the merry little man.

Colom knelt at her feet. "Lady, count me as your vassal," his cherubic face beamed at such noble sounding words issuing from his own lips.

"Master Colom, "the viceroy spoke, amused, but recalling the merchant to his proper, modest title, "I ask these measures not for your advancement alone, but to be certain of you. I am appointing you the acting Mayor of Bordeaux."

"Oh, lord Viceroy!" Colom was overwhelmed. He took both of Simon's hands and covered them with kisses. "Lord Earl, you favor me beyond my merit! And to think that only this morning I complained to Our Lord that you were unjust! Heaven forgive me!" He was breathless with excitement.

After dinner, the viceroy's court opened for the afternoon session. A soldier of the garrison at Bazas arrived. He brought the first news that bore out the full weight of DelSoler's letter.

"Lord Viceroy, the castle of Bazas is under siege! Amanieu d'Albret and Guillaume de Rion, with some hundred knights, attacked us near midnight last night. We beg you, send us relief at once!"

Simon turned to the captain of the mercenaries. "It appears that last night's riot was not a single uprising, but the onset of concerted war. Make your knights ready to march to Bazas."

As the knights were packing their gear and arming, the viceroy received a small parade of Colom boys, and released the Colom men. Guillaume Colom was sworn in as acting Mayor of Bordeaux.

"Lord Viceroy," Colom announced earnestly, "my family and our friends will keep the city safe. You can rely upon the Colom."

"I don't know if he's trustworthy or not," Simon told Eleanor a few moments later in their chamber. She was rubbing oil on his chain mail sleeve to protect it from the still-wet, washed sleeve of his pourpoint shirt. Peter sat on the floor sharpening Simon's sword.

"This is preposterous! We shouldn't even be here!" the countess rubbed hard at the metal in her anger and frustration. "We should be on our way to Aigue Morte. And now you're engaged in some foolish war here!"

Simon took the sleeve from her and put it down. "Eleanor, I did not come to Gascony by my choice. Believe that! I want you to see..." he took her by the arm and drew her to the chamber window. In the courtyard below, the knights' horses were being saddled and bridled and their mantles fitted over their heads. Simon pointed toward the castle's river gate that opened onto the Garonne. Outside the wall, the tip of a mast showed where a ship was moored. "The ship that Henry licensed me to use is loading at the quay. If Colom proves faithless and you are attacked here, take the highest ranking prisoners we hold, and the Colom children, and go to England at once. Don't wait for my return."

Eleanor turned toward him, the gravity of the danger finally reaching her understanding. "You think even Colom may be treacherous?"

"I don't know. Be wise." He kissed her pale, cool cheek.

Peter held out Simon's sword for him. "My lord, it's sharp."

"Heaven help us," Eleanor murmured, reaching for her husband's hand, then kissing him on the lips.

He smiled. "Expect that I shall be back soon." Then he took the sword from Peter, tested its edge and thrust it into its scabbard. "See that my horse is ready," he told Peter.

Eleanor had begun to cry. As the squire left, Simon turned back to his wife.

"This is all Henry's problem!" the countess burst out. "Let's leave here now! Let's go back to the crusade right now! You're pledged to the Cross! And so am I! How dare you risk both of our lives on these trivial, troublesome people! It is the Holy Land that needs you!"

"My lord!" Peter's voice called from the stairs. "My lord, there is a knight here from the garrison at La Reole!"

Simon looked in his wife's eyes. "Eleanor, my soul is at Aigue Morte. But I have no choice!" He turned and went through the door to the stairs where, half way up, a man was bleeding and leaning heavily upon the squire's shoulders. "Bring him in here," Simon ordered. The squire helped the man up the remaining stairs and into the chamber.

The wounded man was another of the English knights who had stayed after his term was done, filling out the garrison at La Reole that de Meulles had set to have a stronghold to the east on the Garonne. His crumpled red and gold surcoat was stiff with blood, and torn where a deep gash laid bare his collarbone.

The countess turned away, toward the window, clutching her brow with her hand to shield her eyes.

As Peter went to fetch his bag of lint to pack the wound, Simon helped the man to sit, and poured a goblet full of wine for him.

The man tried to speak but burst out sobbing. "They are all dead!" he cried in guttural English. "The castellans that we evicted, the Piis... they got in some secret way. They murdered us! It was no battle. It was a sneaking slaughter!"

Peter was back. He began to pour wine into the man's wound to cleanse it, loosening the fabric and the ragged edge of broken chain mail that was dried into the wound. The man screamed. Simon held him and the squire worked carefully.

"Bordeaux, Bazas, now La Reole," Simon said curtly. He glanced to Eleanor. She returned his gaze with a short, angry look, then turned away again to look out of the window.

Servants had hurried in at the sound of the man's screams as Peter probed. Simon left the wounded man for them to hold. With another look to Eleanor, who did not turn around, he left the room and went quickly down the stairs.

In the courtyard the mercenaries, mounted and ready, stood waiting. The viceroy mounted his destrier, which was held in the lead. The gate was opened. Simon with his fifty knights rode out toward the east.

It was the last day of June. The flat fields of the Garonne valley were being mowed of their first crop of hay. Vineyards were in full leaf. Simon and his knights traveled swiftly for all that remained of the day, and rested that night at Langon. The next day the company neared Bazas.

The brilliant southern sun glared in a cloudlessly blue sky. A breeze stroked the tall grass. In the distance rose the half-finished nave of the cathedral, a castle tower, and the beige town wall of Bazas enclosing a cluster of low red-tiled roofs like a penned flock of ruddled sheep. The landscape gave no hint of civil war. But it lay strangely serene. Here not a reaper could be seen in the fields, nor anyone tending the vineyards.

The captain raised his horn to his lips and blew a fanfare for the coming of the viceroy, for the company bore no flag.

In answer, a bell rang from the castle tower.

As the knights approached the city wall, the broad wooden leaves of its gate were swung open. The people of Bazas came pouring out. "Long live the Viceroy Montfort!" "Death to d'Albret!" they shouted. Amid their cries were phrases of the song the troubadour had made when the viceroy came to Bazas to hold court the year before.

Simon rode into the town surrounded by a sea of faces flushed and merry as at carnival. Here, above the crowd, a hand waved a steel cap. A bent, pierced shield bobbed there. The people of Bazas brandished their trophies.

Simon's brow tightened. He did not smile at the gaiety. When he and his knights reached the town square, the men of the garrison, on the tower rampart above, leaned out cheering with the crowd. Simon's knights drew up their horses in formation around the tower door. Pushing the crowd back, they made an opening in which Simon dismounted. The door's iron portcullis was drawn up, the door opened and the Gascon castellan came out.

"What has become of the siege you reported?" Simon demanded, walking through the door.

"We don't know where they've gone!" the castellan hurried after him, clearly amazed. "It has been pitched battle right here in the square! The barons fighting us, the people fighting them! Then d'Albret and his henchmen heard your horn, and they fell away like Jericho before Joshua. The people went to meet you and we don't know where d'Albret has gone." The castellan's sunken eyes and stubbled cheeks bore witness he had been fighting through two nights with no rest.

Simon put his hand on the tired man's shoulder. "You've done well. Would that all this revolt ended so well," he smiled.

The viceroy ordered a search for d'Albret and his followers. As the mercenaries combed Bazas, the people joined in the search. In a short time the barons' horses were found, hidden in a vineyard warehouse that belonged to d'Albret. The baron and his companions had not yet escaped, but were still in Bazas. Soon crowds of people driving carts, riding jennets, donkeys – any mount that they could find, were streaming out the city gate.

"They're going to sack d'Albret's villa," the castellan grinned.

"Have them stopped!" Simon ordered angrily. "I want peace here, not chaos! Have it cried in the streets and in the fields, and at d'Albret's and his friends' holdings, that anyone caught looting commits a crime against the Crown. I'm hereby confiscating all the lords' properties, and placing them under the Crown for safekeeping!"

The castellan looked disappointed. "I'd let the people have their way. It's been a long time coming."

"Complaints are to be settled in court, not in riot and pillaging," Simon cut short his objection.

The captain of the mercenaries came to report, "Lord Viceroy, we've found the barons. We have them trapped. What would you have us do?"

"Where are they?"

"In the cathedral's undercroft."

"Well," Simon smiled, his temper cooling. The cathedral was nextdoor to the tower. He thought a few moments. "Tell them, if they come out by their own free will and present themselves at court, their confiscated properties will be restored, if they're found innocent of treason. I won't order you to go in after them. It is a sanctuary. But see to it they don't escape."

"But Viceroy..." the castellan started to protest. Then he paused, and made a bow instead.

"What is it?" Simon asked him.

"I recall the church at Bezier, my lord. You are very different from your father." The army Simon's father led had burnt to death six thousand Albigensians in the church at Bezier. It was a horror linked with the Montfort name everywhere in the south.

"Castellan, I do not criticize my father's acts," Simon said curtly, "nor do I presume to redeem them."

The captain returned to his men at the undercroft.

Only the chancel and three bays of the cathedral were completed, and even they were still enclosed with scaffolding. Within the structure, around the altar and the entry to the undercroft, there was a wooden shed. Here services already were held. Inside the shed the light was dim, though between the gaps in the board walls the sun cast a few bright, dust-specked beams. Above the altar was a fine embroidered baldachin illuminated by the soft glow of the altar lamp. Several mercenaries stood at the head of the stairs leading to the crypt below the altar. At the base of the stairs was a small oak door.

The captain walked down the stairs and knocked on the door. "Lord Amanieu! The viceroy holds your lands in the king's name. If you and those with you will come with us and have your claims heard in court, if you're found innocent, he promises that all will be returned to you."

There was a pause. Then d'Albret answered, "Does Montfort think returning to us what is ours will lure us to his den? Tell him he must come and take us!"

"The viceroy has done you the kindness of observing your sanctuary," the captain answered, clearly not pleased at the restraint. "He wants no strife, but offers you fair trial. Will you cowards come out!"

A longer pause, then d'Albret shouted, "You can tell the pious viceroy we're taking Holy Orders here. We'll have the bishop hear our case." There was laughter in several voices from behind the door.

The captain went back to the tower to report.

"Keep your guard at the door," Simon told him. "We will starve them out."

But the next morning there was such silence in the undercroft that the soldiers tried the door. It opened, and they found the crypt empty. By enlarging a foundation drainage hole, d'Albret and his friends had escaped.

Chapter Ten

THE GASCONS' NET
1249

THE GASCON REBEL LORDS WERE gone. The siege was over, there was nothing more to be done at Bazas. Simon and his mercenary force returned to Bordeaux before marching on to retake La Reole.

The capital was quiet. The DelSoler faction, except for those held prisoners, had fled. When the castle gates were opened for the viceroy and his company, the new mayor stood waiting for them in the castle yard.

"All's well, my lord." Colom's dimpled face grinned proudly as, like a noble steward, he held the stirrup for Simon to dismount. "The DelSoler are gone and old Rostein is dying."

Simon looked sharply at the mayor and frowned. Colom's hated rival had been quite well when he was taken prisoner.

Colom quickly ceased his grinning. "The old man's over seventy," he said defensively. "His doctor's been to see him. He says it's a tercian fever."

"I'll see for myself," Simon replied. He walked at once across the yard to the river gate where the old man was imprisoned in the barbican.

Rostein's room was bright and white with only a cot and stool for furniture and a few baskets of well-searched clothes, pillows and food brought from his home. Rostein lay on the cot staring at the white ceiling. His eyes were rheumy, his cheeks were pale under a white stubble of new-grown beard. He turned his gaze as the door opened, then raised his head a little in surprise as he saw the viceroy, still in battle dress, come in. Rostein pulled himself up on one elbow. "Lord Viceroy I don't want to die here!" His voice croaked through the mucous in his throat. "Let me go home."

Simon sat on the stool beside the cot. "You've had good care? Your own doctor has seen you?"

"I'm sick. I can't do any harm. Let me go home where I can die with my family around me." He gripped Simon's wrist with his boney hands. His breath had the sweet stench of death.

Simon stood up, prying off the moist, fragile fingers that clung to him. "You're valuable to me as a hostage, Rostein. You know that I can't waste what gains I have." But no sooner had he uttered the pettish words than he felt ashamed. Rostein was pathetic. And too, once dead he had no value as a hostage. "If someone of your family will take your place, I'll let you go home."

Rostein looked at Simon suspiciously. But the sharp, alert gaze ebbed as he gave way to his fever. He lay back. After some moments he murmured, "Tell my son Gaillard to come."

"You would have Gaillard take your place?" Simon asked, amazed that he would name his eldest son as hostage.

"I'm dying. Tell Gaillard to come," the old man repeated.

Simon went down to the courtyard and crossed to the hall. Colom stood ready, smiling, on the dais by the viceroy's chair. But Simon continued through the room and went up the stairs.

As he passed briskly through the hall, a huge man in a leather cuirass and a long, slit riding robe hurried to intercept him. "Lord Viceroy," the man called out, "I must speak with you." It was Amaubin de Barres.

Seeing the baron to whom he had granted Blaye, Simon paused. "Lord Amaubin!" He put out his hands in greeting to the man he deemed the best soldier in Gascony.

Amaubin grasped Simon's hands. "Lord Viceroy, I must beg your help."

"Our guardian of the Gironde has more bad news for me?"

"My lord, I've lost my castle at Fronzac. Gaillard DelSoler, Raymond de Fronzac, young Gramont and a horde of their followers took my steward by surprise. I hold the castle at siege now, but I must have more men if I'm to retake it."

"Lord Amaubin, my garrison at La Reole, men who stayed beyond their term for love of me, are slaughtered. I go from here to avenge them."

Amaubin ran his hand through his thin hair. "I hadn't known the troubles were elsewhere also, my lord. I can hold the siege until you can come from La Reole."

Simon pressed his hand. "Good Amaubin, I trust in you. As it seems we have full war, I want you for my marshal. I shall give you a letter of commission with full powers to act in my name." He turned and beckoned to the clerk who sat on a bench near the dais. Then he started up the stairs again, but paused. "You say that Gaillard DelSoler is at Fronzac?"

"Yes, my lord."

"I'll give you a letter for him also." Simon went on up the stairs with the clerk following.

Eleanor was sitting by the window. She bent toward the light, embroidering a glove. Simon came in with the clerk and shut the door behind them. She glanced up, but said nothing and went back to her work.

Seeing her coldness, Simon turned his attention to the clerk. He dictated the letter of commission, a report to King Henry on all that was happening, and a letter to Gaillard DelSoler, telling him of his father's failing health and of the proposed exchange of himself for his father. Then he dismissed the clerk.

Tight-lipped, without looking up, Eleanor went on with her work.

Simon poured water from a pitcher into a basin on the table to wash himself. "What do you think of Rostein?" he asked, trying to make neutral conversation. "Could Colom have poisoned him?"

She made no answer.

He pulled off his hauberk and shirt and began to wash. "Rostein doesn't seem to think so," he ignored her silence. "I doubt he'd summon his eldest son into the keeping of the man he thought had poisoned him. Washing himself with a soapy cloth, he turned and asked, "What do you think?"

"I sit here with one thought," the countess answered, putting down her work and fixing Simon with a piercing look. "It is that we should be on our way to Palestine. And everything you do ties us here!"

"Eleanor, I'm trying to restore peace quickly!"

She heard the desperation in his tone and said, a little less coldly, "I've looked in on Rostein. He seems to me to be dying of a bad heart and a tercian fever, as his doctor says." She bent to her embroidery again.

Simon said no more but watched her as he washed. Her thin white summer veil fell over her shoulders. Full of the light from the window, its folds held a long stream of sunlight down her back. Her belly, five months from term, was starting to show large. He dried himself with a towel and walked to the window. Gently, hesitantly, he let his hand pass down her veil in a caress that scarcely touched her.

She looked up, tense with anger. "Henry's jealous of you, and you've let yourself be trapped by him!" she hissed. "You could be King of Palestine!"

Stung, Simon drew his hand back. "I see. You are more ambitious for me than I am for myself." His tone was tart. "For me, it's agony enough that I am here in Gascony, and my debt to the Lord goes unpaid." He turned away to dress and did not try to touch her again.

The next day the viceroy and his knights marched toward La Reole. The Piis brothers fled before the army reached the city and the viceroy took the citadel without a fight. He set a new garrison, appointed a mayor for the town and, in two days, returned to Bordeaux.

It seemed that the rebellion, at first so very threatening, was no more than a shadow that the glare of firm action could dispel. With a good steward to govern Gascony, and Barres to patrol the land, Simon thought he still could leave soon for Aigue Morte.

Again at Bordeaux, the lord Amaubin was waiting for him in the hall. "My lord, your message was delivered to Gaillard DelSoler. He would not come. He has escaped from Fronzac with Gramont's son. We followed them to Royan, where they took ship for England." Barres looked very worried.

Simon gave a tired smile. "Good. They've fled into the lion's mouth. I've kept Henry well informed of their rebellion."

"Lord Viceroy, I know these men. They could convince the moon it was the sun! Let me go bear witness to the king against them."

Simon touched the baron's arm wearily. "Amaubin, I need you here. We must retake Fronzac."

That evening Simon went to see old Rostein in his cell. "Your son will not be coming," he told him.

"He hasn't come?" the old man's voice was thin with disbelief. Simon shook his head.

Tears trickled from Rostein's inflamed eyes. "I don't want to die here." He turned on his side, drawing his blanket up to hide his face. Simon could see only the top of his head with its few wisps of hair, pathetic as a baby's.

"Shall I send for your confessor?" he asked.

The head nodded.

The priest came.

The next day DelSoler was dead.

"I cannot understand," Simon remarked to his squire, "that no one of his family would take his place. It is a pity for an honored old man, whatever he has done, to die like this."

That same day the viceroy and his mercenaries rode out of Bordeaux with the Lord of Barres. But at Fronzac they found the siege was broken. The night before, Amanieu d'Albret and his companions from Bazas had attacked Barres' men from the rear. Wounded men were tending to each other as well as they could in their makeshift camp by the castle wall. Fronzac was abandoned.

As Amaubin and Simon entered the hall, the castle's frightened cellarer hurried to his master. "Lord Amaubin, they've drunk up the best wines you brought here. I couldn't stop them! They went down to the cellar themselves."

"I expected no less," Amaubin said curtly. Like most Gascon lords, his wines were his most valued possessions. "All else is well?"

"Oh, I think not!" the cellarer fretted. "I overheard them talking. Some of the lords were going south to join with Gaston de Bearne. They say he has collected a great army. Some others of them follow DelSoler to England. They mean to lodge complaint against the viceroy."

"King Henry won't listen to them," Simon assured Amaubin later when they talked privately. But he was feeling that Henry ought to be supplied with a vivid sense of what was happening. "Lord Amaubin, perhaps it would be best for you to go to England. Take my current report with you, and describe what you yourself have seen and heard. You should also remind the king of the money that he owes me for the land's defense."

Barres left for England with the viceroy's report. Simon returned to Bordeaux.

A few days after Simon reached the capital, a messenger from England came. Colom grinned, "Lord Viceroy, I'll wager DelSoler flew into the lion's mouth just as you said."

"Let's see how the lion has gnawed on him," Simon smiled as he unfastened the parchment tab with the royal seal and opened the king's letter. But the smile drained from his face as he read. Abruptly he rose from his chair and left the hall, motioning for Colom to follow him up the stairs.

Eleanor had gone to the Convent of the Holy Cross to visit the wounded. Their chamber was empty. Simon walked to the window. By its light he read the letter from King Henry again. Then he handed it to Colom.

"My lord, forgive me, I cannot read," the mayor cringed. "Is it bad news?"

'DelSoler is clever!" Simon struck the broad stone windowsill with his clenched fist. "Henry ordered him and Gramont arrested. But they pled they'd come as hostages in exchange for their fathers." He gave a tight smile, "They have accused me of confiscating property and putting men in prison – not for the land's peace, but for my personal gain."

"They will tell any lie, my lord."

"Yes. Well, I have debts that Henry knows very well about, that – to his mind – lend credence to their lies. My contract with the Crown grants me license to send wines to England in my own ship duty-free. He seems to imagine that I've seized these men's vineyards and warehouses to set myself up in the export trade!"

The wine merchant was deeply shocked. "My lord, who could ever think of so fine a nobleman as you going into trade!"

Simon looked at Colom for a moment, then burst out with a laugh. "I tell you, Master Colom, I would rather be accused of turning wine merchant than thief!"

"Let me go to England and throw their lies back in their throats!" Colom's little eyes blazed.

"I've just sent the lord of Barres to the king. But clearly Henry needs more reminding of the truth." Simon thought for a few moments, then "Very well, go to England. Keep Henry in mind that I did not come to Gascony to make my own fortune – but to fight treason against the Crown at his express command! That I have no wish to be here, and if he cares no longer for my services, I will quite gladly leave. Remind him also of the monies that he owes me."

Colom left to join Barres at Westminster. But before he could have reached the Court, another letter came from King Henry. The king flatly ordered Simon to return the lands he had confiscated and garrisoned, and immediately release the prisoners that he held.

The order would undo all that Simon had achieved. He ignored it. He did nothing, and awaited the result of Barres' and Colom's testimony at Court.

Simon waited with the patience of a lion in a net. No quick reverse of the king's order came.

Weeks dragged by. Now there could be no joining Louis at Aigue Morte. No departing with the crusade for Palestine.

Simon sent letter after letter to King Henry. Colom and Barres wrote frequent, hopeful letters. But no word came from the king.

Simon wrote to Louis. Louis, still claiming to fear England's retribution in his absence, would not let him join his crusade without Henry's consent.

Through the last days of summer Simon waited.

In September the crusade sailed from Aigue Morte.

With the rebel barons gone to England or in hiding in the Pyrenees, Gascony was quiet. There was no more pillaging. There were no night raids, no excessive tolls on the roads. Only at La Reole was there any disturbance. The Piis brothers attacked the citadel again and murdered the town's new mayor. The town was thrown into a frenzy of fear and confusion. To restore order, in mid-September Simon moved his court to the great citadel on the Garonne.

La Reole stood on a cliff on the north bank of the Garonne with a commanding view of many miles of flat fields and vineyard lands spreading southward from the river. The castle, built by Richard the Lion Hearted as a stronghold in mid-Gascony, had been renovated by its castellans, the Piis. As aldermen of a rich town, they had furnished it in astonishing *nouveau riche* taste from the proceeds of their graft.

The main hall was a wide, circular room in the largest of the castle's four towers. Its domed and groined ceiling was painted red and powdered with gold stars, its vault ribs gilded. Where the ribs gathered at the ceiling's center, an elaborately carved stone knob in gold, red and green thrust downward like an immense pendant jewel. The vault ribs were supported on the walls by projecting stone brackets fully sculpted in the shape of human heads. Each bracket had a different face painted in lifelike colors. They scowled and leered like devils, or smiled and simpered like lewd ladies at a Court in Hell. The brackets were made to the Lion Hearted's order and suggested an odd humor in the man.

But the Piis had enlarged upon the oddness of the room with a style all their own that seemed learned in a brothel. Murals on the low walls depicted scenes of courtship, the lovers fully clothed but in poses of bold amorousness. Bridging a quadrant of the room's curved wall was a gigantic fireplace before which stood two finely carved oak chairs and an oak table. The table's service was of gold: ewers, goblets, platters, domed chalices and candelabrum. Each piece had, elegantly worked in the design, the form of a scantily clad maiden being ravished by a goat.

Flanking the fireplace, two windows were cut through the eight-foot thickness of the walls. The embrasure of each window was as large as a small room. Broad window seats the size of beds were carved into the masonry on each side of these sunny cubicles, and furnished with thick satin mattresses and heaps of pillows. Providing the alcoves with privacy, heavy, embroidered draperies were hung, their needlework depicting rabbits, squirrels and foxes coupling, and lovers entwined licentiously amid spring sprouting blooms. Long after the Piis had departed, the room's cushions and hangings gave off a strong scent of attar of rose.

There were several prisoners held at la Reole, detained from the preceding year's court circuit and sent here for safe-keeping in the king's strongest prison. The Piis were no friends of the lords. Their seizure of the castle had only made the prisoners' lot the worse. Among the barons held at Le Reole was the Vicomte Arnaud de Gramont.

One evening early in November, Simon, irked by King Henry beyond bearing, had Gramont brought up from his cell. The viceroy would try to comply with the king's order.

"You're looking well, Arnaud, for a man who's been in prison for a year," Simon observed.

"You dredge me up from that stale cell to congratulate me on my health?" the vicomte retorted, looking about the garish room with interest.

"No, to invite you to supper. To remind you of your freedom, and how little stands between you and it."

"You don't need my permission to help yourself to all I have. What is it you want now?"

"All I've ever wanted. Peace in Gascony. But let us dine and discuss the matter in the manner of equals, not prisoner and warder." He motioned to Arnaud to take the chair opposite him at the table, and they both sat.

A page, one of Colom's nephews, offered a gold laver and a fine cotton towel. Simon washed his hands, then poured goblets of wine for Arnaud and himself as the page offered the laver and towel to Gramont. The vicomte washed with care.

Another page brought bowls of pottage for the first course. From a round loaf of bread Simon cut two trencher slices, for his guest and himself, and he began to eat. Seeing Arnaud hesitate, he exchanged the pottage he had tasted for the vicomte's.

"I'm not going to poison you, Arnaud. I only want to talk with you," the viceroy said quietly. "We'll exchange every dish, if that will reassure you."

Guardedly Arnaud began to eat.

"This is a beautiful country," Simon observed as an opening to the conversation. "I believe you can see well across the valley from the window of your cell." He savored the wine, "And the land is very generous."

Arnaud said nothing, finishing his pottage. The boy brought in a roast course. Simon watched Arnaud eat. The vicomte chewed slowly, too proud to show his hunger for the better food.

"Like you," Simon said earnestly, "I too am a prisoner here. If we can work a peace with one another, we can both be free. You from your cell, I from Gascony."

The vicomte said nothing but went on eating, and watching Simon coolly.

Seeing this direct approach got no response, Simon tried a lighter tone. "But you're not drinking your wine? I thought this vintage very fine. My squire found it in the cellar here."

"Indeed, my wine," Arnaud said icily. "By chance in this cellar? Not your confiscation? Sire Montfort, I know the taste of wine from my own vineyard. I remember when these grapes were pressed. Did you mean to torture me with the taste of my lost lands? What is it that you want from me!"

"I know nothing of how this barrel came here, but would assume it was by purchase of the castellans now gone. Nothing of mine is here. And I want nothing from you Arnaud, but your solemn oath of peace and fealty. To King Henry, to me as his viceroy, and to the steward I shall appoint for Gascony. Swear to me, and go home free today."

Arnaud regarded Simon carefully. Then he sat back in his chair and took a sip of wine. "Well, yes, Sire Montfort, let us talk like equals. I could swear fealty to you, like a Colom or a DelSoler, and break my oath the moment that I reached my door. But, as you say, we are equals. I hate you, Simon de Montfort. And I would rather rot in Hell than swear fealty to you! Cut off my ears, as your father did his prisoners! I will not swear to you!"

"Damn you!" Simon, stung to the core, threw his napkin down. "My father maimed his prisoners in answer to the murder of his messengers! Will you southerners obey nothing but cruelty and force?"

"Your temper's short, Sire Simon," Gramont smiled coldly. "You would grant me peace because you're frightened now. I know my son's in England and is well received by Henry. This time next year it will be you who'll be in chains, for throwing us in prison and stealing our lands!"

"Guard!" Simon called out, and the mercenary waiting at the far side of the door came in. "Take this man back to his cell!" Simon ordered, quaking with rage.

Arnaud laughed shortly as the soldier led him away. "Sire Montfort now wants to be rid of me. Is this the viceroy's well-bred hospitality?"

A few days later there was another dinner guest at La Reole, but this time the Countess Eleanor, though pregnant and in her term's last month, was hostess. The guest was the chaplain to King Louis' brother Alphonse.

The good priest held forth throughout the meal with the loudness of a man half-deaf. "The world seems fairly full of news of the triumph of the Good these days," he boomed benignly. "King Louis has already seized Damietta. There's little doubt he'll take the rest of Egypt soon! My lord Alphonse has joined him for the final victory. And now, as if Our Lord meant to set all matters right before His Jubilee Year of 1250, the old heretic Count Raymond of Toulouse has died and gone to his eternal punishment. All evil is being gathered into Hell," he smiled, well satisfied.

Simon forced a smile, but made no answer to the chaplain's happy observations.

Eleanor spoke up bitterly. "Though we've had no part in the victories in the East, at least we need not worry what Count Raymond may be plotting with King Thibaut." She turned to Simon with an acid smile. "I'm certain that is a great relief to your sister-in-law in Bigorre. Perhaps you can stop paying her the seven-thousand marks a year it costs for us to have the honor of protecting her borders."

Simon kept his expression calm, but he was cut. In the strain of their entrapment in Gascony, Eleanor now seldom spoke to him. But when she did her words were aimed to hurt. In an undertone, beneath the deaf chaplain's hearing, Simon said caustically, "I'd thought the grave had silenced the tongue of the queen mother Isabel. But I see it's bequeathed to her daughter's mouth." Then, grimly serious, he added, "If matters grow much worse, we may be glad to have Bigorre for a refuge."

The chaplain missed most of the earl's remark. In confusion he looked back and forth between the earl and countess. Blushing, overcome with embarrassment, he chirped, "Good lady, please forgive me! I should have recalled your own mother's recent passing. I certainly never meant... her among those gathered! It's been a time of passing of so many of the mighty!"

"There's no offense, father," Eleanor narrowed her eyes at Simon, but turned to the priest with a smile. "Tell us more news of the Holy Land. We hope to go there. Some day."

"Indeed?" the chaplain looked to the earl. "May I write that in my letter to my master Alphonse?"

Simon drew breath as if tight cords bound his heart in a knot. "Yes. Tell Alphonse that we mean to come, God willing. Gascony is quiet now. Fronzac is in our hands again. We are obeyed by everyone. If all goes well, we could leave for the East by Saint John's Day."

Chapter Eleven

THE ARCHBISHOP AND THE POPE
1249-1250

IN LATE NOVEMBER ELEANOR GAVE birth to her sixth child, a girl. Simon touched the infant's tiny hand with his thumb as the midwife held her for him to see. The little fingers curled around his thumb and clung tightly. "She's a grasping little wench," he smiled, and his heart warmed to her – more than to any of his children since Henry's birth. She was christened Alice, after his mother.

But the child was sickly. In two weeks, after Simon and his family had returned to Bordeaux, Eleanor learned from the baby's nurse that Alice was dead. She had hoped for a boy, and so completely had she planned on being in the East for the child's birth, that this infant's death was only in keeping with all her other disappointments.

But Simon was stricken. "You should have sent for a doctor!" he raged at the nurse.

"A doctor? For a little baby?" the woman looked at him, incredulous. "Who ever heard of such a thing!" Eleanor rolled her eyes; her husband knew nothing of the care of children.

Fuming, Simon left the women as they prepared the tiny body for burial. For some time he walked about the city, trailed by his bodyguard of knights. When he returned to the hall, he summoned the prior of the Convent of the Holy Cross.

"There is no customary care for young children, beyond what their nurses can give," the Prior answered his question.

"So I've been told," Simon said curtly. His clerk brought a document, written from his dictation while he had waited for the prior to arrive. Simon handed it to the clergyman. It was a charter endowing the Convent of the Holy Cross with the rents of a Leicester fief for the founding of a children's hospital. The endowment was what would have been Alice's dowry.

"Lord Viceroy, this is a great thing!" the prior gushed. But seeing the viceroy's sorrow, he bowed discreetly and took his leave, adding only, "Good Sire, may the Lord bless you. All shall be done as you wish."

In a small grave dug in the aisle of the Cathedral of Bordeaux, baby Alice was interred. Archbishop Malemorte performed the funeral ceremony. The Colom family and numerous others of their faction attended. The service had the quiet beauty of the last rites of an innocent.

Until the little coffin, draped in white, was lowered into the pit. Then Malemorte, in his glittering vestments of white and gold, stepped forward. Pointing at Simon, who was kneeling by the grave in prayer, he proclaimed, "The taking of this child is Our Lord's clear rebuke of the evils of the father! This man, who has imprisoned fathers, sundered homes and families, is being in his own family struck down!"

The mourners, shocked, craned to see how the viceroy would respond.

Two red spots of anger came to Simon's cheeks. Kneeling on the stone, he looked up from his prayers to the archbishop. But he remained silent.

After the death of baby Alice, relations between Simon and Eleanor became still more strained. They argued loudly. Or for days they talked to each other not at all.

In early December, Amaubin de Barres and Guillaume Colom returned from England. They brought with them the long awaited letter from King Henry.

"The king grants you five hundred marks of the money that he owes you. And, though he's freed the traitors who were at his Court, he remands them to you for trial." Colom was quite pleased with his work.

But Simon was not. "Henry owes me four-thousand marks now for the hiring and maintenance of his soldiers! He's sent me five hundred? And young Gramont and DelSoler are free?"

"You can judge them for yourself," Amaubin urged. "They are ordered to appear for trial on February third."

"What will you wager they appear?" Simon retorted.

"If they don't, they'll be defaulters. You'll clearly be in the right in holding their lands." Colom made a little dance of gestures in his effort to appease Simon. "King Henry truly leans to our side now."

"So long as the wind keeps blowing toward us," Simon said sardonically.

"There is a private letter for you from the king." Barres produced another parchment from his sleeve. It was sealed shut with the small royal seal.

Simon opened it and read, then looked up sharply. "When are Gramont and DelSoler to come to trial?"

"On February third, my lord," Barres replied.

"King Henry clearly does not mean for me to hear their cases! He's ordered me to Paris at the end of January, to complete his negotiations for his truce with France. From there, he bids me to visit the Pope in Lyon!"

Simon's temper broke. He threw the letter on the floor. "How am I to be done here, and be his ambassador hither and yon!" Turning to Barres, he ordered, "Amaubin, go back to England. Remind the king of the full sum he owes me. And tell him that I wish to be relieved of service here at once!"

Barres returned to England with the viceroy's request.

King Henry refused. "The Earl of Leicester has a contract with me. I wish him to observe it," he said simply.

When Henry's answer reached Bordeaux, Eleanor shrieked at Simon, "Don't you see! Henry doesn't mean for us to leave so you can heap up fame in Palestine! He's jealous of you! And you've ever been his dupe! You're letting him un-man you!"

Simon clenched his fists and shouted back at her, "Take your vicious tongue out of my hearing!"

The countess pack and sailed for England, returning to Kenilworth.

As January of the year 1250 neared its end, the viceroy named Guillaume Colom Steward of Gascony. Then, with his squire and a small, armed escort, he rode north to negotiate England's truce with France.

The Court was at Melun. Simon met with Queen Blanche there.

The Queen Mother was looking old now. Simon bowed to her. But she put out both her hands and took his hand; she drew him to sit on the dais close beside her chair. Putting her arm around his shoulder, she pressed him to her knees familiarly, almost dependently. "I've heard much news of your good works in the south," her pale lips smiled.

Simon was astonished by her manner. She had never before been so warm with him. He felt abashed. "My reports are not nearly so good as those coming from Louis. I would far rather be with him." He tried to smile, but the pain his words touched was too deep.

"All my sons are in the East. I'm glad you're here." Blanche's look was earnest, "I may have need of you."

Simon kept silent. He dared not speak for fear that the frustration and the rage in him would come boiling out.

Seeing his tenseness, Queen Blanche put her hand upon his head. "You have been nearly as much a son to me as those of my own body. Be a comfort to me, Simon. I am growing old." Her tone sounded pleading. After a while, as he sat silent and lumpish at her feet, she asked, seemingly idly, "How is your wife the countess?"

"She is well, my lady. Though we've lost a child," Simon responded dully. He wanted to speak, to open himself to her. To someone. And Blanche, in her loneliness, seemed more tender to him than she ever had been before. But his anger seethed, kept in hard check, and he dared not open his heart for fear it would spill over. Finally he offered the excuse that he was feeling ill, and left her.

In the next days Simon met with France's Minister of State, Archbishop Odo Rigaud. The terms of the ongoing truce were set, and a copy was sent to England for King Henry's approval.

Simon rode on to Lyon. He was to petition Pope Innocent for relief from the heavy taxes of the English Church. At Lyon, he was to meet the other English delegates: Bishops Grosseteste and Cantaloup, and the king's brother, Prince Richard. Henry had chosen his most forceful arguers.

Grosseteste, Simon's old spiritual counselor, was the person to whom he would open his heart. He looked forward to their meeting. He rode on toward Lyon, the rage tight in him as a smoldering knot so hot he dared not touch it.

Lyon was on the great trade route from Italy to Paris and the countries of the north. At all times it was full of travelers. But with the presence of the Papal Court, the city now was far past its capacities. The inns were filled to their fullest. Everywhere the half-timbered upper floors that projected out above the streets were festooned with the flags of noblemen and princes of the Church from every region in Christendom. And the streets themselves were thronged in a tight-pressed confusion. In any city, mornings when the markets were open, the streets were crowded with every housewife, cook and pantler in the city, buying for their kitchens' needs. Criers added to the press. But with High Mass at noon the markets closed, the streets became relatively quiet, and the more genteel folk could emerge to go about their business with some orderly decorum.

Not so in Lyon now. There seemed no hour under daylight that the streets were passable but at a creeping pace, with body pressed to body whether of high or low degree. The stench of unwashed mankind was extreme. Horses were not of much advantage with the crowding so immovable, and their anxious sweat, urine and defecation added high pungence to the stink.

Simon found accommodations for himself, his squire and his escort at an inn outside of Lyon's western gate. Even that outlying hostel had its rambling facade bedecked with travelers' flags. Simon added his own red lion flag out the window of his room, as was the custom.

He inquired of the innkeeper where the Bishop of Lincoln lodged. His host shrugged. "There are so many here these days. I don't know where anyone is anymore."

Bursting with impatience, Simon went himself, on foot, to find Grosseteste. He pushed his way through the gate and into the teeming street. A man clearly as high ranking as he was seldom seen afoot. He was thronged by beggars who tugged at his black, fur lined cloak and grasped at him. The desperate poor were drawn to the city in great numbers to prey upon the penitents attracted to the Papal Court. Rome could absorb this sort of human inundation. But Lyon could not.

A woman with matted, filthy hair begged a farthing for the infant at her breast. Simon reached for the purse tied to his belt, but found its string was cut and it was gone. He cursed himself for his foolishness in setting out without his guard.

A shoemaker's apprentice, a pair of boots to be delivered clutched against his chest, used his elbows like a prow with a certain expertise and made headway. But a cleric on a mule tried to force his way ahead as his servant on foot cried, "Make way," futilely. A lady's palanquin, carried by four footmen, swayed against Simon and started to capsize, the unseen lady within screaming as its exhausted bearers lost their hold. And the crowd moved slowly, slowly forward, while those going in the opposite direction slowly sifted through.

Simon moved with the crowd from street to street for what seemed hours, no more certain of how to return to the west gate and his lodging, than where to find Grosseteste. He cursed himself over and over again. Then at last he saw, quite near, the See of Lincoln's familiar flag dangling from the upper story of an inn.

The innkeeper sent a boy running up to tell the bishop that the Earl of Leicester had arrived. But Simon followed the boy up the stairs two at a time. Grosseteste opened the door himself. The bishop's thin gray face creased into a smile of delight and he held out his hands to Simon.

The sight of his friend's warm welcome loosed all Simon's pent pain. He reached for Grosseteste's hands, but wrapped his arms around the bishop's narrow shoulders and wept.

Grosseteste was too astonished to do anything but help the earl from the door to the room's one chair. Then he drew up a stool and sat beside him, waiting for the storm to pass.

As Simon regained his self-control, Grosseteste handed him a towel to wipe his face.

"I'm so glad to see you, father," Simon said a little foolishly.

"So I see," Grosseteste smiled. "Now, tell me what it is that's brought on all this gladness, as you call it."

For the next hour Simon opened his heart to his friend. He told how Henry was entrapping him in ever growing debt for Gascony's defense. And of the king's doubts of him, and freeing of the prisoners. But chiefly he spoke of the guilt he felt at not being with the crusade.

"The Gascons are entangling me in intrigues. I see it plainly enough. And the Holy Land is ever further from my reach!" He shut his eyes in pain. "Eleanor is the voice of my own conscience, but I can't bear to hear her. I've driven her away from me."

"If Our Lord willed you to be in Palestine, you would not be barred as you are," Grosseteste said softly. "No. I believe you have a very different destiny. Else you would be in the East."

"I should have refused to go to Gascony at the very outset!" Simon insisted, locked in his own self-punishment, not really listening to Grosseteste's words.

"Were you truly free to refuse? If you had refused Henry, I dare say Louis still would not have taken you with him." The old bishop smiled to himself. "I suspect you are too good a soldier for him." Then he added in a tone with greater force, "Simon, what you do in Gascony may be as sweet to Our Lord as anything that Louis achieves in the Holy Land."

"You're far too kind, father. In any case, everything I do in Gascony is promptly undone by Henry! He shows no steadiness in my support."

"That is what I warned you of long ago."

"Yes. You said I leaned on Aaron's staff, and that it would one day turn serpent and bite me."

Grosseteste's eyes narrowed. "You see now why the land's rule cannot be left to the whims of kings? You see the wisdom of the council I proposed six years ago?"

Simon sighed. He was too weary to resist the bishop. "I doubt a council would have trapped me quite so deftly, then reneged upon my contract with so bold a face as Henry has." He tried to smile.

But he had not come here seeking to be catechized in Grosseteste's politics.

Satisfied the earl leaned that far to his side, Grosseteste went on. "There are a number of us of like mind. We are nearly ready to take action. Cantaloup is having supper with me here tonight. Your former chaplain Gregory de Bosellis and Adam Marsh, whom you know is now Provost of Oxford, will be with us here as well. You will join us?" Seeing Simon was uneasy, he added with a penetrating gaze, "Perhaps you still believe that the caprices of kings must be left untrammeled. Or that ideas of change should remain mere ideas?"

"Father, the notions you have voiced to me are dangerous to act upon."

The bishop's face cleared with a smile. "I have a Good Shepherd Who looks after me, even in the shadows of kings' Courts. But perhaps you fear for yourself? That we might... taint you?"

"No, father. Plainly put, I fear for you, for Walter and for Brother Gregory. As for myself, for love of all of you, I would be your shield if I could."

"Then meet with us tonight."

Making his way through the thinning evening crowds back to his inn, Simon felt calmer. The knot of guilt and rage that had bound up his heart for months seemed loosened. But the bishop's hint at plans for curbing King Henry's misrule left him deeply troubled. He would attend the meeting. If he did not want to see his friends on trial for treason, he had best bring some good sense to bear against their plotting.

When, that night, Simon returned to Grosseteste's room, Gregory de Bosellis was already there and so was Adam Marsh. Grosseteste made amiable conversation about the earl's sons Henry and Guy, who were his pupils at Lincoln. "Henry's doing very well. He has no aptitude for natural sciences, but a fine, quick grasp of ethics, logic and things of the spirit. He should be a candidate for holy orders, he could go far in the Church."

"He has a fine mind," Simon agreed proudly, "but I'd rather Henry found his place close to Prince Edward. What of Guy?"

"A bit slow with his Latin, but a good boy nonetheless," Grosseteste replied, less interested.

"What of Simon?" the earl asked of his second son.

"He finds concentration hard, and discipline almost as difficult. I don't know what to say of him, he does not lack intelligence. And yet his mind is hither and yon... In time, he may grow more self-disciplined... I pray he does."

So the conversation idled until Cantaloup arrived. Walter was amazed at seeing Simon, but thumped him on the shoulder and exclaimed, "How's the lion of Gascony? Devouring the whole country?"

"With indigestion," Simon smiled wearily.

"What! With all that good wine? If I were viceroy, I'd be swilling my way through my revenues!"

Simon grinned. "I'll send you a cask of Armagnac. It's the best thing I've found in all of the south."

Supper was brought. When it was finished, the monks who served Grosseteste were sent away and one trusted man was posted just outside the door. Then the old bishop opened the subject that was on his mind. Simon sat, withdrawn, at the edge of the circle of candlelight. But he listened carefully. The faces of the three Franciscans: the genial Cantaloup, the energetic Bosellis, the scholarly and gentle Marsh, all leaned attentively into the light.

"What is your news from Oxford?" Grosseteste's sharp eyes turned to Marsh.

"The colleges are with us," Marsh said in a low voice. "And so are the brothers of the friar orders, the Dominicans included. They look upon it as no less than the salvation of England."

Simon was shocked, but kept his peace.

"Will they preach our message?"

"To everyone at every school, and market fair, and parish church," Marsh replied.

Grosseteste nodded, well satisfied. "I am going on a tour of the religious houses of my diocese, and of the houses of the Franciscan Order as a whole. Thus, without rousing suspicion, in each region I can also visit the barons who are ill content with the king's rule.

I'll gather them to our cause. The friars, through their preaching, will draw the common people to us. We shall have a force the king cannot resist! If need be, we shall be ready to confront him armed." He turned to Simon, who was silent in the shadows. "What do you think, lord Earl?"

Simon was chewing his thumbnail. He let his hand drop. "If the barons are not with you so far as concerted armed action, what will you do then, father? A plan such as you describe needs more than sympathizers, or it's certain death. You must be sure you have the major part of England's barony with you, or else, I beg you, make no move at all." He hoped this clear, practical advice would dissuade the bishop.

But Grosseteste only smiled. "I know better than to shake a sword without a strong hold on its hilt. I'll sound the barons very carefully."

"Our students at Oxford will take up arms for us," Marsh added.

"Armed students are not a force to set on armored knights!" Simon burst out. "You must have most of the earls on your side, as they control the king's forces. Of the lesser barony, you must have the far greater part of them also, if only to keep them from the king's service. Still, Henry could hire mercenaries abroad. He would find ready support from the Emperor Frederic, and possibly from every king who sees such dissension as a threat to royal power. No, father, force will not work!" he said decisively.

"If it is Our Lord's will to do it so, He shall provide our army. If not, it will be done in peace," Marsh smiled serenely. "We don't presume to choose God's way for Him. But this is certain: change is coming. We will be ready, whichever way He leads us."

"You've been away from Court, Simon," Walter Cantaloup put in. "You don't know what wrongs the king works every day! It has become intolerable! And the king's brothers of Lusignan are like a plague upon us!"

"They beat the monks of Reading Abbey for offering them beer instead of wine," Gregory de Bosellis blustered. "They broke into the abbey's cellar, drank their fill of wine and smashed all of the brothers' casks! And that's but a single instance! They've robbed guests at inns at sword-point! They are common brigands! That's young William de Valence and Guy de Lusignan for you!"

"But worst of all is the queen's young lout of an uncle, Boniface, our Archbishop of Canterbury!" Walter fumed. "He knows no Latin. He can't perform a Mass without having to be told what to do next! And he kicks and cuffs the monks of Canterbury as no decent man would treat a dog!"

Grosseteste turned to Simon. "Complaints to Henry against his kindred meet deaf ears. The Lusignan and Savoyards are given endless wealth and high positions, and are free to do their worst."

"Father," Simon spoke carefully, "I know war, and the strength of Henry's armaments. I beg you! However high injustices may heap, do not consider armed revolt. Or you will throw away all you might gain by peaceful means."

It was late. The meeting ended with no apparent resolution. For Simon, there was now the added burden of fear for his friends, and civil war.

Early the next morning the group met again, this time with Prince Richard. No mention was made of the debate the night before. The delegates discussed how best to present the king's petition for relief of England's churches. Their audience with Pope Innocent was scheduled for that afternoon.

However much Lyon made effort for its revered guest, the Papal Court in exile lacked the splendor of the Vatican. The Archbishop of Lyon, the city's governor, had given up his palace to Pope Innocent for the holding of his trial against the Emperor. Frederic had been excommunicated and condemned – and the result had been that the Pope could not return safely through Italy to Rome. Though the trial was long since ended, he stayed on at Lyon. The archbishop's palace, which never had been meant for such traffic as came seeking the Pope, had grown shabby with wear. The anterooms were crowded and had a bad odor. The satin cushions in the audience chamber were threadbare.

Innocent IV sat in a tall, carved chair, his portly body pressed between the chair's high arms. Over his silk robe he wore a fanciful gold chain, gathered up to the center of his chest and pinned by a fibula from which a richly jeweled cross was hung. A fur cloak was drawn around his mound-like, hunching shoulders, brushing against his smooth-shaved, flaccid cheeks. But though his face was fleshy, Innocent's eyes had an alert and piercing gaze.

Simon had been deeply moved by the holiness of Pope Gregory. Looking at Pope Innocent, he saw a man he could not fathom, and whom he dared not judge. He was very much surprised when, as he stood with his delegation waiting to be heard, a papal clerk singled him out and told him that the Pope would like to speak with him alone that evening.

Bishop Grosseteste and Prince Richard were the chief spokesman for the English plea. They offered their argument. But there was no indication if it was received favorably or not.

That evening Simon returned to the palace at the appointed time. Innocent, in the archbishop's relinquished bedchamber, sat before the fireplace finishing his supper on a large tray. There were the remains of numerous dainty fish dishes and cheese pastries. Though Lenten, the meal was hardly spare. The Pope wiped his fingers carefully on his napkin and gestured to a monk to have the tray removed. Then he looked at Simon.

"My son, I've heard how you've brought peace to Gascony. And how you worked peace, as by miracle, in the Holy Land, before the late misfortunes there. The peace-makers of the world are our greatest blessing in these times of travail." He smiled blandly a moment, but a moment only. "I am a man of few words, and will come to my point. We wish to move our Court to your city of Bordeaux." He tipped his broad face up in something of a challenge. "We will consider your king's petition in a favorable light, if he hears our wish equally."

"Your Holiness," Simon stammered, completely taken by surprise, "the reports of peace in Gascony are very premature. I have evidence that the whole of the province may be at the brink of civil war. From day to day I expect uprisings of the southern barons, who are armed and waiting – for what I know not. It has been my urgent wish to work a stable government for I still hope to join the crusade in the East. But true peace has eluded me."

Innocent became thoughtful, clearly that was not the answer he expected. "Lord Viceroy, we sympathize with you. Yet our wish is still bent upon Bordeaux. Though not to our endangerment. We will do everything in our powers, both temporal and spiritual, to aid you in the quieting of Gascony. There is much we can do. The Lord speed you to Palestine, good Viceroy. You will make certain that King Henry hears our request favorably."

At that the viceroy was dismissed.

The next morning, when Simon met with Richard and the other members of the delegation, he told them what Pope Innocent had said. Throwing up his hands in dismay, he exclaimed, "This is complete madness! Look at what has happened to Lyon! Just what Bordeaux needs, to collapse in utter havoc, is to have all Christendom mobbing its streets as they come see the Pope!"

"Why has Gascony entered his head at all?" Adam Marsh mused.

"Because he wants to leave the realm of France. Queen Blanche is urging him to come to terms with the emperor, for the sake of her son's crusade," Richard, who through his spies always knew even the closest secrets of the French Court, replied. "He has far exceeded his welcome here. And there's nowhere else for him to go with safe passage. The Emperor Frederic, holding both Germany and Italy, has him trapped."

"But how perfect for us!" Marsh concluded. "Now he'll lift the taxes on the English churches, to be in better stead with King Henry."

"Is it so perfect?" Grosseteste asked grimly. "It is a short trip from Bordeaux to Westminster. I can foresee Pope Innocent's hand deep in the Treasury, and Henry's every notion supported with the full powers of the Church. How will England's interests be served then?"

The members of Grosseteste's secret league were struck mute by the prospect. It was Richard who spoke first. "You are quite right, good bishop. Innocent must not come even so near to English soil as Bordeaux. I'll present it to my brother that the Pope wishes this move to strain, and maybe sever, our alliance with the emperor. Put so, he'll never favor it."

"What would you have me do?" Simon asked.

"Fill His Holiness with stories of Gascon assassins in the night," Richard smiled cynically. "No. Better, I'll tell him. I can speak from having been their prey myself. I too am summoned to a private meeting with the Pope."

"Don't put him off entirely," Simon grinned. "He has offered me some aid against the rebels, and I can use all the help I can find."

Whatever Richard told the Pope, the answer to the English plea for relief of the churches was left in suspense. There would be no answer until Innocent was satisfied in regard of Bordeaux. Simon and Richard left Lyon together. They went to Paris to receive, and deliver to the Queen Regent, King Henry's response to the terms of the new truce.

Chapter Twelve

THE QUEEN'S CHAMBER
1250

WHEN SIMON AND PRINCE RICHARD reached Paris, the draft of the truce had not yet been returned from England. Neither was there any word regarding Simon's requested relief from his service in Gascony, the moneys that were owed him, or the funds for hiring the mercenaries who must replace those whose term was nearly done.

But there were letters from Colom in Bordeaux. Gramont and DelSoler had not appeared in court on their appointed day. And in the south, raids, pillaging and high tolls on the roads had resumed. In a swift assault, Arnaud Otton, Simon's steward for Bigorre, had captured a band of raiders led by none other than the Count Gaston de Bearne. Colom and Otton were inquiring what should be done with their prisoner who was Queen Eleanor's favorite cousin.

Simon could not return to Bordeaux, as Henry's response to the truce was expected to arrive any day from England. He wrote instead:

I do not know when I will be able to return, and there is no one now in Gascony of high enough degree to judge the Count of Bearne. You must remand him to King Henry's Court with a full record of his crimes.

His respite in the north refreshed Simon somewhat, and the Pope's promise of aid gave him encouragement.

His mind was filling with new plans for the securing of Gascony. He framed his strategy after the lessons he had learned from the Outremerine lords in Palestine: seek the points of vulnerability in a land held by an overwhelming enemy. To that end, he borrowed eighteen hundred marks in Paris and sent the money south, to be used to strengthen the castles of Bourg, Fronzac and Miremont. And he forwarded the bill to Henry. The king's total debt to his viceroy was over ten thousand marks. The interest alone was consuming Leicester's rents. But Simon had new faith that, with the Pope as his advocate, Henry must give him support.

At last the truce agreement came. It was full of changes. And there was a letter from King Henry to the Earl Montfort:

Sorry we were to receive our Cousin Gaston de Bearne in chains. We have seen fit to pardon him. We are very displeased with your conduct in Gascony. We believe there would be no need for the renewal of the mercenaries had your own actions not roused the land against you. We urge you, when you return to the province, make amends to those you've wronged. And do not look to the royal purse for a solution of the problems your own harshness has raised. As for the monies you have spent already, our rents in Poitou, which have been wrongly confiscated by the King of France, we authorize transferred to you to the amount of our debt.

Simon was with Richard when he read the letter. Stunned, he handed it to the prince. "I cannot understand – he writes as if there were no raids, no pillaging, no treason with Thibaut of Navarre, and all taxes were willingly paid before I went there. The troubles are only of my making?"

Richard read, and handed the letter back. "I'm very sorry, Simon," he said softly. His life had been spent countering his brother's vacillations, his brother's undoings of every capable move he made. No one could understand Simon's frustration better than he. He put his arm across Simon's shoulder and gave vent to a bitter laugh. "Henry certainly knows how to prod us to regain the Poitou rents!"

Simon and the prince returned to the negotiations for the truce, and Henry's demand of the return of the Poitou rents was added to the claims. But the rents were being sent to support Louis' crusade. The queen's ministers and council flatly refused to honor England's claim. Negotiations reached impasse.

On Good Friday a courier arrived with another letter for the viceroy. Simon excused himself from the meeting with the Minister of State, Odo Rigaud, to read the letter privately. Amaubin de Barres wrote from Westminster:

Gaston de Bearne has gone to join Gramont and DelSoler. It is general knowledge that your mercenaries will not be renewed in June. After Pentecost the barons will run raids against all those who have aided you.

Simon returned to the meeting but he was far too troubled to concentrate.

"Lord Montfort, may I be of help?" Archbishop Rigaud asked with concern when they could speak privately. "We know you serve a hard master. I wish, for your sake, that the Poitou rents were not needed in the East."

Simon waved his hand, embarrassed. "How I wish my personal interests were not pitted against the cause I would far rather serve! But my need right now is for a captain. Someone reliable in leading mercenary knights. Someone who could crush an insurrection."

"The man you seek is Bidau de Coupenne. We have had good use of him. You'll find him at the Inn of the Star, in the Rue des Saintes Peres."

Simon sent for Coupenne, hired him and sent him to Bordeaux. Then he wrote to King Henry, telling him of the planned raids.

It is well known that they plan raids by night, and neither sword nor words will stop them. Before I return to Gascony I must speak with you. As I know there are those who have said damaging things about me, you yourself must order whatever I do.

In May, with the negotiations in Paris finally done, the viceroy left for England with the new truce in hand. He would confront Henry face to face.

As Simon entered the hall at Westminster, one of the queen's ladies passed by the door. On impulse, he called after her. He knew he needed influence on his behalf at Court, and some means of buffering his attack upon the queen's cousin Gaston. "Good my lady, tell your mistress the queen that the Earl of Leicester wishes to speak with her."

The waiting woman left with the message, and Simon had the steward announce his arrival.

King Henry was looking better than when he had seen him last, in the meager winter a year and a half ago. His mood was calm. His drooping eye and cheek were no longer so pathetic, for his face had grown a trifle more fleshy. The velvet and fur robe he wore was sumptuous.

Young Prince Edward sat on the steps of the dais, beside the king's feet. The boy, almost eleven now, seemed all awkward, long limbs. His face lit when he heard the earl's name announced. Leaving the dais, he ran down the length of the hall, dodging courtiers, to meet Simon. "Uncle! It's so very good to see you!"

"How you've grown, Edward!" Simon laughed in amazement.

"Father calls me 'Long-shanks.' He says I'm hiding stilts under my stockings," the boy grinned a bit self-consciously.

Simon put his arm around Edward's slim shoulders. His fondness for the boy glowed in his dark eyes. "You'll be big enough for your own armor soon."

"I have my own already! Father had a full suit of mail made for me. And a helmet! Just for practicing. I'm not yet a knight of course. Watch me ride my destrier in the yard tomorrow?" For Edward, the four years he had spent with the Montforts were the happiest of his life. Simon was his ideal... More, the memory of him was the lodestar of his young heart.

"Your own warhorse, so soon? With such a beginning, if you don't surpass the Lion Hearted you shall put us all to shame!" Simon ruffled the boys blond curls playfully.

They had reached the foot of the dais. The Court fool, Avranche, shook his belled scepter in greeting. "The good earl comes with a headache – from consuming the dregs of Bordeaux."

King Henry icily observed Simon's hand around Edward's shoulder. Simon withdrew it.

"We received your letter from Paris," the king said. "We will talk with you regarding the Gascon matter privately tomorrow." His tone was clipped; his gaze, as if he looked upon a stranger.

Simon delivered the document of the truce, and gave report of the slight progress made since Richard had left Paris. Then he was dismissed.

As Simon left the hall, the waiting woman he had met on the way in was at the door. "My lady will see you," she said low, directing him to follow her.

The queen's chamber was in a distant wing of the palace. The sun of late afternoon shone through a stained glass window, casting tints of red and gold across walls painted with scenes of courtly lovers in ancient halls, scenes from the tale of Ronin and Blanchefleur. A large oak bed, curtained with red velvet drapery, and with a coverlet of rich, dark miniver, stood at the center of the room. Upon the coverlet, as if just laid aside, was an exquisite lute inlaid with ivory, the headstock carved in the shape of a woman's laughing face.

The queen was waiting near the door. She put out her hand to Simon, her fingers laden with jeweled rings.

Simon bent and kissed her hand.

"I'm pleased you've asked to see me," she said, her face aglow with a bright smile. Her masses of golden hair fell loosely about her shoulders. She was now thirty, and time had but added to the lushness of her beauty. Her fawn-like high, round brow had not a crease yet, and her crystalline blue eyes sparkled with naughty wit. Her velvet robe clung to the curves of her still slender body. She seemed, in the soft, warm light of that chamber, unchanged since the moment Simon had first seen her on the Canterbury road after her wedding day. Except, perhaps to be yet more desirable. He found that he was staring at her, and had no words to speak. He looked away, trying to turn his mind to what he had come to say.

She glanced to her waiting woman who stood beside Simon, and nodded to her to leave. Then she turned toward the window where old Lady Alice sat on a cushioned bench, reading to three of her young companions. "Please, leave us."

The noble crone raised her eyebrows, pursed her lips, snapped her book shut, got up and left the chamber, with the three girls following and casting curious glances at Simon.

Queen Eleanor laughed lightly at them, and shut the door behind them. "You've been gone from us for so long a time... yet you still wear black?" The queen's small teeth showed in a smile. "No doubt in Bordeaux, or in Paris, you've found fresh temptations to repent?"

"My lady, don't be cruel," Simon said low. "My life has known but one temptation since I married. And were I wholly free of it, I'd dress as other men." He stood with his head bent, looking down, away from her, cursing his stupidity for having set in motion feelings he had worked so long to quell.

The queen walked over to the bed and sat. Taking up the lute, she plucked its strings and, with a sidelong glance, she sang a phrase of a troubadour's song,

She martyrs me.

I am in exile.

My pain is beyond speaking.

With a laugh that tried to sound light and gay but failed, she set the lute upon the floor, then asked, "Well, what is it you have come to speak with me about?"

Simon moved toward her. "I came to ask your help for the campaign in Gascony. Your cousin Gaston gives me a great deal of trouble." He tried to strike a tone of humor, but he was finding his thoughts difficult to keep in mind.

"Why should I help you, when you only think of me as cause for wearing penitential clothes?" She reached out and fingered a fold of his black robe.

He met her eyes as she looked up at him. His voice was hoarse, and barely audible. "I... my thoughts... of you, I fear... give me constant cause..." It was a confession wrung out of the deepest hollow of his heart. "I ought not to have sought to speak with you. I should have known what a foolish... I'm sorry... I should leave." But he did not turn to leave for she held his robe firmly.

"You hurt me badly, keeping distant as you did at Wallingford. And now you want my help?" She slipped her warm, free hand into his, trying to draw him to sit by her on the bed. "Perhaps," she smiled teasingly, "if you confessed these thoughts to me, I would forgive... Let me be your confessor."

Simon looked away from her, glancing at the floor, then at the painted, light-dappled walls with their scenes of lovers in their happiness. Her presence, her nearness, was driving all thought from his mind. His breath caught in the hammering of his heart. At last his eyes met hers, almost pleadingly, "My lady... it has been twelve years... years spent as if with a gaping wound in my side. You know well that you torture me." He realized he was gripping her hand hard, and he let it go.

She let go of the fold of his robe, letting her fingers press against him, stroking downward, then her lips broadened with a smile. "Simon, either you are a fool... or perhaps you presume to be a saint? Saint Francis could hardly equal you!" She gave a small laugh, pressing her hand against him. "Why must you try to be so? When even you know – and I know – that you fail?"

He turned away from her sharply. "Are the laws of treason insufficient? Or do you merely mock me for amusement?"

"I do not mock," she said softly. "I would have you be truthful."

Still turned away from her, he said more quietly, "If you have any true care for me, I beg you, give me what help you can. I am being ruined with debt. And Henry is making peace in Gascony a hopeless labor that I yearn to be quit of!"

She looked down at the floor and her voice was hollow, drained, unmasked. "Simon, you offer me so little. Do you think it's you alone whose life is trouble-filled... and who remembers all to well?" *too*

He turned back toward her, moved by her tone. Letting his guard drop, he said gently, "You, who thought so well of *courtesy's* obstructed love, would have it otherwise?" His dark eyes met hers, open to his heart and heavy with desire. "Admit to me this love is not heaven-sent," he murmured, "but has the very taste of Hell."

She shook her head, her golden curls tossing about her shoulders. "Never! Go! Leave me now! And I shall feed in memory upon your sweet look at this moment," she smiled gallantly. "I will do what I can for you." She stood, and pressed her lips to his.

But he had gone too far in letting his desire out from its imprisonment, allowing it to speak. And now words had released it. Returning her kiss, thoughts of else but her dissolved and all reality was compassed by her touch. The erosion of his spirit, in rage at Henry, and at Gascony, and from ignominy, frustration – and a passion that had not faded but merely lain in wait – brushed twelve years of penitence aside. He knew that when he asked to see her, he had hoped for this.

When love at last was spent, he lay beside her, stunned that years of will, determination, guilt and shame, could mean so little – and the sweet moment so very much. Indeed such sweetness, if it was Hell's reward, seemed recompense enough.

Chapter Thirteen

THE TRAP
1250-1251

SIMON'S MEETING WITH KING HENRY went not well, but better than he had feared.

"Come to terms with the barons and DelSoler," Henry urged. "We know that the world is full of complainers. Our Court is filled with them. Return the properties you're holding and, you'll see, there will be peace."

Simon dug his nails into his palms, but spoke quietly and carefully. Precisely, as to a dull child. "My king, we are speaking of a land that is in rebellion against England. These men have bound themselves by oath to overthrow your rule. The only properties I hold are those of men who have refused to swear their loyalty to you, and who will use the strong towers which I hold from them now, for war against you if they are released."

Henry shook his head doubtfully, but said, "Lord Earl... we'll bear with you a little longer. We believe you mean to govern well. But there can be no peace when you hold such noble men as Gramont as your prisoner without trial."

The king agreed to make good on the eighteen hundred marks Simon had borrowed in Paris, and to renew the mercenary force for one more six-month term.

"Were you pleased with the king's offers?" Queen Eleanor asked archly when Simon came to her that afternoon.

"Our meeting was far better than I'd dare hope," he admitted.

"It was not easy. I think he felt I was betraying my good cousin Gaston in counseling patience with you." She took a sip from a wine goblet, then handed it to him to share.

He drank deeply. Then he drew off his black wool robe with the red cross of crusade embroidered upon it. He was unworthy – no doubt it was his unworthiness that barred him from the crusade. A melancholy had settled over him, a bittersweet resignation that was so tempting in its sweetness that future bitterness seemed worth the price. Tomorrow he would have the red threads of the cross plucked off his robes. But now, the ephemeral, the eternal touch of her governed his will, his thoughts, all his desire.

These languid hours in the queen's chamber were dangerous, and few. Simon had to return to Gascony. And when he left, he did not go to Kenilworth, and did not see his wife.

In Bordeaux he threw himself into his plans and strategies, and did his best to put Queen Eleanor far from his mind. But thoughts of her seeped into every moment that was not fully taken up with work.

He cursed himself for the foolishness that had prompted him to ask to see her. His thoughts, his memories, his desire grew to a scorching obsession. At night he shut his squire Peter out of his chamber. Burning, he found the whip and the hair shirt he kept locked in his traveling chest. Stripping off his robe, he lashed himself. There was a time when pain had seemed to cleanse, to give him mastery of desire. But no longer did he have faith in the sureness of that cure.

He wore the hair shirt constantly again. In the southern heat and sweat it chaffed and salted the whip's cuts. But now the pain merely reminded him of his passion. Concentration on the task of Gascony's defense was his only relief.

The raids that Amaubin predicted had not yet begun. The viceroy deployed his defenses eastward, fortifying Mouleydier, Castelmoron, and Montcuc-sur-mer, and westward to Fronzac, Cubzac and Blaye. At every vulnerable point, Gascony was readied to meet civil war. The prisoners at Saint Sever, Dax and La Reole were moved out of the province entirely, to a castle Simon rented on the Isle d'Oleron, an island off the coast of Poitou.

Arnaud de Gramont, old Bertrand d'Aigremont, the handsome young Vicomte of Soule and the barons of the Adour and Labour valleys were sent under heavy guard. Their hands were bound, their ankles manacled with heavy chains that passed under their horses' bellies. Laden with iron and surrounded by armed guards, the lords were a piteous sight as they passed along the roads. The common people did not jeer, but closed their shutters rather than look upon their fallen masters going by in chains.

In July a letter arrived from King Henry. He had heard that Raymond de Fronzac was planning raids. He warned Simon that he must take precautions.

"If I tell the king of insurrection, it means nothing!" Simon roared to Guillaume Colom. "Let him hear it from somebody else, and he writes to me as if it were a revelation."

Pentecost was long past, but the expected raids had not occurred. With the viceroy's mercenary force renewed and Gascony well fortified, the rebels stayed in hiding. Simon prepared to seek them out.

Then in August there came news that changed everything. Little by little, since early summer there had been dark rumors from the East. Three Genoese spread panic, claiming that King Louis' crusade was lost. In the collapse of confidence, they bought goods cheaply and sold them dear. Queen Blanche had the men hanged.

But vague and sinister reports continued. And, inexplicably, there was no direct word from the crusade.

Then irrefutable news came. On Easter Sunday morning, as Louis had moved up the Nile from his base at Damietta, his immense army had divided – and had been destroyed. Of the army's forty thousand men, only three hundred survived. Among the dead was the old, noble William Longspee, the head of the English knights. Piers Mauclerc, the Count of Brittany, was also dead, as were Count Hugh of La Marche and his son Hugh le Brun. King Louis' own brother, Robert of Artois, was dead.

The few who still lived, King Louis and his youngest brother Alphonse among them, were prisoners held for ransom by the Saracens. All else that was known was that Louis was feverish again, and that he had been tortured for his faith.

Simon's first thought was to gather all the men he could and go at once to the East. But the finest knights of Europe had been on that crusade. To lead a hastily raised force against such power as the sultan now apparently possessed would be merely to lead more men to their deaths. And, if attacked, the Saracens might kill their prisoners.

Thoughts of Queen Eleanor receded to the dark corner of his mind where they had rested for so many years. Rescue of the crusade became his one concern. He wrote to Queen Blanche, asking her to tell him what she would have him do. She answered with a request that he help raise funds for the ransom.

With all the zeal he would have spent slashing with his sword among the Saracens, Simon used the circuit of his courts to raise money for Louis. If there was any way that he might yet redeem himself, this seemed his chance. The slightest infraction of the law – leaving wood in public streets, letting pigs or chickens roam – incurred heavy fines beyond anything ever known before. In two months the viceroy sent the funds he had collected to Aigue Morte, where Blanche's treasure ship was waiting to set sail for Damietta.

By the end of October there was news that Louis was freed. The remnant of the crusade was safe at Acre.

The autumn passed. Gascony remained quiet. Gaston de Bearne was in England again. There were no raids, no movements at all by the rebel lords.

Simon drafted a new treaty for Bordeaux. It seemed the time had come to let his hold upon the province ease. The partisans of DelSoler, held at Bordeaux, were offered their freedom. They could return to their homes, provided they swore fealty to Henry, and gave boys from their families as hostage-pages.

Early in December Simon wrote to Henry, asking for the funds to pay his mercenaries through the spring.

The King's answer came back sharply:

Our cousin Gaston de Bearne has made it known to us that you deport to unknown places the lords whom you hold prisoners. We say again, peace cannot be found through hiring foreign armies or imprisoning noble men.

No further monies will be sent in support of these policies. We urge you to make peace with those you have harmed.

With misgivings, but no choice, Simon saw his mercenaries leave. Apart from the garrison at Bordeaux and Amaubin de Barres knights, the viceroy's forces dwindled to the city's militia, men commended now by Colom – and to other Colom partisans. Still Gascony was quiet.

On New Years Eve, the last day of the year 1250, Simon knelt in his bedchamber in Bordeaux, but no prayer issued from his heart. None had for some time. His rage at Henry drew a knot tight in his chest. And desire had made havoc with his soul. He covered his face with his hands. After some moments he rose to his feet heavily and sat at his table. Taking up a quill and a sheet of parchment, he began to write to his wife. He had not seen her for more than a year.

As he was writing, a distant horn sounded. He thought at first it might be revelers greeting the new year. Then there was pounding at the gate. In a few moments he heard soft knocking at his door. "My lord, " his squire Peter called, his tone sounding urgent. "My lord, Sire Amaubin is here and must speak with you at once."

Slowly, Simon got up and unlatched the door.

Amaubin de Barres came in wearing full battle dress. He was heaving, out of breath. "Lord Viceroy the raids have begun! I was attacked at Castillon. The force was large, well armed. As I came here, just outside Bordeaux I saw bands of armed men. The city is about to be besieged!"

Simon ran to the spiral staircase that led to the tower's roof. Amaubin followed him. The stairs wound upward in complete darkness to the castle's parapet. Once on the roof, a few lights glimmered below in houses as late celebrants welcomed the year. Most of the city was black, sleeping, lulled by the quiet tapping of the curfew wardens' staffs.

But in the distance there were strange, faint sounds. Simon peered toward the city's gates. A yellow flame sprang in the darkness as a warehouse of Colom's, by the Ayres Gate, was set ablaze.

"They waited only for the mercenary forces to be gone," Simon remarked bitterly.

As he spoke, a horn sounded an alarm. Then, from gate tower to gate tower, horns answered all around the city's walls. The bell at the Saint Eloi Gate rang wildly, calling the militia. Bordeaux was under siege.

"The militia will hold the city," Amaubin said hopefully, watching the streets below coming to sudden life. Moving splashes of light, men carrying torches, hurried with cross-bows to their appointed places on the walls.

"We will withstand them here," said Amaubin.

"And let the barons hold the countryside?" Simon asked tartly. "No, it's very clear, we must have an army, or England must relinquish Gascony."

They went down the stairs. Colom was in the hall.

"Guillaume, I leave you as Steward of the province, and Amaubin as Marshal. Hold Bordeaux as best you can. Or, if you must, make terms with the barons until I return. Peter!" Simon called his squire, "tell the captain of my ship to make ready to sail at once. We go to England!"

The squire ran to the river gate where the small ship Simon rented to send wine to Kenilworth lay at her mooring. Before dawn Simon, Peter, and the mercenary captain Bidau de Coupenne, the only man of the hired force remaining, went aboard. The ship caught the morning tide and sailed down the Gironde.

On Twelfth Night, January sixth of the year 1251, the viceroy reached the royal Christmas Court at Winchester.

The king was hearing a complaint against the queen's young uncle Boniface, the Archbishop of Canterbury. Queen Eleanor sat on a chair on the dais by Henry's side. Simon strode through the assembly with Bidau de Coupenne following. They went up to the dais unannounced.

"What?" Henry exclaimed at this breach of the Court's custom.

"My lord, Gascony is in revolt!" Simon shouted for all to hear. "I left the city of Bordeaux besieged, as Sire Coupenne here can bear witness! This is the doing of Gaston de Bearne, Amanieu d'Albret and their allies who've made league against you! I've paupered my own resources, but though I've wrung the revenues of Leicester dry, I cannot wage this war without support!"

Henry, flustered by his viceroy's sudden appearance, blurted out, "Gaston's chaplain was just here. He confirmed Bearne's pledge of loyalty..."

"My king," Simon's tone became cold and measured, "these people who would like to have you think them friends, lie and betray you! Just as they have always done! When you were in danger in Poitou, when the queen was sick and poisoned at Bordeaux, these people didn't trouble themselves about you. They took all they could from you! Yet these are the people whose word you believe over mine!"

Shaken, Henry admitted, "By the Head of God, lord Earl, what you say is true. You've fought well for me, and I won't refuse you help." He rose from his chair, trying to recover his mastery of the moment. "But there have been complaints against you. We're told that lords who answered summons from you in good faith were put in chains and sent to death!"

"Sire, the Gascons' treachery is well known to you!" Simon thundered. "Yet you still believe their lies!"

The Court was silent, tense, watching the shouted exchange. Queen Eleanor put her hand on Henry's arm to calm him and said gently, "The Earl of Leicester has been much in danger in our service. I pray you, give him what he asks. Or recall him and send someone else in his place."

"Whom should I send!" Henry turned upon her angrily. "Whom!"

But the queen had no ready answer.

He turned back to Simon. "We'll give you the funds for your mercenaries, but we mean to find out the truth! Investigators will go to Gascony and send us their report. I'll find what's truly happening!"

"My king," Simon said icily, "send all the investigators you wish."

Henry waved his hand as if to shield himself from Simon's glare. "I'll send Nicholas de Meulles." Since serving under Simon, de Meulles had been loud in the earl's praises. "And Drogo de Barentin," Henry added. Barentin was no friend to the earl.

"Lord Montfort," the queen spoke up in the strained moment, "though it is hard news that brings you here, know that we pray for your safety, and mean to do all that we can to help you to enjoy peace."

Her smile was soft and, in Simon's ear, her words were double in their meaning. But he had no intention, under Henry's gaze or otherwise, of giving her encouragement. He dared not succumb now. He bowed to her in formal gratitude. "I'm sorry I could bring no better news, especially of my lady's cousin." The words sounded stiff. The queen looked at him archly.

In the next days Simon formed his plan for his return to Gascony. Messages came from the queen. He burnt the bits of parchment without reading them.

Word arrived from Barres. He still held Bordeaux. The revolt was not so well coordinated or widespread as it had been two years before. And the viceroy's precautions were effective. None of the outlying garrisons had fallen. The rebel barons had withdrawn to Castillon. From there they made raids on the nearby countryside.

Simon worked with Coupenne, forming his campaign. With his plan in hand, a full list of the forces he would need, and an estimate of costs, he met with King Henry.

The queen was also present at the meeting. "I, too, wish to hear how you mean to retake our province, lord Earl," she nodded. There was the slightest edge in her tone.

Simon met her eyes uneasily as he proceeded to describe his strategy. Questions and answers were exchanged till all seemed clear. Then, just as Henry was about to come to a decision, the queen interrupted. "Let us not conclude these issues in haste. Would it not be better to let commitment rest upon a day's deliberation?"

Simon bit his lip in annoyance. But Henry put decision off.

That afternoon Simon received another message, brought by Lady Alice. The old waiting woman refused to leave him until he had read it. The note was brief. The queen wished to speak with him privately. Lady Alice murmured, "I'll bring you to her after vespers."

"You were quicker to find your way to me before," Queen Eleanor observed when Simon was shown into her chamber and her waiting woman left them in privacy "Did you go then so unhappily?"

"I went with shame."

She smiled, and sat upon the bed, smoothing the fur coverlet with her jeweled hand. Only the fireplace and one tall candle on an iron candle stand gave light. Her face was partly shadowed. "I suppose I'd rather that than mere annoyance," she laughed softly.

"Have you no fear of the risks of summoning me here?"

"Risks of the heart? Ah, yes. Risks otherwise? Have you no notion of the risk it is for me to speak out in your favor?"

"You're reckless then."

"You are supposed brave."

"Not foolhardy. You must not summon me now. And I must go."

"Why are you so harsh?" she asked, her voice starting to tremble. Her desire, and her fear, were slipping past control, welling over her easy-seeming air. "Have you not thought of me these months?"

"Would that I had not! Be pleased, if you will, to know our last meetings have cost me all peace..."

"Then why do you speak to me so... your voice cold and hard. Should I believe it? What more cost could there be to you, in the touching of your hand...?" she placed his hand upon her breast.

He groaned at the sensation of her soft warmth. "God help us," he breathed.

She bent her head to press kisses upon his hand, whispering, "You must, you know... you must..." and she drew off her robe.

As they lay together, he whispered, "That such sweetness, and such wrong, are one... You are the one sweetness of my life."

She smiled into his dark eyes, shadowy in the dimness of the light. "And you, my whole desire. Give me... of you. Again." And she drew his head down to hers, kissing his lips. Her breasts were large but her belly flat, for she had lost a child: a child begotten when they were together before.

The next day, in the presence of the full Court, Queen Eleanor said to King Henry, "The Earl of Leicester has served us so well and faithfully, that I urge you to find in his favor and grant what he asks."

Simon, who was standing near the dais, talking with the young Earl of Gloucester, Richard de Clare, looked up, surprised.

The handsome Clare remarked with a smirk, "It is an able man who knows best how to serve our queen."

Simon glanced at him sharply, but Clare turned away.

Henry overheard the remark. With his drooping eye he studied the queen, then Simon. "We see you have an advocate."

"The Earl of Gloucester, who does nothing, is jealous," the queen said slyly.

"My king," Simon offered, "my aim is to hold Gascony for you, as you have bidden. I did speak with the queen, as her cousin is involved."

The Marshal Roger Bigod was talking with several lords, none of whom had any fondness for the Gascons. He called out in his bluff way, "By God's Head, grant him what he asks! Or it will take five hundred men to do what he can do with fifty!"

The other lords joined with the marshal in a clamoring agreement.

King Henry called for a clerk of his Treasury. Then, to Simon, "Let's see again the list of funds you ask." Simon gave the bill once more to the king, and each item was reviewed.

"The original two thousand marks, the fee for the earl's service, must be reimbursed, as he has spent it in our service," the queen reminded with a sparkling glance to Simon.

But Henry left the reimbursement out of the accounting. Simon received three thousand marks, towards the nearly twelve thousand now owed him for the raising and supply of troops, and five hundred and fifty more for a new force of mercenaries.

As the session ended, the king motioned for Simon to go with him to a private chamber off the hall. Simon, tensing, followed.

He suspected someone might have seen him leaving the queen's chamber.

Inside, Henry turned upon him abruptly. "I hope you've informed our holy father the Pope about this insurrection. His legates press me every day to grant him leave to move his court to Bordeaux."

Simon sighed, relieved to hear it was only this the king wished to discuss with him in privacy. "I've been reporting to His Holiness in as discouraging a tone as I can strike. But I've not yet written to him of the raids. I will do so at once."

The viceroy collected his funds from the royal treasury and sent them on with his captain, Coupenne, to Paris. He already had learned that the two hundred mounted infantry he wanted, at the price of fifty knights, could not be assembled until March. Barres' letter showed there was little he could do before the mercenaries came.

De Meulles and Barentin were on their way to open their investigations of his doings. He decided to remain in England until March, so no one could claim that he had interfered with the investigators' work. If the rebels made use of his absence to run raids, so much the better that they did it before the king's own witnesses.

He would stay in England, but not at Court. Temptation and danger were both far too great. Simon went home to Kenilworth.

Chapter Fourteen

THE INVESTIGATORS
1251

THE LAND WAS EARTHY BROWN, winter fields already turned and planted with the first wheat seed; fallow fields stubbled from the last harvest of grain; spring fields where cattle still grazed as the plow ridges awaited planting. The road to Kenilworth passed endless seeming vistas of brown, dotted here and there with gray hayricks, sky-colored pools, crofters' plots of bare fruit trees, and thatched roofs clustering round the gray spike of a steeple. Occasionally the humble world of gray and brown was livened by the peaked gables of a manor house, a darting fox, or a hawk motionless high in the air, waiting-on.

The weather was lightly chill. The earth at mellow peace. With his squire following, Simon let his palfrey amble at an easy pace as he sank deep in thought. Thoughts painful, and thoughts that gave him shame. Regrets for his anger and his separation from his wife for causes that seemed distant now and meaningless. The loss of the crusade had changed everything. And now again he had betrayed himself. Betrayed himself and others. The countess had been right, He never should have gone to Gascony. He should have died in Palestine.

It was almost two years since he had seen his wife last. He would beg her forgiveness – which she would be right not to grant.

As they neared Kenilworth, Simon sent his squire on ahead to give word of his coming, and he rode on alone.

The bell in Kenilworth's tower began pealing joyously. "The master's come!" a villein in the field shouted, and ran toward the village to spread the news. As Simon passed along the road lined with crook-timbered thatched cottages, one after another the cottage doors swung open. People hurried to greet him. He was England's best loved, and most ill-used, hero. They were proud to have him as their lord.

The earl nodded, smiled and called those whom he knew by name. He spoke to them in English, though it came to his lips haltingly, unaccustomed to it as he was for so long. The villeins followed him through the woods, and as far as the swing bridge to the castle's causeway, where he bade their shyly smiling faces and their clumsy, bobbing bows farewell.

In the castle's inner court, with several of the castle's servants hovering behind her, the countess stood waiting, her face beaming with welcome, her mantle clutched around her in the breeze. Peeping from within the billows of her cloak was the inquisitive face of little Eleanor. The countess held six year old Amaury with her free hand.

"Who is this tiny chick who peeps from her mother's feathers?" Simon grinned as he dismounted, handing his horse to the kitchen boy, Slingaway, to take out to the stable. The earl swept his little daughter up in his arms and she let out a shrill squeal of delight. Setting her down, he bent and kissed the curly brown hair on the top of his small son's head. Then, hesitatingly, he touched his wife's hand.

All at once the countess burst to laughter and tears. "Your coming like this... so unexpectedly, has utterly undone me!" She wiped her cheeks. "It's good to have you here." She put her arms around his neck.

He held her to him. "It's never good for us to be apart." He glanced uneasily away from her, and reached out to the two children. Taking the boy and girl each by the hand, he went up the foyer steps to the hall. "Bishop Grosseteste wrote that Guy is doing well now, but that he has sent Simon back to you. Where is he?"

"Out hunting," the countess answered, following them. There was a hint of disapproval in her tone. Their second son had grown aloof and ever more unmindful. He worried her.

Later, having heard the bell, young Simon came into the hall. He was ten, a sturdy boy with his mother's soft brown hair and large nose and mouth, but his father's intense eyes. He held a partridge he had killed. Seeing his father standing in the room, he did not run to him but made a stiff, shy bow.

The countess frowned. "Take the bird out to the kitchen shed, Simon. You know you're not to bring dead things into the hall." When he had gone, she turned to her husband. "I'd send him back to Lincoln, but the bishop doesn't want him there, he's too disruptive. Perhaps you ought to keep him with you."

"I have enough problems in Gascony without a wayward child."

"He says he's the wild man Ivain," little Eleanor tittered.

"I'm considering taking young Henry back with me," Simon remarked. "I don't want him to grow up a pale cleric."

The countess looked down, clearly not pleased. "I'd rather you didn't."

"You're thinking of Grosseteste's raving at his baptism? That Henry and I would die on the same day, and by the same hurt?" Simon laughed shortly. "I won't live separate from my eldest son for fear of that!"

"Then I pray God keep you both," the countess said softly.

Touched by the warmth of her tone, Simon took her hand. He paused uncertainly, then kissed it. "I thank you for your prayers. I am not worthy of you."

That night, as they lay together in their great, curtained bed, the countess spoke of what most held her mind. "Simon," she whispered in the darkness, "I've given the Lord thanks, time and again, that we were spared from the crusade. Can you forgive me?"

He drew a deep, thoughtful breath. "Perhaps it is as Grosseteste said. I wasn't meant to go. But it is I who must ask your forgiveness. All that you said was true."

In the next days the countess ordered feasting at Kenilworth in celebration of the earl's return. Henry and Guy were brought home from Lincoln. The boys arrived accompanied by Adam Marsh, the Provost of Oxford whom Simon had met in Lyon.

"How are the bishop's plans proceeding?" Simon asked when he could speak with Marsh alone.

The Provost rolled his eyes toward Heaven. "The barons see the light, but dare not step toward it. They speak against the king, but they don't want to be troubled from the comforts of their lives to take action." He shook his head in wonder at human docility.

Simon gave a sigh of relief. The church fathers would not be able to raise civil war.

Marsh brought with him a copy of Grosseteste's work, *On Kingship and Tyranny*, which the bishop had given him for Simon, along with a large volume of Saint Gregory's *Commentaries on the Book of Job*. "The good bishop sends these to you, to give you comfort in Gascony."

Seeing the titles, Simon gave a curt laugh. "The bishop knows well how to comfort me."

Through the winter days at Kenilworth Simon hunted with his three sons in the manor's chase, or looked over his steward Seagrave's reports of his fiefs. In the quiet of the evenings, young Henry read aloud in Latin from the bishop's book on Job. The family listened, Guy openly admiring his brother, little Eleanor and Amaury playing on the floor, young Simon bored and toying with his hunting knife.

Simon, contented, watched his children, and looked to his wife. Eleanor drew her proud gaze from the grave young reader and took Simon's hand. In the peaceful surroundings of his family, the temptations, the passions that had haunted him, faded like mist in warm sunlight, and his spirit healed. He wished to the depth of his heart that this, and this alone were his whole life.

But with the coming of March he would have to return to Gascony. Simon dared not be alone in Bordeaux as he was before. It was agreed that the countess would follow him in three weeks time, and bring young Henry.

Simon went to Paris first, hiring a corps of archers in addition to his mounted infantry. At the head of his mercenary troops, on the twenty-fifth of March, the viceroy re-entered Bordeaux.

All was in good order. The city and most of the nearby countryside were still held by Barres.

At the castle Simon found a surprise. The Bishop of Agen was waiting for him. "His Holiness received your letters from England," the bishop told him. "He is eager to support your fight against this fearful uprising."

Simon read the documents the bishop delivered to him. They set out a list of formidable powers, including dissolution of the vows the rebel lords had taken to oppose him and, quite stunningly, automatic excommunication of anyone who attempted to oppose his rule.

"I shall write at once to His Holiness and tell him of my gratitude," the viceroy bowed low to the bishop. Then he excused himself and went up to his chamber to consult with Colom and Barres.

"Had I known we had the heavenly phalanxes ranged on our side, I'd not have bothered hiring mere men," Simon grinned, handing the documents to Barres.

Barres read aloud to Colom. When he finished he turned to Simon in amazement. "Truly the Pope does mean to come here. He's just short of taking up the cleric's battle mace and morning star himself!"

"Where are the king's investigators, de Meulles and Barentin?" Simon asked.

"They've gone out to Castillon. The rebels all have gathered there to have their complaints heard."

"How very helpful for us. We shall take all of them at once. The investigators can bear witness how politely we require their surrender."

The day before the viceroy marched on Castillon, the countess and her son Henry arrived.

The next day, as morning sunlight bathed the buff stone of Saint Eloi bell tower, the viceroy, on his battle-mantled destrier, passed through the gate with his son riding by his side. Henry was eleven. His young face shone with excitement as he watched the rampant lion flag of Montfort, and the royal flag of golden lions *en passant,* billowing before him. Behind was the rhythmic, concerted din of an army in motion: the tread and jangle of mounted infantry; the double row of archers marching with their bows slung on their backs, their rustling wicker screens slung on their left arms and overlapping like a moving wall; the rumbling wheeled-platforms that bore two steel-springed mangonels; and last the creak and rattle of the wagons of supply. Henry looked to his father, who was dressed in his black suit of steel chain with his two-edged sword, famous in trouveres' songs for the blood it had drawn at Sainte and at Veyrine, buckled to his hip. The boy's heart felt near to bursting. Though he had thought to be a priest, he knew now he would be a knight.

A bright blue sky dressed the spring day with a clarity that gave the distance sharp outline. To the east, yellow cliffs rose up against the blue like a jaw of sharpened, carious teeth. The first green tinged the vineyards where ancient, gnarled grape stumps were coming into bud.

By afternoon the army rode past marshes and flat fields of emerald hue. And by that evening, as the viceroy's army crept over the crest of a gentle slope, Castillon's tower appeared across a shallow valley. Atop its battlement there flew a tiny speck of white.

"They're begging truce already," Barres noted with satisfaction.

The army drew up to encamp at a little distance from the walls of Castillon. The horses were tethered on long lines, tents were set up, supply wagons were unpacked and campfires were made. Fascinated, Henry wandered amid the hubbub, watching the professional fighting men go about their ordinary tasks. When everyone had settled to make supper, he found his way to his father's red and white striped tent.

The viceroy, his son and Barres were sitting on camp stools, eating by their campfire as squire Peter poured their wine, when the two investigators, led by guards, walked into the circle of their firelight.

"The Gascons beg peace with you," de Meulles told Simon. "They've asked to submit their charges against you to the judgment of the Archbishop of Bordeaux, the Bishop of Agen and ourselves as the king's representatives."

"Their charges against me? It is I who charge them with breaking the laws of this province," Simon looked up at de Meulles. "As viceroy, it is my court to which they must submit. And I mean to hold them here at siege until they do."

De Meulles and Barentin went back to Castillon with the viceroy's answer.

During the night Simon moved his troops into siege formation. He had the barons' horses taken from where they were grazing in the fields. In their place he set up his two mangonels and his archers' screens. The lords in Castillon were cut off from escape and from supply.

The next morning the white flag was lowered. The flag of Bearne rose in its place. De Meulles and Barentin came back to the viceroy's tent.

"They say they will not fight you. They only want their hearing, judged by the archbishop, the bishop and ourselves." This time Barentin was spokesman.

"You've heard what I have to say. They'll have their hearing in my court."

De Meulles and Barentin began a shuttling life between Castillon and the besieging camp. No blows were struck, and there was no surrender. The barons would not give themselves up to the viceroy, and the viceroy would not leave. April passed. May dragged through the mid-point. Castillon's supply of food was nearly spent.

"They will pledge to come to court anywhere, at any time, provided an impartial tribunal hears their cases. What they're asking isn't unreasonable!" de Meulles pleaded with Simon.

"Nicholaus, you were here with me when I first came. You saw how these men keep their pledges! And the harm they do!"

"But they're starving! I have my report to make to King Henry. For God's sake, let them have their terms!"

"You would make report against me? If I don't take these men into custody, they'll never come to trial. Before me or anybody else!"

"Don't be so hardhearted, Sire,"

"Nicholaus, you've been as loud as thunder in your praise of me, but you're as sturdy as a reed in your support! Very well," Simon bellowed, "tell them they may have their terms! If that's the only way to stay the knife you would thrust in my back with your report!"

A truce was made. Out of the castle came Amanieu d'Albret, Raymond de Fronzac, Geoffrey and Elie Rudel, Guillaume de Gramont, Gaillard DelSoler, Gaston de Bearne and the entire company of rebels. They were rumpled and thin, some of them weak with hunger. One by one, in the viceroy's tent, in the presence of the king's two investigators, they pledged to appear in court and were appointed times of hearing.

"We will regret this," Amaubin de Barres said grimly, watching them set free.

The lord Gaston de Bearne, his fat gone with the siege diet, his clothing hanging on him like bed draperies, came to the tent last. He bowed to de Meulles and Barentin, ignoring the viceroy. "I cannot take this pledge, as my equal isn't present," he announced as though it were a fact that everyone should know.

"You claim the privilege of kings, Gaston?" Simon asked crisply. "Make your pledge!"

"King Henry is my nephew, and a most loving one I might add," the lord of Bearne said in a mincing tone calculated to annoy. "He wouldn't countenance the extraction of my pledge by force." He turned to leave.

Simon, rising from his chair with combat speed, grasped Bearne by the wrist. "Pledge, or stay my prisoner."

"Let go of me or I will see thee thrashed!" Gaston hissed.

Simon's face grew red with anger, and his strong hand tightened in a grip crushing the bone.

Gaston blanched with pain and gasped. To Barentin he spoke between clenched teeth, "You see! The man's a beast!"

Barentin pursed his lips. "My lord, you did promise to pledge."

There was a long, tense moment. Then the viceroy let go of his hold. The lord of Bearne, rubbing his wrist tenderly, made his pledge.

As Bearne left, Barentin muttered under his breath," The Gascon bastard."

Summer, through September, was given over to the proceedings of the court, witnessed by de Meulles, Barentin, the Bishop of Agen and the Archbishop of Bordeaux. Several of the lords appeared on their appointed days, but most did not. Among those who did not appear was the lord of Bearne. The king's investigators returned to England with a lengthy report.

Early in October King Henry's answer came. The viceroy was recalled. The letter was vague, cloaked in the announcement of the wedding of the king's eldest daughter. The child would marry the young King of Scotland at York in December. The Earl and Countess of Leicester must attend.

"Henry wants presents," Eleanor said cynically. "No doubt he's found no better way to raise money." The marriage of the king's eldest daughter and the knighting of his eldest son were the occasions of the Great Aides, when donations of a specified high value were owed by the king's vassals to the Crown.

"I hope this summons is no more than that," Simon said darkly.

On the morning of the fifth of November the earl and countess were at Wissant, waiting at a crowded inn for a windy storm of several days' duration to abate and permit crossing of the Channel. As they sat amid their traveling bundles with young Henry and their servants, warming themselves at a brazier in a corner of the inn's common room, a cheery cry of "Ha, there! Sister!" greeted them.

A swarthy, good looking young man waved over the heads of the clusters of travelers. It was Guy de Lusignan. Rain-soaked from the road, he pushed his way across the room. "I'm so glad to find you here! All the ships are fully booked for days ahead and I must be at Dover with the first crossing."

"We're on the first ship. If you leave your attendants to cross later, we could leave one of our people to come along with them, and you could cross with us," Eleanor offered.

"Bless you, sister!" Guy kissed her hand. "The king is to meet me at Dover. I've just done him a service for which he is most grateful!"

Coolly, Simon observed the youth whom Bosellis described as a brigand. Guy exchanged his look briefly, but gave no further notice of the earl, spending his attentions entirely upon Eleanor.

The countess arranged passage for him with her family. The storm quieted in a few hours and their ship left port. Buffeted across the Channel by high winds, it reached Dover late that afternoon.

Indeed the king had come. And he had brought nearly the entire Court with him. A crowd in noble finery was waiting on the quay when the ship docked. Guy left the Montforts and ran down the gangplank into Henry's arms.

"My good brother!" King Henry embraced him, and walked off with his arm around Guy's shoulder.

The king had seen the earl and countess, Guy had been standing beside them on the deck. But he did not pause to greet them.

Simon and Eleanor walked down the plank, young Henry following. The courtiers on the quay spoke not a word to them but looked away, embarrassed, or smirked and whispered among themselves. Eleanor went pale and hurried through the crowd. Simon took his son's hand and walked with his head high, greeting those he knew, if they acknowledged him or not.

Young Henry watched as people moved away from them. "Why are they not speaking to you, father?" he asked in a small, frightened voice.

"Because I am in disfavor," Simon answered him.

The Court returned to Westminster. As did the Montforts, but they went alone.

Simon presented himself before King Henry and the Court to give his formal report on Gascony. The queen was in attendance. She sat beside Henry. Her fingers picked nervously at the carving on the arm of her chair, and she kept her gaze cast down.

Even she, it seemed, would not look him in the face. A flush rose to his cheeks, but he collected himself and made his report with an assumed dignity that, as it was forced, was stiff in the extreme. "My king, I know de Meulles and Barentin have made the results of their investigations known to you. Whatever they have said, I do not feel I need defend what I have done. I've acted within the bounds of my commission, which granted me a free hand for seven years to bring peace by whatever means I could. There is now peace in Gascony, save for the seditions that you yourself have kept alive by freeing the wrong-doers when they were in my hands. Yet if you wish to terminate my service, I am very willing."

Henry smiled coldly. "We have other matters of more pressing concern at the moment. But, lord Earl, you are not to leave the country. The Masters of the Cinque Ports have orders not to let you pass." Simon was dismissed.

The Montforts traveled on to Kenilworth.

December came. The highways were filled with travelers to York for the marriage of the King of England's eldest daughter to Scotland's young king. Tents in all colors bloomed on the wintry hill that rose up to York's city wall. The gray stone city, topped by dark slate roofs, sat like an ancient beldame on a gay primrose knoll. High above her granite shoulders, the creamy Caen stone of the new Minster gleamed gold in the northern winter sun. Boats on the rivers Ouse and Foss were trimmed with ivy and holly, and freighted with merrymakers in bright colored robes and furs. Music sounded everywhere: the pipes, drums and tambourines of troubadours, and the trumpets of the noble parties at the gates.

Within the city, the streets were aflutter with the flags of noble visitors, and the narrow lanes, where cantilevered upper stories nearly met across the way, were canopied with swags of evergreens. At dark, the city glowed with flares. Candle lanterns lit each windowsill. The northern night descended in mid-afternoon, its darkness lingering like a languid reprobate until mid-morning, but the revelers made festival that never ceased.

Amid the mass of visitors, sellers of all sorts cried their wares: strolling piemen with trays heaped with pork and sausage pastries, or honeyed sweets; fruiterers with baskets of dried apples and prunes; toymen with tall frames hitched to their backs displaying wooden swords, horses, dolls, small flags, trumpets and drums. Mountebanks set up their stalls of holy medals, pills and tonics: cures for everything from gout to impotence. Jongleurs tossed flaming torches, casting arcs of streaming fire through the midnight air.

Brewsters and vintners offered beer and wine from casks strapped to their chests, a single cup serving for all. And drunken knights stumbled in the alleyways long into the morning.

The wedding took place at the high altar of the York Minster. Two solemn children, dressed in spreading robes of cloth of gold, pronounced their vows. Princess Margaret and King Alexander of the Scots were both nine years old.

"It's fortunate King Alexander is as young as his bride," the Earl of Gloucester, Richard de Clare, remarked bemusedly at the wedding feast. "What a bore it would be for a grown man to have to wait years for his bride to be his wife. It's practically a license for adultery."

"I quite agree," the Countess Eleanor said warmly, thinking of her own first marriage at age nine. "The Church promotes sin, making children wives. What do you think, my lord?" she asked her husband.

Simon's attention had been wandering about the room. They were seated as far away from the royal party as people of their rank could be, with the exception of the Earl of Pembroke who was always in disgrace.

"What do you think, my dear?"

"Of what?"

"That the Church promotes adultery."

"I wasn't of that impression."

"You haven't been listening!"

As best as his nearsighted eyes would permit, he had been watching the royal group, made up of the queen's uncles Peter of Savoy and the Archbishop Boniface, and the king's half-brothers of Lusignan, Guy, William and Aimery. Though he could not see the features of their faces, he recognized them well enough by general shapes and gestures. They were all men accused of abuses, and there was not one Englishman among them. Even the king's full brother, Richard of Cornwall and his wife, the queen's own sister Sanchia, were seated down the row.

"Henry is making a very grave mistake," Simon muttered.

The Earl of Gloucester looked where he was gazing and caught the drift of his thoughts. "Henry has his fawning foreigners drawn round him tightly as a noose. Some day they'll all hang."

Simon looked sharply at Clare.

The young earl returned his look with an easy smile. "Well, not *hang* of course. But how long do you suppose this tyranny will be tolerated?"

"Did Bishop Grosseteste visit you?"

Clare nodded, his look unwavering. "I see the bishop spoke with you as well."

"He did."

"I'm glad to see you're with us."

"I have better sense," Simon said curtly, turning away to watch the revelers and bring the topic to an end.

"Don't be a fool, Earl Montfort," Clare pitched his voice low. "Henry has more reasons than Gascony for placing you so shamefully far down the board."

The days after the wedding were spent in the presenting of the wedding gifts. Court met at the Minster's old Chapter House. The royal colors of red and gold draped the building's walls. Tents covered the square. All of the nobility of England and Scotland gathered, finding old friends, hearing the latest news, and what each other was giving for the Great Aide. It was an immense reunion of the noble families of two neighboring lands. Friends who seldom saw each other gossiped avidly. The elderly brought stools and blankets to sit out all day. Peddlers wove through the crowd, hawking their hot cakes and ale from trays hung round their necks.

Simon stayed away from the public gatherings, talking with the Bishops Walter Cantaloup and Grosseteste in their rooms. But he was alone at their own lodging, reading, when Eleanor came in one afternoon very upset. She had been holding her hood up to shield her face but, reaching the room, she let it drop and let her cloak fall to the floor. Her eyes were red and wet with tears.

"What's happened?" Simon asked, getting up and going to her.

She shook her head and covered her face with her hands.

"Tell me!" he insisted, thinking someone had offered her insult.

"I was at the square by the Chapter House," she began slowly, struggling to keep from crying. "Two ladies whom I didn't know mentioned your name. I joined them, thinking they might have heard something of Barentin's report. But that was not the subject of their talk." She paused, struggling painfully. Steadying herself, she managed enough composure to go on. "They spoke of you as the queen's lover. They said everyone is talking of it. That you are said to be the father of the child she bore in October."

Simon went pale.

"They will spread any lies to harm you!" Eleanor blurted.

He looked at her, holding her fingers tightly in his hands, but he could find no words.

She stared at him, amazed at his silence. "There can't be any truth to it..." she searched his face.

"I've tried..." the words caught in his throat and tears filled his eyes. He let her hands go.

She turned away from him and faced the window, her arms crossed, clutching herself. "It is not an utter lie? Not a lie at all?" Tears began freely running down her cheeks again. After some minutes she straightened, and almost managed to laugh. "It certainly explains why Henry has been treating us so badly! And I thought it was because of Barentin's report!"

Simon put his hand upon her shoulder to turn her toward him, but rested his forehead against her neck instead. The shame that he had kept tight-held poured out in tears. "It is ended," he wept. "By God, I pray it's ended."

Moved by his pain, she touched his hair then slowly leaned her cheek against his head as he wept.

After a few moments, she said in a quiet voice, "I know that I'm a plain woman. And shrewish... I felt that I was fortunate beyond measure when you loved me. Every woman thought were you the handsomest of men she'd ever seen." She paused, then, "But like goes to like. Somehow I cannot feel the outrage that I ought... when I think of you with the queen. If it is over, as you say, let's say no more about it. And live as best we can through what may come."

Simon took her hands and pressed them to his tear-wet lips. "You are too kind... God blessed me with you. Far above what I deserve."

The Earl and Countess of Leicester attended Court at the appointed time to present their gift to the king. Also in attendance on that morning, and clearly not by chance, were Goeffrey and Elie Rudel, with the collected offering of the lords of Gascony.

King Henry and Queen Eleanor sat upon a pair of finely carved tall chairs set on a high dais canopied and draped with heavy silks in red and gold. Though dressed in a sumptuous cloak of blue velvet and ermine, the queen looked pale and kept her eyes downcast upon a little book of hours she held in her lap. The king peered about with the alertness of a bird of prey.

"Good King Henry," Geoffrey Rudel bowed with an elegant flourish, "the lords of the Labour, Adour, Dordogne and Garonne valleys, of the Pyrenees and the Medoc, bid us as their representatives to deliver this poor gift on their behalf. They bear the shame that it is of so small a worth. The fault lies not with them, but with your viceroy." He turned and looked to Simon, "He has robbed them of their homes, and has wrung every shilling out of Gascony!"

The king stood up. A whispering went through the Court and everyone looked at the earl. But Simon, standing to one side with Eleanor, took the accusation coolly.

"Lord Montfort, do you hear what this man says?" Henry demanded.

"I hear it, my lord. For three years I've been living in the midst of the deceits that are the common currency among these people," Simon answered, loudly enough for everyone to hear.

"It is no lie!" Geoffrey Rudel threw back. "My king," he knelt before Henry, "we wish only to be your faithful subjects. But this, your viceroy, cannot be forborne! If you won't grant us relief from him at once, we've sworn to join in war against him and his people.

Yet we are no rebels, my king! Only your loyal subjects, fighting for our lands and lives!"

Simon made his way to the open space before the dais. "If what this traitor says is true, my lord, I beg leave to return to Gascony. Your truly loyal subjects are in danger!"

Henry looked down on Simon with a frown that twisted his drooping eye and cheek. He too spoke loudly, so that no one in the hall could mistake his words. "I've trusted you as I would my own brother, Earl Montfort. I've given you high office, and been patient when there were complaints. You've never ceased to pump the royal purse for money! Now tell me – you've had free use of all the tax monies of Gascony for these three years, and not a cent of it have you remitted to the Crown – where has the money gone!"

Simon was dumbfounded, "Where has it gone? You know I've stripped my own estates for Gascony's defense! At your command and in good faith! It isn't I who should be made to answer to this traitor's accusations!"

"Sire Montfort, we sent you to bring peace to Gascony," Henry said icily. "Instead, we find you are the center and the cause of ongoing unrest. The rumors and the cries against you are unceasing. We must suspect," he gave a tight smile, "that where there are so many shouts of smoke, there is a fire."

The king turned to his secretary John Mansel. "Draft a commission for Henry Wengham to go to Bordeaux." Wengham was the king's agent for searching out evidence of high treason.

Simon tensed. "You mean to send your prying spy to Gascony to look into my conduct?"

"If your innocence is so evident, lord earl," Henry replied with mocking archness, "why should you fear his inquiry? It will only make your glory shine the brighter."

Chapter Fifteen

SIMON ON TRIAL
1252

IN JANUARY, WHILE THE VICEROY was detained in England, in Gascony full war broke out.

At London Simon's ledgers and account roles were demanded for inspection. The king named a commission to conduct a full review.

Through February, Simon met with the investigators: Richard of Cornwall the king's brother; the king's half-brothers of Lusignan Guy and William de Valence; and the Bishop Walter Cantaloup. The commission seemed balanced, with an even count of those who thought well of Simon and those who did not. The earl produced his personal financial accounts. But the records of the taxes and the fines he had collected remained in Bordeaux. He begged leave to go and fetch them.

In Gascony, Wengham had reached the leaders of the revolt with letters from King Henry, ordering the complainants to appear at Westminster to bear witness against the Earl Montfort. A truce was called. In mid-March, as Simon arrived in Bordeaux, Wengham, shepherding the witnesses he had collected, was on his way to Westminster. Accompanying the king's agent were Amanieu d'Albret, Gaillard DelSoler, Guillaume de Gramont, Raymond de Fronzac, Guillaume de Rion, the aldermen of Dax and Saut, and even the Piis brothers of La Reole and the Archbishop Malemorte of Bordeaux.

When Simon, returning with the tax records, reached Dover, the Master of the Port delivered a summons to him. He was ordered to appear on April ninth to answer charges before the king.

Simon was at the great hall at Westminster at the appointed time, but he found the Court was not in session. A bailiff directed him to a private chamber. There, the clerk Mansel worked at a trestle table heaped with documents. Henry sat in a tall chair, resting his elbows upon the chair's arms, his fingertips stroking his forehead, his eyes looking down. As Simon was shown in, the king did not look up, but let his secretary speak for him.

"Lord earl," Mansel stood and addressed him, "the king hereby informs you that his majesty's good subjects of Gascony have given presentment of high treason against you."

Simon cast a sharp look at Henry, but the king kept his eyes down.

Mansel went on. "You are to submit yourself for trial thirty days from today. As treason is a high crime, entailing the penalty of death, you are granted one month to prepare for your defense."

My lord, the charge is treason?" Simon asked hollowly.

The king made no response.

"You mean to use against me the witness of men whom you know are traitors? Who have admitted so before you, and raised war while I was here?"

Henry looked up, meeting Simon's eyes. "Is it not true that you've repeatedly betrayed me?" he said quietly.

The question, and the look in Henry's eyes, went to the core of Simon's heart. He could only answer, "I've served you to the best of my abilities in Gascony."

Henry gave a short, sardonic laugh. "Your protests don't blind me, Simon." He motioned to his secretary.

Mansel handed the earl the summons with the royal seal attached. "On the ninth of May, lord earl, at noon at Court in Westminster, you must surrender yourself for trial."

Simon left the palace, numbed. He went to Worcester House, where he was staying with his friend Walter Cantaloup.

Walter was waiting for him. When he heard of the trial and the charge of treason, he remarked grimly, "Henry has been cosseting the Gascons like precious favorites. I feared something like this might be the outcome. What will you do?"

Simon's face was empty of expression, his feeling clouded, vague, withdrawn. This was the outcome that his conscience had long expected. The lashings, the hair shirt, the penitential clothes, those were for his own soul, and he had never doubted earthly justice would make its demand as well. What he had tried so hard to resist was having justice strike in this guise. Yet he had little will to fight it.

"What can I do? The records of Gascony are with your commission now. I could find witnesses, Barres, Colom, the warder of my prisons on the Isle d'Oleron, the former governor of Gascony, Richard de Gray – d'Urberville died in Egypt..." He looked in his friend's eyes, "But what use are witnesses, when the judge already has determined my fate?"

Walter's broad jaw tensed. "Bring your witnesses, Simon. Let justice show itself! If the king is determined upon this outrage, let it be seen by all. And so much the worse for Henry!"

Walter wrote to Grosseteste, and the two wrote to all the lords they knew who were displeased with King Henry's rule. They urged them to attend the trial. "The wrong that may be done the Earl of Leicester threatens every Englishman who serves the Crown," Grosseteste warned.

The barons came. Some were roused to fury, and some were merely curious. They crowded into the hall at Westminster on the ninth of May. So great and uncommon was the attendance that Henry ordered the place of venue changed at the last moment, to the far smaller refectory of Westminster Abbey, to limit the spectators.

The trial took five weeks. The abbey's refectory had a shallow, vaulted stone ceiling that rang deafeningly with the excited, high-pitched voices of the Gascon accusers. Except for a chair for Henry, and the writing table and benches for the clerks, there was no place to sit. The lords who packed the room for hour after hour of the hearings stood on the stone floor, cramped together in the stifling heat, dim light and stale air.

Outside, in the adjacent cloister garden, the spring weather was bright and cool. A young laburnum tree was in full bloom, its drooping yellow blossoms flickering with bees. A woody rosemary was flecked with purple flowers. Thyme, basil and winter savory gave off theirs pungent scents and myriad healing herbs made the air fresh. In the center of the abbey's herb parterres a stone fountain plashed and birds came to drink. But inside the refectory it was hot, foul and hellish.

A little space in front of the king and the clerks was kept open by the bailiffs for the witnesses. Simon stood beside the open space. One by one the Gascons gave their evidence, shouting loudly and gesturing in his face.

"This man, our viceroy," Geoffrey Rudel sneered at Simon, "deprived me and my brother of our inheritance of Blaye, to give it to his friend Amaubin de Barres!" Rudel produced charters that proved Blaye had been held by the Rudels in unbroken succession for four hundred years.

"He took from me my fief and town of Bezaume!" Guillaume de Rion accused. "My claim was that I held from d'Albret. D'Albret claimed that he held Bezaume outright. But neither of our charters meant anything to Sire Montfort! He gave Bezaume to the lord of Bergerac who bribed him!"

"What proof have you that I ever took a bribe!" Simon demanded.

"Here are our charters with our clear claims!" Rion slapped the vellum documents with the back of his hand, then thrust them toward a court clerk. "Bergerac had nothing! What more proof do we need!"

"That is no proof!" Simon bellowed back.

King Henry cut him off before he could say more. "Earl Montfort, you were not asked to speak!"

The aldermen of Dax stepped forth as a group. "Good King," their spokesman opened, "this man, your greedy viceroy, wrung the shillings out of us without a shred of mercy! Panting after gold to fill his treasure chests, he had his knights search our city, demanding preposterously high fines for the smallest, slightest things amiss! We paid unheard of rates for minor wrongs that never before had been fined at all!"

The court records of Dax were presented. They clearly showed the huge sums Simon had raised in the summer of 1250: money he had sent to the East to ransom the lost crusade.

Simon stood silently as the condemning records were read.

Gaillard DelSoler entered the witness space. His voice quavering with emotion, he pointed at Simon. "This man, Simon de Montfort, took my father prisoner. My father was seventy, but in good health. In the viceroy's hands he died within a week!" Gaillard fell to his knees before the king. "I beg the royal pardon for not delivering myself to take my father's place in prison, as your viceroy ordered. But I feared for my life! I beg of you, my lord, grant me revenge for my father's murder!"

The Vicomte de Gramont's son Guillaume, a young man barely twenty, was the next witness. His eyes were filled with tears. "My father also was in Sire de Montfort's keeping. But DelSoler is fortunate. For my father, there is no place even to mark where his body was thrown! May justice be done to his assassin!"

"My king, grant me permission to speak in my own defense," Simon begged.

"We are hearing your accusers," Henry answered icily.

The dark-browed Archbishop Malemorte came to Gramont and put his arm comfortingly around the young man's shoulders. Glowering at Simon, with a booming voice well practiced at echoing off the stone vaulting of his own cathedral, he intoned, "Life is nothing to the Earl Montfort! In his boundless thirst for wealth, he has seized our people's lands! And when they have resisted him, he's crushed them unto death! His greed and lust for power is insatiable! He is as a Leviathan that would drink Jordan dry!"

Picking up from the archbishop's prompting, Gramont wiped his eyes and went on with his testimony. "I can bear witness how he spends the money that he's wrung from us," he offered earnestly. "My father, in the last letter that I had from him, described the viceroy's lodgings. At La Reole the viceroy lives sunk in every luxury! His table service is all gold, fashioned in lewd designs. His furnishings might serve a house of shame. In the great chamber there are large alcoves with draperies embroidered with the most lascivious designs. Even the roof has corbels shaped like leering heads."

Henry turned and looked at Simon with a hint of amazement.

"Good brother!" Richard of Cornwall, standing among the observers at the front, protested, "this does not sound at all like the man we have known well for many years!"

"Then perhaps we have not known him well enough," Henry replied.

"My king, let the earl speak in his own defense," the Marshal Roger Bigod tried to insist.

"This is no trial, brother, where the accused is not permitted any answer!" Richard pressed.

"This is no trial!" the Earl of Gloucester cried.

Simon stood silent, his head bent. All around the room the spectators were crying out and making angry gestures.

King Henry scanned the shouting onlookers uneasily. He could have had his bailiffs clear the court, but these were the men on whom his kingdom depended. They could not just be herded off as if they were the commonality. "Very well, we will hear whatever the earl may claim in his defense."

Simon raised his head. After a pause he spoke. "I am accused of wringing Gascony to indulge myself in pleasures. To this, my answer is the fiscal records I've submitted to the king's commissioners. I have waged war for the king, at his command. And war is very costly."

He stopped speaking for a moment. Then, "As for the furnishings at La Reole, which Sire Gramont describes so vividly, I occupied the citadel exactly as I found it. It is a royal property, not for me to change."

There was a gasp at his implication, and then a snickering went through the crowd.

Simon turned toward the lords, "It is very true that I've seized lands and castles, and put men into prison. When I first went to Gascony, those castles, as the king's own captain Nicholaus de Meulles and the former governor of Gascony, Richard de Gray, can well attest, were centers of sedition. Their locked chambers were filled with victims of a land at civil war. I took the castles for the royal keeping, using their lords' own fines and the lands' taxes to support royal garrisons. I've taken nothing for myself. The records I've submitted prove this.

"I put the lords in prison without trial because they would not pledge themselves to the king's peace. They were, and are, sworn traitors. If there are any others I've detained without fair hearing, I plead in my defense the disorders of a land at war, which hindered me from holding court as regularly as in times of quietness."

"What of the huge fines you levied on the towns!" an alderman of Saut cried out.

Simon turned upon him. "Shall I have the records called for Saut? You refused to pay your taxes even into the king's own hand!" Then, turning back to Henry, he added, "I confess I used my powers in excess in the heavy fines that I collected in the summer of 1250. I've given your commissioners the full accounting. The monies that, I do admit, were truly wrung from Gascony, I sent to pay the ransoms of our Christian knights who were prisoners in Egypt. Of this crime I am most guilty, both for having done it, and for not informing you, my lord."

There was a moment of uneasy shuffling among the spectators. Then someone shouted, "God bless the Earl of Leicester!" The shout was taken up throughout the room.

"Murderer! He's a murderer!" DelSoler protested.

"Simon wheeled on him. "Whom have I murdered!"

"My father!" DelSoler screamed.

"Yes," Simon nodded. "Rostein did die in my keeping. A man of seventy years. His own doctor's opinion was that he died of a tercian fever. A fever brought on by his leading a night raid of the armorers' shops on the Rue Saint James – to arm an uprising of rebels against King Henry!"

"And what of my father!" Gramont exclaimed. "You poisoned him as well!"

Simon smiled bitterly. "I poisoned the Vicomte de Gramont? I offered him wine from his own vineyards, I didn't think it all that bad."

A spasm of laughter bubbled through the room.

Simon turned back to the king. "I've brought a witness as to the well-being of the prisoners I hold, the Vicomte de Gramont among them. May I call the Castellan of Oleron?"

Henry would have refused, but young Gramont was so earnest in his concern for his father that the witness was permitted. The castellan was brought in. He swore the prisoners in his keeping, reading name after name from his list, were all safe and well.

And so the trial went on. Simon explained his reasoning in granting Blaye to Amaubin de Barres, since he had forces to secure it and was faithful to the Crown. As for Bezaume, his having let the common people choose their lord was not a welcome notion to any of his listeners. But he refuted point for point every accusation that the Gascons brought against him.

The commission investigating the earl's finances was called to make report. They were divided: Prince Richard and the Bishop Cantaloup insisted every shilling was accounted for in costs of war. The Lusignan brothers denied it.

Simon's brow gathered tightly in a frown as he heard Guy de Lusignan and his brother William testify against him. What they claimed had no relation to the facts, they were wild fabrications.

"My king, "Simon turned to Henry when the Lusignan were done, "by my honor and my faith, the records give a full and true account. If I am still doubted, I have no recourse but to beg to have the truth tried by old custom." He faced the Lusignan and Gascons. "I will submit myself to Heaven's judgment in the ordeal of hot irons, if any of my accusers will submit himself also."

No one spoke or moved.

Henry waved his hand. "We are not beasts. We don't ask anyone to suffer more who has been wronged already."

"My lord," Simon turned to King Henry again, " I cannot prove my case but in those ledgers and accounts. Or in God's Own judgment! If I may not be granted trial by ordeal, then I beg trial by combat." He turned to the Gascons again. "I will meet any one of you, and will fight you unto my death or your submission."

The Gascons, mute and frozen, stared back at him.

"My lord," Simon turned on his heel in disgust, and looked to Henry again, "how can I clear my name?"

"You have committed high treason against the Crown, Sire Montfort..." Henry spoke the dark preamble to the death sentence.

"Brother!" Richard interrupted him, "there is no proof of that! The evidence does not support it!"

"The Earl Montfort has mortally abused our trust!" Henry threw back.

"He has waged war for you!" the Marshal Bigod shouted. "Montfort has done more to secure England's lands than all the rest of us have ever done!"

"He's earned a traitor's death!" William d Valence shrieked.

"There are no proofs!" the Bishop of Worcester boomed over him.

Order in the crowded room was crumbling.

"Free the earl!" the shout went up, with cries, "This is no trial!" "This is a mockery of justice!" The mass of spectators began pressing forward threateningly.

Alarmed at the angry faces moving toward him, Henry got up from his chair and started toward a nearby door. But the crowd closed around him. The lords were shouting, gesturing, enraged.

Trapped, King Henry looked wildly about him for an instant. There was no way of escape. Straightening, striking as masterful a pose as he could, he raised his hands. "Good lords of England!" he cried loudly. "Peace! Let there be peace! I grant you there is insufficient proof!"

The crowd stopped its forward pressing as the king spoke, and quieted enough for his last words to be heard. There was a moment's pause. Then a low rumbling sound swelled, a roar, a cheer loud-doubling beneath the vaulted ceiling.

Simon was surrounded by the lords and lifted off his feet. Tears of amazement, and of sudden relief, ran from his eyes. Triumphantly the lords bore him on their shoulders out of the trial room, out of the abbey, and through the streets of Westminster to freedom and victory.

Chapter Sixteen

REVENGE
1252

SIMON LOOKED UPON HIS RELEASE as a miracle. He was guilty of treason. A treason he felt certain lay behind Henry's intent in bringing him to trial, though it had not to do with Gascony. And though he had escaped from sentencing, he was not truly free. His contract with King Henry bound him to serve for three more years as viceroy. Clear, written relief from his commission was needed. Early the next morning he presented himself at Court.

The Gascon lords were in attendance. D'Albret and the Rudels sat on the dais steps by Henry's feet. Fronzac, Rion, Gramont and the Archbishop Malemorte stood nearby, engaged in animated conversation with the king. But all stopped speaking when the Earl of Leicester was announced.

There were others in the room also: Prince Richard, the Earl of Gloucester Richard de Clare, the Marshal Roger Bigod and a few more of Simon's supporters.

Simon went to the dais. "My king," he bowed, "I've come to ask your wish regarding my return to Gascony."

Henry gazed at him coldly. "My trusty viceroy is ready at my service so early in the day?" he asked sardonically.

"My lord, I've given you loyal service in the past, and I hope to do so again," Simon said quietly. "Our rift before was mended. I served you well at Sainte, when the King of France might have entrapped you."

"I recall your service at Sainte. It was bloody. When I need a vicious dog, I shall remember," Henry replied caustically.

Simon blanched. The determined grip he had upon his feelings was badly strained. "My lord, you bid me crush the Gascons as my father did the Albigensians. Those were your words. If you wish a milder governance, I can carry that out willingly. I ask only that you be consistent, and not make me the butt of your changes of mind." As the earl's voice rose, his partisans drifted toward the dais. "If you would rather appoint someone else," Simon went on, "I ask only that you reimburse the monies that I've spent in defense of your honor."

Knowing Simon's temperament, and that his hold upon himself was fragile, Henry goaded him. "You arrogantly lay the ills of Gascony to changefulness on my part? And not to your willful arrogance, lord Earl?"

The Gascons standing no more than an arm's length from Simon, grinned and suppressed laughs.

"Yes, my king," Simon said measuredly. He held his hands behind him, one hand clutching the other wrist hard. He must pass through this ordeal calmly. "Your words should be stable and trustworthy, my lord. Keep your contract, or relieve me of my office and repay the monies that I've spent. It is well known that I've impoverished myself in your defense."

A smile twisting his lips, Henry glanced down to d'Albret who was sitting by his feet. "If I'm so changeful as you accuse, lord earl, be sure I will not honor a contract with a traitor." He raised his head, meeting Simon's eyes. With a look of private, intimate meaning in that most public place, he added, "It is right to break one's word with those whose words are false. And to deal without shame with those who are shameless."

The words cut deep, and pierced Simon's restraint. The rage and the frustration of weeks, of years; the ooze of all his pain and his despising of Henry, burst out and he stepped forward shouting, "That I ever broke my word is a foul lie!"

Richard and Bigod had moved close to him. They grasped his arms and held him where he was. Struggling to break free of their grip, Simon cried out, "If you weren't protected by your title, this would be a dark day that you called me a liar!"

"Stop baiting him, brother," Richard shouted at Henry. To Simon he hissed, "For God's sake, don't you see what he's doing! Control yourself! Or he will have your head!"

At Richard's words, Simon stopped struggling. Breathing heavily, wiping his face with the back of his hand, after several moments he regained some mastery of himself. Henry had good cause against him, whatever the excuses that he might choose to use. He looked at Henry almost pleadingly, his heart as open as it could be before the eyes of the assembled Court and the Gascons who were grinning at him. "My king," he met Henry's gaze, "are you not a Christian? Do you know the meaning of repentance? Have you never confessed?"

"*I* have," Henry replied coldly.

"Then what is confession without repentance and atonement?" Simon spoke of his struggle with his penitence as plainly a he could.

Henry looked on him with disdain. "I never repented any act so much as I repent ever having let you enter England!"

The Gascons loudly hooted their approval. But Henry's Minister of the Treasury, de Riveaux, standing behind the throne, stepped forward, "My lord, don't stoop to answer him," he cautioned.

Richard, still grasping Simon's arm, urged, "Come, my friend. There's nothing to be gained here now, and much to lose." Clare joined the prince and Bigod, and the three drew Simon toward the door at the rear of the hall.

Looking back at Henry, who was talking with d'Albret and Malemorte, Simon went with them without resisting.

But as they reached the door, the king called out, "Lord earl, I order you to return to Gascony." And he added with biting sarcasm, "There, you who are so fond of wars may find enough of them, and return to us with that same reward your father received at Toulouse." As everyone there knew, in the war against the heretics, Simon's father had been killed at Toulouse.

The Gascons jeered and hooted their approval even more loudly, with whistles and gestures of derision.

Simon shook himself free of Richard's and Bigod's hold. He straightened, and with dignity he turned to face the Gascons and his king. "I will go there willingly, my lord," he replied. Making a slight, ironic bow, he added, "Nor will I come back until, ungrateful though you be, I've brought your Gascons to submission, and made them your footstool!" He turned and left the Court.

With Amaubin de Barres, Colom and the castellan of Oleron, Simon left London that same day. He went south to Kent. The Countess Eleanor had come to London with the children for the trial, but the stress had been too much for her and she had gone to their manor at Sutton, in Kentshire.

Simon had sent his squire Peter at once to tell her of the trial's outcome. When she saw her husband and his friends dismounting in the yard, she hurried out with all the children, and threw her arms around her husband's neck. Henry, Guy and young Simon stood smiling with relief and gladness, and the smallest ones, Eleanor and Amaury, embraced their father's knees.

Alone together that night, sitting by candlelight at a table in their chamber, Simon told Eleanor the details of the trial's amazing end.

"Praise Heaven for Richard," Eleanor said softly. "If this child I bear now is a boy, let us name him for my brother who has twice saved your life."

Simon nodded, pleased. But he added bleakly, "I pray I live to see him born."

Eleanor frowned at his grim remark. "You're safe now!"

"Henry has ordered me to return to Gascony."

She stared at him. "He sends you back?"

"He's giving me no funds for fighting men. He knows my credit is spent; I can no longer hire men myself. And it will be full war. Or whatever a war against me alone may be called," he gave a wry smile. Simon's dark lashes shaded his eyes, his elbow on the table, his chin pensively resting on his fist.

Eleanor watched him, his broad, strong hand, beautiful in the light and shadow of the candle's glow; the fine features of his face, his deep eyes full of thought. She thought of how audacious this present moment was, how full of life, of substance and reality so seemingly unending. And how very strange it was that death would make that face, that hand, into nothing. She touched his hand.

He looked up and smiled into her eyes. "There are ways to recompense an army when you have no funds," he said. "I know where I can find help. I won't return to Gascony alone."

"Let me go with you? I want to be with you."

"No," Simon shook his head. "But I will take our son Henry."

"No! Please... take Simon, or even Guy..."

He spoke quietly but with determination. "I would have Henry with me."

The next day, with his squire, his eldest son who was now almost thirteen, and his three companions, Simon left for France. They went secretly, by way of Winchelsea where the Master of the Port held the earl in high regard, and had no love of the king. He could be trusted.

Landing at Boulogne, the castellan returned to Oleron, but Simon and the rest did not go south. They ambled through Normandy, visiting the noble families who, for generations, had been allies of the Montforts, who had been with Simon's father on the Albigensian Crusade against the southern heretics. Most had lost lands in England, earned in the Conquest in 1066 but confiscated by King John or Henry. Their hatred of the King of England was surpassed only by their loathing for the southern French. Though Louis remained in Acre, many had returned from the East, coming home nearly penniless. They had contributed, to the extreme that their estates could yield, to go on the crusade, and their families had entailed their rents for years to come for their ransoms. Simon's offer could not have been better timed.

To the many who gathered at John Harcourt's manse, Simon said, "Come south in arms with me. Help me retake Gascony and, as viceroy, I will not object if the land is sacked of every golden cup and tun of wine."

From one noble's household to the next he made his offer. Word spread quickly. As Simon rode toward Paris, he left behind him a widening wake of knights readying for war.

At Paris he visited the Court at once. Queen Blanche received him warmly. "Ah, Simon!" she reached out her hands to him. "We've heard of your misfortunes. How good it is to see you safe!"

He kissed her hand, noticing how frail it had become with age. The skin lay thin, almost transparent, over the blue veins and white bones.

"Will you stay with us now?" the queen's deep, hollow eyes searched his face.

"For my honor, I cannot. Though it would be my greatest happiness. But I must finish in Gascony."

"You'll come back to us after that?" Her tone was almost pleading. "I ought never to have sent you to England." She used the personal "I" and spoke hardly above a whisper. It seemed as if she was asking his forgiveness. Then she changed, becoming softer still. "I want you here, Simon. This past year has tried me beyond my strength, which is but little now I fear." She tried to laugh. "I grow too old."

"Your son Alphonse is here," Simon said gently, for Alphonse had returned with many of the others from the East.

"Yes, Alphonse," she nodded without cheer. "But Louis will never come back. He breaks my heart! He's sworn to stay in Palestine as penance for the deaths of those who followed him." She looked intently at Simon, "He has no pity for the pain he causes France, and me."

Simon had never thought to see Queen Blanche so frail, so vulnerable. He knelt beside her, pressing her fingers to his lips. "Louis does what he believes is right." His heart was full for her – the woman who had been a mother to him for almost all the early years he could remember. He promised her, "I will come back."

She put her hand upon his head. "You have been like a son to me. In some ways a better son than those of my own body." Her long fingers trembled as she stroked his dark hair. "We have riches and honor to offer you, as fine as any King Henry can give." She seemed to be trying to make up for having sent him away so long ago.

It was her image that took the place in memory of the true mother whom he lost when he was eight. And Blanche was the mother he adored and lost again when he was seventeen. She had never spoken to him with such tenderness before. "I willingly would stay by you," he murmured earnestly, "though it leave me the poorest man on earth in earthly things, for my heart would be happiest." It was very true.

"But you must go now to Gascony?"

"I must."

"We will give you every help we can. Take care! Henry is unworthy of you." Later, she directed her Minister of State, the Archbishop Odo Rigaud, to give the viceroy all the funds he asked.

Simon was amazed when he met with Rigaud. "I never expected to find such help."

Rigaud cautioned him. "It must be kept a close secret. We don't want to engage England in outright war, even for your sake," he smiled.

With money from France's treasury, Simon hired forces of mounted infantry and archers. Then with his son Henry, Colom and Barres, the viceroy rode south. Following him was an army of Brabant mercenaries, and Norman knights each with their bands of foot soldiers.

It was the middle of July of 1252, one month since his trial had ended, when Simon reached Gascony.

He had sent a summons ahead to his liegeman Arnaud Otton at Lourdes, ordering him to gather all the news he could of the rebels' plans and movements, and come to him at Bordeaux.

"The lords who went to England have not yet returned," Arnaud told him. "But, during the truce for your trial, Gaston de Bearne went to the Courts of Aragon and Navarre. He raised an army there of some seven hundred men, and he's brought them into Gascony. Two days ago they crossed the Garonne. They march now along the north shore of the Gironde, northward of Blaye."

Simon turned to Amaubin, who knew the shores of the Gironde as well as his own yard. "Could a ship come to land in the Gironde north of Blaye?"

"No. But a ship could anchor and be met by boats to come across the shallows. You think he's gone to meet the lords coming from England?"

"That, or perhaps he means to attack Oleron. Most likely both. We'll follow him," Simon decided.

After a day of rest, the viceroy's army left Bordeaux, crossed the Gironde and easily picked up the route the lord of Bearne and his seven hundred men had taken. Scouts were sent ahead.

In the early hours of the morning a few days later, the scouts found Gaston's army camped upon the beach. In the dawn mist a ship lay at anchor on the smooth gray waters of the estuary. Rowboats glided across the water, ferrying the Gascon lords to land.

By the full light of morning, a few miles from the landing Simon brought his army to halt along the road down which the Gascons and Bearne's troops must pass. A mile to the rear he ordered a camp made for his wagons of supply, and he left young Henry there under the squire Peter's care.

The land was parched yellow and gently rolling, with three low hills like the swells of waves. Riding ahead with Barres, Simon saw the dark mass of a grove of stunted pines and brush on the slope of the western, furthest valley.

"I could hide fifty horsemen in that thicket and attack the enemy's rear guard once they've passed," Barres suggested.

"You would prevent them from fleeing back to their ship," Simon smiled. "Take fifty men. But don't show yourselves until the Gascons meet our main force in this middle valley."

With Barres's ambush in place, Simon stationed a lookout in a lone pine tree to signal when the enemy entered the far side of the middle valley. When they reached the valley's lowest ground he would attack. He deployed his men upon the slope just over the hill and out of sight of the valley that would be the trap for the Gascons and Bearne's army.

The morning became bright and beating-hot. Locusts sang a steady droning as heat rippled in the breezeless air. The lookout sat staring at the far hill where it curved over the crest of yellow grass. The valley where Barres waited in ambush was out of sight beyond the next hill after that.

There was a flap and jingle now and then as a horse shook it mantling. As time passed, the riders held their reins loose so that their mounts could graze. The heat was stifling. The sun, blazing upon the steel, made ovens of the knights' helmets. One after another, the men untied their laces and took their helmets off, wiping their red, sweat-soaked faces with their surcoats. They did not put their helms back on. Now and then a knight dismounted to piss, or talk in low tones with his foot soldiers.

Hours passed. The heat, the stillness, the steady hum of insects dimmed the senses. As they waited, and waited, battle tension sank.

The sun dragged past noon.

"My lord, it's possible they'll camp for some time on the beach," Arnaud Otton suggested.

"If they've not come by nightfall, we'll send forward another scout. But I would rather meet them here where the land gives us advantage."

Then suddenly the lookout shouted, "Lord earl, a knight is coming on at speed!"

"Probably come to tell us they've made camp," the knight John Harcourt sighed to Simon.

"Perhaps..." But Simon was perplexed. His mind dazed by the heat.

In the time it took to cross the valley at full gallop, the rider appeared, dashing over the hill's ridge. His horse was swift and soon he cut across the field directly toward the viceroy. "My lord," he gasped, reining his mount and turning it so hard its rump collided with the viceroy's horse, "My lord, the Gascons have captured us! Someone betrayed our ambush! The lord of Bearne is coming on to give you battle!"

At that moment the lookout in the tree began waving and shouting, "They are come! They come on quickly!"

Simon was jolted from the heat's lethargy. "We're waiting here too long!" he cried to his trumpeter. "Sound the advance!" He laced on his helmet and put spurs to his horse.

At the trumpet call, the archers and the mounted infantry and knights fumbled with their gear and helms and hurried to remount.

Simon galloped to the top of the hill. The wind blew from the south, carrying sounds away toward the sea, but Simon's horse was tense, alert to the shaking of the earth from the hoof beats of the army coming on. In the valley below, the army of the enemy was moving at a swift trot down the farther slope, the vanguard was already crossing the valley's floor. Knights from Barres' company were dotted among the forward riders, hunched figures disarmed and tied to their horses, their slumping posture apparent even at a distance.

Squinting hard through the eye slit of his helmet, Simon could make out among those in the fore a rider with the barred blue and white surcoat of Barres. Squeezing vision from his nearsighted eyes, he saw the riders flanking Barres broadly gesturing. They seemed in high spirits. Barres cringed away as one struck him in the head.

The earth trembled and a din like thunder came up with the breeze as the viceroy's army on the far side of the hill began moving forward at speed.

For the Gascons, the sound was lost amid the rumble and jingle of their own advance. But Barres looked up, and his glance caught d'Albret's attention. What they saw upon the slope was a single knight in black chain mail and helm, with the red lion mantel of Montfort. D'Albret and Bearne stopped their talk and stared, dumbfounded, as the rider came at them alone at full volant.

"My spy must have gotten the viceroy's horse," Gaston de Bearne remarked at the amazing sight.

"He rides as though the hounds of Hell were after him," d'Albret observed.

"Or with him," said Malemorte. The archbishop, his rotund body in chain mail although his horse wore the caparison of a holy day parade, drew up beside d'Albret.

Bearne motioned for the march to halt.

The knight neared without reining in his horse. He drew his sword. Gaston quickly turned from his way. The blow fell on d'Albret's shield with all the force of the oncoming gallop, carrying the Gascon and his mount back. Simon was beside Barres.

"My lord?" Barres gasped in disbelief as Simon' sword slashed through the cords that bound his hands and neck. Gaston de Bearne was closing. Simon stopped the blow with his shield. But now d'Albret was moving in again. And the Archbishop Malemorte, unhooking a studded morningstar from his saddlebow, was swinging it for aim. Barres kicked d'Albret's horse, spoiling his aim at Simon as the viceroy met Gaston's next stroke with his sword. The Archbishop's morningstar came down on Simon's horse's flank. The animal reared, stopping d'Albret's second blow with its neck. The white mantel spurted red. D'Albret and Bearne closed over Simon as his mount staggered and sank under him.

Barres tackled the morningstar out of Malemorte's grip. Mightily swinging the chained ball right and left at d'Albret and Bearne, he shouted, "It is only right I rescue my rescuer!" He battered the horses and swung at the riders' backs, and caught Gaston de Bearne a blow between the shoulder blades. Gaston fell forward, coughing blood, and his horse pushed from the fight.

As Gaston moved out, Barres could see Simon kneeling, crouching against the body of his dying horse. His shield was hacked and broken but still covering him. "My stirrup's free! Climb up!" Barres shouted, catching d'Albret's blade with a swing of the morningstar and wrestling the chain-wound sword as the studded ball swung wildly. Simon climbed up behind Barres' saddle.

Now the viceroy's army was pouring over the hill. Bearne's army charged to meet them. Barres let go the handle of the morningstar and dug his spurs into his mount. The heavy-laden horse reached out its legs and galloped for the slope, passing between the on-coming riders.

"Is the viceroy hurt?" the knight of Vernon called out.

Simon waved his sword and shouted cheerfully," Not scratched! Lay on to the devils for me while I get another horse!"

It was not true he wasn't scratched. In his tent at camp, the squire Peter carefully removed his master's chain hauberk and sleeves, and his bloody pourpoint shirt. He gently dressed the cuts on Simon's shoulders, neck and back, packing the deepest wounds with boiled lint.

Simon saw his son watching him with wide eyes. He grinned at the boy. "Don't think too much of it, Henry. It doesn't hurt. At least not till the battle's done." He was exhilarated, even merry.

Barres sat nearby on the cot. "I never before saw anything so mad as that!" He ran his hand over the bald spot at the top of his head. "It was like a wild man! You came down the hill and took on the whole army by yourself!"

Simon laughed. "My brains must have been baked."

"For certain! I'll wager your father the Crusader never led a charge a full mile ahead of his men! It's God's Own work you're still alive."

Young Henry listened, and looked at his father in wonder.

Bandaged, dressed and armed again, Simon took a sturdy roan horse that had no mantel, and went back to the battle. As he and Barres rode out, he called to his son, "Henry, come and watch the battle from the hill. Learn what battle is. That's why I've brought you."

Henry ran fast to his palfrey, mounted and rode up the hill.

The field was full of disordered action. Foot soldiers, who had followed the charge as best they could, now clustered around their knights, fending off with their short swords blows aimed at the horses. The knights, above them, traded blows and parries with their long two-edged swords. Pairs of fighters, and larger struggling knots of men and horses, were scattered all over the field. But as many as fought, that many and more, mounted and on foot, stood looking around. Here and there a downed horse lay thrashing in the grass, straining to get up. Wherever a man was fallen, men on foot hurried to him, sometimes with a horse to carry him away.

Some of the wounded came up the hill, passing Henry on their way back to the camp. At the outskirts of the battle there was a constant flow of men coming and going, though more going than coming. The baggage of the Gascons and Bearne's army's supplies were in wagons drawn up on the field's far side. Like a magnet gathering metal filings from a heap, this Gascon camp drew most of the departing riders. They arched their way around the battle to disappear among the wagons and their grazing, hobbled oxen.

Now and then the glimpse of a familiar mantel drew Henry's attention to a particular knot of the battle. He had learned the Gascons' arms when he and his father were at Castillon. And those of the Norman knights he had studied well on their trip south from Paris. He could just make out the blows exchanged as the lord of Vidame fought Raymond de Fronzac. He could see the arms of Noailles and Harcourt engaged with the Rudels. But chiefly he looked for the roan horse with no mantel, whose rider wore black chain mail. Toward him the battle clustered. Henry peered at the shifting struggle around the speck of black that disappeared and then appeared again, always in the midst of the densest fight.

The breeze shifted to the north, blowing across the valley toward the hill where Henry stood. The boy's palfrey snorted. The air brought up the sounds and smells of battle. The acrid smells of sweat, horse dung and blood. The unintelligible din of voices, clashing metal and jingling harness, through which sometimes a shout rang clear. Then the breeze dropped. But the shadow play went on, thinned by incessant draining at the edges. Henry saw riders leaving from the Gascon camp by twos and threes on fresh horses that galloped away at speed.

The warm light of late afternoon was gilding the grass. The battle slowed. The tired figures seemed to move with the deliberation of a dance. The golden light, the slowness of the movement would have made the scene seem beautiful, but for the dying horses struggling to rise and the bloodied bodies being carried from the field.

Gradually the slow motion of the battle came to halt, There was a final burst as men darted away. Then there was milling movement. Those remaining on the field divided, some coming up the hill toward Henry, the rest going toward the barons' baggage camp. Henry strained to see the knight on the roan horse. He thought he caught a glimpse of him moving toward the Gascons' camp. But figures and colors were becoming indistinct. The failing light was turning the whole scene to blue. Henry searched for the roan, then gave his palfrey a kick and started down the hill.

Among those coming up the slope was the knight John Harcourt. He took off his helmet as he saw Henry. "We won the day!" he shouted. "Your father's gone to take possession of the Gascons' baggage train."

Henry gave a cry of joy and dug his heels into his horse, galloping down the slope and onto the field. He skirted the hard-trampled ground littered with gear and the bodies of horses. There were men there too. Men crushed under the haunches of their horses. He forced himself to look at their gaping mouths and staring eyes as he rode by.

He reached the baggage camp and found his father, smeared with dirt and drying blood, sitting exhausted on a wagon wheel. His knights stood or sat around him on the grass, in council. Shyly, Henry found a space among them and sat down.

"When the lord of Barres has made a full list of the prisoners, the wagons, their contents and the horses, we shall divide the ransoms and the spoils by lot," the viceroy said.

Some of the Gascon barons had escaped. Among them were Gaston de Bearne and Amanieu d'Albret. But the victors held most of the knights of Aragon and Navarre, and many of the rebels.

"Did anyone see which way Bearne fled?" the viceroy asked.

His son spoke up timidly, "I saw him with some other riders leaving from this camp. They all went that way," he pointed to the east, the opposite direction from Oleron.

Simon nodded to his son approvingly, then said, "We will return to our camp for tonight, and follow after them tomorrow."

In the deepening blue light the oxen of the Gascons' baggage train were hitched to their wagons and were driven across the battlefield, over the hill and into the viceroy's camp. The captured foot soldiers walked in file, tied by their wrists to long ropes strung between the wagons. Prisoner knights rode tied to their horses, their horses' legs hobbled so that they could move only slowly. It was night when the slow-moving prize cavalcade crept over the hill's crest and crossed the little valley into the camp. There, bright fires were lit. The squires had helped themselves to sheep grazing nearby, slaughtering a hundred of the animals and roasting the carcasses on spits. The victors were feasting.

The viceroy, his son and Arnaud Otton had ridden back to their own camp as soon as the council was ended.

Henry noticed that his father rode stiffly. He clearly was in pain though trying hard to conceal it. When they reached the red and white striped tent, Henry jumped from his palfrey and held his father's stirrup, helping him dismount.

At his son's worried look, Simon gave a strained smile and said softly, "After the battle's done, it can be troublesome." He spoke in an undertone so no one else would hear and be alarmed.

Henry did not dare help him, but walked beside him as he went into the tent.

Cautiously, the squire Peter drew his master's hauberk and chain sleeves off again. He applied a clean rag soaked with wine to the blood-caked pourpoint shirt, then gently peeled it back from the wounds. The bandages beneath were torn, a mass of cloth and blood, and there were new bruises and large open cuts. With more soaking, Peter cut and peeled the ruined bandages away.

Sitting on a campstool, Simon took gulp after gulp of Otton's armagnac from a goatskin flask. Henry saw his father becoming very drunk. But Peter was both gentle and expert, and finally the bandages were removed. Blows from blades not sharp enough to cut through mail had battered and split the skin. Peter daubed away the blood and packed the larger wounds with lint, but whole areas were purple and swelling.

Bleary, Simon looked to Henry, "You had better bring me something to eat."

"Better not, sire. Eating now will make you sick," Peter warned.

"I've had too much to drink already," Simon said thickly. "And I'm going to drink more. I want something to eat."

Henry looked to Peter. The squire rolled his eyes upward and shrugged. Henry went to fetch some roasted mutton.

As he went through the camp, everyone asked how the viceroy was. "He's not seriously hurt," Henry assured them, wondering if it were true, he had so many hurts. But he sensed from his father that he must lie if need be.

He came back with a thick piece of meat. Simon ate it hungrily, Then almost at once threw it up, with much of the armagnac. Peter looked on coolly, holding a shaving basin as his master retched.

His head clearer, Simon lay down carefully, prone, on his cot. "It hurts," he grumbled as he let Peter spread great quantities of an herb unguent. The squire laid clean bandages over his salved back, then, having him sit up, he spread more unguent on the cuts on his chest, shoulders and neck, laid on more bandages, and wound long strips of linen around his back and chest. Simon lay down prone again, the pain subsiding, and he fell asleep.

"Is he really going to be all right?" Henry asked in a whisper.

"The worst will be the headache that he has in the morning, from all he's drunk," the squire answered hopefully.

Chapter Seventeen

MONTAUBAN DE CASSEUIL
1252

IN THE MORNING SIMON ROSE from his cot very stiff and with a throbbing headache. But he dressed and went outside his tent so that his men could see that he was not seriously wounded. Sitting on a campstool, sipping a hot decoction of ground valerian root that Peter claimed would ease the pounding in his head, he talked with Barres, Arnaud Otton and Harcourt. "Did you learn anything from the prisoners last night?" he asked, taking a sip and grimacing.

"Before they left England, King Henry called a truce," Barres replied. "Apparently he had a change of mind after you left. They say he's coming here himself in October."

Simon raised his eyebrows.

"But that's not the strangest of the news, sire," Arnaud Otton put in. "He has truly transferred Gascony to Prince Edward, as he promised years ago. He made the lords all pay their fealty to Edward."

"If you stay here, they say that Henry means to take the field against you himself, in Prince Edward's name," Barres added.

Simon set his cup on the ground and straightened his back painfully. "Well, if he means to treat me as a renegade, so be it. I've known he wanted my earldom back, to enrich his Poitouvins or Savoyards with it." He turned to Otton, "Have you learned any more of where the enemy has gone?"

"My scouts say they retreat toward La Reole, which Gaston took last spring and has been using as his northern base."

"We'll march to La Reole," Simon decided.

After breakfast, the tents were furled, the wagons packed and the army moved on with its prisoners and booty.

As they traveled, Simon's pain and stiffness grew worse. The beating summer heat made his bandages chafe, sodden with sweat. By the next day his lips were dry, his face burning with fever. "I must stop," he whispered to his son. "Bring the lords Amaubin and Otton to me – quietly."

Henry turned his horse and trotted back along the line of march until he reached each of the lords with his message. They moved their horses out of the march and trotted forward. Barres reached Simon first.

"I must stop and rest. Is there any fortified place near here?" Simon asked him.

"Yes, my lord." Barres eyed the viceroy's flushed face with concern. "Montaubin de Casseuil isn't far. It is one of the Lion Hearted's small towers, and is a holding of mine."

"Take me there. I'll keep my prisoners and five of the mercenary foot soldiers with me." He turned to Otton, who had just ridden up. "Arnaud, lead the army to La Reole and open siege. I'll join you there after I've had a day of rest."

Road

Only a few miles from the main rode, as Barres had said, a small stone tower stood. In the middle of a lush pasture, the structure rose with no outbuildings or ditch or bailey wall. It looked like a chess rook dropped in a green vale. An iron-shod portcullis was suspended over the main door. Sunk in a hollow at the rear of the tower was a small postern door bound and studded with ironwork. Long arrow-slit windows looked over each entrance. The roof displayed a toothed battlement of merlons and crenels.

The caretaker, a servant of Barres's, opened the portcullis for his master and the viceroy. With his squire and young Henry's help, Simon dismounted painfully.

Barres and the five foot soldiers led the viceroy's prisoners around to the postern door which gave entrance to the tower's cellar: a room that was no more than a pit, furnished with a few wine casks, the caretaker's straw bedding and a small iron brazier. A chink in the wall let in a beam of sunshine. In this narrow light two hens sat thoughtfully on a box filled with straw. Strings of garlic, onions and sausages hung from the ceiling. Stairs of wooden slabs set into the wall's masonry led from the cellar to the upper floor, a round, empty, dusty room lit dimly by the two slit windows. From there, stone steps carved out of the curving wall led up to the roof, where stood a rain cistern and the winch that raised and lowered the portcullis.

With the portcullis raised, Simon walked stiffly through the main door into the upper room. Thanking Barres, he dismissed him to rejoin the march to La Reole, and he ordered his baggage to be brought in. As Barres turned to leave, Simon told him, "I'll rejoin you in a day or two, after I've rested here."

Peter hurriedly assembled the earl's cot, campstools and table. Outside, the horses were unpacked, unsaddled, hobbled and left to graze. There was not so much as a shed for stabling.

After Barres had gone, Simon sat down on the cot. He smiled to Henry. "At last I can groan without a thousand eyes turning and worrying."

Peter helped him to take off his clothes. The squire removed the bandages, peeling them back from the thick salve as Simon lay on the cot, letting the cool air soothe his skin. Henry sat upon the floor, watching his father.

"Read to me, Henry," Simon said.

Obediently, the boy got up and dug out of his father's traveling chest the volume of *Saint Gregory's Commentaries on the Book of Job*. "Where shall I begin?" he asked.

"Read about Job's boils," Simon grinned. "No. Start again. From the beginning."

The boy opened the massive book and began to read. Peter brought out cold roasted mutton and bread for their supper, and wine from one of the casks in the cellar. Henry read into the night, by candle light until, tired but healing, Simon fell asleep. Henry and the squire made beds for themselves out of the blankets from the chest, and went to sleep on the floor.

On the roof the tired foot soldier appointed for the watch slept too.

Below, in the cellar, guarded by the soldiers and the unhappy caretaker, the viceroy's prisoners spent the night as best they could on the damp earth floor. Though Simon had offered to divide the prisoners by lot, his Norman knights insisted that he take the most high ranking. The miserable prisoners in the cellar were Elie Rudel, Raymond de Fronzac, Guillaume de Rion and the Archbishop Malemorte.

At dawn everyone was wakened abruptly. There was a clangorous banging at the portcullis.

Henry sprang up and peeped out the narrowing opening of the arrow loop. Directly below, a crowd of armed men stood around the door and one was pounding on the iron bars with the flat of his sword. "Come out, Earl Simon!" he called out. "We have you besieged!" It was Amanieu d'Albret.

Simon, wrapping his blanket around him, went to the arrow loop and looked out. He motioned to Henry, pointing to the loop across the room. "Henry ran and looked out there. Softly he said, "There are three men by the postern door, father. And there are more coming."

One of the soldiers and the caretaker had come up from the cellar.

"Barricade the door!" Simon ordered them. "What is in the cellar?"

"Casks of wine, pretty heavy," the soldier replied.

"Most have gone to vinegar, except the one the squire opened," the caretaker glared at Peter.

"Use them to block the door," Simon ordered. As they went down the stairs, he called after them, "Bring me the archbishop!" Holding the blanket around him, he climbed the stairs to the roof to check the portcullis's machinery. The winch was only slightly rusty. The main door seemed secure. He went downstairs again.

The archbishop stood in the middle of the room in his vast chain mail shirt, his crumpled, dirty traveling cloak and robe. His hands were tied, his hair disheveled, and a day's growth of beard bristled on his jowls. "The Lord's requital is upon you, Lord Montfort," he said darkly.

The viceroy ignored his remark as Peter salved his wounds and bound fresh bandages around his chest, shoulders and back, then helped him to put on the blood stained, tattered pourpoint shirt. Simon drew on fresh drawers and padded leggings.

Peter frowned as he put the weighty chain mail hauberk over his master's head. "You ought not to be covering these wounds so heavily, my lord."

"Had I a choice, I wouldn't. Move quickly!" Simon chided, and handed him the chain mail sleeves, holding out his arms for the sleeves to be pulled on and knotted to his hauberk. As Peter fitted on his chain leggings, Simon looked at the archbishop. "Father, do you tell lies?"

"I tell the truth!"

"Then remember what you've said of how I treat my prisoners. Give thought to what your share will be."

"I am prepared to die," Malemorte said with dignity.

"And your friends in the cellar?"

The archbishop made no reply.

"I give you a chance to win your freedom. Fail, and it will be the worse for you. Amanieu d'Albret is at the gate. Negotiate our safe passage from here, and you and the others will come to no harm."

He took his sword belt from Peter and buckled it on. Then he stepped close to Malemorte, looking in his heavily browed eyes. "If d'Albret attacks us, I will kill my prisoners, with you the last to watch the death-throes of the rest."

"The Lord will punish you!" Malemorte spluttered.

"May the Lord help you avert it." Simon roughly took the archbishop by his bound arm and pushed him up the stairs to the roof.

The guard who had been sleeping cringed at sight of his commander. But Simon ignored him, hurrying Malemorte across the roof to the crenel that was directly over the portcullis.

At sight of movement on the roof, the Gascons let fly an arrow that arched over the battlement and buried its point in the cistern's planking. Simon stood shielded by the merlon of the battlement, and thrust Malemorte out into the square gap of the crenel.

"Hold your arrows!" the archbishop cried franticly.

At that moment a crash resounded at the rear of the building. Simon pulled Malemorte across the roof again and shoved him, head downward, through the crenel above the postern door. The archbishop let out a piercing shriek. Terrified, he wobbled his great body in the stone slot, trying to regain his footing as his boots waved in the air. The men below stared up, dropping the tree trunk they were using for a ram.

"Tell them to withdraw," Simon ordered Malemorte.

"Good men, withdraw!" the pinned archbishop gasped.

The men began to talk among themselves and one ran to get d'Albret. In a moment the Gascon lord came around to the postern door.

Simon held Malemorte head down far out over the parapet with his sword's edge at the archbishop's neck, clearly visible to those below.

D'Albret called up, "Earl Simon! Lord Beast! Surrender! Don't add the death of a high lord of the Church to all your other sins!"

"Your words mean nothing to me, d'Albret! This man is no lord of the Church, but an excommunicate! As you all are by dictum of the Pope for raising hand against me!" He pressed Malemorte hard against the stone, forcing him to lean further out as the blade cut a thin red line across the fleshy neck.

"Fall back, lord Amanieu!" the archbishop pled desperately.

D'Albret walked back a little way, talking with his knights. Then the besiegers at the door were called away and guards were posted.

The Gascon lords withdrew into the meadow, but the tower was close-held. D'Albret's men set up tents to stay.

Peter had come up to the roof.

"Bring two of my soldiers here." Simon heaved a heavy breath, his energies near spent from his exertions. When the men arrived, he posted them as watch, then shoved Malemorte to the stairs and down to the hall.

In the darkness of the circular room, dim lit compared to the bright sunlight on the roof, Henry looked to his father, frightened.

"They hold us at siege, but I doubt they will attack us for the present," Simon answered his son's look in as easy a tone as he could put into his voice. He looked out the narrow loop window. Where his horses had been grazing, the barons' tents were going up. He saw his horses gathered with the Gascons' mounts on tether lines at the far side of the camp. There would be no chance of reaching them.

He went to the cellar stairs. "Come up here!" he called to a soldier who was looking up the stairway from below. As the man reached the upper room, Simon ordered him, "Take this man back to the cellar and keep your prisoners bound securely." He turned to the squire Peter. "We're going to have to measure out our food. Confiscate whatever the caretaker has and lock it in my traveling chest."

"He has two hens, for eggs... "Peter gave a questioning look.

"Good. Bring them up here too."

The squire, the soldier and the archbishop went down the stairs.

Henry turned to his father. "What will happen now?" he asked, his face tense with fear.

"As we have nothing but our swords, there's little we can do but wait. And pray Barres and Otton miss us soon."

His wounds burning and aching and his head throbbing, Simon sat on the stone floor, leaning his least hurt shoulder against the wall.

Peter brought up the sausage, the strings of onions and garlic and the two hens. The birds walked about, cocking their eyes at the dust, searching hopefully for insects.

Henry crouched beside his father, his back against the wall, his long, thin, stockinged legs doubled in front of him. He stared at the middle distance.

"Read to me, Henry," Simon said to get the boy's mind off his fear.

Henry got up and fetched the book, then sat down by his father again. He opened the big book and began to read aloud where he had left off the night before. But soon he looked up. "When will the lord of Barres come back for us, father?"

"When he sees we are late reaching La Reole. If he comes at once, he could be here in three days. Or he may have learned that d'Albret has turned back. In which case he may be not far away right now. Read, Henry," he said gently.

The boy read.

Simon listened. Idly, with a straw he drew in the dust on the floor. He made the outline of a shield, then drew lines within it, and scratched them out. Drawing another shield, he carefully outlined a flower of three petals.

Henry looked at the drawing, then at his father questioningly.

"When we reach La Reole I must have a new shield made," Simon mused. "I'll have it painted with a lily. In white on an azure ground."

"Not our red lion?" Henry asked, dismayed.

Simon shook his head. "I want the lily that Saint Gregory writes of – that grew among the tares, like Job who lived among the wicked folk of Uz but kept his faith."

Henry looked down at the drawing of the lily shield in the dust.

"When we leave here," his father made a point of speaking of the future, "I will adopt the lily for my device. At least so long as we're in Gascony."

"When I'm knighted, should I have the lily too?" Henry asked.

Simon smiled. "No. You keep the lion rampant of Montfort. It is the device of our house. The lily is my special token."

They sat silently for some time, listening for sounds outside. Despite talk of the future, they both were thinking of Grosseteste's prophecy at the boy's baptism: that they would die together on the same day, and by the same hurt.

At last Henry could keep quiet no longer. "Ought I to confess, father?"

Simon put his arm around his son's thin shoulders. "Not yet. And not to me. Would you confess to the archbishop?"

Henry wrinkled his nose.

"Not every dying man has an archbishop in his cellar to hear his confession," Simon grinned.

The boy smiled.

"Don't think of dying, Henry. We are not beaten yet."

The soldiers and the squire took turns as lookouts on the roof and warders of the prisoners. The soldier who had slept when the Gascons had come up, now was earnest in his sleeplessness. But nothing more happened that day. The Gascons kept their guards at the tower doors, but otherwise stayed in their camp. At evening, in the tower, an egg, some sausage, bread, onions and mutton were cooked together and divided equally among the thirteen men besieged.

The next morning d'Albret came offering terms. "Let your prisoners go," he shouted, "then we'll let you leave."

"What guarantee will you give me of our safety?" Simon called down from the roof.

"Our word!"

Simon laughed loudly. "You'll have to offer more security than that!" He now stayed on the roof so he could see the Gascons' guards and camp.

The day passed. Its ration of food, drinkable wine and water from the cistern were consumed. And night came on.

It was a bright, warm night, lit with a broad splash of stars. Simon lay stretched out on the roof, looking up at the sky. From time to time he got up to squint at the Gascons' campfires. The dots of orange shimmered in the light breeze.

Simon kept a prisoner by him now. A rope binding the prisoner's hands behind his back was extended a little distance and tied around the waist of the soldier on watch. That night the prisoner was Elie Rudel.

The slender, young lord whom Simon had deprived of Blaye leaned against the parapet, looking at the stars and singing to himself.

Simon half listened and half dozed... till a soft, rustling sound near the foot of the tower, just below where Rudel stood, prodded him to alertness. Silently Simon stood up and crept across the roof, behind Rudel's back. He glanced over the wall.

Below, figures were moving quietly, piling tinder up against the postern door.

With the speed of battle reflex Simon pitched Rudel over the parapet. The soldier on watch, sitting at a few feet away with the rope tied around his middle, was jerked across the roof as the man fell. Simon caught the rope and braced himself against the parapet. The soldier scrambled to his feet and ran to help him. They looped a turn of the rope around the merlon.

His shoulders wrenched out of their sockets, Rudel hung screaming over the pyre of branches, dangling by his wrists behind his back.

"Set your fire!" Simon shouted down.

The Gascons stood back, shocked. Rudel was bellowing in agony.

"Haul him up, for pity's sake!" d'Albret called up. "We won't attack!"

Simon watched until the last of the kindling was taken away. Then he and the soldier hauled Rudel back onto the roof. Elie moaned with pain, both his shoulders were broken.

"Have Peter come up and see what he can do for him," Simon ordered the soldier. "And bring another prisoner to take his place."

The squire came and took Rudel, crying and groaning, down the stairs. And the soldier brought up a very frightened Guillaume de Rion.

The third day of the siege passed. The barons made no move, but kept the tower closely held. Food was running out. The hens, confined with little to eat, lay no more eggs. They were roasted on the caretaker's brazier, on a fire made of the empty wine cask staves.

Simon gazed toward the road all day, but Barres did not come.

On the fourth day of the siege no food remained except a few onions, garlic and the casks that indeed were vinegar, as the caretaker had said.

Sitting on the roof, sleepless and hollow-eyed, Simon came to a decision. He called his son to him. Henry squatted down beside him. "I'm going to offer the Gascons terms, Henry," Simon said quietly. "I'm going to offer them the archbishop in exchange for your freedom."

"Father I want to stay with you!" Henry protested.

But Simon had more to say. "They've let the horses off the tether lines to graze. As soon as you're outside the door, run as fast as you can to my destrier. I dare say he will be the fastest. Fly to our garrison at Cubzac. It's some fifteen or twenty miles further along the road from which we turned to come here. Tell them what has happened, and have them send a messenger to Barres at la Reole." He looked at the slender thirteen year old boy. "If the lords take hold of you, it is possible they'll try to use you in a way to force me to surrender. Do you understand?"

"Yes, father," Henry said gravely.

"I know you can run fast. And my horse will let you ride him without a saddle. Don't pause until you reach Cubzac."

"Yes, father." Henry spoke hardly above a whisper. He put his slim hand into his father's hand.

"I know you're brave," Simon tried to smile.

The agreement was made with d'Albret. As the Gascon lords stood at a little distance from the main door, the portcullis was raised, the inner door opened, and the archbishop and the boy stepped out.

The barons started to move forward. The portcullis dropped and Henry ran as fast as his long legs could carry him. With the swiftness of a sparrow he darted around the barons, past the camp and to the horses in the meadow. He hurled himself upon the familiar, great white destrier, clutching its mane and scrambling till his legs gripped its back. The horse, surprised, bolted and ran wildly for an instant. Henry, sprawled upon its neck, reached for its halter and pulled its head around to face the road. The animal, seeing the open road ahead, collected itself and leapt forward at full vollant.

The horse and the boy were gone. Several men ran from the Gascon camp with saddles, cinched them quickly on their horses, mounted and rode after them.

Simon watched from the tower's roof. When the last of the pursuers galloped out of sight, he turned to his squire, as pale as if his heart had not beaten since the boy stepped from the door. "Pray for him, Peter," he said low. "If they catch him, I shall not bear to see him hurt."

An hour later the Gascons who had ridden out returned. Henry was not with them. Simon, watching by the merlon, sank down to the roof and openly wept with relief. In a while he fell asleep, the first true sleep that he had slept for days. The soldiers and the squire kept watch through the night.

The cool air of dawn awoke Simon. He stood up and looked over the parapet. The Gascon guards stood and sat around the tower's doors. At the camp, a few men were beginning to emerge from their tents, prodding guttering campfires to life. Suddenly they seemed alert, pausing, listening. Some started back toward their tents.

In moments knights came riding through the camp, shouting and flailing with their swords. The Gascon barons ran. Men, half-dressed and naked, dashed out of their tents, scattering in every direction, running for their lives. The siege was routed. The lord Barres, on his sweated, steaming horse, was at the portcullis.

"Lord Viceroy, you're safe!" Barres cried, clearly well pleased with his morning's work.

Simon leaned over the parapet. "Is my son safe?"

"Henry's safe!"

"Why are you so late!" But before Barres could answer, Simon waved his hand. "I'm coming down. I've had enough of this place!"

Chapter Eighteen

King Henry in Gascony
1252-1253

"My son is safe at Cubzac?"

Amaubin nodded. "And he'll be glad to see you!"

As Simon breakfasted heartily with Barres in the Gascons' abandoned camp, he had the archbishop, who had been seized again, brought to him. "I'm releasing you," he told Malemorte. "I regret that you've suffered at my hands but, as my king has made me a renegade, I dared not risk surrender."

"May the Lord's curse be upon you!" the archbishop's heavy-browed eyes blazed. "You are an evil and an impious man, Sire Montfort!"

Barres, aggravated, stamped his foot at Malemorte. "Leave here, old frog! While you can still croak!" The archbishop hurried to the big horse that was held for him, and galloped away.

Barres continued, "We've had hard battling at La Reole. Bearne still holds the castle. When you didn't come, and it was clear d'Albret was missing, I came back as soon as I could. We met your messenger from Cubzac on the road last night. We didn't pause till we got here."

After paying the unhappy caretaker at Montauban for the consumed sausages, garlic, onions and the two slaughtered hens, Simon and his men and prisoners left, escorted by Barres and his knights. They rode on to Cubzac.

Below the massive towers of Cubzac young Henry sat on the grass, staring up the road. He had been at his lookout spot all morning. When he saw the company of riders coming, he got up and ran as fast as his legs would carry him until he reached his father's side.

Simon leaned down and pulled the boy up onto his saddle. Henry put his slender arms around his father's neck. They rode on, neither speaking, until the boy, his anxiety finally ebbing, said proudly, "I rode your destrier here all the way at a gallop bareback."

"You did well," Simon smiled.

Henry's face shone with pride.

Leaving his prisoners in Cubzac's strong fortress, Simon, his son and Barres' men went on to La Reole.

The bailey wall of the great castle on the Garonne had been undermined when Gaston de Bearne had taken it in the spring, but it had been repaired since then. From the road Simon dispatched a messenger to Bordeaux, ordering Colom to send the two mangonels at once to La Reole. The machines came the day after his own arrival there. Now he battered La Reole's hastily rebuilt wall until it collapsed again.

But by the time Simon seized the main tower of the castle, Bearne and Amanieu d'Albret had fled.

"They slip through my fingers like little fishes!" Simon raged. "Well, I know what they care for that cannot escape." He held meeting with his Norman knights. "For reward of your services to me, you may go to the villas of the lords Gaston de Bearne and Amanieu d'Albret, and all their followers. Take and do there as you please. But do this for me – cut off the grapevines at the root. Destroy the vineyards. I mean to serve these Gascons in a way they shall never forget!"

Simon, with his mercenary troops, remained at La Reole, rebuilding and fortifying the castle to be ready for full war in October, when King Henry was to come. Even Bacon's bronze device he ordered brought from its warehouse in Bordeaux and had it mounted on the roof of the castle's great tower.

But most of all Simon rested. His wounds were not healing well, with all of the exertions of the siege and its sleepless nights. His squire probed and sponged away infections with strong wine, and applied his herb salves thickly. Simon let himself be cared for. He slept much, and began to truly heal.

It was at La Reole that King Henry's agents, the Master of the Templars in England Rocelyn de Foss, and the royal secretary John Mansel, found Simon. They had been searching for him in England and in France for more than a month. No one in England knew where he had gone when he left King Henry's Court. They presented him with a royal order, commanding that he observe the truce the king had made with the Gascon lords.

The earl read the order with a look of mock surprise. "But how can I observe the truce when the Gascons attack me? Have you not heard? I was held at siege at Montauban when these good subjects of the king found me poorly guarded. As Henry well knew when he ordered my return to Gascony, I must defend myself as long as I am here."

"If you won't observe the truce," the Templar Foss said dryly, "we bear orders from the king that you resign your office of viceroy, relinquish the country to Prince Edward, now the Duke of Gascony, and place all castles that you hold into my keeping, as the king's and the duke's marshal."

"This seems more of caprice than reason," Simon smiled genially, after looking at the second letter that the Templar offered him. "No doubt King Henry's changed his mind a dozen times in the weeks since he issued this. I would be remiss in my duties if I paid any attention to it."

At Foss's and Mansel's stunned looks, Simon added blandly, "Good sires, as I'm sure you know, I have a contract with King Henry, often renewed and upheld, requiring my services here for seven years, almost three years of which remain. If Henry truly wished to terminate my services, he knows that he need only pay me what he owes for the debts I've incurred on his behalf, and I will gladly leave. Otherwise, I have no choice but to continue here as viceroy, with my own army which, thanks to the largesse of war, I can maintain indefinitely."

"You're holding Gascony to ransom!" Mansel burst out.

"I'm keeping my part of my contract," Simon said firmly. "Let the king keep his!"

Mansel and Foss returned to England with the earl's answer.

King Henry summoned his barons to declare the Earl of Leicester a traitor, a renegade in revolt against the Crown. He ordered the lords of England to arm for war.

But, gathered in the great hall at Westminster, the lords, as usual, had their own views.

"You ask for our services *and* this sum of seventy marks per man?" Ralph Basset raised his voice in dismay. "If we give our service, what is the money for?"

"The price of your passage," Henry answered the Warwickshire knight flatly.

"I can cross to Wissant for five marks," the knight persisted.

Henry rose from his chair. "Your objections are impertinent, Sire Basset! We cannot cross at Wissant and then march through France! Your passage directly to Bordeaux, with your men and horses, is seventy marks." He sat down again, crossing his legs and pettishly turning away in disgust at the quibbler.

But his reply had brought the room into an uproar. The Minister of the Treasury, de Riveaux, came to the edge of the dais, trying to calm the din of objections. He raised his hands, "We must sail to Bordeaux! Queen Blanche will not permit us to march through France to Gascony."

"Seventy marks from each of us amounts to a fortune!" The Earl Humphrey de Bohun snorted. "How much does the Crown owe the Earl of Leicester anyway?"

"The full and actual sum is now nine-thousand, two-hundred-and-thirty-two marks, including the interest owed to the Hospitallers at Leicester for the first loan," Prince Richard answered promptly, having Simon's account books in his keeping from the trial. Henry shot an angry glance at him, but Richard looked back coolly.

"Let's pay the nine-thousand-some-odd and stay home!" Bohun cried back. "We'll save ourselves money, war and possible injury."

Henry stood up, glaring at Bohun. "We go to war against Montfort!"

"He'll leave Gascony if he's paid what he's owed!" Roger Bigod shouted back. "Go fight him if you want, we'd rather pay him off!"

Seeing the meeting reeling out of order, Henry waved his hands, "Very well!" he shouted. "I'll offer Montfort his declared terms. We'll pay him what he asks! And we'll see if he vacates Gascony! You'll end by paying more, and going to war too!"

King Henry sent to Simon the offer of full reimbursement, on condition he quit Gascony.

Guillaume Colom was with Simon at La Reole when he received the royal messenger. The earl read the letter aloud.

A broad, dimpled grin spread over Colom's face as he listened. "The tail that wags the dog is twisted in your hand, my lord, and the dog yelps. If you hold out for a hundred thousand marks as price of leaving, I'll wager you will get it."

Colom's leering suggestion shocked Simon. "I ask only what is owed me."

"You're passing up a fortune!" the merchant looked dismayed. "A hard earned one at that!"

"I want only that my contract with the king be kept. I don't intend to make base use of my advantage."

Colom gazed at the earl as though he were a madman. "Advantage is the whole point of life," he muttered.

Simon sent his answer to King Henry, accepting his offer. He directed that the money be put to his credit at the Hospital of Saint John in Paris.

While he waited at La Reole for Henry's reply, a courier came to Simon from Queen Blanche. He delivered a small strip of parchment with no seals, but written in the queen's own hand which Simon knew well enough, though this sample was feeble and erratic. The note was brief.

I am ill and hope to struggle no more with this world. I must speak with you one last time. Come to me at once at the Abbey of Maubuisson at Pontoise.

The courier urged, "Good earl, my lady the queen is very weak. It is not possible that she can live much longer. I am to beg you, in her name, to come at once."

Simon waited no longer for Henry's answer. He gave command to the sergeants of his garrison that, if he did not return in two weeks, they were to obey Prince Edward's stewards when they came. He bade his Norman knights to wait two weeks, and then go home if he was not back in that time. Keeping his mercenaries for a bodyguard, he rode north with his son and squire, out of Gascony.

Pontoise was wrapped in the held breath of expectation. Even the keeper of the abbey's gate spoke in a hushed voice. A quiet had seeped through the countryside as though in deference to the impending death, and spread from Pontoise throughout France. Simon moved through the eddying gray silence to the sickroom at its heart.

In a grand, canopied bed Blanche lay, emaciated, paralyzed. She had suffered a stroke and could move only her fingers and her eyes. Expressionless but still aware, her eyes followed Simon as he came into the room.

"The queen has not spoken for a day now," the nun tending her told Simon.

Blanche's fingertips reached out, quivering above the bedclothes. Simon took her hand, gently pressing its smooth, chill skin in his warm hand.

Her eyes seemed to smile. A noise came from her throat as she tried to form words. But the effort was too much.

"Good Earl, the queen spoke of you to the Archbishop of Rouen before the paralysis came on," the nun told Simon. "I know she wished to speak to you directly. Perhaps he knows whereof."

The bony hand pressed Simon's in acknowledgment, and the eyes took on an urging look.

Not wanting to leave her, Simon sat on a stool by the bed, holding her hand. But she clearly wanted him to go and find the archbishop, and he soon went.

Odo Rigaud greeted him solemnly but warmly. "It is very good you've come. France is in a sorry way, with Louis in Palestine, his heir so young, and the Queen Regent dying." He paused, looking at Simon earnestly. Then, "Queen Blanche has directed me to ask you to remain in France – as Regent. Should King Louis ever return, she has advised us to offer you the title Steward of France."

Simon was astounded. "But what of Louis' brother Alphonse?"

"He is not suitable," Rigaud said in an undertone. "The queen and I know well that were he placed in power, the lords would not accept him, whereas they hold you in highest regard. For our young prince's sake, we ask you."

Simon's lips began to tremble, he felt weak as if the world had turned beneath him, leaving him afloat and in confusion. "You have such faith in me..." he knelt and kissed the archbishop's hand. Since he was a boy, serving as page in France's Court, Rigaud had been chief councilor of France. Now Rigaud was placing the power of the Crown into his hands. Overwhelmed that there were those who thought so well of him, after such danger and such ignominy as he had been enduring, he felt breathless, overcome, unsure if a great weight was lifted from him, or a far greater one was descending to crush him to the ground. But most of all, he felt like an exile finally permitted to come home, and home to an honor higher than any he could ever have imagined.

The archbishop put his arm around Simon and raised him up, murmuring, "Queen Blanche has great faith in you. Go! Tell her that you will accept."

Simon went back the queen's bedside. He tenderly took her hand again, "Yes, I will stay. I'll serve you, and the king and prince, as regent or Steward of France." His voice broke and he began to weep. Sinking down to the stool again, he buried his face in the coverlet, beside her hand.

Blanche moved her fingers to stroke his hair. Between the clenched teeth of her rigid jaw she formed the words, "You are good, Simon."

A few hours later Queen Blanche died.

The mourning Court in solemn progress conducted her catafalque to Paris. At Saint Denis, among the ancient kings of France, Blanche's body was set to rest with grand and tender ceremony, as if she were a saint.

A few days later the Archbishop Rigaud, as Minister of State, summoned all the lords of France to Paris.

The deaths of so many of the lords on the crusade had stripped away a generation in its prime, and brought their sons and younger brothers to the Great Council of France. They had come together for the first time at Blanche's summons to raise the ransom for the survivors of the crusade. They had met again to receive word of Louis' pledge that he would never leave Palestine. They had watched as the Queen Regent sank toward death. Now Rigaud convened them to receive their new Regent. It was the first hope of a stable, sustained governance that they had known. They welcomed Simon with an unpent flood of relief.

On the Isle de la Cite, in the vast double gabled hall of the palace, Simon, in his black robe, knelt on the steps of the dais before the two empty chairs of the dead queen regent and the absent king. Beside the chairs stood the Archbishop Rigaud and a frail boy, also dressed in black: nine-year-old Prince Louis. Solemnly Simon renounced his fealty to England and pledged himself to France, to King Louis and to his heir. The boy pressed his chill hands around Simon's clasped hands, and the archbishop bestowed his blessing.

There was no celebration. The Court was in deep mourning. Simon quietly took up the business of the State. He met the next day with the Great Council. Though his nearsightedness could distinguish few faces beyond the first row of the clergy, the sea of young lords all seemed welcoming. The lords of Brittany and La Marche, those who chiefly had thought ill of Simon, who had been his enemies, were dead – except for Thibaut of Champagne and Navarre, and he did not respond to the summons.

France was placed in Simon's hands, with no opposition. Even Prince Alphonse seemed relieved.

But Simon's heart was grave, not triumphant. Through the long winter the Court remained subdued, sunk in mourning.

Living in the palace, walking alone freely through the long series of rooms and corridors that terminated in the dead queen's or the absent king's chambers and the winter desolation of the garden, Simon felt like a page again, not master of France. Early lessons that

Louis was king, and he only his servant, weighed him like an anchor dragging somewhere far below the waterline of consciousness. He longed for Louis' return. He longed to serve as Steward for his friend. Not as Regent, as though Louis were dead.

He took the sickly prince to his father's chamber, and had him kneel at the prie-dieu. "Pray for your father in the Holy Land," Simon told the boy, his hands upon the child's blond head. "Pray that Our Father in Heaven keeps him safe, and brings him back to France." And he added a prayer of his own silently for Louis' fragile-seeming heir.

With the first spring convoy of ships to Palestine, a letter from the Great Council was sent to Louis, informing him of his mother's death, and of the regency of Simon de Montfort. The letter begged the king's return, and informed him of his mother's wish that, should he return, Montfort be named Steward of France.

The letter was the work of Simon and Rigaud. But no one really thought that Louis would break his vow and come home.

As regent, Simon set about putting France into better defense. Knowing England's never-ending wish to regain her lost duchies in France, he sent funds and plans for the improvement of the Crown's castles, from Coucy to Frontenaye and southward through Poitou. As he had done in Palestine, he took measures to encourage trade, using the Crown's taxes to repair roads and see that travel was secure. The lessons he had learned as Mayor of Jerusalem and Governor of Outremere during his years in the East, he applied now to France, fostering prosperity and loyalty to the Crown. And France indeed prospered.

In February, the Countess Eleanor arrived in Paris with her children, her servants and all that the Montforts owned that could be moved to France. Their life in England was ended.

For Eleanor, the regency bestowed on Simon was the final proof of her brother Henry's failure to see her husband's worth. She was elated, full of victory over the petty wrongs and mortal dangers that had filled their lives in England. But the countess's heady spirits clashed with her husband's subdued frame of mind.

"Surely it was for this that your life was spared from the crusade! Regent of France! All but king yourself!" Her face beamed with extreme satisfaction. "You were clearly spared to serve your own country. How fitting!"

"Perhaps," Simon tried to smile. "Yet I feel the burden far more than the honor."

But the countess's spirits were in tune with the Court's rising mood. The gloom that had hung over France ever since the loss of the crusade, was lifting. The Court, which had long lived in dread of what would happen after the old queen's death, had found new life. Mourning was still worn by the regent's own command, but a spirit like a fresh spring breeze gave lightness to the courtiers' tread. Open smiles met Simon everywhere. Secretly, Court gossip spoke of Louis as abandoning France. He was unworthy of the Crown. The nobles looked hopefully at their regent.

Simon knew their thinking, and was not pleased.

But there was one matter that brought a smile to his lips. If King Henry truly had believed his viceroy was the cause of Gascony's unrest, he had been shown the lie. News from the south was that the province was in complete chaos. No sooner had Simon left, than the lord of Bearne had gone to King Alphonse of Castile, betraying Henry and offering Spain his homage. Again the raids, the extortionate tolls on the roads, the holding of travelers for ransom had brought all travel and collection of taxes to a halt. By February, Gascony was again as Simon had first found it. He was much amused.

There were rumors that King Henry planned to command an army himself, to retake the land from the queen's rebel cousin Gaston de Bearne.

Then summer brought the first returning ships from Palestine. An answer came from Louis. The King of France would leave the Holy Land, and return home to his throne. He was reinforcing Outremer, rebuilding the defenses of Caesarea. When he was done he would set sail – not later than the coming year, 1254.

There was a private letter for Simon. Louis thanked him warmly for his services as regent, but in a wording strained with care, he said the office of Steward of France already was bestowed by him upon a young knight who had served him in the East, the lord of Joinville. Louis made no compensating offer.

Simon sat a long time with the letter in his hand. He read its brief message again and again. The countess found him sitting in the garden, staring at the letter.

"What can be the matter?" she asked with concern.

He looked up at her. "There is no recompense. I was not with the crusade, and nothing I do here can compensate that failure." His voice was hollow, echoing from the pit of his heart. He shook his head. "Louis will be back. And there will be no place here for us." He handed her the letter.

The countess read. "What is this? But surely Louis knows what you have done for him! How can this be! How can he do this!"

"He is free to bestow office as he wishes," Simon said bleakly.

"What sort of man is he who vows to stay in Palestine, then breaks his vow to come back here and upset everything!" she railed. "And this person Joinville. Who is he to be Steward of France!"

"When you have only a few men left to you, even the least among them becomes precious. It is my misfortune that I was not one of the few."

Crushed by Louis' letter, Simon moved through the days dully, forcing himself to pay attention to the business of the Court. But when his time was his own, he sat on the garden's parapet, sunk in thought, watching the creamy brown waves of the Seine rising and falling against the castle wall below. The heavy roses in the garden's parterres flooded him with their perfume, a scent freighted with memories of his childhood and his youth: of afternoons with Louis when they both were boys; of Queen Blanche when she was fresh and lovely, surrounded by her ladies; of Johanna, the Princess of Flanders, his betrothed. Thoughts of the life from which he had been parted haunted him, setting in sharp focus the strangeness, the hardness of the life that had befallen him since he first left France. He lingered in the pleasant recollections of his early life, unable to make sense of how Fate toyed with him since then, unable to bring his mind to bear upon the present, or the future. For, once again, his future was a void.

He tried to focus on where he should go, what he should do, when Louis returned. Henry had seized Leicester and Kenilworth. And, of course, when he left Gascony, Henry ceased to feel the need to pay him the nine thousand marks. Simon's mind, wearied, crippled with disappointments, sank into despair.

In August news came to Paris that King Henry had reached Bordeaux. He brought with him the army of England's lords to prosecute the war against the Gascons and Gaston de Bearne.

One day in mid-October Simon sat in the garden with Grosseteste's book, *Saint Mary the Egyptian,* in his hands. Like the saint of the story, he found himself an aimless wanderer in a world of emptiness, brought to such helplessness that faith alone must be his guide. Stripped of purpose, of expectation, even of hope, he found comfort in Grosseteste's tale.

He was turning the pages pensively, feeling something of the settled peace of those who resign themselves to faith, when the Countess Eleanor came striding angrily out of the chamber door. A messenger in England's royal livery followed her.

"Here is audacity!" she declared, gesturing at the messenger.

"Don't abuse him," Simon frowned at her. "You have a letter for me?" he asked the cringing messenger.

"A letter from His Majesty the King of England, if you please, good Earl." He offered a parchment with the large royal seal closing its tab.

Simon broke the tab and unfolded the letter. In Mansel's tidy handwriting it said,

"We command and request that you come to us in Gascony to discuss matters with us. If you think that it befits neither our honor nor yours to remain with us, you may withdraw when you please without incurring our displeasure. Knowing that the roads are dangerous for you, we have directed the Earl of Norfolk our Marshal, the Earl of Gloucester and our brother Guy de Lusignan, with other of our knights, to conduct you safely to us, and from our company if such be your wish. Throughout the time that you remain with us you shall have nothing to fear from those who wish you ill."

When he had finished reading, Simon, with an ironic smile, showed the letter to his wife. "Here is someone who values my services more highly than Louis does. Henry summons me to Gascony."

"You won't consider going, surely!" She was horrified. "It can be nothing but a trap!"

"Is it not Our Lord's command to turn the other cheek?" he asked grimly.

Simon met with the Archbishop Rigaud for his advice regarding Henry's letter.

"As you must know, I'm deeply disappointed with the outcome of the stewardship," Rigaud said heavily. "But since Louis offers no provision for you here, we cannot urge you to remain with us. God be with you, Simon! Had I a son, and you were he, I could not love you better. But I cannot countermand King Louis' choice. You must do what is best for you."

"I've searched my mind for what I am to do. In France I've felt as one who is at last permitted to come home. And yet I know no place or purpose for me here. Or any future for my sons. It may be best that I find what King Henry wants of me. And what he offers."

Rigaud embraced him, "May Our Lord guide and protect you!" He placed his hand on Simon's head in blessing.

In a few days, after formally transferring the power of the regency to the able archbishop, Simon took his leave of the French Court.

He rode south with his squire to meet the earls Bigod and Clare and Guy de Lusignan at Angouleme. He found the three idling over a game of dice in the common room of the town's largest inn. De Clare and Bigod were both wreathed in smiles at seeing him. Even Lusignan gave him a hearty welcome.

"I had not thought that life would bring me into your company again so amiably as this." Simon looked around, "Where is your guard to arrest me?"

"Far from it, lord Earl," de Clare assured him. "It's a wonder that Henry didn't send heralds to make your way, with strewn rose petals and a fanfare of horns."

"The truth is, we don't gain an inch against Bearne and the Gascon bastards," Bigod said bluntly. "Not an inch since we arrived! Henry looks to you as someone who works wonders. If ever there was a model of contrition!"

"Truly? But he declared me a renegade..."

"All is forgiven and forgotten," Guy de Lusignan smiled broadly.

Simon looked to Clare, whom he had come to trust as a sharer in the king's disfavor. "Can I believe this?"

Clare met his eyes earnestly. "You know better than any other man that the king is changeable. Right now he looks to you to defend his very life. But, above all, *we* would have you in England again. You are needed."

Simon met Clare's look. He understood the young earl spoke of Grosseteste's plans against untrammeled sovereignty. "What you ask for England, I've no wish to take a share in. I'm not the man you want."

"Lord Earl, such modesty," Lusignan broke in. "Who else can thrash the Gascons as you have?" His bluff camaraderie made it clear he had no knowledge of the meaning of Simon's words addressed to Clare.

"Have you heard? "Clare asked. "Our beloved Bishop Grosseteste has died."

The unexpected news struck Simon like a blow. "I had not heard..."

"He had great faith in you," Clare said with freighted meaning.

"A faith misplaced I fear... Yes, I would wish to go to England... to pay my respects at his tomb." He sighed. "Very well, I will go with you to Henry, and if it is God's will that I return, so be it."

"Ah," Bigod breathed with relief. "I don't know how we'd face Henry if you didn't come back with us."

Where is the king?" Simon asked numbly.

"At La Reole," Bigod replied.

"With that as his stronghold, he can't be in so very bad a way," Simon tried to smile.

"His stronghold!" Bigod scoffed. "We're on the outside trying to get in. And praying that we do before Bearne's army from Castile comes up and takes us from the rear!"

Simon, with his squire, went south with the two earls and Lusignan, surrounded by a guard of royal knights.

In the trampled and uprooted vineyard across the river from the fortress of La Reole, Simon was ushered into the king's tent.

Henry was dressed magnificently for battlefield in a gilded chain mail hauberk covered by a surcoat of red velvet with the strutting lions of Plantagenet worked in golden thread. Partly sitting, partly leaning against his camp table, he held in his hand a heavy steel arrow, a quarrel, which he studied with apparent concentration. "Have you ever seen such a thing as this before?" he asked, as if his brother-in-law had just stepped out, and returned after no more than a half-hour's absence.

Simon frowned at Henry's way of dealing, or not dealing, with the situation. But he took the steel quarrel and looked at it. "Yes. I had these made."

"I should have known that these were yours," Henry gave a mock scowl that almost closed his sagging eye. "The devil's own handiwork! At least a dozen of them have been hurled at us amidst the most colossal burst of thunder anyone has ever heard!"

"Really?" Simon's interest was piqued.

"How do they loft them?" the king asked.

"They can be fitted to a mangonel. It was for that I had them made," Simon said warily.

"No mangonel ever caused a noise like that," Henry took back the quarrel and turned it butt-end up. "Look at this. It's burnt."

"Did any of them hit their mark?"

"One struck a squire. But most fell short of us, burying themselves in the ground. I suspect you know quite well how they were lofted." Henry raised his one moblie eyebrow and gazed at the earl.

Simon smiled at Henry's coy approach. "There is, up on the fortress's battlement, a bronze device, a copy of a weapon that the emperor has. Round stones, small missiles that are charge for a catapult, or quarrels can be put into the vessel's mouth. Fire is set to a wick in the vessel's side, and it belches with great force and sound." He omitted any mention of the black powder. "How many successful shots have there been so far?"

"Four or five, if you can call such an infernal, ill aimed thing successful."

Simon looked amazed. "That many? I'd have thought by now the weapon would have proved more deadly to the men loading it, than to us."

"To us? Then you are with us?" Without leaving time for an answer, Henry raised his head so that his drooping eye looked in Simon's eyes. "I owe you an apology. Never have I been so wrong as to believe the Gascons, and doubt you. Can you forgive me? Let me restore your earldom to you. And reward you, as I now fully, and most painfully, understand you ought to be rewarded. Will you permit me to make amends?"

Simon looked away from the king, chagrined. "My lord, I ask nothing more than what I have always asked. To have my rightful English titles, to be cleared of debt, and to live in peace."

"Three months! That's all I ask of you. Before, in just three months, you laid Gascony beneath your feet. Give me three months time again, and then go home to Kenilworth."

Simon agreed.

Taking command of England's army in King Henry's name, he opened his campaign to retake Gascony yet again. He undermined La Reole at the point in the wall he knew was weak. The wall was breached, and in a day the castle was retaken. Then, with that citadel as base, he pursued d'Albret, Fronzac and their allies, laying waste to every place that gave the Gascon barons refuge as they fled.

The Bishop of Hereford, Peter Aigueblanche, and the royal clerk John Mansel were sent as ambassadors to the Court of Castile, to sever the Gascons' alliance and cut off their source of aid. When the ambassadors returned, the bishop, beaming smiles, presented Henry with the draft of a new treaty with Castile.

"King Alphonse values peace with England far above any gain that he might have from Bearne," Aigueblanche reported proudly. "He goes so far as to insist the bond be sealed by a royal marriage.

He asks that the Prince Edward wed the Infanta, King Alphonse's own sister."

Henry and Simon both looked at Aigueblanche with astonishment. Alphonse of Castile was a man of advanced years.

"The king's sister in question is a maid of but eleven years of age," the bishop added quickly. "She seems both modest and devout. Alphonse is very set upon the match."

"This seems hasty," Simon cautioned. "Edward is only fourteen years old."

"I know Edward's age," Henry said rather testily. "It would be most suitable if you – in your capacity as Steward of England – determined if this term of the peace can be accepted. As I recall, you didn't approve my choice of bride," he smiled ironically. "You may be wise for Edward, for your heart is in the issue."

Simon's dark eyes studied Henry, but there seemed nothing threatening in his manner. "Indeed I'm fond of your son the prince. I'll gladly fulfill the commission, with England's and the prince's good in mind," he bowed.

"We're certain that you will," King Henry smiled.

Simon went with Aigueblanche and Mansel back to Castile. In three weeks he returned to La Reole.

"The treaty is accepted by King Alphonse, complete with your amendments," he reported. "I see no reason to bar this peace treaty between England and Castile."

"What of the Infanta?" Henry asked. "You found her acceptable?"

"Castile is noted for its ladies well-brought up. Queen Blanche was of Castile..."

Henry interrupted with a wave of his hand. "I know your nearly sainted foster-mother was King Alphonse's aunt. I'm certain the child reeks of piety. But is she at least pretty?"

"She is beautiful. With the face of an angel and a spirit to match," Simon grinned. "She would make a gentle and wise queen for any monarch. And, you'll be pleased to know, her name is Eleanor."

"Another Eleanor!" Henry laughed outright. "Let Edward have her then. Eleanors are to our taste, are they not my Steward?"

End: Book III

Historical Context

IN HIS YEARS AS VICEROY of Gascony, 1248 to 1253, Simon de Montfort developed the skills that enabled him later to seize England and transform its government. He may also have learned, from his painful experience in Gascony, some moderation of his military skills if any long term success was to be achieved.

The events of this book principally follow the Bemont biographies of 1884 and 1930 as they are the fullest in reproducing the surviving records of the period. But I have used many other sources, and have made point to be influenced by what Simon was reading as evidenced by the covering letters, preserved in the *Monumenta Franciscana*, that came with the loans of books from his Franciscan friends.

A note about names and numbers:

Simon de Montfort the Earl of Leicester has been variously numbered by scholars as Simon de Montfort III, IV, V and even VI. These numbers are becoming more confusing than helpful.

In any case, 13th century usage reserved numbers principally for kings. The repetitiousness of names within a family commonly was overcome by the use of descriptive appellations. Thus the Simon with whom this book is concerned was known as Simon de Montfort the Earl, or Earl of Leicester. Before his receiving his titles, Henry refers to him simply as "our Simon de Montfort." His father was Simon the Crusader, his son: Simon the Younger or Simon Fils.

Except in the chronicles and some official documents, King Henry was not usually referred to as Henry III, but simply King Henry. He referred to himself, when trying to identify himself during the Battle of Evesham, as Henry of Monmouth after the place of his birth. Queen Eleanor was designated Eleanor of Provence.

Eleanor, Simon's wife, was often Eleanor of Pembroke after her title of Countess of Pembroke from her first marriage, even though she was widowed at age fifteen. Simon's daughter Eleanor was designated Eleanor la Demoiselle.

"we have no choice but to relieve him of the burdens...": Though Henry deprived Richard of his dukedom, he did not formally invest Edward with the title until the prince had come of age at thirteen years old. Richard was nearly shipwrecked and drowned on his flight back to England. See Matthew Paris, *Rerum Britannicarum*, Vol. V, pp. 291-293 and Maddicott, *Simon de Montfort*, p. 116.

"I'll make good my sister's rents out of the royal purse" See: Bemont, *Simon de Montfort*, 1930, p. 68 for reference to the contemporary documentation of this. Also: "At the request of countess Beatrice of Provence, King Henry's mother-in-law, who came to England at the end of 1243 with her youngest daughter Sanchia, the fiancée of Richard of Cornwall, the king consented to perform certain 'acts of bounty' towards his sister, the countess of Leicester..." Translated from *Bibl. nat. Ms.lat., 9016, number 6*. See Bemont, *Simon de Montfort*, 1976 reprint, p. 335-339 for the original document, and Maddicott, *Simon de Montfort*, pp. 32-33.

He spent hours with the master builder: Building of the new abbey was commenced in 1245, and was ultimately to cost an estimated 450,000 pounds. A loaf of bread (to use Adam Smith's calculations of wheat as the basic value of an economy) at that time cost a farthing. There were four farthings to a penny, and 240 pennies to a pound. 450,000 pounds equaled 108,000,000 pence, or 432,000,000 farthings. I purchased a loaf of bread today (January 30, 2010) for $2.50. At that rate, Westminster Abbey in today's dollars would have cost $172,800,000. At this evening's exchange rate that is 107,217,314 pounds, or 124,675,321.33 Euros.

as Christmas neared, the royal revelers moved on to Wallingford: In his usual, laconic way, Brother Matthew describes Richard's wedding and the celebrations at Wallingford. "In the year of grace 1244, which is the twenty-eighth year of the reign of King Henry the Third, the same king was, at Christmas, the guest of his brother, Earl Richard, at Wallingford, when a sumptuous banquet was given, to which nearly all the English nobility had been invited: this was the finish of the festivities commenced in London, where everything that could be thought of was brought forward to terminate worthily the nuptial ceremonies." Matthew Paris, *Chronica Majora,* trans. J.A Giles, Kessinger reprint as Matthew Paris's English History, V1, p. 478.

In February of 1244 King Henry called a meeting of the barons. See Matthew Paris, *Rerum Britannicarum,* Vol. IV, p. 294. Paris's interest in this meeting of the barons is chiefly regarding the protests of the bishops of Lincoln, Worchester and Hereford against King Henry's continued harassment of the See of Winchester, where the monks of the Chapter refused to agree to the king's appointing of a bishop.

The preceding bishop, Peter de Roche, was a Poitouvin and Henry's principal guardian during his childhood. De Roche had used his position to enrich himself tremendously. Henry's intent was to place one of his relatives as bishop and take for himself the riches Roche had accumulated and which now were the property of the See of Winchester. This issue dragged on for years, with the monks choosing their own bishop, whom Henry drove out of England. With the death of this Bishop of Winchester in France, Henry finally succeeded in placing his own candidate, his young half-brother Amaury de Lusignan, as bishop. (*RB,* Vol. V, p. 343.) This episode became one of the clergy of England's chief causes of complaint against the king's "tyranny".

The Lusignan brothers' criminal misdoings are recorded in irate detail by Brother Matthew pp. 343-345. It was common practice for them to demand free service at inns, and at one time they tortured and murdered their cook. However, as adept poisoners themselves, they may have had cause in the case of the cook.

According to Paris, the king did establish a "council" – consisting of John Mansel, his secretary, and Lawrence of Saint Martins, of whom we know little else. Such a "council" would have been a travesty of the body of representatives of the barons and clergy that Grosseteste had in mind. See also Maddicott, *Montfort*, p. 34

the Emperor means to grind money out of Henry. The Holy Roman Emperor, Frederic II, claimed kingship over the Christian kingdom of Outremere in Palestine. Since the First Crusade had established a permanent Christian community of knightly families, their Crown of Jerusalem had been bestowed upon their elected king, but the sovereignty had devolved upon a single family whose heiress, the twelve-year-old Yolanda of Jerusalem, the Emperor Frederic had married.

Not observing the custom that child marriages should not be consummated until the bride reached maturity, Frederic impregnated Yolanda and she died giving birth to a son, Conrad. Frederic might have properly claimed the regency on his son's behalf, but he claimed the kingship for himself outright, much to the outrage of his subjects, the lords of Outremere, who tried to refuse him their fealty. Through his own Order of Teutonic Knights, Frederic maintained his hold on Outremere and a precarious balance of power. As King Henry's brother-in-law (he now was married to Henry's sister Isabel) and ally, he often turned to Henry for aid in money or fighting forces.

A people called the Khoresines: Also referred to as Khwarismians and Choermains, these people were from Persia, displaced by the Mongols of the Khan Ogodai. In 1244 they captured Jerusalem and defeated the lords of Outremere decisively near Gaza. See Labarge, *Saint Louis*, p. 97, and especially Runciman, *The History of the Crusades*, Vol. III, pp. 249-254 for a full discussion of the internal politics of the Khwarismians, of the Mongols, and the impact of the invasion upon Islam. The letter of Robert the Patriarch of Jerusalem, describing the debacle, is printed in Matthew Paris, *Chronica Majora*, trans. J.A Giles, Kessinger reprint, pp. 522-529.

There also has been preserved a letter from the Emperor Frederic on this subject giving a fair sample of his florid style: "Frederick, by the grace of God, emperor of the Romans, ever Augustus, king of Jerusalem and Sicily, to his beloved brother-in-law Richard, earl of Cornwall, greetings and the assurances of sincere affection – 'In Rama was there a voice heard, a lamentation and weeping, and great moaning;' – a voice which report before spread abroad as the forerunner of our sadness... There were numerous peals of thunder which resounded about Jerusalem, and announced the future tempest, the bloody extermination of Christ's followers..." Frederic refers to the invaders as "Choermains." See Matthew Paris, Kessinger reprint, pp. 491- 496 for the full text. Matthew follows with further description of the debacle and a letter from the Master of the Hospitallers of Jerusalem, pp. 496-500.

the Pope begging asylum in France. He fears the emperor. The conflict between the Holy Roman Emperors and the Popes persisted for generations, with the supporters of the Popes known as the Guelfs, and the Emperors' faction known as the Ghebellines. Frederic II was born after his father's death, and his mother died in childbirth. Brought up in the care of his mother's Moslem physicians, he had an insouciant attitude toward the Church and felt freer to harass the Popes than had his predecessors. Principally it was his disrespectful behavior toward the Church that earned him the name *Stupor Mundi*, the Wonder of the World. Among his provocative actions, he seized papal lands claiming he was merely relieving the Pope of worldly cares.

the Montfort household went on eyre of the Leicester manors. It was customary for an entire lordly family to move from one to another of their fiefs in the course of a year. This was considered good practice to discourage graft and pilfering, and to retain the loyalty and good will of their villeins.

It has been suggested that the purpose of the eyre was to use up the local produce of each fief, rather than cart it to a single manor. But moving the whole household from fief to fief surely was more costly and troublesome than carting each fief's produce to a single location. For when the lord's household moved, *everything* was moved. His manors were not furnished separately. Very nearly all the furniture (*meubles* movables): every bed, chest, chair and cooking utensil had to be moved, and meals and lodging had to be provided while the family and most of their servants were on the road.

Beds were disassembled to bundles of boards, and loaded with their straw or feather mattresses into wagons or the freight saddles of sumpter horses – a specific horse designated to carry each bed. One horse bore the furnishings of the lord's chapel. Several carried the clothing, straw mattresses and bedding of all the lesser folk of the household. Still others carried the food to be prepared while traveling, and bags of horse fodder. There were horses for kitchen utensils and a horse for each disassembled table. Alternatively, large wagons might carry the household utensils, clothing, bed curtains, armaments, valuable documents and records, table clothes and napkins, and the silver serving vessels that were packed in barrels stuffed with straw. How large such wagons could be is evident from a law of King Henry's that roads should be wide enough for fourteen knights to ride abreast, or two wagons to pass each other.

The Montforts' fiefs at Desford, Chilton, Hinkley and Ashby were fairly near Leicester. Kenilworth is some twenty miles from Leicester, but a stopover at one of the outlying fiefs easily could have been accomplished in a day's travel from Kenilworth. But travel from Kenilworth, in the midlands, to Odiham, in the south, would have taken about a week, if the route were direct and passed through Oxford. The Montforts' Chawton is about ten miles from Odiham. Chawton is better known as Jane Austin's village. Her brother resided in the lovely little manor that had been Simon's lodge. The Montforts, with all their baggage, frequently traveled the even longer route from Kenilworth via London to Odiham, which could have added another week to the travel time. Paris records an incident when a Montfort wagon went off the road at Dorking, which is on the Odiham – London route.

With their flag borne at the head of their progress, lordly families rode palfreys with gilded saddles, with heavily padded saddlecloths and mantels of satin that reached to their horses' hooves. A noble eyre through the countryside was the grandest spectacle that most country folk would ever see, and if they were near a main road they saw many.

The family's waiting women, stewards, clerks and clergy rode horses or mules, while the footmen, porters, stablemen, kitchen boys, maids and other servants walked beside the wagons, which were pulled by teams of oxen. Dogs, hawks and extra horses were brought along, with their attendant kennel men and stable boys. The lord's chief stableman and farrier were responsible for keeping the horses well fed, healthy and shod, and the wagons in good repair on the march. The cook and kitchen staff had to prepare two meals each day for everyone no matter where they were, and the household steward kept accounts of all expenditures on the road.

The average speed for a lordly eyre was about fifteen miles a day. Covering that same ground, a messenger, traveling day and night and changing horses, could travel sixty miles. According to the witness of his seal, given one day in one place and another place the following day, Simon at least once traveled a distance of seventy-five miles in a single day.

The leisurely amble of an eyre, with its very slowly changing scenery, was undertaken chiefly in the summertime and looked upon as a great treat. Servants could chat and flirt. The lord and lady could fly their hawks at small game that might be added to their dinner menu. The young folk were freed from their books to develop their riding skills, or practice on their lutes or harps, their horses easily following in the parade without much need of hands on reins. The lord's cleric would dole out alms to the poor who knelt beside the march to beg. Gaudily dressed, strolling trouveres or troubadours might join the progress, bringing news and gossip, and tales of chivalry as well as their songs. Peddlers offered food and drink, or trinkets. The road itself was something of a traveling fair.

There were inconveniences of course. Drivers of freight wagons were notoriously rude. Wagon breakdowns, the passing of too many lordly eyres, and the driving along of wandering pigs, sheep, geese and cattle on market days caused traffic jams. But if stops were necessary, almost no stretch of road in the heart of England lacked inns at more than five-mile intervals. The roads passed down the main streets of every village on the way. See Labarge, *A Baronial Household of the Thirteenth Century.*

"There is matter I would have you negotiate for me in France," Henry told him. *"The Truce of Blaye will end soon. Treat with Louis for renewal of its terms."* See Bemont, *Montfort,* 1930, pp 70-72. During this stay in Paris Simon probably met Roger Bacon. It was at this time that the university applied to King Louis to expel Bacon from his rooms for making foul odors. See below, note on the use of cannon and gunpowder: *Roger Bacon had succeeded...*

Genoese shipbuilders were commissioned... King Louis' extensive preparations for his crusade are thoroughly described in Labarge, *Saint Louis,* pp. 98 to 105.

"...mend matters for me in Gascony and I shall grant you whatever you ask." See Bemont, Montfort, 1930, p. 76 and footnote 1: "We have indeed the original patent of Henry III granting the earl (1 May 1248) everything he asked. This patent, interestingly, is not mentioned in the Calendar of Patent Rolls. The original is in the *Bibliotheque Nationale, Clairembault 1188."* See also: Maddicott, *Montfort,* p.108; and LaBarge, *Gascony, England's First Colony, 1204-1453,* p. 19.

"My lord, these are the men who were given me. They are all true knights. But most of them were prisoners of the Crown." See: *Calendar of Patent Rolls 1247-1258,* pp. 2, 9 and 31; and *Close Rolls 1247-1251* p. 119.
Close Roll 1247-1251, p. 85 provides the example of Hugo de Tywa, who was in the king's jail, held by the sheriff of Yorkshire for his inability to pay a fine of 100 pounds, the penalty for a crime of which he had been found guilty. Hugo's brother John volunteered to serve in Gascony until Easter on his brother's behalf. Presumably Hugo was ordered released.

In all likelihood, John, for his kindness to his brother, lost his life with the other English knights at La Reole. The wall of the fortress, where it overlooks the river, in Simon's time would have been fitted with roofed hoardings, like a long shed cantilevered out from the parapet. This structure would have served as barracks for the garrison. I was told by my guide at La Reole that this parapet is haunted, and the cries of the murdered English knights occasionally can be heard.

On the first day of court, held in the town's castle, Dax's overdue taxes were delivered at once. See Bemont, *Montfort*, 1930, p. 77. The ransom Simon imposed upon the lords of Labour was 7,000 shillings Morlaas, an amount they could not pay and so remained in the viceroy's keeping with their castles confiscated. British Museum, *Additional Charters*, number 3303. Simon's court and military actions in Gascony in 1248 all follow Bemont.

Roger Bacon had succeeded in analyzing and compounding d'Urberville's mysterious black powder. This use of the cannon is not usually credited to Simon. The trail of evidence is very circumstantial but the facts are these:

Gunpowder and cannons were first used in China. The first Western use appears to have been by Islamic forces battling the Christians on the Iberian Peninsula in the thirteenth century. Arab trade with China at that time, with dhows sailing to Canton and junks sailing to Aden, was quite active, and most likely brought the technology to Arabic domains. But apparently cannons and gunpowder remained very secret weapons in the West.

The Emperor Frederic was educated by and remained close to Arabic scholars and scientists. At his siege of Milan, Frederic's army deployed a strange weapon that reportedly lofted missiles amid smoke and a thunderous roar. This same Milanese siege, at which Simon was serving, was commanded by Henry D'Urberville, Simon's former commander in Wales. D'Urberville was Simon's immediate predecessor as governor of Gascony.

Before going to Gascony, Simon was serving as ambassador for England at King Louis' Court. During the time of his stay there, the university brought charges against Roger Bacon for making foul smells in his room as a by-product of his alchemical experiments. They wanted him evicted. Bacon next turns up established at Oxford, which is then under the care of Robert Grosseteste's protégé Adam Marsh: Grosseteste's and Marsh's existing letters to Simon show an extraordinary degree of familiarity with the earl, they undoubtedly were his closest friends. It seems likely that Simon was the link between Bacon and Oxford. In his Magnum Opus, essentially an encyclopedia, Bacon describes explosives, and includes a drawing of a bronze vase-like vessel, the prototype of the European cannon.

Simon's defeat of the mountain fortress of Mauleon was so miraculously swift that it was attributed to supernatural agency. Later, in 1253, when King Henry was trying to raise funds from his barons for his war in Gascony, he displayed to them steel arrows, quarrels, which had been lobbed at him amid thunderous noise from the roof of the fortress of La Reole – which previously had been occupied and fortified by Simon. The butt ends of the arrows were blackened as from a fiery explosion.

A cannon, very similar to the one Bacon illustrated in his writings dated 1248, appears in *De Nobilitatibus, Sapientii, et Prudentiis Regum*, by Walter de Milemete in 1326. But the use of cannon and gunpowder by the English is not widely recognized until the battle of Battle of Crecy in 1346.

"Bigorre shall be yours..." See: Bemont, *Montfort,* 1930 pp. 79-82 for a thorough discussion of Simon's arrangements for Bigorre. Bemont sees these arrangements as containing Gaston de Bearne, who had intentions to claim Bigorre on Pironelle's death. His wife was Pironelle's daughter by her fifth and last husband Boso de Mathe. While Simon may well have been acting with such foresight, his immediate achievement was to detour the trade and pilgrim routes, specifically depriving Bearne of access to travelers. See also Labarge, *Gascony,* p. 19.

Historical Context

Simon moved on to Ainhoa, on the border of Navarre. There he was to meet King Thibaut. The meeting between Simon and Thibaut was on October 30, 1248. The rather one-sided agreement, giving Henry the final judgement, was ratified by King Henry February 6, 1249: See Bemont, Montfort, 1930, p. 81 and footnote 5.

"It's common for the warder..." It is not known exactly what Simon and Thibaut said to each other at Ainhoa, but the quote given was well known and might have been a great temptation. The stanza of Thibaut's poem actually is as follows:
"Coustume est bien quant on tient un prison
qu'on ne le veut oir ne escouter
car nule riens ne fet tant cuer felon
con grant pouit, qui mal en veut user"
And twenty-two lines later:
"Vou savez bien qu'en ne conoisten lui
ce qu'en conoist en autrui plainement"
See Frederick Goldin, *The Lyrics of the Troubadours and Trouveres,* song 34, pp. 462-64. See also Labarge, *Gascony,* p. 19.

Bacchus lounged with his wild bacchantes: Murals were the customary decor of the wealthy, but exactly what the subjects of Savoy's murals were at this time is not recorded. Brother Matthew only advises us of the outrageous opulence of the Savoy Palace, which was notorious. Inventories of its treasures in the time of the Black Prince exist, and still raised public consternation. The Savoy Theater, of Gilbert and Sullivan fame, was named for, and built on the site of the Savoy Palace.

While King Henry's choice of the crusaders' Battle of Antioch for the murals at Westminster Hall is historical, the mural description here is fictional. Peter of Savoy was highly cultured and would have been likely to flaunt his sophistication. Classical influence enjoyed something of a renaissance in Europe in twelfth and thirteenth centuries, and in Provence classical culture never had fully vanished. The duchy of Savoy was located in what is now northern Italy, bordering Provence. It is possible that Earl Peter favored classical imagery over the usual Christian or Arthurian subjects. Cataline's misdoings would have been well known from Cicero, whose orations were studied in the medieval discipline of rhetoric – a part of any good education. The Vestal Virgin whom Cataline was accused of seducing was Cicero's sister.

While Paris's *Chronica Majora,* (Giles, Vol. V, p. 48,) is our source regarding the shocking extravagance of Savoy's festivities, and of the hero's greeting Simon received there, he does not record the specific conversations.

he can't afford his own household expenses! King Henry's self impoverishment at this time, and his shameful reduction of the royal hospitality, is recorded by Paris, *Rerum Britannicarum*, Vol. V, p. 199. In some ways there was no pleasing Matthew, he rails against both lavishness and penury. Much of the money Henry was saving was going to build Westminster Abbey Church.

"We wish to move Our Court to your city of Bordeaux." See Paris *Rerum Britannicarum*, Vol. V, pp. 110-111 and 180-190.

"Master Colom's here! He says there's fighting in the city!" Precisely which faction began the uprising is very muddied by the partisan accounts of each side. Simon would first have heard Colom's alarm.

Bemont, *Montfort,* 1930, pp. 82-83, presents the DelSoler argument that it was the Colom who initiated the violence by seizing the marketplace. No doubt it was such an accusation that enabled DelSoler to rouse the mayor and militia to his side. The truth was probably unascertainable at the time. But since the Colom were royalists, it seems unlikely they would make such a disruptive move right after the return of the viceroy. And the subsequent, apparently coordinated rising of the Gascon lords all over the country makes it probable that their partisans in Bordeaux were attempting a night raid on the armorers' shops to supply their civil war.

Washing himself with a soapy cloth, Soap was a fairly recent innovation, a luxury product that came from Spain and would have been available to the wealthy in Bordeaux. Personal cleanliness since Roman times had been accomplished by rubbing the body with oil, then scraping the oil, dirt and sweat off with a dull, curved blade called a strigil.

Laundry was washed with washing soda: sodium carbonate, which was derived from the ashes of plant material. Where washing soda wasn't afforded, laundry was simply beaten on rocks in a running stream. When I visited an ancient village in the Massif Central region of France there was a covered arcade with huge stone tubs into which water from the nearby stream could be fed. Within living memory the laundry in this village was washed twice a year, as a great community activity of the housewives. But the practice ceased when a woman died as a result of the extreme cold of the stream water.

Dry cleaning, in the 13th century, was sent out to be done by professionals who had dry cleaning solution formulas that they kept secret. There were also professional services for shearing the "pills" off of woolen garments. The principal source of information on de-pilling is the Countess Eleanor's own expense roll. See Labarge, *A Baronial Household.*

La Reole stood on a cliff on the north bank of the Garonne. It still does, and I had the good fortune during my research travels in 1978, to be welcomed by the Viort family, the fortress's castellans, and given a tour of the castle.

The fortress is comprised of four towers, and actually bears the name Les Quatre Soeurs. Its massive walls tower over the flat land beside the river (and the railroad tracks entering the town.) The town rises in cobbled streets with ancient semi-circular shop windows, to a gate which opens onto a broad, walled courtyard. Whether this courtyard was composed of fill to the depth of the base of the soaring walls on the outside of the castle, or the original topography was a cliff which had been faced with the castle's masonry I don't know. But the outer wall's parapet overlooking the river, at the time of my visit, was a completely enclosed, tile-roofed gallery on the courtyard side of the wall.

The large main tower was the Viort family's residence. The main hall was as I have described, though in 1978 the stone walls, magnificent vaulting and astonishing carved brackets were not painted – nor of course was the hall furnished as I have portrayed it. I was shown onto the roof, which offered a view of the countryside to the south that gave vivid meaning to the word "commanding."

"Count Raymond of Toulouse has died..." Raymond died of illness. Paris, *Rerum Britannicarum*, Vol. V, p. 90.

"May I write that in my letter to my master Alphonse?" Boutaric, *Saint Louis et Alphonse de Poitiers,* pp. 69-77 for the chaplain's letter: "... we spoke to my lord Simon about his passage overseas and heard that he intended to go at the Feast of Saint John. And know that he holds Gascony in good estate, and all obey him, and dare undertake naught against him; and he has taken the castle of Fronzac..."

"It is well known that they plan raids by night." Royal Letters, Vol. II, p. 52. Rather colorfully, Simon warns *"ni poet ni chevalier"* will stop them. Since the letter exists, it must be granted he did on occasion write and speak like that.

Louis never swore, and Simon almost never. But there is another instance of Simon's rising to poetically vivid language in the heat of the moment. It is years later when his sons have arranged for a tournament *a outrance* and he forbids it as politically explosive. On that occasion he warns Henry, Simon and Guy that he will put them where they "will have the benefit of neither sun nor moon" – presumably the wine storage cellar in the corner tower of Kenilworth which King Henry had fitted out with manacles. The threat was quite effective and the tournament was disbanded.

Simon's letters to King Henry during his viceroyship, and the king's responses, are reprinted in Bemont, *Montfort*, 1884, pp. 286-296 from *Archives Nationales. J. 1028, number 13.*

H I S T O R I C A L   C O N T E X T

King Louis' crusade was lost. See Runciman, *The History of the Crusades,* Vol. III, *The Kingdom of Acre,* pp. 264 to 271, for a brilliant description of Louis' entire preparations, campaign and defeat.

Louis landed and seized Damietta, an important port city on the westward side of the Nile estuary. By this time the Khoresines, who had sacked Palestine and been the original spur to the crusade, were long gone. The Sultan Ayub and his relatives were in control of the Holy Land and at civil war with each other again.

Louis' plan was to march east, taking the whole of the estuary and blocking the sultan's main ports of supply. He had considerable success in this, though it meant crossing numerous streams and rivers, until he came to the banks of the widest of these branches of the Nile, with the city of Mansourah on the opposite bank.

During Louis' advance, Ayub had died (November 23.) His son Turanshah was far away in Jezirah. But his sultana, Hajar ad-Durr, managed to establish Turanshah as the rightful heir and to organize a campaign against the invading Christians. Louis, hearing of Ayub's death, assumed the civil war would become far more ferocious and complex, offering him a fine opportunity if he just waited. Hajar's appointed general, Fakhr ad-Din, brought his forces up to Mansourah, camping right across the river from Louis and disabusing him of that happy thought.

The armies stared at each other across the impassable river until a traitor to Hajar showed Louis a fording point upstream. Early in the morning of the 8th of February Louis' forces forded the river and surprised Fakhr's camp. The assault was led by Louis' brother Robert of Artois, despite his having been told not to move forward until the whole army was across the river. But fearing he would lose the advantage of surprise, Robert and his knights attacked right away. Fakhr was killed along with many of his soldiers. The rest fled into the city, with Robert and his knights in pursuit.

Mansourah was a city of narrow, winding alleys. Its inhabitants took to their roofs and pelted the Christians to death with stones and arrows. Nearly all of Robert's force was destroyed, including Prince Robert himself. With him, William Longspee, the head of the English contingent, Count Hugh of la Marche and his son Hugh le Brun, and the Master of the Templars died. Only five of the two-hundred and ninety Templars who were with Robert's contingent survived. The Count of Brittany, Piers Mauclerc, was mortally wounded but succeeded in escaping the city and riding back to tell Louis what had happened.

Louis' army had not yet completed crossing the river. He had drawn up his mounted forces in order to cover the building of a pontoon bridge to enable his archers and foot soldiers to cross. Now he was struck by wave after wave of attack by the sultana's army, which had almost instantly reorganized under the command of Rukn ad-Din.

With the arrival of his archers, Louis pushed the Arab forces back, and camped where Fakhr's army had camped in front of the city. Three days later there was a fierce battle, but Louis held his ground.

Louis' supply line was by boats from Damietta. Now Turanshah, recognized as sultan, sent his own boats and cut off Louis' supplies. By April 5th Louis' camp was rife with starvation, dysentery and typhoid.

Louis began his retreat toward Damietta. Rukn's forces pursued, harassing the Christians' march. Louis, conscience stricken at the loss of his brother and so many of those who had followed him, insisted on marching with the rear guard where he was most exposed to the enemy. By the second morning of the march he was so sick with the return of his dysentery that he could hardly remain in his saddle. Nearly all of his soldiers were sick. Rukn's army easily surrounded them.

Philip de Montfort was in the midst of hopeful negotiations with Rukn's representatives when a French knight rode among the halted Christians shouting that King Louis had surrendered. The army surrendered to Rukn without Louis' permission, and he was taken prisoner with all his remaining forces.

Queen Margaret, pregnant and close to term, had remained at Damietta. Now, in the very act of childbirth, she learned of the capture of the army, and had to negotiate the terms of Louis' and the army's ransom. The price was the relinquishing of Damietta, and the payment of one million gold besants. See Paris, *Rerum Britannicarum*, Vol. V, pp. 105-108, 130-134, 138-144, 147-175, 202-204, 211, 218-221, 239, 257, 342.

help raise the funds to pay the ransom. See Paris, *Rerum Britannicarum*, Vol. V, pp. 239, 257 and 342. The ransom was sent in 1251. Queen Margaret, in the midst of childbirth, probably had not been in a frame of mind to drive the hardest bargain for the ransom. Nonetheless, her accomplishment was heroic. Shortly before she was required to negotiate with the sultan's ambassador, she had managed to persuade the Genoese ship captains, who had brought the crusaders to the East and who were in actual control of Damietta, not to give up the city to the Saracens but keep it as a bargaining asset. Had she not shamed the Genoese into agreeing not to abandon her and the city to the enemy, the ransom would have been far higher.

Louis was freed. Louis' and the survivors of the crusade's release in 1252 is recorded by Paris, *Rerum Britannicarum*, Vol. V, p. 342.

"these people, who would like to have you think them friends, lie and betray you!" This exchange between Simon and King Henry is quoted from Bemont's translation, *Montfort*, 1930, p. 91. The original document recording their words is reprinted in Bemont, *Montfort*, 1884, pp. 313-317: *British Museum, Additional Charters, number 3303.* See also Paris, *Rerum Britannicarum*, Vol. V, pp. 208-210.

"I am in disfavor." Paris records King Henry's warm greeting of Guy de Lusignan, and says nothing of Simon but that Guy sailed with him after all crossings of the Channel had been delayed for days by storms. See *Rerum Britannicarum*, Vol. V, p. 263.

the wedding of the king's eldest daughter to Scotland's king. Margaret's marriage at York is recorded by Paris, *Rerum Britannicarum*, Vol. V, 266-268 and 272. King Henry left his daughter in the care of Robert de Ros, Stephen Bauzon and Mathilde de Cantaloupe in Scotland. These three also oversaw the governing of Scotland for the child king Alexander. It appears that from this stewardship that Henry established, the title Steward evolved into the family name Stuart, and hence became the royal line of Scotland.

Wengham had reached the leaders of the revolt. Paris records the Gascons' conspiracy against Simon, the investigation, and Simon's return to Gascony and siege of the Gascons, which the investigators Wengham and Meulles witnessed. Paris, *Rerum Britannicarum*, Vol. V, pp. 276-284.

"On the ninth of May, lord Earl, at noon at Court in Westminster, you must surrender yourself for trial." Simon's trial is here largely rendered from Matthew Paris, *Chronica Majora*, Vol. V, pp. 287-296, H.R. Luard, Rolls Series, 1876-82; and the letters of Adam Marsh: for translation see Green, *Princesses*, App. IV, pp. 448-453 See also: Labarge, *Simon de Montfort*, p. 119; Maddicott, p.115-17; Labarge, *Gascony*, pp. 21-22. Paris, *Rerum Britannicarum*, Vol. V, pp. 276, 289-296. That he was rescued by the protests of the barons, led by Richard, as King Henry was about to pronounce sentence, is history.

treason is a high crime, entailing the penalty of death, As Simon well knew, the penalty of death for high treason was hanging, drawing and quartering. The victim was cut down from the hangman's noose before he was dead so that he might witness the "drawing": the cutting open of his belly and drawing out of his intestines. While still often surviving this, he was then quartered, his body butchered into four parts, each one with a limb attached. In the case of a man who tried to assassinate King Henry III, the four quarters were then allotted to be dragged by horses through the streets of the ancient holy cities: London, Canterbury, York and Coventry. What remained of these parts was then thrown into ditches and left for dogs to eat.

"My king," he bowed, *"I've come to ask your wish regarding my return to Gascony."* Paris describes Henry's action as like King David sending Uriah out to die in battle, and gives the entire exchange between Simon and King Henry. See Paris, *Rerum Britannicarum,* pp. 295-296.

Matthew renders Simon's words in Latin: *"Ex ego libenter ibo. Nec, ut credo, revertar, donec tibi, licet ingratio, rebelles subjugando ponam inimicos tuos scabellum pedum tuorum.* (The underlining is Paris's.) Simon is quoting Psalm 110:1: "Till I make of thine enemies thy footstool." *Rerum Brtiannicarum,* in its marginal notes, cites Psalm 109, which is not accurate, but probably was very familiar to Simon at this time – and why he could so readily quote Psalm 110. Psalm 109 includes:

"Hold not thy peace, O God of my praise. For the mouth of the wicked and the mouth of the deceitful are opened against me; they have spoken against me with a lying tongue. Thy have compassed me about also with words of hatred; and fought against me without cause.

Regarding the curious passage where Simon asks Henry if he knows the meaning of repentance – it seems hardly credible there is not a hidden meaning intended. Given the chronically rebellious condition of Gascony, Henry's previous order to him to "treat them as your father did the Albigensians," his letters to the king and his self-defense at the trial, it seems highly unlikely that, the day after the trial ended, Simon was repentant about his actions as viceroy. Like Henry's ravings at the Churching of the Queen after the birth of Edward, the words make sense if Henry believed Simon to be the queen's lover, and Simon was admitting some truth of the relationship, and his repentance.

"Come south in arms with me. Help me retake Gascony..." See *Rerum Britannicarum,* Vol. V, p. 313, and Bemont, *Montfort,* 1930, p. 113, for Simon's raising of funds in France, and invitation to the knights of Normandy to join him for the sake of booty.

what they saw upon the slope was a single knight in black chain mail and helm with the red lion mantel of Montfort: The account of how Simon came single-handed against the army of the Gascons is vividly told by Matthew Paris, and the telling here follows his description, including his rescue of Barres, what Barres said and Barres's rescue of Simon. See Matthew Paris, *Chronica Majora*, Giles, Vol. V. p. 31, *Rerum Britannicarum*, Vol. V, 314-316, and Bemont, *Montfort*, 1930, pp. 113-114.

Assuming it did happen more or less as Matthew tells us, the heat of the day and the long wait seem the best explanations for Simon's irrational single-handed assault. It is evident from his extraordinary detour to Montaubin, that his wounds from this battle caused him great suffering, and he did not venture such a foolish thing ever again.

"Montaubin de Casseuil isn't far. It's one of the Lion Hearted's small towers. I have the Viort family, the castellans of La Reole during my visit there in 1978, to thank for my information regarding the general physical appearance and situation of Montaubin de Casseuil, which had been in the keeping of one of their cousins. See Bemont, *Montfort*, 1930, p. 114 regarding this siege. Upon his return to Bordeaux, Archbishop Malemorte furiously excommunicated Simon for the abuse he had suffered at his hands. But Simon was fully protected by the special powers granted him by Pope Innocent. Paris, *Rerum Britannicarum*, Vol. V, p. 334.

"I want the lily that Saint Gregory writes of: that grew among the tares, like Job who lived among the wicked folk of Uz but kept his faith." Maddicott shows interest in Simon's reading of *Saint Gregory's Commentaries on the Book of Job*, p. 94. Adam Marsh had particularly recommended the work to Simon's attention in a letter preserved in the *Monumenta Franciscana*, Vol. 1, pp. 266-268. The significance of Simon's briefly adopting the lily as his shield's device after the siege at Montauban suggests he may have been thinking of this particular passage.

but how can I observe the truce. Simon's amusingly disingenuous response to the king's order is the beginning of a pattern of behavior that becomes most striking in his answers during his trial for treason in 1260. He is maturing, and finding humor a far more effective defense than blunt rage. Secure now in the knowledge of his own remarkable capabilities, he behaves with far fewer extremes of temper hereafter. For his full response to Henry, see Bemont, *Montfort*, 1884, p. 343 for a reprint from *Bibliotheque Nationale, Ms. lat. 9016, number 5.*

"Let's pay the nine thousand and stay home!" Paris records Henry's seeking of funds for war against Simon and the barons' refusal: *Rerum Britannicarum*, Vol. V, pp. 335-338; and the uprising of the Gascons, which began on April 19, 1253 (*RB* V, p. 370.) After a false try delayed by weather, Henry finally departed in arms for Gascony on August 6, 1253, arriving at Bordeaux on August 15, and proceeding to lay siege to La Reole. (*RB* V, pp. 381-388.)

"Queen Blanche has directed me to ask you to remain in France – as Regent." Matthew Paris heard that Simon had been offered the position of *Seneschal*, the term for Steward, which, in the absence of the king, would have powers eqiuvalent to that of a regent or viceroy. Matthew believed that Simon refused the title on ground it would be incompatible with his liege to King Henry. He was aware that nobles of France were so pleased with Simon that they wished to have him replace Louis, whom they considered to be abandoning the interests of France by his vow to remain in Palestine for the remainder of his life.

Simon would certainly have rejected any move to place him on the throne, but he appears to have taken up the position of Seneschal and to have done well, with Archbishop Rigaud continuing as Minister of State. His powers were intended for the interim before Louis' return, or before the majority of nine-year-old Prince Louis. As it happened, young Louis died in 1260 and never came to the throne. *Rerum Britannicarum*, Vol. V, p. 366, 371-372. See *RB* pp. 280, 307-310 for France's dissatisfaction with Louis. (See also above for how the stewards (Seneschals) of Scotland transformed into the royal line of Stuarts.)

"We command and request that you come to us in Gascony." This letter is verbatim from Bemont, *Montfort*, 1930, pp. 119-120. It was written October 4 at La Reole, where Henry had been attempting to besiege Gaston de Bearne since September 7. See *Roles Gascons*, number 2111, and *Calendar of Patent Rolls, 1247-1258*, p. 244.

"The treaty is accepted by King Alphonse," When Simon left for France, King Alphonse of Spain claimed Gascony: *Rerum Britannicarum* Vol. 5, p. 365. The surrender of La Reole, and the treaty by which Edward was betrothed to Alphonse's sister Eleanor, are recorded by Paris, *RB* V, pp. 396-397. On February 6, 1254, Simon's seal appears for the last time attesting his witnessing royal documents issued from Gascony.

Bibliography

Primary Sources:

Montfort Archive, Bibliotheque Nationale, Paris. There is preserved, in this boxed archive of original documents, a brief autobiography by Simon written in 1260 in preparation for his trial before King Louis for treason against King Henry. (In the event, the trial was actually heard by Queen Margaret of France.)

Publications:
Calendar of Charter Rolls, Vol. I, 1226-1307, Public Record Office. Kraus Reprint, Neldeln/Liechtenstein, 1972.

Calendar of the Liberate Rolls, 1226-1240, Volume I, Public Record Office, 1916.

Calendar of Patent Rolls, 1232-1272, Henry III. Public Record Office. Kraus Reprint, Nendeln/Liechtenstein, 1971.

Eccleston, Thomas of, *The Coming of the Friars Minor to England, XIIIth Century Chronicles*, translated by Placid Herman, O.F.M., Franciscan Herald Press, Chicago, 1961.

Excerpta e Rotulis Finium in Turri Londdinensi Asservatis Henry III, 1216-72, ed. by C. Roberts, Public Record Office. 1835-36.

Exchequer: The History and Antiquities of the Exchequer, Madox, Greenwood, 1769- 1969, Volumes I and II.

BIBLIOGRAPHY

Goldin, Frederick, *The Lyrics of the Troubadours and Trouveres,* Original texts with Translations and Introductions, Anchor Books, New York, 1973.

Grosseteste, Roberti, Episcopi quondam Lincolniensis Epistolae, ed. by H.R. Luard. Rolls Series, 1861.
Dicta Lincolniensis, ed. and trans.: Gordon Jackson, Grosseteste Press, Lincoln, 1972.
R. *Grosseteste Carmina Anglo-Normannica: Robert Grosseteste's Casteau d'Amour and La Vie de Sainte Marie Egyptienne,* Burt Franklin Research and Resource Works Series No. 154, New York, 1967.

Laffan, R.G.D. *Select Documents of European History, 800-1492,* Volume I, Henry Holt and Company, New York.

Matthew Paris's English History, from the year 1235 to 1273, translated by the Rev. J. A. Giles, Henry Bohn, London, 1852. See also Kessinger Publishing's Rare Reprints. www.kessinger.net.
Rerum Britannicarum Medi: Aevi Scriptores or *Chronicles and Memorials of Great Britain and Ireland During the Middle Ages,* Kraus reprint 1964.
Matthaei Paris, Monachi Albanensis, Historia Major, Juxta Exemplar Londinense 1640, *verbatim recusa,* ed. Willielmo Wats, STD. Imprensis A. Mearne, T. Dring, B. Tooke, T. Sawbridge & G. Wells, MDCLXXXIV (1684)
Matthaei Parisiense, Chronica Majora, Kraus reprint, 1964.

The Chronicle of William de Rishanger, of the Barons' War: The Miracles of Simon de Montfort. ed. J.O. Halliwell, Camden Society, 1840.

Royal Letters, Henry III, ed. W.W. Shirley, Rolls Series, 1862.

Strassburg, Gottfried von, *Tristan; with surviving fragments of Tristran, of Thomas,* trans. A. T. Hatto, Penguin Books, New York, 1967.

BIBLIOGRAPHY

de Troyes, Chretien. *Arthurian Romances*, trans. W.W. Comfort, Everyman's Library, Dutton, New York, 1975

Secondary Works:

Baker, Timothy. *Medieval London*, Praeger Publishers, New York, 1970.

Bemont, Charles, *Simon de Montfort, Earl of Leicester*, translated by E. F. Jacob, Oxford, Clarendon Press, 1930
Simon de Montfort, Comte de Leicester, Sa Vie (120?-1265), Slatkine-Megariotis Reprints, Geneve, 1976. *Reimpression de l'edition de Paris 1884.*
Roles Gascon, 1242-1254, 3 volumes, pub. Francisque Michel, 1885; and Supplement 1254-1255, 1896.

Boutaric, Edgar. *Saint Louis et Alphonse de Poitiers*, 1870.

Chrimes, S.B. *An Introduction to the Administrative History of Medieval England*, Basil Blackwell, Oxford, 1959.

Cosman, Madeleine Pelner. *Fabulous Feasts: Medieval Cookery and Ceremony*, George Braziller, New York, 1976.

Furnival. *The Babees' Book: Medieval Manners for the Young*, ed. Edith Rickert, Cooper Square Publishers, Inc., New York, 1966.

Green, John Richard. *Green's History of the English People*, Lovell, Coryell & Company, New York, Volume II, 1878-80.

Green, Mary Anne Everett, *Lives of the Princesses of England*, London, 1849.

Homans, George Caspar. *English Villagers of the Thirteenth Century*, Russell & Russell, New York, 1960.

BIBLIOGRAPHY

Howell, Margaret. *Eleanor of Provence, Queenship in Thirteenth Century England*, Blackwell Publishers Inc., Malden, Mass., 2001.

Johnson, Mrs. T. Fielding. *Glimpses of Ancient Leicester in Six Periods*, Simpkin, Marshall. Hamilton, Kent & Co., London, and John and Thomas Spencer, Leicester, 1891.

King, Edmund. *England, 1175-1425*, Charles Scribner's Sons, New York, 1979.

Labarge, Margaret Wade. *Simon de Montfort*, Eyre & Spottiswoode, London, 1962.
A Baronial Household of the Thirteenth Century, Eyre & Spottiswoode, London, 1965.
Saint Louis, Louis IX, Most Christian King of France, Little, Brown and Company, Boston, 1968.
Gascony, England's First Colony, 1204-1453, Hamish Hamilton, Ltd., London, 1980.

Maddicott, J.R. *Simon de Montfort*, Cambridge University Press, 1994.

Nagler, A.M. *The Medieval Religious Stage*, Yale University Press, New Haven, 1976.

Nicoll , Allardyce, *Masks, Mimes and Miracles: Studies in the Popular Theatre*, George A. Harrap & Company, Ltd., London, 1931.

Power, Eileen. *The Wool Trade in English Medieval History*, Oxford University Press, London, 1965.

Powicke, Maurice. *Medieval England: 1066-1485*, Oxford University Press, London, 1931.

Pye, N., ed. *Leicester and its Region*, Leicester University Press, Leicester, 1972.

BIBLIOGRAPHY

Renn, Derek. *Norman Castles in Britain*, John Baker: Humanities Press, New York, 1968.

Runciman, Steven. *A History of the Crusades, The Kingdom of Acre*, Volume III, The University Press, Cambridge, 1955.

Salisbury-Jones, G.T., *Street Life in Medieval England*, The Harvester Press: Rowan and Littlefield, Sussex, England, 1975.

Slaughter, Gertrude. *The Amazing Frederic: Stupor Mundi et Immutator Mirabilis*, The Macmillan Company, New York, 1937.

Waddell, Helen. *The Wandering Scholars*, Henry Holt and Company, New York, 1927.

Author's Note

MONTFORT, OF WHICH THIS VOLUME is Book III of five, is a work of thirty-three years of research, rumination and writing. Not only is the original source material fragmentary, though surprisingly abundant considering the passage of seven hundred and fifty years, but it is highly partisan. Simon's detractors are legion, extending from his early lifetime even to the present. Matters that are the reports of Simon's contemporaries differ drastically in regard of what ought to be incontrovertible facts. But anyone who has served on a jury dealing with the testimony of several eyewitnesses knows that such differences are commonplace. What witnesses see is colored by their expectations. When the extreme emotions that Simon generated around him, ranging from intense hatred to, at the end of his life, the adoration of a religious cult that considered him the risen Savior, are taken into consideration the possibility of objectivity is nil.

I have sought to present Simon's story as close to the way he might have wanted it told to a twenty-first century readership, were he in a particularly confiding mood. That historians will find faults I don't doubt, but I have not found any two historians who agree with each other on all points of Simon's history.

My intent is not to write a definitive biography, but to rouse public interest in a man whose life truly changed the world – who has effected all of our lives up to the present, and will into the future, as long as governments seek their authenticity through a body of the people's elected representatives.

Made in the USA
Charleston, SC
01 June 2010